UNDER NAMELESS STARS

"Christian Schoon knows h[illegible] has everything a sci-fi lover [illegible] forms to quantum entanglem[illegible] stellar YA heroine. Zenn's moxie an[illegible]ination make this a debut to remember. Highly recommended!"

Phoebe North, author of Starglass

"Reading *Zenn Scarlett* is like venturing into a gargantuan alien animal in one of the in-soma pods Zenn uses to provide veterinary care: delightful, bizarre, and occasionally terrifying."

Mike Mullin, author of Ashfall

"Many young people want to become veterinarians because they love animals. All future veterinarians will want to read *Zenn Scarlett* and her adventures with veterinary medicine on alien animals."

Temple Grandin, author of Animals in Translation

"Mars, monsters, and mysteries: *Zenn Scarlett* is a thoughtful and thrilling science fiction adventure that's perfect for readers who think they've seen it all! It's refreshing to encounter an original young adult story that defies expectations, and the breathtaking conclusion will leave you desperate for more."

EC Myers, author of Fair Coin

"Both animal lovers and science fiction fans will enjoy the unusual and imaginative story of Zenn Scarlett. This is the challenging life of a trainee exovet, in an inventive future where alien creatures are harnessed to send ships between star systems."

Janet Edwards, author of Earth Girl

BY THE SAME AUTHOR

Zenn Scarlett

CHRISTIAN SCHOON

UNDER NAMELESS STARS

STRANGE CHEMISTRY

STRANGE CHEMISTRY
An Angry Robot imprint
and a member of the Osprey Group

Lace Market House
54-56 High Pavement
Nottingham
NG1 1HW
UK

Angry Robot/Osprey Publishing
PO Box 3985
New York
NY 10185-3985
USA

www.strangechemistrybooks.com
Strange Chemistry #28

A Strange Chemistry paperback original 2014

Cover design by Steven Meyer-Rassow
Set in Sabon and Refrigerator Deluxe by Argh! Oxford

Distributed in the United States by Random House, Inc., New York.

ISBN 978 1 90884 487 3
Ebook ISBN 978 1 90884 488 0

Printed in the United States of America

9 8 7 6 5 4 3 2 1

To Kathleen, my guide-star.

ONE

When Zenn came to, she was floating, weightless, in a very dark place that smelled of animal. She hurt all over. Every breath pulled in bits of drifting dirt and debris. She spit out a long piece of straw, and the next second something unseen closed around her wrist in a powerful grip. Reacting in blind panic, she flailed, twisting in the air. She broke free and kicked away from whatever it was, brought her arms up in front of herself, fists balled, ready to fend the thing off if it came at her again.

"Nine Hells, Scarlett," a male voice swore from the darkness next to her. "You nearly kicked my teeth out."

"Liam," she said, relief washing over her. "Sorry. I couldn't see, didn't remember where… I didn't know it was you."

"Who else *would* it be?" he hissed.

A rumbling grunt sounded somewhere behind Liam. Then, an angry, ear-splitting roar. Adrenaline and fear jolted Zenn fully awake. She remembered where she was: in a shipping cage-crate. With Liam and a full-grown sandhog boar. In the zero-gravity hold of an orbital ferry, high above Mars.

Another roar – louder, shaking the air.

"He's waking up, Scarlett," Liam said.

"I know that," she said, reaching out into the dark. "I can't find the seda dish."

"Here. It's right here." She felt Liam press something into her hands: cold, metallic – the sedation field unit. The hog roared again. "Turn it on," he yelled.

Zenn fumbled for the control surface on the back of the dish, then contorted her body and aimed the device at the sound of the sandhog. The sedation field took effect; the roaring softened to a growl, then an idling snore.

"OK, he's out," she said. A frightful new thought arose. Katie!

Zenn looked around frantically, turning herself in the air, searching. Her eyes were adapting to the dim light now, and she strained to see through the darkness.

"Katie," she said out loud, even though she knew it would do no good. The rikkaset had been deaf since birth. "Katie, where are you?"

Something downy-soft bumped against her hand. A warbling trill sounded. The air in front of her shimmered lilac-and-cream, and the form of the little rikkaset took shape, allowing herself to become visible again now that the commotion of the ferry's launch was past.

Zenn hugged the animal to her, then released her into the air again.

"Is Katie good?" Zenn signed with one hand; with the other, she tried to keep the seda-dish aimed at the hog. The size of a house cat, the rikkaset had a round-headed, sharp-muzzled face, and large eyes the amber-green-gold of a ripe peach, all crowned by big tufted ears. With mental abilities a little greater than an Earther chimpanzee, Katie had quickly learned the basics of sign language when still a cub.

"Katie good," the rikkaset signed to Zenn, the slender, black fingers on her front paws spelling out the words as she tried to keep her body oriented toward Zenn. "Bad sounds. Too loud. Shaking. And floating. No fun for Katie."

"Bad sounds finished," Zenn signed, also speaking the words aloud so Katie could read her lips. But even as she said this, the sandhog emitted another deafening roar. In the confines of the metal-walled crate, which was a little smaller than Zenn's dorm room at the cloister, the animal sounded like it was close enough to touch.

"I thought you said he was asleep," Liam said, reaching out to pull Zenn away from the noise.

"He was," she muttered, repeatedly pressing the activation switch again on the back of the seda unit. "The dish. It's old. Doesn't always take at first."

It wasn't her fault. The seda-dish, like almost all the other things in Zenn's exovet field kit backpack, were either hand-me-downs or borderline-expired meds she'd scavenged from the storeroom at the cloister. After the Rift with Earth cut off trade, supplies of any kind were desperately hard to come by on Mars. She'd been proud of herself for scraping together what she could from the odds and ends Otha had no use for at the clinic.

A loud banging sound rattled the cage-crate.

"Sounds like he's trying to claw his way out," Liam said. "Better get that thing back online before he floats this way."

A harsh hum now sounded from the seda dish. Zenn shook it, then hit it hard with the heel of her hand, producing a brief shower of sparks in the dark air, followed by quieter humming.

"Damn, Scarlett, don't break it."

"I didn't. It's working now."

She swept the dish's beam onto the hog, and he immediately stopped thrashing. His vocalizations dropped to a breathy rumble as Zenn dialed up the strength of the field. She double-checked the dish output level. Even though sandhogs were considered "domesticated" animals, they were still big enough, and unpredictable enough, to kill a person when provoked. And after the tumult of the ferry launch from Mars, this hog was plenty provoked.

She could just discern the creature's outline, now; it had drifted up into one corner of the cage-crate, looking like a misshapen, sofa-sized dirigible. With a body something like a manatee, or maybe a rhinoceros-sized grub, a sandhog's most prominent feature was a pair of immense digging claws on its fore-section. They had no hind legs, no neck to speak of and a broad, concave face, with five small, spider-like eyes and a vast, gaping cavity of a mouth. The hairless, muscular body was covered in calloused-skin armor plate and tapered down to end in a powerful stub-tail, used to push the creature through the soil as it burrowed.

"So, guess we survived lift-off," Liam said. "I must've blacked out. You too?"

"Yes. From the g-forces," Zenn said.

The hog snorted in his sleep.

"You sure Tiny, there, is out for the count?"

"Yes. But don't let yourself get close to him. In case he drifts out of the seda-field."

"Don't worry. The smell alone will keep me away."

Zenn reached out and pulled Katie to her. The little marsupial clung tightly to the front of the oversized worker's coveralls Zenn wore. She'd found the coveralls hanging on the wall of the warehouse in Pavonis and put them on over her pajamas after she was kidnapped from the cloister. Kidnapped. Her. The whole thing was simply too preposterous. Senseless.

Not now, she told herself. Focus. First things first...

Dialing up the seda-field another notch just to be sure, Zenn pushed off the nearest wall, and coasted to park herself in the opposite corner, where she looked out through one of the vent-holes in the crate. There was a porthole in the ferry's bulkhead. Blackness filled it, punctuated by a few blazing stars. Then, something else came into view as the ferry continued its silent ascent. A starship – the *Helen of Troy*.

Though she could only see part of it through the porthole, Zenn knew the starship was a good quartermile long. Pressing her face against the side of the crate, she watched as the multilayered darkmatter collection panels at the bow swam into view, hanging like a deck of playing cards suspended in mid-shuffle. Then the passenger decks and crew quarters slid past, bulging gracefully in smooth, sculpted lines along the ship's mid-section. Next came the huge, blocky Indra-hold, suspended at the stern of the ship on a thin stalk, far enough away to protect the passengers from the Indra's radiation output when it tunneled through space. There was no sign of the Indra from the outside, of course. The mighty stonehorse would be resting now, burrowed down in the metal labyrinth of its warren, gathering itself for the task ahead.

"What do you see?" Liam asked, rising up to position himself next to her. The towner boy was a little older than Zenn, tall for his age, with longish blond hair that, like Zenn's red locks, now rose up freely around his head in the absence of gravity. His face, sunburned from his work helping out around the cloister, was open, friendly. He was still dressed in the patched heavy cloth pants and homemade hemp-cloth shirt he wore for doing chores.

"It's the ship. We're coming into dock with it." She moved aside so he could look.

"Whoa," he said. "It's huge. You ever see anything that big before?"

In fact, she had.

"Yes. Another starliner. When I was nine." Her voice grew quiet. "My mother was aboard, treating the Indra..."

"Oh. Right. Sorry, Scarlett." Liam pushed himself back and faced her. "I'm an idiot to bring that up."

"Liam, it's OK. I've... learned to deal with it." Not entirely true, but at least now she could talk about it without seizing up entirely. "Like Otha said once, afterwards. Mom was doing what she loved, trying to help an animal that needed her. And she knew the risks. She knew accidents happen."

"Yeah, but to be inside an Indra and then... They ever figure out what went wrong?"

"There was an inquiry. They said it must have been the

in-soma pod's autopilot. Software bug. Apparently the pod rerouted itself, took her into the Indra's skull. The Indra's immune response triggered. Whatever was making it sick might have made the response more powerful than usual."

"And so the Indra just, like, vaporized?"

Zenn flinched at the word. Over the years, she had more or less sealed off the memories of that terrible day, encapsulated them within a sort of protective cyst in a far corner of her mind, away from the light, where it couldn't hurt her. Liam's questions and the sight of the *Helen of Troy* opened the cyst and released its contents in a stomach-twisting rush of emotion. But she knew it wasn't healthy to push the memory down inside her, to let it fester. It was better to talk. At least, that's what she'd been told.

"When the blast shield in the pilot room retracted, the Indra chamber was empty. Mom, Vremya, the Indra... were just gone."

"Vremya?"

"Mom's lab tech. She was in a vac-suit, inside the chamber, monitoring the pod-insertion."

"So, you being on the ship. How'd that happen, anyway? You were just a kid."

"When Otha and my dad drove to the ferry launch port to go up to the ship, I hid in the back of the truck."

"You?" Liam laughed. "I don't believe it."

"They couldn't leave me at the port. So they had to take me along."

"You little sneak."

"Liam, I was nine."

"Yeah, that's what I mean. Mule-headed from an early age."

"Mules are highly intelligent creatures, I'll have you know."

"Fine. You're a know-it-all mule."

The ferry fired its braking jets, jostling the craft. Liam's attention was drawn back to the porthole.

"So, you've actually seen a live stonehorse, huh? What are they like, in person?"

"Well, they're impressive. The one I saw was a full-grown female, must have been seven-hundred feet, with that kind of snake-like, flattened body."

"But, what's it like to look one in the eye?"

"Sort of eerie. They don't have eyes, really, but three sets of full-spectrum radiation sensor slits where eyes would be. They can perceive everything from infrared through visible light all the way up to ultraviolet."

"Damn, I'd love to see one up close."

"Well, if we get away with this," Zenn said, thinking about what they were actually attempting, "maybe you will."

"What? Get into the pilot room? I thought they didn't let mere mortals in there."

"Uh huh. Usually just the Indra grooms and their sacrists. Maybe a VIP passenger now and then."

"And exovet moms and their smart-alec kids," Liam said, grinning. Then, adding quickly: "Geez – sorry. I did it again."

"I told you. I'm dealing."

He put his face against the crate wall again to look out.

"So, the ship's big bulge at the end of the long tube, that's where the Indra lives."

"Right. The Indra warren."

"And how do they get the thing to do what it does? You know, take everybody to the next stop?"

"The Indra groom summons the Indra, and it enters the chamber, the front part of the big bulge. Then the groom communicates the coordinates to the next star system. The Indra responds by turning dark matter into warping catalyst. And about a nanosecond later, they open what's called a tunnel and the entire ship is transported across... You probably don't care about all this. I'm just rambling."

"No. Really," he said. "I'm gonna be on that ship out there. Won't hurt me to know how it works."

"I know, but sometimes I just sort of spew out information."

"Hey, I asked for it, OK? And I'm serious. I've never paid much attention to, you know, the sciencey stuff. Like why do some people call Indra stonehorses? They don't look anything like a horse."

"Well, the head kind of has a sort of seahorse look, if you use your imagination. But they got their name because in the wild they live inside asteroids. Big ones, made of metals like iron and nickel. They keep these asteroids in front of them when they tunnel, as particle shields. So, the grooms call them stonehorses."

"Yeah, that's another thing. The grooms. They go into some sort of trance, don't they? Some kinda spooky mumbo-jumbo?"

"Their rituals, you mean? They say it's part of their communing with the Indra. Dates back to when the first abandoned Indra-drive ship was discovered. I think it's just to make up for the fact that no one really understands all the aspects of tunneling. When people don't understand something in nature, they invent things to make sense out of it."

"Well, whatever works."

"How close are we to the docking port?"

Liam let Zenn take a turn looking out. The ferry was near enough to the ship to let her examine the vessel. The details now visible betrayed its history. Along one section of the underbelly, a rust-eaten pattern of unrepaired micrometeor damage speckled the alloy hull; farther along, billowing filaments of silvery insulation had squeezed out of a vent opening and dangled in long streamers that glinted as they unfurled against the jet-black backdrop of space. This aging ship had seen better days. She must have been built over a half-century ago, during the heyday of the huge Earther shipyards. The same bitter tide of anti-alien sentiment that brought the Temporary Executive Authority to power on Earth had also spelled the end of those imposing orbital assembly platforms and the titanic machines they produced.

But the age and condition of the *Helen of Troy* didn't really matter to Zenn. All that mattered now was getting safely aboard. Then she would try to locate the Skirni who had kidnapped her father and then her. She would follow him. If he didn't lead her to where Warra Scarlett was being held, she would find a way to make the Skirni tell her where he was. She knew it wasn't much of a plan. But she was her father's only hope. She had to find him. It was that simple.

If Liam could help her do what she need to do, she'd take advantage of that. But talking with him here, she felt herself falling back into old habits, bantering as if he were the same, easy-going towner boy she'd known for years on Mars. The fact was, she'd thought she knew who Liam Tucker was. She'd been wrong. And this mistake had almost destroyed her home, her school and the alien animals she was caring for. He claimed he'd seen that he was wrong, and he seemed genuinely sorry. So, maybe he really had changed. But until she knew for sure, it made sense to be careful. She would keep her guard up.

A grinding noise came from outside the hull as the ferry docked. She turned to watch the floating sandhog, but it continued its fitful slumber. There was the groan of a hatch opening, a whoosh of inrushing air, then the rattle of a machine approaching, followed by scraping sounds. Then the crate heaved into motion and, a few seconds later, she, Katie, Liam and the hog all dropped to the floor of the crate, pulled down in the grip of artificial gravity.

She'd done it. She was aboard the *Helen of Troy*. Now, all she had to do was track down a single three-foot-tall Skirni among the starship's thousand or so other passengers, follow the alien to find her father, free her father from his captors and get away again, all while first avoiding discovery and being sent back to Mars. Right.

With the sandhog's slow, raspy breathing the only sound, she and Liam sat silently on the floor of the crate and waited several minutes in case anyone should come. Finally, Liam stood and cautiously peered out through one of the holes in the crate wall.

"Looks empty," he said quietly.

"Katie hungry," the rikkaset signed at Zenn, big eyes blinking. Then she went to Zenn's field kit backpack where it lay on the floor and began pulling at the cover flap with her deft little paws. "Friend-Zenn have treats? Treats for Katie in bag?"

"No. Sorry. Treats later," Zenn signed. "Wait a little."

Katie huffed at her, sat down and wrapped her long, striped tail around her body.

Zenn went to where Liam stood and looked out to survey the scene. They were in a vast, dimly lit cargo hold, with containers of all sizes and shapes piled to the ceiling as far as she could see. The sandhog rumbled and twitched in his sleep; the movement made the entire crate rock back and forth.

"Hey, I've got a wacky idea," Liam said, regarding the hog. "How about we get outta here before Tiny rolls over and mashes us?"

Zenn eyed the hatch on the crate's ceiling.

"OK," she said. "But we'll need to keep him asleep until we're both through the hatch."

"So, what's the problem? You leave your knockout ray pointed at him and we climb out."

"I can't just leave him under permanent sedation," she said curtly. "It could kill him."

"Oh, can't have that. I guess."

And besides, she thought but didn't bother to say, it's my equipment and I'm responsible for its proper use and maintenance. Otha had drilled this fact into her on countless occasions during her classes back at the cloister. Back on Mars. Back with all the people and animals and places she loved and was already starting to miss. At least she had the backpack, the one Otha had given her to use as a field kit. The Skirni had grabbed the pack off the desk in her room. Immobilized by whatever weapon he'd used on her, she'd seen him sweep a stack of her computer mem-shards into the pack, just before he'd thrown her over his shoulder and made his escape. When she'd retrieved the pack in the warehouse, the shards were the only things missing, as far as she could tell. But why take the shards? More to the point, why take *her*?

"So," Liam said, "how do we get outta here in one piece?"

Zenn thought for a few seconds, then crouched by the backpack and searched in it. She found what she was looking for and stood again, a length of hemp-braid rope in her hands.

"What?" Liam said. "You're gonna lasso him?"

She didn't answer but stooped to secure one end of the rope around the seda-field unit. She then knotted the other end around her wrist, then signed for Katie to get into the pack and, once she was settled, hoisted the pack up, slipping one strap over her arm.

She nodded at the hatch in the ceiling. "Give me a boost up."

"Oh, sure. I'll just hang out down here with the giant killer-hog."

"He's not a… Just lift me up, will you?"

Liam gave her a look, then laced his fingers together. She put one foot into his hands and he easily lifted her up until she could reach the latch of the feeding hatch. She opened it, grabbed the lip of the opening and, with a final push from

Liam, was up and out. On the roof of the crate, she quickly slipped off her pack, lay down flat and reached in for Liam.

He was trying to jump high enough to grab her hand when the seda-field dish emitted a loud crackle, spat another burst of sparks and puffed out a large cloud of white smoke – followed by silence.

"The dish – it's dead," she whispered. "Liam, get out. Grab my hand."

"I'm trying."

Beneath her, Zenn felt the crate shift as the hog started to regain consciousness and move.

"Hurry!"

With his next jump, Liam's hands took hers. He was too heavy to lift off the floor, but by pulling with all her strength as he jumped, he reached high enough to grab the edge of the hatch opening with one hand. Zenn stood, repositioned her grip, and began to pull on his arm with both hands. But as she struggled to lift him up through the hatch, the sandhog gave a savage bellow, followed by the sight of a huge digging claw swiping across her field of vision, hooking Liam's body, breaking her grip and throwing the boy out of sight. She heard him hit somewhere on the far side of the cage. She dropped to the opening again, leaned down into it, but couldn't see him.

"Liam!"

A loud thud of metal hitting flesh came from the dark, then Liam's face was beneath her, his hands reaching up.

"Now would be good," he gasped.

Zenn extended her arms as far as she could and he took her hands again.

Pulling with all her strength, she was able to help him regain a grip on the edge of the hatchway.

The creature's furious roar just underneath him prompted Liam to fling himself up in a frantic effort to get away. He'd just cleared the edge of the hatch and rolled away onto the roof of the crate when the hog threw himself upward, the impact shaking the container beneath them.

"It's OK," Liam said, breathing hard as he got to his feet. "He came at me and I nailed him with the knock-out dish. Kinda pissed him off, I think."

"Sounds that way."

Zenn quickly began to reel in the rope connected to the dish, but, a moment later, she was jerked violently to her knees, the rope cutting into the flesh of her wrist.

"I'm caught," she said. "The hog – tangled in the line."

Another tug from the sandhog and she was sliding across the roof of the crate, toward the open hatch.

"He's pulling me in!"

TWO

She felt Liam's hands around her ankles, felt him straining, lifting both her legs into the air as he leaned back. Zenn clawed at the knotted rope with her free hand, but it was no use. A powerful jerk from the animal and they were both hauled forward. Another tug, and Zenn was over the opening, the snorting, growling hog beneath her in the dark, his acrid scent sharp in her nostrils. Then she was tugged backwards, just a bit. She saw Liam had braced his feet against the raised metal lip that framed the hatchway.

"I can't hold him, Scarlett," Liam said. "What do I do?"

"My backpack. Can you reach it?"

He let go with one of his hands, grunting with exertion.

"Too far. Can't get to it," he said. "Unless I let go of you."

The hog pulled on the rope. She and Liam held out against the force. Barely.

"You have to get the maze-caut cutter," she told him. "When I say so, go get it. Ready?"

"Scarlett, I don't–"

"Liam. Ready?"

"OK, OK."

One more pull from the hog, the rope peeling flesh from her wrist, then a bit of slack.

"Go!"

As soon as Liam loosed his grip, Zenn's legs fell. She spun around, jammed both feet against the far side of the hatch opening and braced herself.

"Scarlett?" Liam shouted, panicky. "The cutter thing – looks like a…?"

"Like a… It's like…" What did a maser cauterizer look like to someone who'd never seen one? "A cylinder… a tube… A flashlight. Like a flashlight."

"This?"

She twisted enough to see him holding up a large-gauge dermal infuser.

"No! It's metal! With… a pointy tip. And buttons."

The hog's next jerk on the line snapped her forward at the waist, the force strong enough to bang her head down hard on her knee. The hog's next pull would be too much for her. Then Liam's arm was around her waist.

"Scarlett," he breathed through clenched teeth, his face close to hers. He held the maze-caut in his other hand. "Where's the on-switch?"

Zenn snatched the cutter out of Liam's hand, pressed the power pad, and saw the blue-white maser tip crackle to life. The hog tugged again, and her trapped hand, with the rope that held it, was pulled out of sight into the hatch.

"Liam, I can't see to cut. Pull up hard. Now!"

The towner boy's arms were strong around her. He heaved backward with all his might, crushing the air from her lungs. But the effort brought her arm up far enough to see the rope. The sandhog gave one more powerful jerk, the line went painfully taut, and she swung the cutter blindly.

With the sudden release of tension that followed, she and Liam flew backward from the hatch, rolled awkwardly and came to rest several feet away, lying next to each other, exhausted, Zenn's wrist burning.

A chattering, scolding noise came from nearby.

She raised herself up to see Katie, perched on the backpack. The rikkaset was sitting upright on her haunches, vocalizing in high-pitched squeaks and signing a stream of words that equated roughly to "Friend-Zenn being silly. Katie doesn't like. Stop now."

Zenn got to her feet, massaging her shoulder, which felt as if it was nearly dislocated by the hog's final pull on the line. She scanned the surroundings. The ship's storage hold stretched on for hundreds of feet, the stacked containers arranged with narrow walkways between them. There was no one in sight.

She moved cautiously back to the hatch. The animal raised itself up to snarl at her, then dropped its bulk onto the seda-field dish, crushing it flat, before retreating out of sight to a dark corner of the crate. Liam joined her and together they hefted the hatch lid shut.

"Well, Tiny seems fine. But I think your knock-out ray is toast."

Zenn just nodded and started to work the knotted rope off her wrist.

"Bad hog-thing! Stinks," Katie signed.

Zenn had to agree.

"Yes," she signed, then spoke aloud for Liam's benefit. "Sandhogs have a strong odor."

"You got that right," Liam said. "I've come across road-kill that smelled better." He sniffed at his own shirtsleeve. "Ugh. Now I reek as bad as he does."

"It'll wear off," Zenn told him.

"Not soon enough. I mean, why bother with these damn things, anyway? I know: they turn useless sand dunes into soil for crops. I'm not totally dense. But there are chemicals for that. Those are cheaper. And won't kill you."

"Sandhogs don't kill people, Liam."

"Oh?" He gave her a hard look.

"Your dad? That was an accident, you know that."

Intending to steal a valuable generator and sell it to pay off his gambling debts, Liam's father had mistakenly crept into the wrong shed on Gil Bodine's farm one dark night. It was his last mistake.

"Yeah. I know," he said. "But that doesn't mean I have to like the things. Or their stink."

While her uncle Otha was fond of saying hogs weren't worth the trouble, the truth was that resource-strapped colonists on Mars needed all the crop-growing soil they could make. In fact, Zenn had been assisting her uncle when he went to treat this particularly troublesome sandhog boar out on Gil Bodine's farm. It had burrowed out of its enclosure the night before. After it suddenly reappeared and almost attacked Otha, Gil said he was through with sandhogs, that he was going to send the creature back to its owner on Sigmund's Parch. That piece of information had come in handy. Hiding in the Pavonis warehouse, she'd heard her abductor talking to someone about her kidnapped father, saying that the Skirni was going to take her up to the *Helen*. After that, it was just a matter of hiding in the hog's cage-crate and waiting till it was loaded on the orbital ferry. So far, so good.

"C'mon." Liam sat down on the edge of the crate. "Let's make ourselves scarce before someone comes. I think I see an exit over there." He pushed himself off to land on the floor.

Zenn went to where Katie sat.

"What this place?" Katie signed at her.

"A ship. A big spaceship."

"Don't know word: space-ship."

Zenn thought for a second.

"A big, floating house. In the sky. Many people in it."

"Why Friend-Zenn comes here? Why brings Katie up in sky?"

Good question, Zenn thought, wondering at the impossible events of the past weeks, trying to bend them into some sort of logical order. They resisted being bent. And she'd hardly had time to catch her breath, let alone think things through, since the moment she was kidnapped.

That word again. Who could possibly have any reason to kidnap her? She opened the backpack and rearranged the meds and supplies inside to make more room for Katie.

But maybe that's how quickly a person's life can turn upside down, she thought. One minute, you're minding your own business, living in the cloister where you've always lived, where your whole world is a small corner of a pressurized canyon in the Valles Marineris on Mars, where your only problems are too much homework, passing the next test or treating the next patient in the cloister's menagerie of animals.

Well, she allowed, her life also presented a few other problems to consider. Like Liam Tucker. Like her foolish abandonment of her time-tested routine of keeping other people out of her life, or at least holding them at a safe distance. Or, the uniquely unsettling problem of Liam's embrace and the kiss that she should've seen coming but blind-sided her completely. Or, a few hours after that, finding yourself slung over the shoulder of a stocky, pug-faced little alien and taken from your dorm room in nothing but your old, worn-out pajamas.

Pajamas.

"I need to find some real clothes," she said. She made sure Katie was securely settled, hoisted the pack onto her back and tightened the straps around both shoulders. Then she sat down as Liam had done, and he reached up to help her down off the crate.

"What's the matter?" he said. "Orange clashes with red hair?"

"I kind of stand out in this," she said, indicating the coveralls. "I'll need to blend in if I'm going to follow that Skirni without him seeing."

"Right," Liam said, looking down the nearest row of crates, boxes and shipping containers. "Let's see what we can find." He went to the nearest container that had an unlocked door latch and pulled it open. It was full of large plastic sacks labeled "Gen-Soybeans. For Export Only".

After trying four more containers filled with either bulk food products or crated machinery, they finally found one stacked with passengers' trunks and suitcases. Zenn flipped up the lid of a case, feeling a twinge of guilt. It was full of men's clothing. She opened another and held up a silky green evening gown.

"Pay dirt," Liam said, looking on.

"Not exactly low-profile. And way too big."

They continued down the row, opening more crates.

"So, Scarlett. This whole thing with you and the Skirni, back on Mars. He went to a lot of trouble. To find out about you. To sneak into the cloister. To kidnap you. Why would he do that?"

"From what we overheard the Skirni say, it's because of something called a nexus. And thanks to you, *Liam*... he didn't have much trouble at all finding out about me. And apparently, whatever it is, it's important enough to kidnap me and my dad."

She felt her irritation with Liam rising again, then became angry with herself once more, for confiding too much in the towner boy, for opening up to him about what had been happening between her and the clinic's animals.

She brushed by him to the next unlocked container. The first trunk she opened held girls' clothing, roughly her size. She dug deeper. At the bottom of the trunk, she found a full-body jumpsuit, made of some dark synthetic material that felt almost weightless. She held it up to measure against herself; it was a little big, but close enough.

"Stylish," Liam said, attempting humor. "It's you, Scarlett."

"At least it's close to the right size. And all the pockets could be useful," she said. "It'll do. But I still need shoes."

She bent back into the trunk but found nothing. They went to the next container.

After two more suitcases, she turned up a pair of pair of heavy leather, lace-up boots and a long blue-and-black silk scarf.

"A scarf? Really?" Liam said, smirking.

"To cover my hair and face," she told him. "Low-profile, remember? Now…" She gave him a significant look. "Do you mind?"

"What?" he said. She held up the jumpsuit. "Oh, right. I'll just… go check for a way outta here," he said, and walked off.

When he'd gone, she pulled off the coveralls, then the pajamas. The jumpsuit fit well enough and was, frankly, so new and fashionably current, Zenn felt uncomfortable wearing it. She was lacing up the boots when Liam returned.

"Very nice," he told her. "In fact, probably the best-dressed I've ever seen you."

"Thanks a lot," she said. But he was right – everything she'd ever worn back at the cloister was either homespun or secondhand. Still, he didn't have to rub it in.

"C'mon," he said. "That door leads into a corridor. I opened it a crack. There are lots of passengers going past. We should be able to slip into the crowd."

"And then?"

"Then… then we try and spot your Skirni and follow him and… Nine Hells, Scarlett," he swore. "I don't know. We'll make it up as we go."

Resigned to the fact that this was also about as far as her own planning had proceeded, Zenn followed him to the nearest wall of the cargo hold. She watched as he opened the door a few inches and peered out. Over his shoulder, Zenn could see passengers flowing by in either direction, most of them chattering excitedly.

"C'mon." But no sooner had he stepped out into the corridor than a high-pitched voice spoke from close behind Zenn.

"Excuse me! You there, young human." Zenn froze, her heart leaping. "If you don't mind my asking, what is your business here?"

THREE

Zenn slammed the door shut, her last sight that of Liam standing in the teeming corridor, his expression panicked. She turned, holding the door latch, shielding it with her body from whoever had spoken. In her hands, behind her back, she felt Liam rattle the latch. She held it shut.

The voice she'd heard belonged to a Gliesian. He was dressed in the crisp white uniform of a ship's steward. Roughly Zenn's height, the amphibious alien regarded her suspiciously with two globular eyes that protruded from its broad, froggish face like a pair of glassy grapefruits. The smooth facial skin was a brilliant lime-green with indigo blue dots spattered across it like paint flicked from a brush. His two large flippered feet were clad in a kind of sandal.

"I'm sorry, but passengers are not allowed in the cargo hold. This is for your safety. You can identify yourself, please?"

Zenn's mind raced.

"I'm... Zz... Zora. Zora Bodine."

"And may I ask your reason for being here, Guest Bodine?" The little steward's voice was childishly high, but his vocabulary and almost total lack of accent indicated expert and expensive language instruction at some point in his career.

"The sandhog," she said. It was all she could think of. "My father's sandhog. In there." She pointed lamely to the hog's crate. "I was checking on it. I wanted to make sure it was OK. You know, all set for the rest of the trip. To Sigmund's Parch."

The steward regarded her for a moment, then padded over to the hog's crate. He stopped several feet away, eyed it suspiciously and pulled a v-film out of his coat pocket.

"Yes." He looked up from the film. "This animal is listed as belonging to a Bodine. And it is going to Sigmund's Parch. But your presence here... this is not according to regulation." The pupils in the Gliesian's globe-eyes narrowed, as if deciding what to do about her.

"And the hog, our sandhog," she went on mindlessly, "he does seem good, so that's fine, he's just fine, everything's fine with him." She felt Liam trying to open the door again. She leaned back hard onto the latch to keep it shut, and he stopped.

Take the hint, Liam. Just get away.

"Hmph," the steward huffed, grapefruit eyes fixed on her. He glanced from her to the crate, the pupils now widening slightly. "Um... so, you have looked in to view this animal? And all is well with it?"

"Yes. He's fine."

"You were able to approach closely, in such a way that I... would possibly not be required to verify this?" Zenn understood now. He was afraid of it. Her theory was confirmed when, a second later, a booming roar from the crate caused the steward to leap high into the air, landing several yards away, his body lowered into a protective crouch.

"Ha-ha..." He laughed a high, musical laugh. "This was unexpected." He crept closer to her again, not taking his eyes off the crate. "And how could you do this? Evaluate the animal, to know that it was well?"

"I was able to because I'm an exoveterinarian." It was almost not a lie, Zenn told herself. She was a novice exovet, at least. OK, not a full novice, but over halfway through her novice year. The steward stared at her blankly. "That means I'm a doctor for alien animals. Like sandhogs. I have medicines." She indicated the pack on her back. "They can make the sandhog sleepy so you can get close and examine it. Then they won't attack you. Usually."

The Gliesian shifted anxiously, looking at the crate. The hog snarled menacingly.

Zenn went on, "So, that's why I came down to take a look. Alone. By. Myself," she said loudly. Hopefully, loud enough for Liam to hear. "And I'd say there's no need for you to bother yourself with checking on the hog. He's doing fine."

To Zenn's immense and instant relief, the little steward now gave her a big grin filled with teeth like tiny black icepicks.

"You are qualified, then. To evaluate the animal. To say it requires no further attention."

"Yes," she said. There'd been no further jiggling of the latch. She hoped Liam had finally given up. "He's just a little agitated by the ferry ride from the surface, but that's normal. We're very pleased with his conditions here. And that's to your credit. We're very satisfied with the service. Mister Bodine and I."

"Your satisfaction, you could possibly make mention of this, perhaps? To the Captain?"

"Oh. Of course, I'd be glad to."

The steward smiled even more broadly at this, rocking back and forth on his heels.

"Very kind of you. Very kind." The Gliesian gave the crate one last glance. "I can now help you? To your cabin? Do you have luggage?"

"Oh, no," Zenn said quickly. "I… The luggage… has been sent up my cabin. Our cabin. But thank you."

"And I thank you," he said, beaming at her. They stood looking at each other for a few moments. "And what is your deck, then?"

"Deck… eight?" Zenn ventured.

"Ah, this is fortunate. I serve on decks five through nine. Please do not hesitate to call on me for anything you may require. I am Deck Steward Yed. In point of fact, I am called in Gliesian as Yed the One Who Consumes Fat Meal-Larvae With Lip-Noises of Pleasure. But for our valued guests, I am Yed."

"Right. Yed. Got it," Zenn said. "So, I'll just go on up. To my cabin." She turned toward the door.

"Guest Bodine," the steward said. Zenn stopped. "Deck eight is this way, please." She smiled sheepishly and squeezed past him. He pointed to a door in the opposite wall, and she headed for it. "Yes. That way, thank you."

Zenn gave the grinning steward a final wave, took a deep breath, opened the door and stepped through.

The corridor Zenn emerged into was narrow, with barely enough room to contain the river of passengers streaming in both directions. They were mostly human, but with a scattering of Asents – Alien Sentients – mixed in, both humans and Asents conversing as they ebbed and flowed around her. The carpeting on the floor was dingy and worn, and the walls could do with a fresh coat of paint. The nearest ceiling light flickered on and off, and the stale air smelled of artificial freshener.

With no idea how to reach the corridor Liam had entered on the opposite side of the hold, Zenn chose a direction at random and let herself be swept up into a group of about two dozen passengers. There were both adults and children, and she hoped she'd just blend in. From their excited chatter, she decided they were probably Earther colonists from the mining outposts on the moons of Jupiter, Saturn or the larger asteroids.

Shuffling along with the colonists, she tried to order her thoughts. Her first priority: getting herself out of sight. Next, try to locate Liam, then get word to Otha down on Mars, so he, Sister Hild and Hamish wouldn't worry. Otha would surely be mad, but at least he'd be relieved to hear from her. Especially when she explained she had been kidnapped from her room. On the other hand, he'd want to know why she didn't get in touch or come back to the cloister as soon as she escaped. And, like when she first told him about her mental "links" with the animals, there was the distinct possibility he wouldn't believe her about any of it. But she didn't really have a choice. If she'd let the ferry blast off without her, she'd have lost her only chance to find her father. She'd also have to carefully time her communication with her uncle so that he couldn't have her sent back.

Amid passengers ahead of her, she now saw a small, squat form swathed in a garish array of colored robes, assorted jeweled necklaces and heavy rings on every stubby finger. The Skirni who had abducted her! What had Liam called him? Brokt? Pog?

Her heart rate galloped at the sight of the alien, and she dropped behind the passengers nearest her, then stepped into a recess off the corridor and watched. The three-foot-high creature's black-and-white mottled bulldog face and under-slung jaw were thrust forward as he shouldered his way through the crowd, his short, hairless tail dragging behind him as he hobbled along.

She maneuvered her way through the corridor to what she thought was a safe distance behind him, wrapping the silk scarf up around her head as she went. She tucked her long hair out of sight inside it, then brought the end up across her lower face. Not a foolproof disguise by any means, but it would have to suffice.

The Skirni veered off into another passage and Zenn followed. A short way on, he stopped and spoke to one of the cabin doors that lined both walls. Zenn was too far away to overhear, but the door responded and opened. After he entered and the door shut, she got just close enough to read the cabin number and turned to leave.

Intent on following the Skirni, she hadn't noticed the activity behind her. Another uniformed Gliesian steward had come into the far end of the corridor. He was stopping passengers and asking them something… to show their tickets. She retreated in the other direction, but found herself at a dead-end. Trapped. She would have to pass the steward to get away. He was stopping everyone. Soon she would be the only one left.

The steward was close enough now to be heard.

"Boarding passes, please. Thank you."

There were fewer than half a dozen passengers between her and him. Zenn spoke to the cabin door nearest her. No response – it was locked. As were the next two. Three passengers remained in the corridor. She didn't think the steward had noticed her yet. But he surely would in the next few seconds.

She spotted an archway between her and the steward. It appeared to lead into some sort of public room. Quickly, she walked down the passage and ducked inside.

It was a lounge of some sort, with a bar along one wall. Passengers sat on stools, drinking at the bar and at half a dozen tables. Zenn pushed her way to the back, where another archway opened into a smaller, more private space.

The room was half-obscured by a fog of low-hanging smoke that smelled of cherry and tobacco. She was able to make out the near end of a table. Seated at it was a long, upright reptilian form: an Alcyon. He held a fanned array of playing cards in one clawed hand.

"Looking for someone?" The Alcyon spoke in a deep, wheezy voice, his long jaws and lack of flexible lips causing him some difficulty with his enunciation. "The Lieutenant? Or Master Vancouver?"

"Yes! Master Vancouver," Zenn said, picking a name, any name, anything to get her as far as possible from the steward.

The Alcyon glanced at her, flicked his long forked tongue into the air three times in her direction and turned back to his cards. He sported a bright red-and-blue tinted crest of skin that rose like a small sail on his scaled head. This marked him as a mature alpha male of the human-sized crocodilian species from Hyria Nine in the Alcyon star system. From the size of the crest, Zenn guessed he was most likely a clan leader of some sort and, judging from the golden chain mail vest he wore, a wealthy one.

"Ah, you can perhaps distract Master Jules for me," the reptile said, lifting a long, claw-tipped digit to indicate the outline of a barely visible figure at the far end of the table. The Alcyon took a long drag on a flexible tube connected to a large hookah resting on the floor next to his chair, then puffed out double plumes of smoke through his nostrils and added, "He is too quick in the eye to allow my cheating." The reptilian's short, sharp laugh was a low-pitched coughing sound, accompanied by another cloud of smoke.

A voice sounded from the other end of the table, now partially visible through a gap in the haze.

"Yes! Do distract Master Van-coo-vehr for us, will you?" At the sight of the speaker, Zenn recoiled involuntarily – another Skirni. "Perhaps you could wave at him some old fish-heads. Har." His voice sounded as though he was gargling oil as he spoke. He was short, like all Skirni, and more rotund than usual. He wore a heavy green velvet robe, and a thick half-circle of carved ivory dangled from the septum of his snub nose. Several of the teeth jutting up from his lower jaw appeared to be made of some copper-tinted metal. "Fish heads! That would draw his attention, would it not, Lieutenant?"

The one he called Lieutenant, a human, now became visible through the smoke. The human didn't smile at the Skirni's joke and looked up just long enough to give Zenn a quick once-over. Zenn guessed he was late-thirties, his clean-shaven face tanned and handsome in a square-jawed sort of way, with close-cropped light brown hair. His crisp crimson uniform jacket bore golden epaulets on each shoulder, with a black leather strap cutting a smart diagonal across the chest. The immediate impression should have been the very model of a dashing, archetypal young hero, but there was something... unusual... about his appearance. Zenn found herself staring, and only pulled her gaze away when the curtain of drifting smoke lifted enough to reveal the farthest end of the table. Seated there was possibly the last creature she expected to see on a starship orbiting Mars.

FOUR

A whimsically smiling face looked up from playing cards held in a big, four-fingered mech-hand. Two jet-black eyes set against downy gray skin caught sight of her, and two sounds emerged as the creature spoke: one sound, the fainter of the two, like a rusty gate hinge mixed with stuttering laughter; the other, louder sound was a synthesized Transvox voice.

"Is the female biped noun mammal seeking personal pronoun my own identity?" he said.

"I'm... sorry?" was all Zenn could manage.

The Alcyon interpreted. "I think Jules meant to say, 'Were you looking for me?'"

Before Zenn could respond, the Transvox voice went on, "Personal pronoun me am here verb transporting two circular sugar-candies on paper-sticks into colloquialism the washing machines."

"And that," the Alcyon said, "was to say, 'I am about to take these two suckers to the cleaners.'" The Alcyon reached over the table to tap on the cybernetic arm extending from the upper-body area of the one called Jules. “Adjust your Transvox again, friend. You speak nonsense.”

One of Jules Vancouver’s mech-hands fiddled with a control pad on his other mech-arm, and he spoke quietly, as if talking to himself. Again, the fainter liquid chirps and squeaks were overlaid by the Transvox voice, but then the squeaking sound grew softer as the unit’s frequency dampers kicked in, allowing the artificial voice to be heard more clearly. “Testing, testing… Under the wide and starry sky, dig the grave and let me lie… It was the best of times, it was the worst…”

Satisfied the device was working properly, he looked up at her and the Transvox voice said, “I apologize for my translating device. It requires fresh soft-codes. And I’m eager to know who you are and your purpose. But look…” One mechanical hand gestured at the pile of colored discs on the table in front of him. “I’m winning. Please, sit.” He gestured to a chair by the wall, then bent his smiling, beaked face back to his cards as if he’d known her for ages and she’d just stopped by for a friendly chat.

Zenn couldn’t help herself.

“You’re a dolphin,” she blurted. The others all looked at her. “I mean…” Her mind scrabbled this way and that, searching for something sensible. “I mean, Father didn’t say you’d be a dolphin. When he told me. About you.”

“Your father? I will assume he and I are acquainted?” the dolphin said as one mech-hand counted through his piles of discs.

“Oh, yes, you’re definitely acquainted,” she lied as innocently as she could manage. “From Earth. From his time on Earth. Where you’re… from.”

Several silent seconds passed. Jules the dolphin looked up and blinked at her expectantly.

"But," Zenn said, "I don't want to intrude. On your game." She smiled idiotically. "Why don't you just go ahead and finish? I'll wait."

Jules took another look at his cards, pushed the mound of colored discs forward and peered at her again. "You have a quantity of freckles across the skin of your nose and facial area. They are distinctive."

"I suppose they are," she said, smiling in spite of herself beneath the scarf, which she now checked nervously to ensure it was still in place. She was beginning to get the hang of listening to him speak. She had to ignore the twitter of his natural vocalizations and force herself to listen only to the Transvox speech coming from the two small speakers attached to his walksuit's harness.

Zenn had studied basic dolphin physiology as part of Sister Hild's class on Earther marine ecology back at the cloister. She knew a little about dolphin culture, about their somewhat troubled history of contact with human society on Earth. She also knew that walksuits like the one he wore were hugely expensive and only available on a limited basis. The suit consisted of two legs and two arms, both powered by hydraulic micro-actuators at the joints, with a central web-like arrangement that cradled the sleek, gray body of what Zenn judged to be a young, six- or seven-foot-long bottlenose dolphin.

"I am calling your bets with my cards," Jules declared to the others. "Peruse them and commence weeping." He released the holographic cards he held and they hovered up into the air, where they floated in place for a second before rearranging themselves into a flying wedge. With a short burst of mechanical-sounding trumpet music, three of the cards transformed themselves into small silver scepters that flew in quick circles around the other two cards, which converted themselves into a pair of spiked balls affixed to short wooden handles.

"Scepters over maces," the dolphin said with evident satisfaction.

The Skirni snorted in disgust. "Blast and pestilence." He glared at the dolphin and threw his cards at the table, where they landed with a soft, buzzer-like bleat of defeat.

The Alcyon released his grip on his cards, and they spread out in the air over the table. "Scimitars over tongs," the reptile hissed. "I am afraid the weeping will be yours. Salty tears for your salty sea-home. Ha."

More mechanical music sounded as the Alcyon's cards turned into four small curved swords and a tiny set of blacksmith tongs. The swords twirled through the air toward Jules's still-hovering weapons, neatly sliced both the scepters and maces in half and, to a short fanfare of victory music, rose a foot higher before they and the fragments of Jules's items became cards again and dropped to stack themselves neatly on the tabletop.

The Alcyon laughed another short, harsh laugh and swept the discs to his side of the table. Jules shook his head, his permanent dolphin smile unable to mask his disappointment.

"Crap," he muttered, giving the traitorous cards a stare.

The Skirni pushed his chair away from the table. "That's it. I'm done."

"But Master Thrott," Jules said, "I have lost a significant amount of my chips here. You are stopping now, without allowing me to regain my lost funds?"

"Yes," Thrott grumbled. "It is called quitting while I'm ahead." He hopped down out of his chair, pointed at what remained of his chips on the table and said, "You. Pick these up; we're going."

With a start, Zenn thought he was addressing her. Then she saw a figure crouching against the wall behind her. The creature had been so still and the smoke so dense, she hadn't noticed. The Fomalhaut was a female, much taller than Zenn but only about half her weight, the slender humanoid form dressed incongruously in a shabby black tuxedo several sizes too small, her yellow crescent-moon eyes focused permanently on the floor. The delicate features of the Fomalhaut race always made Zenn think of an elvish child's doll stretched lengthwise in a funhouse mirror.

"Don't muck about! Pick those up, I said." The Skirni raised a hand in threat, and the Fomalhaut scurried to the table, gathered up the discs and bowed her head in submission before moving to stand a few paces behind the Skirni. Slavery had been outlawed on all the planets of the Local Systems Accord centuries ago. But with no home world of their own, the wandering Skirni mainly lived aboard a scattering of starships in the Outer Reaches, beyond the oversight of most LSA laws; the law governing slaves aboard starliners remained unsettled. Subsisting on the grudging acceptance of the other races, they scraped out a living selling questionable medicinal potions, arranging marginally honest transactions, telling fortunes to the gullible and generally doing the jobs no one else would do. Their Fomalhaut slaves were given the jobs even the Skirni balked at.

"So, Master Van-coo-vehr, you wish to recoup your losses?" the Skirni leered at Jules.

"Earnestly."

"In that regard..." Thrott said, bringing his hands together with a clink of heavy rings. "I have a proposition. I own an animal. A fighting slug. It is nothing special, a feeble thing, actually. Wins so seldom I don't know why I waste my time with it. But if you wished to put a creature of your choice up against it, accompanied by a suitable wager, you could regain your losses several times over."

"A fight between animals?" Jules said, surprise audible in his tone. "Such events are illegal, are they not?"

"We are star travelers. In the arms of the mother-void," Thrott said, gesturing broadly at their surroundings. "The legalities in space are, shall we say, murky. With a little discretion, we could arrange–"

"It *is* illegal! And it's cruel," Zenn said. All eyes in the room turned to her. She instantly regretted her outburst.

"Oh, are you a qualified expert on the subject?" Thrott gave her a mocking, thick-lipped grin. "You practice interstellar law, do you?"

"No," she stammered. "But... I know animal fighting is banned. On all the planets. And it's inhumane." Her face burned hot.

"But I am no human," the Skirni said. "And so cannot be inhumane, har. Who are you, in any case, to lecture me? What right do you–"

"She is correct to speak." Jules cut him off. "And I agree. I will not wager on any such animal battles. It is regretful to hear you request such an event."

"Oh, I apologize for disappointing you," Thrott sneered, sarcasm twisting his face.

"The dolphin and the girl have it right." The soldier gathered up his own colored discs as he spoke. His voice was… what? Commanding, Zenn decided. "We're still in Sol space. Solar conventions in this case apply until we move out of the system."

"Ah, conventions. They are formulated to be interpreted, are they not?" Thrott gave the soldier a jowly grin.

"The law's the law," the soldier said, unsmiling. "When laws are clear, interpretation doesn't come into it." Zenn realized then what it was about the young officer that kept his appearance from that of a cookie-cutter hero: his eyes. They were pale gray, almost silver. And she couldn't define it, but there was something about them that seemed able to take in everything about whoever he looked at, as if he had some uncanny skill at reading those around him. Thrott's own eyes looked away from the challenge of the soldier's piercing gaze.

"It is your loss, then," Thrott growled at Jules. "And I will go now and spend your money on a jug of your excellent Earther tequila. Har." The dolphin was about to reply to this when another voice sounded behind them.

"Boarding passes, please."

Zenn turned around. The Gliesian steward was right behind her, his webbed, three-fingered hand outstretched. Panic washed all thought away and she drew back from him like a hunted animal.

The Alcyon, who had been quietly observing the confrontation between Thrott and Jules, now unfolded himself from his chair. He thanked Jules for inviting him to the game, showed the steward his pass and left.

Thrott brusquely showed his own boarding pass and moved toward the exit.

"Forgive me; boarding pass, please," the steward said to the Fomalhaut trailing behind Thrott.

"This thing?" Thrott said, waving one hand at the cowering alien. "It is a slave, obviously. It cannot be expected to have a pass."

"I am sorry; all passengers must show a pass before ship's departure from orbit."

Thrott sighed heavily and gave the steward an indulgent smile.

"My good friend–" the Skirni reached up to drape one arm around the steward's shoulder and with his other hand pulled his credit relay from beneath his robes "–I was mistaken. I have that creature's pass right here. Shall we say... five units?"

The steward glanced nervously around at the others in the room. Jules and the soldier both suddenly found something else to look at.

"Five units?" The steward quickly showed his own relay to accept Thrott's funds. "Yes. All is in order here. Thank you." He then gestured for them to exit.

Thrott gave the soldier a gloating grin.

"There. You see? Even in Sol space, the interpretation of law has its place." With that, he grunted at the Fomalhaut to follow him and waddled off.

The soldier stood and flashed his pass at the steward. As he moved to the door, he had to wait for Zenn to step out of the way. He watched her, the pale eyes regarding her with what seemed like a bit more curiosity than before.

"You mentioned your father knew the dolphin here – on Earth," he said. "You don't sound quite like a citizen. Do I detect a Martian accent?"

"Oh," Zenn said, grasping for an answer. "Yes. We… moved. When I was young."

The soldier considered this.

"Well, thank your for the game, Jules," he said. He gave them both a quick smile and was gone.

"Yes, if I may trouble you–" the steward popped his glass-globe eyes at Zenn "–boarding pass?"

Her heart sank. It was over. What could she say? That she'd lost her pass? There was no convenient sandhog to serve as a distraction this time.

"Your… boarding… pass?" the steward asked again, speaking slowly, as if to a young child. "If you please."

Out of the corner of her eye, Zenn saw the dolphin suddenly sweep one mech-hand across the tabletop, pushing his discs onto the floor.

"Oh," he said loudly. "Look at this. You." He gestured at Zenn. "Pick this up. Immediately obey me and pick these gambling materials up." Zenn stared at him. So did the steward. "Are you such a lazy slave? Pick this up, I command you."

It took Zenn another moment to understand. Stooping, she gathered up the discs and clutched them in both hands. Then, she bowed her head as she'd seen the Fomalhaut do and moved to stand meekly behind the dolphin.

"Yes, she is an unsatisfactory indentured servant, this one." The dolphin shook his large head at her disapprovingly and held out his pass for the steward's inspection.

"Ah, I see, Guest Vancouver," the steward said, looking from the dolphin's pass to Zenn and back again. "They allow this? For dolphinkind to possess such an... item ? To possess an Earther human as slave?"

Jules had no reply to this.

"I'm not an Earther," Zenn said. She added, in what she hoped was a suitably slavish tone, "Forgive me speaking, but as I said, I'm from Mars. Not Earth."

"Yes, a Martian," Jules said. "Perfectly allowable, you will agree. For me to have a Martian slave not from Earth."

The steward bulged his eyes at them. She could see he was wavering, trying to decide if their story made sense.

"And for your understanding," Jules held up his credit relay. "Please accept this gratuity. Five units, shall we say?"

Without hesitating, the steward brought out his own relay to accept the "tip".

"Yes. This is in order," he said, pocketing his relay. Zenn was quite sure she'd just witnessed the second blatant bribe the steward had accepted in the last few minutes, which, apparently, neither dolphin nor Gliesian viewed as unusual in the least. "Thank you, and I trust you will have a pleasant journey onward with us." The steward flashed them a black-toothed grin and left them.

"Thank you. For doing that," Zenn said, watching the steward make his way out of the bar. "I must have forgotten my boarding pass. In my cabin."

The dolphin looked at her for a moment. "You are welcome, Miss..."

"Bodine. Zora Bodine."

"Zora Bodine. And your father is, then, Mister Bodine, I will assume."

"Yes. Bodine. Um, you don't remember him?" she said, clinging to the desperate hope that she could feel her way to something like solid conversational footing.

"No, I'm afraid I don't," the dolphin said brightly. He must know by now she was lying, but he seemed unconcerned. "I associated with only a few humans on Earth. None were named Bodine. Or are in any way likely to be your father."

"No, of course not. My mistake." She felt her face flushing hot beneath the scarf and moved toward the doorway.

"And I am wondering, Zora Bodine, if you would like me to call the steward back... perhaps he could help you return to your cabin and locate your pass?"

"No," Zenn said quickly. "I can find my way. It's not a problem. I'm sorry I bothered you."

"But there is some problem, isn't there, somewhere?" The dolphin crossed his mech-arms in front of him. "I hazard to guess that you are in a form of trouble."

"No. I just came in here to..." It was no use. She knew it. And this dolphin knew it as well.

"I will tell you what I see as the facts," he said, hydraulic legs whirring into action as he stepped closer, bright obsidian eyes fixing on her. "You wished to be seen as someone who knew me through your father. A father I have never met. You also show reluctance to interact with the ship's authorities to display your boarding pass or to go to your own cabin. My surmise is that your trouble is awaiting you at your cabin. Possibly, you have no ticket. Yes. Or no cabin, even! Furthermore–" he clapped his mech-hands together in growing excitement "–I will wager you that you are... a stowaway." He again held up his credit relay. "Shall we say ten units?"

"You... want to make a bet?"

"I would win it, would I not? You *are* a stowaway. I am correct?"

Zenn nodded miserably. With enough misery, she hoped, to evoke sympathy. If she could just convince him to keep her secret, she might still be able to remain aboard somehow.

"Yes, correct." He seemed deflated at the thought. "It would not be a fair bet now that I know the truth of the situation. I withdraw the wager." He lowered his relay and looked at her for a moment. "So, a stowaway," he said, with what to Zenn sounded almost like admiration. "But this is thrilling. Are you running from unjust persecution? Is that it? And you could not buy passage on this ship... because you have no funds? You are impoverished, a poor wretch living only on your wits? Have you had your rightful inheritance stolen by low scoundrels, perhaps? And you are now seeking your remedy in an escapade formulated to right this wrong? I have read of similar events. In the printed-on-paper novels of several ancient Earth writers. It is the stuff of imagination and adventure. Is it like that with you?"

"No, not exactly," she said, wondering at his enthusiasm but recalling that dolphins could be prone to impulsive behavior and fixations on certain elements of human society. While he appeared harmless enough, she simply didn't know how much she should divulge. "I'm looking for my… for someone. That's why I stowed away. I followed somebody aboard who might know where this person is."

The dolphin bobbed his head at her. "Truly? By coincidence, I am looking, too. For someone. But that is another story. An adventure of its own, I can say, with drama and twists, and like yours, not yet finished." He stood before her, hydraulics humming softly. "And you are alone here? What of the remainder of your family? You are young, and they would be missing you, would they not? I'm sorry, but you see how my need to satisfy my curiosity requires my asking."

Zenn did see. It was perfectly understandable.

"But I am rude to impose my questions without offering hospitality," he said. "Please, accompany me to my own cabin and we will discuss the mystery of your situation further." He gestured to the door, but Zenn hesitated. The dolphin's fixed smile and inexpressive eyes made it impossible to read him. "There is no need for anxious concern." He raised both mech-hands in the air. "I am eminently worthy of trust, I assure you. It is a large and spacious cabin where we will be most comfortable as we speak. And we have established your own options at the moment are limited. What is there to lose? Nothing at all. This way."

Without waiting for her to answer, he strode out of the room, mech-legs hissing and clicking, his tail flukes held aloft behind him as he walked. He was absolutely right, of course. There really were no other choices for Zenn to consider. Suddenly, she felt the full weight of where she was, the hopeless task she'd set herself. And then, despite everything she'd been telling herself since leaving Mars, she desperately, and irrationally, longed for the reassurance of Liam Tucker's self-centered, annoying, towner-boy presence. OK, a little less annoying since he'd tried to come to her rescue back on Mars. So, where was he now? Had he found a place to hide? Or had he, like her, been confronted by a steward's demand to see the boarding pass he didn't have? If nothing else, Liam was a solid connection to home, to safety, to all she was leaving behind. She could try to find him. But where would she even begin to look? Besides, she couldn't risk being distracted from her primary aim: find a place she wouldn't be noticed. Then locate her father.

Focus, Zenn. Focus.

Realizing she still clutched Jules Vancouver's gambling discs in her hands, she stuffed them into her jumpsuit pockets and hurried to follow the dolphin out into the passageway.

FIVE

Zenn wasn't sure what she had expected a starship passenger cabin to look like, but the dolphin's accommodations still left her looking about in wonder. Unlike the shabby corridors open to the general public, this large suite of rooms was well maintained and sumptuous. The walls were ornamented with richly embroidered tapestries and antique oil-on-canvas paintings of rural landscapes and portraits of people dressed in old-fashioned clothing. In the central room stood furniture with plush cushions. On a long table by the wall was a ceramic bowl filled with apples, bananas, kipfruit and what looked like an assortment of dried fish morsels wrapped in clear plastic. One wall held a large viewscreen that currently displayed a changing display of the ship's various passenger decks, recreation venues, retail shops and other areas. Off to one side of the main room were three doorways leading to what Zenn assumed were the bath and sleeping quarters.

"As you can see, a plentitude of space," Jules Vancouver said, gesturing at the room. Zenn just stood, looking around herself. She felt herself beginning to relax. Was this Jules someone she could trust? She was beginning to think he was. "Please, you must unburden yourself. Sit, do." He watched her as she slipped off her backpack, set it down on one chair and sank into the cushions of another.

"So, Zora Bodine," he said, pouring them both glasses of an orangish-pink liquid from a cut-glass decanter on the central table. "You must tell me of your adventure. How you secreted yourself aboard this ship. And why. Perwynk cider? It's freshly crushed."

"Thank you," she said. She unwound the scarf from her head and took the offered glass.

"Your hair. It is quite red," Jules said, leaning in for a closer look. "Is this a true color? Or have you altered the hue artificially?"

"No," she said, smiling at him. "This is its natural color."

"I am sorry. Do I presume upon you too much with my personal questions? I am intrigued, you see, by your situation. I am eager in fact, to hear your tale if you would tell it. Would you? Tell it to me? Or do I insert my nose in where it is unwelcome?"

"No, of course you don't," Zenn said. "You kept me from being thrown off the ship. You have every right to know what I'm doing here." In fact, she thought, without this obliging cetacean, her so-called "plan" to save her father would have been over before it started. There was only one course to take: she settled back in her chair and started talking.

She told him everything. How she was in her novice year of exovet training at the Ciscan Cloister training school that her uncle Otha ran on Mars. How she'd recently found herself sharing thoughts with some of the alien animals being treated at the clinic, and how these "links" became so intense her uncle thought she might be having a mental breakdown. She told him about Vic LeClerc's attempt to have the clinic closed so she could steal the Cloister's land for growing crops to feed the struggling colonists in the Arsia valley. She explained how the woman forced her nephew Liam to help her, and how Liam had finally changed his mind and exposed the plot, causing Vic to be arrested along with her thuggish foreman, Graad Dokes. Then she told him as much as she could recall about how the Skirni had paralyzed her with some sort of toxin and then kidnapped her, how she'd woken up afterward imprisoned at the Pavonis launch port, and how Liam had found her there. Finally, how she, Katie and Liam had smuggled themselves aboard the *Helen of Troy* in the sandhog's shipping crate.

"Kidnapped. This is simply amazing. But why?" Jules asked, pouring himself another glass of juice. "Why come onto this starship at all? Why did you not escape back to your home place?"

"Because when the Skirni was in my room at the cloister, I linked with his mind and… saw his memories. I know how that sounds." She held up her hands to stop his incredulous objection. None came. "I saw my father, on Enchara, being taken. I saw him held in some kind of room, a room with medical equipment. Unusual equipment. Later, I overheard the Skirni say he was going to the *Helen of Troy*. I had to follow him."

"You believe you saw this Skirni's memory... of your father... kidnapped? Truly?" the dolphin exclaimed. Zenn was certain he was about to tell her the story she was spinning was simply too far-fetched and impossible to waste any more of his time on. Instead he said, "But this is most marvelous and deeply fascinating." He rubbed his big mech-hands together excitedly. "And what transpired then?"

"You... believe me?"

"Why shouldn't I? What reason would you have to relate lies to such a stranger as me? No reason I can discern. Besides, let us be honest: if you wished to deceive me in some way, you would have constructed a more plausible and convincing narrative, of which your tale is neither. Please, enlighten me about your life at this healing cloister. How does one so young become entrusted with the care of such colossal and imposing life forms?"

Jules listened with rapt attention as Zenn went on with her story, interrupting occasionally to ask for clarification.

"And you have flourished among these immense alien animals since your earliest moments? So, you are well familiar with non-Earthly creatures. And your very own mother was also such an exoveterinarian expert. But as you lived at this Ciscan Cloister home by yourself, your entire life, you had no friends to visit and interact with you?"

She considered his question. She loved her uncle Otha and Hild, of course, and Hamish and she had been friendly... but were they actually friends? Wasn't a friend someone you talked to as an equal, someone you could share experiences with, share secrets with, feel... friendly with?

"There was one person," she said, almost reluctant to bring it up, but feeling it was something she needed to talk through, if only to clarify in her own mind. "Liam Tucker. The human boy I came aboard with."

"Yes, he was your close and tightly bonded friend then?"

"We were friends,"she said slowly. "And then things got complicated."

"Complications. I have read all about such things." The dolphin emphatically set down his glass and began to pace the room with excitement. "Yes. Yes. It begins with two characters of opposite gender meeting by accident. This initial interaction reveals you are utterly incompatible, and so this is followed by a lengthy period of sparring back and forth, tit for tat, you say one thing, he then says its opposite, culminating in a crisis point of some argumentative variety. But this was a misdirection. Upon encountering some new and even higher crisis, both of you are struck as by lightning that you do not hate each other, but instead – and quickly, magically it would seem – find you are both looking with the other's eyes and, with a shock of knowing-all-at-once, realize you are in fact soulmates. Seeing that you are destined one for the other, you now commence to share your long, long, happy lives as one. The end."

He took a deep breath and stood, mech-hands on mech-hips, nodding his head up and down, watching her expectantly."I am correct, am I not?"

"Not quite," she said slowly, reluctant to dim his enthusiasm.

"No? This is puzzling. I have encountered this behavior repeatedly in all manner of the old adventures and romantically inclined mysteries-on-paper. I assumed it was standard."

"Well, it was complicated, like I said. Vic's foreman, Graad Dokes, forced Liam to do the bad things he did, so in a way it wasn't his fault. But when I said I had to tell my uncle Otha what was going on, Liam asked me to wait until he could get proof to clear himself. And then he kissed me. And then he ran off and didn't show up again, so I thought he'd been lying to me. I thought his kissing me just–"

"I knew it." Jules slapped his hands together. "It is the budding of the romantical element."

"No, it's really not. It wasn't."

"It was not? But the moment of kissing is always the budding moment. Oh, I see... he took you by force. He imposed his pulsing will upon you and this then became the moment of passion, uncontrollable, you felt swept away on the rising tide of–"

"No." Zenn stopped him. "It was nothing like that. This kiss was more of a 'thanks for not turning me in to the authorities' kind of kiss."

"Interesting," Jules said, his voice calm again. "So. What then did you feel?"

"Baffled, mostly. Not that it was... bad. It was OK. I can appreciate the fact that Liam is my age, he's not terrible-looking, he's kind of... intriguing, in some ways. But he can also be really exasperating."

"And yet, unless I am mistaken, you do wish to be reunited with this person," Jules said. "So, perhaps he has demonstrated that he worthy of your friendship. Is he? Worthy?"

Zenn hadn't considered the situation in quite this way. The truth was, she'd hardly had time to consider the situation at all.

"Well, Liam did admit he was wrong about helping Vic and Graad. And he came to warn us that Graad had tampered with the sunkiller's restraints in the infirmary."

"Ah, so he is not an entirely vile and disreputable person, then?"

"No, he isn't, not at all. And then after the Skirni took me from the cloister, Liam followed him to the warehouse and tried to rescue me."

"A rescue attempt," Jules said approvingly. "This is surely the sign of his affection and care for you. Maybe this Liam is in fact worthy of your trust."

"Well, you might have a point," Zenn conceded.

"You are smiling at this thought," Jules said, regarding her. "It makes you feel better?"

Zenn had to laugh at this. "Well, I suppose it does. But let's not read too much into it, OK?"

"Yes. This is wise, especially since you deny there was any romantical element."

"I think it's safe to say my upbringing might not have equipped me for the romantical element. Does that make sense?"

"Ah, your faulty and cruel upbringing has crippled your development into a social being. I have read of this tragic issue as well."

"Not cruel," she said. "My mom and dad were great. But faulty? You might have a point. The truth is, I really never made friends when I was very young," she admitted. "I played with kids from town, from Arsia City, like when we went in to barter crops for supplies. But I don't even remember their names. And later… I didn't want to go into Arsia, anyway. Because of how the towners acted. They didn't like that we had off-world patients – that we treated alien animals at the clinic. There's a lot of prejudice against off-worlders of any kind on Mars right now."

"Yes, the influence of the Temporary Executive Authority government on Earth." Jules sounded thoughtful. "Their campaign to ban all non-Earthly creatures made for unpleasant times for many beings. It is certain the situation would have been more dire had the New Law faction prevailed. The New Law would have seen aliens of all sorts on Earth simply exterminated, if the rumors were credible."

"But the New Law faction never had any real power, right? My uncle says they're just a small group of Earther fanatics, too crazy for even the Authority to listen to."

"Honestly, I do not know the pertinent details," Jules said. "Politics was never one of my interests. I simply recall there was considerable fear among the off-world beings during the time of the purge. And after the embargo of the Rift was imposed, no Asents or their alien animals at all remained on Earth. It seemed an empty world then. Emptier, at least."

They were both quiet for a moment.

"But we were discussing your sad and failed socialization on Mars," Jules said. "So, you are not in love with this Liam?"

"No, I'm pretty sure I'm not," Zenn said. "Liam and I were just… friends."

"Yes. The 'just friends' phrase. But your expression communicates the situation still contains the complexity mentioned earlier."

Zenn sighed. "You could say that."

"I also see that you tire of this subject," he said. Quite perceptively, Zenn thought, feeling addled and vaguely embarrassed by the topic. "Tell me this, then: how did you adjust to it – growing into your upper years in the absence of peer-group interaction?"

"I had my uncle and the Sister. And Hamish, our sexton. He's a coleopt – basically an eight-foot tall beetle. He was someone I could talk to, at least. But I was busy, too. With my chores and with school. And I had the animals, of course. They gave me more than enough interaction. Too much, sometimes."

"I can understand," he said. After a brief pause, he went on. "Now, there is the fact of these interludes during which you and some of your animal patients shared thoughts together. And the memory-thoughts of the Skirni. Do I understand correctly? Shared thoughts?"

How absolutely ludicrous it sounded to her, spoken aloud. Still, she found it easier to discuss the subject with this amiable dolphin than with Otha. Her uncle was a scientist through and through, and espousing a belief in anything remotely like ESP was simply not something one did around him. And Zenn had always been the same way. She was raised to base her convictions on sound evidence, to assemble the facts, weigh them carefully and draw conclusions from what the real world told her. But the links she'd experienced with the animals were infuriatingly beyond the logic she'd always depended on. No matter how she approached the issue, there was no denying the fact that she'd "felt" the emotions of these creatures. It was impossible. But it had happened.

Science, for the first time in her life, seemed to offer no answer. And this was as deeply distressing to Zenn as anything else that had taken place over the past few unnerving weeks.

Jules sipped his juice, then lowered his head to stare directly into her eyes, as if looking for something. "So, you are an insane person, perhaps?" he asked her matter-of-factly. "Deranged in some way, out of your mind, a raving lunatic, hearing voices?"

"No," she said, a little too insistently. "Of course not."

"Yes, but a deluded person would respond as you just did, I believe. They generally fail to see their own mental disintegrations, do they not?"

"Well, yes, I suppose that's true, but–"

"No," he interrupted, waving one mech hand in the air. "I am of the opinion you are not a deranged and gibbering psychotic. There is something unusual affecting you, however; that we can say with assurance. You are convinced you share thoughts with these animals? That is a fair descriptor: to share?"

"Yes. It's sort of like sharing," she said. "But not thoughts, really. More like sharing what they're sensing at the moment, but definitely more than just me being sensitive. There's a connection happening. A real mind-to-mind connection. It doesn't make any sense, I know."

"Or possibly the sense it makes is not comprehended by us at present," the dolphin replied, with perfectly sound logic. "Are there any common features among the times you experienced these events?"

"Common features?"

"Such as environmental factors. The weather? The location? Your mental state? Anything to bind together the events when they occur?"

Zenn tried to think, but her mind was too unsettled. "No, I can't... There's nothing that seems similar. I just get this weird sensation, like being dizzy or confused, and then I'm in touch with the animal on some different level. It's hard to describe. And there was pain in my eye, with the whalehound, and on my face when the Skirni was in my room. Katie attacked him, and she scratched him. And I felt the pain that he felt, here." Her hand lifted to the skin on her cheek.

"I see. Are you in pain now?"

"No, no, it's nothing."

"But you were hurt, then, when this sharing happened?"

"No, not me. The Skirni was in pain, and I... it was like..." The realization struck her at once. She jumped up from the chair. "That's it..."

"It is?"

"Yes! They were all in pain. Or... or afraid. That's the common element – the thing that was happening every time. That must be the trigger. Why didn't I see it before?"

"I am not understanding you."

"Each time I linked with an animal, it was in trouble," she went on, speaking fast, wanting to get it all out, to see if the pattern held. "Katie was trapped. The hooshrike stuck in the cage bars. The whalehound's eye." She thought back, ticking off each event, trying to remember them all. "Gil's sick sandhog. Zeus, Liam's cat, when he was injured. Then the Skirni when Katie attacked it.

They were all in pain or distress. That's when the link happened. That's when they connected with me."

Jules cocked his big head at her. "So, an animal's pain creates a mental state that allows them to reach into your thoughts? Every time you encounter such a situation?"

"No. At least, I don't think it's every time. It must be when I'm especially focused on them or something."

"But how? And why? Why would they connect up with you? Is your brain in some way special among humans?"

"Not that I know of," Zenn said, combing her fingers back and forth through her hair in agitation, as if that would shake loose some helpful insight. "All I know is I've connected with certain animals. And maybe it's because they were stressed when it happened." She sat down and put her head in her hands, suddenly weary. "Or maybe I *am* just a deranged lunatic."

"Possible. But unlikely, I would say. In any case, it is a mystery. Something to be turned over in the mind and considered. You will perhaps understand it at some later juncture. Or perhaps not."

The dolphin was quiet for a long while, watching Zenn, head tilted to one side, as if working something out in his mind. At last, his legs whirred into action and he strode over to stand before her.

"If I may be so bold," he said, soundly oddly formal all of the sudden. "Your story has brought me to propose a path forward. It is my conclusion the best way would be for you to reside here, in this cabin, while you search out your father. I have rooms too many for my use. We will not be overcrowded."

"You'd do that? Let me stay, here, with you?"

"I would! It will be our adventure, the two of us who are seeking others."

A wild rush of surprise and relief flowed through Zenn, followed quickly by the image of her uncle saying on more than one occasion that anything which appeared too good to be true generally turns out to be just that. But she could see no alternative.

"Can you agree to this proposal?" he asked.

"You know what? I can," she told the smiling dolphin. "I can agree." She wanted to hug him. Do dolphins hug?

"Outstanding decision," he said, extending a mech-hand. "We must clasp hands to seal our new association. It is customary among friends." She took the metal-and-neoprene hand and marveled at the delicacy of its touch.

Yes, she thought, smiling up at him. This is what a friend would do. Something just like this.

Still holding her hand, he put his large head down close to hers. "Your hair really is quite red. Shocking, almost."

From the chair where Zenn had left her backpack, there was a trilling sound, followed by the appearance of a violet-and-cream rikkaset. Katie yawned, then climbed out of the pack, sat on the arm of the chair and gave Jules an intense, inspecting look. She signed at Zenn:

"Walking-fish-man have food for Katie?"

SIX

After Zenn introduced Jules and Katie, the rikkaset was given an apple from the bowl of fruit to nibble. Jules showed Zenn to one of the cabin's bedrooms. It was small, but displayed the same opulence as the rest of his quarters, with fine, colorful weavings covering the walls. At first, the dolphin looked on from the doorway as Zenn stowed her backpack in the room's small closet. But when she looked up again, he was gone. She found him standing before a large mirror in the small hallway leading to the cabin's exit door. He was twisting his body awkwardly in a futile attempt to check the back portion of his walksuit.

"These devices are always getting out of alignment," he muttered, gingerly poking at one of several dozen small nozzles mounted at various points on the suit. The nozzles periodically puffed out tiny mistings of water onto the areas of his skin not covered by the suit itself. "If they are not properly directed, I get dry patches..." Zenn couldn't suppress a grin.

"Mister Vancouver, I just wanted to thank you again. For letting me stay. For trusting me, when you don't even know me."

"'Mister Vancouver'?" The dolphin threw back his head in an open-jawed, chittering laugh. "You make me feel like a family-elder with dull, broken teeth! I am Jules, please."

"OK. Jules. Thank you."

"It is my own pleasure to have your company. And the small one Katie as well. As for trust…" His bright eyes narrowed just a bit. "I have this positive feeling concerning you, Zora Bodine. And I am generally correct in my impressions."

"Zenn," she said, coming to a decision. "My name isn't Zora. It's Zenn. Zenn Scarlett. You should know my real name."

"A secret name? But this is even better. This is a key ingredient in the printed-on-paper adventure novel, you know. Secret names. Kidnapped persons and scoundrels. I wager you are also carrying… a treasure map. Am I correct? Do I win?"

"Um, sorry, no. No map." And she actually felt a kind of remorse at failing to fulfill his expectation.

"I see. I neglected to state an amount of this wager. Which I have lost, fairly and squarely. You may name a reasonable amount." He produced his credit relay and held it out.

"Oh, no. That's not necessary, Jules."

He quickly put his relay back in its compartment on his walksuit.

"That is very generous of you. To allow me to get down off of the hook, as they say. Thank you."

Zenn grinned at him. She was starting to feel that, yes, this dolphin was in fact eminently trustworthy.

They went back out into the main room, where Katie had fallen soundly asleep, curled into a ball in one of the chairs.

"So, Jules, you're going to Enchara?"

"I am not pointed at Enchara. I travel to the water-planet Mu Arae. I search for a friend. A close friend."

"A friend from Earth?"

"Yes, my First Promised. She was on a ship bound for Mu Arae in the past year. It went missing. One of the vanished Indra craft, you understand. I intend to find her. It matters."

"Jules, I'm so sorry."

Zenn had met only one or two others who'd lost anyone on a hijacked Indra-drive ship. The ships had been disappearing periodically for two decades, leaving no trace or any indication of the cause. Lately, the frequency of these events had increased alarmingly. It was getting bad enough to start threatening communications and trade with some of the outlying planets of the Accord.

"Yes, the vanishing of Indra-type spaceships in our Local Accord is a serious and growing dilemma. And yet, all investigations have produced to date no hope of a resolution."

"I know. But people are trying," Zenn said. "My mother, Mai, was actually working on the Indra problem when she... when she was lost. She specialized in treating Indra."

"I am saddened to hear of her passing. When was this terrible event?"

"Four Mars years ago. Almost eight Earth years. I was only nine. I don't remember all of it. No." She stopped herself. "I do remember. I just don't want to."

"Then we will not speak of it."

"So," she said then, more than willing to change the subject. "By First Promised, you mean promised as in marriage, to have a family, that kind of 'promised'?"

"A family? No, I think not. But as in marriage and lifemate, yes. Inga was scheduled to be my first wife, you see." He stepped over to the bowl of fruit and began unwrapping bits of dried fish. He popped several into his mouth, swallowing them whole. "The first is the most important of the wives that will follow. It makes the most sense."

"I'm sure it does," Zenn told him, determined not to be judgmental about cetacean mating customs.

"So you see it concerns me intensely that I find her."

"Of course. But, Jules, do you have any information to go on? The missing ships – they just disappear. No real leads have been found about the cause. Do you have some reason to think you'll learn where she is when you get to Mu Arae?"

"No. No good reason, actually." Another morsel of fish. "It is the one clue I possess, however. There seems to be no other place that makes the most sense to go looking. Where would you look?"

He appeared genuinely interested in her opinion on the matter, which made Zenn feel even sorrier for him.

"No, I'm sure you're doing the right thing. It just seems… It must be very difficult for you."

"It is difficult. She is an outstanding mate prospect, and we became very good friends before she went on her voyage.

She overlooks my wearing of the walksuit and going about on land, which others of my kind criticize me for. But I belabor my own problems, which is rude behavior, isn't it? I will speak of something else." He looked around the room, as if he might spot something that would suggest another topic of conversation. The last piece of fish disappeared into his smiling face with a clack of his jaws.

"This Skirni, the one you followed here," he said. "You saw in your dream-sight that he was with your father? And you believe your father could also be aboard this ship?"

"I don't know. Maybe. At first, Dad was in his office, I think, on Enchara, in the… dream-sight. And then he was in some room with medical equipment."

"But what of this Liam Tucker person? He is helping to locate your father?"

"Not really. Liam has his own reasons for wanting to get off Mars. It's kind of a long story."

"Are you thinking of finding this Liam? Could he help in your searching?"

"Well, yes, I'd like to find him. I mean, yes, he has tried to help me before. And I can use all the help I can get if I'm going to track down my dad."

"I have a concept to aid in your searching," Jules said. "I will put a tail on the Skirni."

"A tail?"

"It is an expression of craft in certain of the antique printed-on-paper-novels involving criminals and those who detect clues in order to apprehend them. I will follow the Skirni surreptitiously to gather information about his activities. I will then make my report to you. Yes! It will be our case together."

"Our case..." Zenn was a little dubious about the cetacean's childlike enthusiasm for what, to her, was very serious business.

"Why not? Tailing and reporting the accumulated clues form the basis for almost all successful mysterious adventures of this variety. It seems the best way until we come upon some better solution. Now..." He lifted a bunch of bananas from the fruit bowl, looked underneath, but found no more fish. "I am exceptionally hungry." His attention had shifted abruptly once more – a trait Zenn thought she should probably get used to. "The food on this ship is quite adequate. And in main dining areas they do not ration the amount one consumes. Are you hungry as well?"

Zenn realized that she was, in fact, famished. Deciding it was best she remain in the cabin, Jules hurried out into the corridor and Zenn found herself alone with the sleeping Katie.

She went into her bedroom amid the sudden silence, which was then broken by a faint chiming tone that sounded from a hidden speaker somewhere in the cabin, followed by a bland female voice.

"Greetings to our recently arrived guests, and welcome aboard the LSA LumiLiner *Helen of Troy*," the voice intoned. "The ship is commencing orbital exit maneuvers. We will soon be departing Mars and Sol Sys space for Sigmund's Parch, Luveern Transfer Hub, Enchara and Fomalhaut, with connecting services to Mu Arae, the Moons of Altair and the Outer Reaches. Our estimated transit time to the Sol space tunneling coordinates is two standard days, seven hours. Thank you for traveling with LumiLiner, and please have a pleasant voyage." The message then began to repeat, first in the hissing, sibilant sounds of Alcyoni, then in the low, melodic tones Zenn recognized as the language of the Zeta Reticulans.

So, this was it. She was really leaving. For the first time, she was now truly on her own, beyond the reach or assistance of anyone back on Mars.

She sat on the bunk to think. There was still the problem of letting Otha know where she was. What would he say? What would he do? And Liam. Was he looking for her? Was he even still aboard? A sinking hollowness opened deep inside her. But at the thought of her father, helpless, imprisoned, maybe hurt, she stood up again, her entire body electric with fury and resolve. Yes, she was on her own. And whatever happened from now on was up to her and her alone.

She went to the cabin door, hesitated just long enough to wrap her scarf around her head and lower face, took a deep breath, and stepped up to the door. Looking back to see that Katie was still asleep, she quietly asked the door to open, leaned out into the passageway and checked both directions. No one. When she had followed Jules to his cabin earlier, they'd passed a viewport just down the corridor. Deciding that one last look at Mars didn't necessarily mean she was already homesick, she hurried down the passage.

The perfect disc of Mars hung suspended in the circular, floor-to-ceiling viewing window, a majestic expanse of browns and rusty reds rotating slowly far below. Gauzy white clouds trailed from the higher volcanoes like ragged pennants. Here and there, thin lines of green zigzagged through the barren wastes – pressurized valleys where the colonists maintained their fragile toehold on the planet. Zenn scanned the surface, trying to get her bearings and locate her home valley and Arsia City.

Something moved into view from one edge of the scene outside – a ferry, dropping away from the starship. Zenn assumed it was the one that had brought her, Katie, Liam and the sandhog up from the surface. Glinting in the stark sunlight, the little craft emitted a silent burst from its thrusters and fell toward the planet. Zenn watched the ferry grow smaller and smaller before it disappeared into the atmospheric haze.

A moment later, another bell-like chime sounded three times. Far off in the depths of the ship, she heard the rumble of machinery – that would be the sound of the ship's immense solar sails deploying, folding out like a vast, glittering gold umbrella with the ship like a handle in its center. Propelled by the solar wind, the huge sails would take the ship to the void between the asteroid belt and Jupiter, where the Indra and its groom would have the room required to commence tunneling.

The panorama framed by the window slowly shifted as the starship veered out of Mars's gravitational pull and began the slow ballet of orbital exit. She wrapped her arms tightly around herself and watched her world sliding away. She recalled the scent of fresh-cut switchgrass, of Otha waving at her as he drove his beloved old pickup truck into the cloister's dusty courtyard, Hild's weathered face glancing up from her workbench after firing up a near-dead diagnostic computer; Hamish in the brew house, holding four mugs of ale aloft in his four upper insectoid arms, saying he'd named this batch "Sexton's Very Best Bitter". She saw her mother and father laughing together, joking with each other the way they did, before... She thought of her father after Mai Scarlett's death, the permanent cloud that seemed to veil his moods, even when he tried to make her think he'd found the trick of being happy again. More than anything in the world, she'd wanted him to find that trick, to have her father back, the father she'd known when he still had her mother to be so deeply, amazingly in love with.

Mars continued to drift sideways in the portal, then vanished from view as the starship pointed its bow toward open space. The viewport filled with stars burning in the blackness, the nothingness shot through with unblinking, pinprick light-holes.

She leaned against the corridor wall, and the ship's mechanical systems thrummed against her back, beneath her feet. She had just two days before the starship would pass through the asteroid belt. Then, in the empty space that lay beyond, the Indra would work its uncanny sorcery. The immense "stonehorse" would awaken and uncoil its body into the cavernous Indra chamber. The groom would perform the arcane rituals of astronavigation, and the Indra would open the wormhole-like tunnel, dissolving the fabric of time and space. Once the interdimensional pathway materialized, the Indra would cross the threshold and, in an eyeblink, take the *Helen of Troy* across the unimaginable distance to Sigmund's Parch and, in its next tunneling, onward to Enchara.

So, she had two days before they would leave Sol Sys space. What if she hadn't found her father by then? She couldn't imagine where she would finally end up if she failed, what she would do, how she would ever get back home. And, she realized with cold, clear logic, if she didn't find her father, none of the rest mattered.

SEVEN

Zenn was back inside the cabin a short time later when Jules returned, carrying a large tray draped with a linen cloth. Beneath the cloth was an array of plates and dishes containing pasta with a tomato sauce, various vegetables, half a loaf of bread and several other varieties of food Zenn couldn't identify. Jules explained he had eaten while in the dining hall, and he now watched her intently as she ate, neither of them speaking. She devoured almost all of the food she could recognize, and some she couldn't, until she was unable to eat any more. She put a small dish on the floor for Katie, which the rikkaset sniffed skeptically.

Zenn waved at Katie to get her attention, then spoke aloud to her, talking slowly and exaggerating each word.

"Katie? This is good food for Katie."

The rikkaset watched Zenn intently, then signed back at her.

"Certain good? Good for Katie?"

"Yes. Katie will like."

"She can hear you, this Katie?" Jules said. "I thought she had no hearing?"

"We've been working on lip-reading," Zenn said. "We've only just started, but she's picking it up really fast."

"She has a smart brain in her, then." Jules peered down at the rikkaset. "Well done to you, Katie."

Katie ignored him and took a tentative bite of the food before her. Deciding it would do, she ate eagerly.

Jules pointed to another covered dish on the tray – a treat for Zenn. He held the dish out for her approval. On it was what looked like a small, leathery-skinned fruit with a delicate orange-and-aquamarine coloring.

"Can you guess what this is?" he said. Zenn peered more closely at the dish and its contents. "I will wager you cannot guess," he said, taking out his relay and brandishing it at her. "Shall we say one unit? As a wager between friends?"

Zenn laughed and took out her own relay.

"Only one unit?" she said. "How about two... between friends?"

Jules bobbed his head in agreement.

"So, how many guesses do I get?" Yes, eating had definitely left her feeling much more like herself.

"Only one guess, of course. It is a wager."

"Just one guess?" she said. "Gee... let's see... could it be... a Lyran Rooloo?"

Jules's beaked jaw fell open for a second, then snapped shut.

"You knew its identity the full time."

"Yup. But the betting was your idea," she said, smiling as she watched Jules's relay blink on and off again, transferring the winnings to her account.

"Yes, true enough and well done," he exclaimed. So, dolphins were good sports, at least.

"Answer me this: have you ever coaxed out a Rooloo?" She shook her head no. "It's an experience to be had." He crossed his mech-arms in front of him and watched her. She gave the tiny sphere a tentative poke with her finger.

"Hold it in the palm of your hand," Jules instructed. She obeyed. It was dry and cool to the touch. "Now breathe on it."

She gave him a puzzled look.

"Like you were breathing on a mirror to clean the surface."

She opened her mouth wide, held the fruit up to her face and huffed on it. The Rooloo vibrated softly against her palm and, with a soft "whump" of rind and juices, it exploded. Zenn jerked back in her chair, her face covered with a sticky wetness like popped bubblegum, except the gum was moving – it was alive! In alarm, Katie leaped up on the table and uttered a fierce little growl at the offending Rooloo.

Zenn peeled the clinging thing from her cheek and held it at arm's length. It looked like a sort of turquoise starfish, and it quivered and wobbled as it tried to get a grip on her hand and crawl up her arm. With some effort, she scraped it off into her empty water glass. She put a plate on top to keep it from getting out. Katie eyed it closely until she was certain it couldn't escape. Then she hopped off the table and returned to her dish of food.

Zenn realized that the chirping sound in her ears was Jules's staccato laughter. Across the table, he was shaking his large head rapidly up and down, obviously relishing his little surprise.

"You did that on purpose," Zenn said. She mopped at herself with a napkin. Jules had stopped laughing, but he couldn't keep his head from bobbing with pleasure.

"You should have seen your countenance and its expression. This was an excellent example of humor based on the unexpected. Do admit it."

"I don't admit anything of the kind." But Zenn's outrage was now totally manufactured, and she struggled to keep herself from laughing. The stories she had heard about the dolphin sense of humor were apparently true. "You might have warned me."

"But that would entirely undo the purpose of humor premised on the element of surprise."

"Oh, right, silly me. So, what do we do with this little guy?" She pointed to the Rooloo crawling up the inside of her water glass. Jules bent down to watch it, leaning forward slightly. "Oh, no, you don't," Zenn told him earnestly. She snatched up the glass. "You're not eating him. He's way too cute. I know it's just walking fruit, but it's still too cute to eat."

"Did I say I intended to ingest it?" Jules protested, a little too strongly. "I have seen that the galley kitchen here keeps a Rooloo breeding colony. We'll purchase its freedom and put it out to pasture. There is rind-juice on your chin..." Jules picked up his napkin and handed it across the table to her. "My First Promised enjoyed Rooloo. It was a favorite of hers, even though it was not fish-based. We were to serve it at the bonding ceremony."

Zenn took the napkin from him and dabbed at her face. "If you don't mind my asking, Jules, how old are you?"

"I am eighteen years on the moonrise of the coming migration season," he told her. "But as I grew up at the institute facilities away from my birth pod, I won't undergo the usual initiation."

"The institute?"

"Yes, the Claussen Institute. It is a research unit of the TerrAqua Corporation. TerrAqua is the company that designed and built this walksuit. The business was owned by Per Claussen. He was kind to me, much like a father, in fact. But he died."

"Oh, I'm sorry."

"During my growing-up period at the Institute, I assisted in refining the workings of the newer suit models." He raised both mech-arms. "Upon Per's passing, he arranged to leave me this newest model. As well as a good deal of his money." The dolphin lowered his head slightly, his gaze growing distant. "In any case, it is his gift of funds I now use to pay for this starship ride and this comfortable cabin. It was his final kindness to me."

"But you were taken away from your family when you were young? And you didn't mind? You didn't miss your family group, your dolphin pod's initiation and all?"

He leaned closer to her and dropped his voice. "Don't tell it far abroad, but the pod initiation is a ritual I am pleased to avoid. There is no small amount of biting and slapping with tail-flukes involved. And, as you have seen, with my years of practice, I am most expert in the operation of my walksuit. This mobility upon land was a... great side-benefit... to..."

The dolphin's voice trailed off and he slowly closed

one eye as his beaked chin dropped. A sound like a softly deflating tire emanated from the blowhole on the top of his head. It sounded like... snoring.

"Yes, I'm sure it was a benefit," she said. "And so, were there other dolphins at the Institute?" Jules didn't respond, but continued his soft, rhythmic breathing.

Zenn was about to ask again when she noticed one of his mech-arms had dropped to his side, and the hand-unit was trembling in little waving motions. She leaned over the table to ask him if he was OK, and saw that he had one eye open. It followed her movement. Then, the other eye popped open and he sat upright.

"Oh... excuse me," he said, clearing his blowhole by exhaling in a short burst. "I dozed away for a second."

"You were asleep? But your eye was open. I saw you watching me."

"It's how dolphins sleep."

"With one eye open?"

"Yes. The term is called unihemispheric slow wave sleep. 'Uni' meaning 'one', 'hemi' meaning 'half', and 'sphere' indicating–"

"Jules. I know what a sphere is."

"Naturally you do. In any case, this kind of sleep arose in dolphins to permit us to rest and yet breathe at the same moment. One half of our brain goes into light sleep mode while the other stays awake. One eye is open to keep us oriented toward the water surface so we can breathe and watch for predators – such as sharks and, before the Cetacean Cooperation Treaty, killer whales. First, we rest one side of the brain; next, the other. Generally this goes in eight-hour cycles during nighttime, as with humans. But I've been off my cycle a little lately. With the trip and its dislocations."

"I've heard about this. But only in birds. This isn't just more dolphin humor? Like, 'ha ha, humans will believe anything'?"

"I assure you it's not." He sounded indignant. "If I were executing a verbal jibe, the humor would be self-evident."

"Right," Zenn said. "And I'm sorry. I know you weren't expecting to have a roommate on this trip. I'm sure that's not helping your internal clock get back to a regular routine."

"You mustn't apologize. It was my decision," he said. "But yes, I believe we can both use some sleep rest. Let us make a decision to eat our breakfast meal together when we awaken. We can talk about what our plans will be. Yes?"

"I'd like that," Zenn told him, and with a small tip of his head that looked something like a bow, the dolphin went into his bedroom.

In her own room, Zenn fell back on the bed. Katie came in and hopped up to lie on the pillow beside her, just as she'd always done back at the cloister. Zenn thought again about contacting Otha, and how she would accomplish this. She thought of dolphins reading old Earther adventure novels. She thought of her father, of the Skirni who had taken him – the Skirni who was possibly sleeping right now in his own cabin several decks below. The sounds of the starship's mechanical systems rumbled and creaked distantly, like a giant metal beast, restless in the dark cold of space. She wondered yet again what had become of Liam. Before any other thoughts came, she was asleep.

After Jules had brought her breakfast the next day, she entered the suite's sitting room just as the dolphin opened the door to the corridor. In the passageway beyond stood a Gliesian steward pushing a small cart piled with dishes.

"Your dishes, please?" he said. "If you are finished and have any dishes I would be happy to–"

Before Zenn could withdraw back into her room, the steward spotted her. She froze.

"You," he said, grapefruit-eyes going wide.

Katie, who'd been lying on the back of one of the easy chairs, leaped to her feet and went into rikkaset blending mode, vanishing from sight.

Zenn felt the blood drain from her face. She'd been discovered. Her stomach clenched, an acid taste filling her mouth. Caught. After coming so far. How could she be so careless, so stupid, to let herself be seen this way?

Then the steward's wide, amphibian face split in a broad, needle-toothed grin.

"Bodine? The animal doctor. Yes?"

It was the steward from the cargo bay – that's how he knew her. Was she safe?

"Yes, that's me. And you... are Yed, right?" she said, forcing a smile. Jules looked at her, saying nothing. He stepped aside to let the steward enter.

"Yed, yes. You are finding your time with us pleasant so far?" Zenn heaved a sigh. She hadn't been found out. The steward set a metal tray on the table and began stacking their dishes on it. Katie rematerialized and cautiously approached the little Gliesian, sniffing.

The steward was apparently familiar with rikkasets.

"Ah. You have a vanishing-appearing rat-cat. These are magical animals, are they not?"

"Well, no, not magical," Zenn said. "Their fur bends light so they can camouflage themselves, that's all."

"Yes. Magical. May I ask if you have everything you require?"

"I do. Thank you."

"And you as well, Guest Vancouver? All your needs are met?"

"I am well taken care of. The cabin is more than satisfactory."

"And, Guest Bodine, your own cabin is to your liking? For you and your father Bodine?"

"Um, yes. My father and I are quite happy. With our cabin. *On deck eight*." She shot Jules a look, hoping he'd catch on.

"So, you and Guest Vancouver are long acquainted?"

"Yes," Jules said. "Because of course she is my slave–"

"No," Zenn cut him off. Confused, the steward looked from one of them to the other. "I mean, yes," Zenn stammered. "I'm… slavishly devoted to Mister Vancouver. As a good friend should be. It's a figure of speech."

"Of speech, necessarily," the steward said, nodding, but still looking puzzled.

"Yes. Indeed. We share a long and well-known friendship," Jules said, realizing her intention. The steward's eyes took on the smallest shadow of suspicion at this odd exchange. Jules noticed and quickly produced his relay. "And, to signify our satisfaction in all areas of accommodation and service, you must allow me to give you a monetary tip." The steward's face brightened, any sign of doubt instantly erased.

"Thank you, sir! For your generosity," he said, holding up his own relay. "Guest Bodine, it is a happy accident, my finding you. If I may impose, might I ask a question?"

"Of course."

"As an animal doctor, would you perhaps know of the creatures called mudlark?"

"Mudlarks. Yes. They're native to Tandua."

"I've never heard this name," Jules said.

"It's a little misleading," Zenn said. "They're actually fungal animoids. A plant-animal hybrid. Sort of like a big mushroom. They inhabit the tidal zones of Tandua's Great Swamp Sea."

"But larks are avians of Earth," Jules said. "Do these mudlarks fly?"

"No. But they sing. That's where the name comes from," Zenn told him. "And they're mimics. Like parrots or mynah birds. But instead of just being able to copy a person's voice or a single melody, they can mimic dozens of sounds at once. They can be trained to sing entire symphonies, and they sound just like the real thing. I've only heard recordings, but it's really amazing."

"My asking is due to our Captain. Captain Oolo," the steward explained. "For, you see, he possesses such a mudlark. But it has a problem lately. It languishes and does not eat. It occurred to me that you, as an animal physician, might be in a position to determine what ails it."

Zenn understood now what was on the steward's mind and began to wonder if maybe she shouldn't have mentioned being an exovet.

"But does not the *Helen* have its own creature-physician aboard?" Jules asked.

"Yes, I wouldn't want to step on anyone's toes." The steward regarded her blankly. "I mean, I wouldn't want to make the ship's exovet mad by treating one of their patients. It wouldn't be professional."

"Ah, no, this is not a concern," the steward said eagerly. "Our ship's animal doctor is absent for this most recent leg of our voyage. He left us at Zeta Reticuli and was unable to rejoin. So you can see the Captain would clearly be most obliged for you looking in upon his pet animal. He cares deeply for it."

Leaving Jules's cabin would be a risk. But, on the other hand, there might be a useful trade-off to be had. A steward's goodwill could be a valuable commodity.

"I suppose I could take a look at it. But I might ask for a small favor in return."

"But of course. What service can I perform for you?"

"I'd like you to find out some information for me. About a passenger. A Skirni. I have his cabin number."

The steward hesitated at this, his wide lips pursing.

Jules saw his reluctance, and raised his credit relay.

"Yes. It is crucial we detect important details about this passenger. Will five credits facilitate this undertaking?"

The steward raised his relay, reluctance replaced by a conspiratorial smile.

"This is most suitable, and I thank you, Guest Vancouver. How can I assist you in this matter?"

Zenn explained that she wanted to know the Skirni's destination, where he first got on the ship and any details about who he associated with and his other activities since he'd been aboard. "While you are about this," Jules said, "be certain your sleuthing about does not raise red flags of interest from the Skirni. You must move as a rubber-shoed cat burglar, slinking in shadows."

"I must... slink?"

"Just don't let anyone know what you're up to."

"Ah, to be discreet. Of course. I am a starliner steward. Discretion is simply one of my duties."

"Thank you, Yed," Zenn said. "Now, tell me more about your Captain's mudlark. What sort of symptoms does it have?"

"I know only that for three days now it has been silent. Total and complete. And it refuses its feeding. This I am told is a bad sign for these animals."

"Yes, this could be something serious. Any change in dietary habits can mean there's a problem. And they usually vocalize several times a day. At least, in the wild."

"What is the ailment? You can heal it?"

"I won't know till I see it. Where is it?"

"Normally, it resides within the Captain's quarters. But it has now been removed to the ship's main sickbay due to this illness. Our ship's doctor, the doctor for our passengers, has been unable to help it. I could take you there, even now. Unless it's inconvenient."

"No, now is good," she said. "The sooner we diagnose your mudlark, the sooner we find out what that Skirni is up to."

Five minutes later, the three of them were riding a lev-tube to the *Helen's* deck eighteen. Making an excuse about being chilly, Zenn had once again wound the scarf around her head.

When they arrived at the sickbay door, it was locked. The ship's doctor was apparently out, and after the steward entered a manual passcode on the door's touchplate, it opened and they entered. The sickbay was spacious, with three examination tables in the central area and various treatment devices and supply cabinets against the wall.

Yed indicated a doorway at the rear of the room.

"Captain Oolo's mudlark is within," he said. "Its name is Cleevus." The steward made no move to enter the room. Zenn was on her own.

"OK, let's have a look," she said. The door to the smaller room slid open. It was a dimly lit storage closet with a large, rectangular aquarium-like enclosure set against one wall. Barely visible in the low light, the mudlark squatted in the center of the aquarium, anchored to a spherical rock that jutted up out of six inches of water filling the bottom of the clear-walled box.

Zenn had just felt her way through the near-darkness to the edge of the cage when the dizziness spun up within her. Even after the half-dozen previous times, she was still unprepared for it. Her knees buckled slightly, her thoughts tangled in sudden confusion. The next instant, her vision flickered, then vanished entirely. She was blind! Blind as a… mudlark. And she had become instantly thirsty, an aching thirst that emanated from somewhere outside of her but, at the same time, inside. Yes, it was happening again. She was feeling what this creature felt, their minds somehow linked, somehow sharing sensations, emotions… blindness. It was impossible. There was no scientific explanation for it. But she felt the mudlark's overwhelming thirst and discomfort as if they were her own.

"…are you unwell?" Jules's voice sounded miles away, but it was enough to bring her back. The feeling fled from her. Vision returned.

"No. It was just…"

"You were sharing thoughts?" Jules bent his head low, bringing his dark eyes close to hers. "Just now, is that it?"

"Yes. But only for a few seconds. I'm better now."

The little steward was wringing his hands. "You are not ill, Guest Bodine? You are well?"

"Yes." She patted him on the shoulder, and he relaxed. So, whatever was afflicting her around animals in distress, she hadn't left it behind on Mars. No. That would've been too simple. She indicated the mudlark. "I'd say that Cleevus seems to be badly dehydrated."

After another moment to clear her head, and several breaths to steady herself, Zenn pulled a lightpatch from her backpack, adhered the patch to her forehead and turned it on. The mudlark reacted to the beam of light, shrinking into itself slightly, but it made no sound. The creature's central stalk was several inches thick and about a foot and a half high, topped by a foot-wide cap punctuated with multiple small openings – but all the many aspiration orifices were shut tight. The coloration was a deep, muddy green with iridescent purple streaks. This was clearly a diagnostic symptom. A healthy mudlark should be a light, greenish-beige with no streaking.

"I think it's got a mineral deficiency," Zenn said, rummaging in her kit and hoping she was right about the facts from her basic course on Tanduan hybrid fauna.

Zenn found the foil pressure-pak she was looking for and attached it to the smallest-gauge pneuma-ject syringe she had. Leaning down into the mudlark's cage, she injected the animoid with the potassium booster solution and stood back to wait.

As they all watched the creature for any reaction, Yed explained how the Captain had taught the mudlark a variety of musical pieces, and how he enjoyed showing off his pet's abilities to dignitaries and guests.

Further conversation was interrupted by a soft, unidentifiable sound, something like bagpipes played inside an echoing cave. Zenn bent down to shine her lightpatch into the cage, where the mudlark had undergone a startling transformation. It stood taller now, the last hints of purple streaks fading, the stalk's surface flushing with healthy new color even as they watched. The many breath-holes on the cap were open and slowly vibrating. The wheezing sound it was making changed, became more defined and increased in volume, growing until it filled the small room with what could only be described as the sound of musical instruments, accurately reproduced down to the strings, tympani drums and woodwinds, all playing a complex and beautiful melody.

"This music, I know it," Jules said after a few moments. "It is Master Beethoven's of Earth. His number six symphonic composition. The '*Pastoral*'." The dolphin closed his eyes and raised his mech-arms, waving his hands in the air as if directing a performance.

"Yes, it sings, it sings." The steward started to dance to the music, hopping as he spun in a circle, clapping his hands. "The Captain will be joyful. And Yed will be his favored one. I will be favored."

Zenn smiled at the impromptu celebration, the miraculous music washing over them all, the mudlark swaying back and forth to the rhythm of its many-throated song. It was while she was peering into the sickbay from within the closet that the new thought came to her in a single flash of recognition.

"A sickbay…"

"A sickbay," Jules said, arms paused in midair. "Yes, it is where we are."

"No. That's what I saw, what the Skirni was remembering. During the break-in at the cloister," Zenn said, moving out into the main bay and walking to the bank of instruments on the wall. "In my vision, when I saw my father, on that table. It wasn't a hospital room. It was the sickbay of a starliner. And not just any sickbay. It was *this* sickbay. I saw this same exam table, the same kind of equipment, the same sort of cabinets and decorations on the wall."

She turned around to see Jules and the little steward staring at her outburst.

"Don't you see? My father must have been here. He was here!" But even as she said it, the thought was replaced: if Warra Scarlett had in fact been here… where was he now?

EIGHT

"Again, I must thank you for the miraculous result you have achieved," the steward said to Zenn as they rode a lev-car back down toward Jules's cabin.

"I'm just glad it worked," Zenn said, smiling with relief. But seeing Yed's concerned expression, she added, "I was pretty sure, of course, that it would. Work."

"As I have said, it is our very good fortune you came on board the *Helen*," Yed told her. "Lucky for the Captain's Cleevus. Cleevus is lucky in many ways. This animal lives a very good life on this ship. Unlike some other animals, I must say… Ah, we come to Guest Vancouver's deck."

Yed opened the lev-car's door and gestured for them to exit.

"Wait, what did you say?" Zenn asked.

"Oh. I speak out of turn." The steward's bright green brow creased, and he looked away. A guilty look? "Yed? What did you mean about the other animals?"

He muttered something and looked down nervously at his webbed feet.

"I am sorry, Guest Bodine. I merely spoke my thought aloud. It is of no account."

"Yed." She sounded as firm as she could. "Are animals in trouble? Are they sick? You need to tell me if they are."

"But… I am paid not to say," He popped his round eyes at her and wrung his hands.

"Steward Yed?" Jules held his credit relay aloft. "What sum are you paid not to say?"

"Twenty-five units," he said reluctantly, blinking at them.

"Here then is thirty," Jules told him. Yed held his own relay up. "You are now paid to say."

Yed blinked a few more times, then looked down at his relay.

"It is an animal fight I am paid to be quiet about. The Skirni, guest Thrott, has arranged it. Below decks in the steerage levels of the ship."

"A fight?" Zenn asked. "With what kind of animals?"

"Guest Thrott pits his trained slug against a waspworm. The wasp is owned by a Fomalhaut freedman. There are wagers being placed on this event."

"When, Yed? When are they going to fight?"

The steward looked at his sleeve-screen.

"Soon. In the next hour."

Zenn didn't have to think about it. "You need to take us there now."

"You? Take you?" Yed looked from her to Jules. "I am not certain this would be… in order…"

Jules raised his money relay again.

Yed slowly raised his relay too, then he spoke to the lev-car.

"Steerage level three, please," he instructed the car, shaking his head. The doors slid closed and the car started down.

Zenn knew that tickets for passage on the steerage level of starships like the *Helen of Troy* were much cheaper than those for the upper decks. As they stepped out of the lev-car and into the corridor, she understood why.

The smell that assailed them when the car's doors opened was her first clue: heavy with the exotic odors of cooking foods and thick with the scent of living, sweating beings, both humans and Asents. The passageway before them flowed with moving bodies, a dozen different races thronging in both directions, most of them talking, some shouting, Alien Sentients calling and human infants crying, others hooting, mewing, everyone jostling.

With Yed leading the way, they forced themselves out into the crowd. As they pushed their way through, Zenn saw that here and there along the passage, enterprising individuals had set up small, portable kiosks. At these makeshift stands they loudly hawked all manner of goods to the milling passengers. At one stall, black metal pots set over gas flames boiled and seethed with some sort of stew, attended to by a caftan-clad female Zeta Reticulan – a human-sized biped with a vaguely cow-like appearance. The Reticulan's boxy head was covered in a downy pelt and bore a double set of flattened horn-like protuberances that curved down over her face, the large, gentle eyes blinking out at the world from beneath this built-in helmet. At another stall, an elderly human male with a long, dingy gray beard tried to get Zenn to buy a gigantically oversized pressure suit, while at the next kiosk an Alcyon busily arranged his table-full of dangerous-looking knives, spare particle-weapon parts and other odds and ends of military hardware.

They came to a turn in the passage, and after a short distance Yed stopped at a large double door marked "Storage Rm 9, Sub-3 – Authorized Personnel Only". He glanced up and down the corridor and, when the passing crowd thinned, spoke a series of numbers at the door. It swished open.

"Yes, please, enter quickly. I will wait for you here," Yed said. "It is not good that I should be seen at such an event, you understand."

The room held perhaps thirty passengers of all races and sizes. They stood around a central open space that was illuminated by a single, powerful light shining down from the ceiling. There was a barrier between the passengers and the center of the illuminated space, thrown together from an array of shipping crates and barrels. Some of those in the room shouted out bets; others waved their credit relays in the air to take those wagers.

Zenn forced her way to the front. At the far side of the circle, she saw the Skirni Thrott, standing next to a large, clear-walled ballistiplast cage set on a wheeled luggage cart. The Encharan fighting slug in the cage was six feet long with glistening, tawny skin lined with burgundy stripes that warned any would-be attacker of its toxic slime coating. When Thrott banged on the side of the cage, it reared up on its fleshy pseudopod, slid its rasp-toothed radula from its mouth, retracted its eyestalks and threw itself against the cage wall with a fleshy thud. The impact left a fresh, dripping film of caustic acid.

The writhing slug drew a shout of approval from the crowd. Then another shout went up as a tall, willowy Fomalhaut male, dressed in a tattered uniform of some sort, emerged from the shadows beyond the boisterous circle. The crowd drew back quickly to allow him to pass. Scuttling along at his side, held by a heavy chain leash, was his waspworm. Its blue-black body moved low to the ground on twelve short, spindly legs, its swollen abdomen carrying at its tip a venomous foot-long sting. The animal vibrated its four overlapping wings as it walked, creating a threatening buzz.

"Har," Thrott scoffed as the Fomalhaut brought his fighter into the center of the circle. "This will be no contest at all. Watch as my creature pulls the sting off this bug."

The crowd reacted to this with a mix of cheers and boos. Zenn, her heart beating wildly, climbed up on one of the crates lining the circle.

"Stop!" she yelled at the top of her lungs. "You can't do this!" To her great surprise, the entire room instantly fell dead silent, all eyes upon her, no one moving, the only sounds the gurgling of the slug and the buzzing of the waspworm. "Animal fighting…" she went on, righteous anger making her voice shrill, "…is illegal."

"Oh, noooo," the Fomalhaut shrieked in a put-on falsetto voice, clapping both hands up to his face. "It's ill-leeegal." The room erupted into laughter.

"You." The Skirni Thrott jabbed an accusing finger at her. "You have no business here."

"These animals will be hurt," she yelled into the din, her face flushing hot. "You have no right to–"

"We have no right?" An especially large Sirenian coleopt stepped out of the crowd to approach her. The towering insectoid raised two of his upper arms at her, his plume-like antennae quivering atop his head, the great multifaceted eyes glinting in the low light. "Who died and made you Queen Spawn-Mother, eh?" The crowd guffawed. "Go back where you came from, hyoomun."

Zenn's face glowed hotter and she yelled again for them to stop, but by then no one was listening. No one even looked at her, and the hubbub grew even louder as everyone resumed their betting.

Then, amid the tumult, came a voice that sounded distinctly familiar.

"Scarlett?" Yes. Someone calling her name. It couldn't be. She searched the crowd for the speaker. No. Yes!

"Scarlett, over here."

Standing at the far side of the circle of humans and Asents was a tall, fair, sunburned Martian towner boy.

"It *is* you," Liam Tucker called, swiping at the sheaf of hair that hung down in his face as he made his way toward her. The sight of Liam, wide grin on his face, striding toward her, sparked an instantaneous surge of relief in her. Yes. No doubt about it. This Liam was a friend who she was very glad to see once more.

"I can't believe it," he said. "You got away, in the cargo hold. I thought you were pinched for sure. What in Nine

Hells are you doing down here?"

"We heard about the fight," she said, raising her voice above the noise in the room. "I came to try and stop it."

"We?" Liam looked Jules up and down. "You with this guy? I can't wait to hear *this* story."

"He sort of... bailed me out," Zenn said. "He's letting me stay in his cabin."

"Really? Nice work. I thought they'd have you on a ferry headed back to the surface by now."

"What about you? How'd you end up down here?"

Liam dug in his pocket, then held up a credit relay. "Just call me *Victor* LeClerc."

"You stole Vic LeClerc's credit relay?"

"Victor, Victoria, who'll know the difference up here?"

"But how'd you get it?"

"I 'borrowed' it when I took the lease papers from Vic's ranch. Figured I'd need it. I knew I was gonna have to make myself scarce if I blew the lid on what she and Graad were up to. Pretty much maxed it out to bribe the first steward I met after you slammed the door on me back there. But it was enough for a discount ticket to the cheap seats down here. Not exactly the lap of luxury. Hey, it's off-planet; that's what counts."

"But what are you doing in here? This is wrong, and someone needs to..."

A particularly raucous shout went up from the crowd, and Zenn looked over to see Thrott preparing to release his slug into the makeshift arena.

"We have to do something," she said. "Those animals will cut each other to ribbons. We have to stop this."

"But you have already attempted this," Jules said, leaning down so she could hear him above the din. "These gamblers are not concerned with statutes governing this sector."

"Yeah. What a shock," Liam said, looking around at the motley crowd of bettors. "This way." He nodded at her to follow, then shouldered his way out through the crowd. At the far wall, he pulled himself up onto a tall container, pulled a small square of metal from his pocket and held it up to the ceiling. Zenn saw then what it was: an old-fashioned cigarette lighter. She heard a clicking sound as Liam held the lighter up, now with a small flame rising from it. "They don't give a damn about the law, do they? But ya know what? I'll bet they give a damn about *this.*"

He played the flame across the surface of the ceiling. A moment later, the room was filled with a cloudburst of water, streaming down like a heavy rainfall from invisible openings in the ceiling. The shock of the cold water hit Zenn like an icy, wet blanket – but Liam was right: the crowd responded as a single organism, breaking in a chaotic surge for the room's two exit doors. Shoving and pushing, they slid crazily on the water-slick floor, colliding with each other in their haste to leave, as a digitized voice from somewhere intoned loudly: "Emergency. Unidentified combustion detected in storage room 9, sub-deck 3. Emergency..."

Thrott went by, wheeling his caged slug in front of him. As he passed Zenn, the Skirni shot her a withering glare.

"This is your doing." He pawed water from his face, sodden robes clinging to him. "You meddle in affairs of which you know nothing. And yet you meddle."

"This is incorrect," Jules told him. "This person here is an exovet of the novice rank and knows much about slug types and all variety of creatures."

"I care not if she is exovet master rank! She meddles. She cost me my winnings. Thrott Larg-Skirnik will not forget."

Zenn recoiled at his venomous rage, then found her voice.

"It's against the law," she said. "And it's cruel."

"Bahhg! Law. In the mother-void? What law? You will pay. Thrott will not forget." Then he shoved the cage through the door and was gone.

"Come on," Liam said as the last of the room's occupants slipped out into the corridor. "We don't wanna be here when they find out it's a false alarm." He reached up to help Zenn down from the crate she stood on, his strong hands on her waist. Lifting her down to the floor, his hands stayed in place as she looked into his eyes. Zenn wasn't sure how to read what she saw there, but the moment seemed to call for something from her.

"That was… quick thinking. Thanks."

"Hey, just trying to make amends."

He continued to hold her close, his body warm against hers as the icy water sheeted off them.

"Please, come with me now," Yed called, peering in from the passage outside. Zenn pulled away from Liam's grasp.

"That's Yed. He brought us down here."

"We must go. And quickly," the steward said, waving them on. "I cannot be noticed here. I will summon the lev-car." He padded on ahead of them, disappearing into the throng.

"Liam, this is Jules Vancouver," she said as they walked. "He has a suite on the upper decks."

"Nice," Liam said, his usual smirk returning. "If you've got the credits."

Ahead at the lev-tube, Yed was holding open the door.

"We must go back now, yes, please? It is close to curfew, and we cannot be down in steerage after curfew."

Zenn and Jules entered the car. Liam remained in the corridor.

"Coming?" she asked.

"No, please," the steward said, holding one webbed hand up to keep Liam from boarding the car. "This ticket does not allow him to pass above steerage level."

"Yeah, I'm stuck in purgatory," Liam said. "But don't worry about it. I'm adapting. And the Reticulan stew –" he jerked one thumb toward the alien fussing over her bubbling cauldrons a short distance away "–is almost edible."

"Please! I must return to my duties. It is late. And getting no earlier."

It occurred to Zenn that Yed was right – it was late. And despite all the excitement, she was getting punchy from lack of sleep, not to mention being soaking wet and freezing.

"I'll come back soon as I can," she said. "We'll figure out… a plan."

"A plan. Good idea. I'll look forward to it." He slicked his wet hair back and gave her a grin. "And Scarlett?"

"Yes?"

"I lied about the stew. Not really edible. Bring some decent food with you."

NINE

The next morning, she and Jules discussed developments over a hasty breakfast eaten in their cabin.

First, there was the appearance of Liam down in steerage. There was no denying how seeing him again had lifted her spirits. But what to do now? She felt sorry for him, forced to survive in the conditions of the lower decks. Should they try and smuggle him up to Jules's rooms? Maybe he'd be more use moving about freely down there. No. It wasn't fair to just leave him there. She'd have to think of something.

Then there was the mystery of what Zenn had just learned about her father. Even after she and Jules examined the problem from every conceivable angle, it still made no sense. How could a full-grown man be held in a starliner's main sickbay and go unnoticed? Was she certain it was the *Helen's* sickbay? It had to be, didn't it? When the Skirni was talking on the com in the warehouse, it was clear his unknown accomplice was waiting for him up on the *Helen*. He also said he was going to bring Zenn up to the ship.

It seemed logical to Zenn that they had taken her father there as well. And from what Zenn remembered from her linking with her abductor, the *Helen's* sickbay had exactly the same layout, contained the same equipment, all in the same positions, down to the ornamental designs decorating the walls. But if this was true, then what had become of Warra Scarlett?

Any further dithering over what to do about either puzzle was prevented when the cabin's door announced the arrival of a visitor. It was the little steward.

"Greetings," Yed said. "I bring you several pieces of news."

"Then you'd better come in," Zenn said.

"I have found details on the passenger about whom you inquired. The guest in cabin 786 of deck 5 is registered under the name Pokt Mahg-Skirnik."

"Yes, Pokt," Zenn said. "That's what Liam called him."

"He has booked second-class passage through to Enchara. Also, I spoke with our ship's physician. He has seen no red-haired Earth male suiting the description you gave me. Nor has he noted any visit from Guest Pokt to the *Helen's* sickbay unit."

This was disappointing. And perplexing. At some point in the not-too-distant past, the Skirni must have been in the sickbay with her father. But when? And why wasn't he seen?

"Furthermore," Yed went on, "it is my pleasure to convey salutations from Captain Oolo. He was very pleased to hear his Cleevus singing and in good health again."

"I'm glad I was able to help," Zenn told him. "Please tell the Captain it was no trouble."

"As it turns out, you can tell him yourself."

"I can?"

"Yes. You are both requested to accept Captain Oolo's invitation to dine at the Captain's table with him this very night, at the pre-tunneling party. It is a costume gala. This is a ship's tradition of long standing. I can say you accept?"

Zenn's smile froze on her lips.

"The Captain's table," Jules said. "This is quite an honor, I believe."

"Yes, it is..." Zenn said, searching for a reason to decline. "But I really don't deserve it, do I, Jules?"

"But you assuredly do," Jules extended both mech-hands toward her. "You repaired the Captain's favorite creature. And now a costume party. These events are enjoyable. I have attended them in the past."

"Yes, please, it is most appropriate. To accept this invitation." Yed's tone now became fretful. "It would be your chance to tell our Captain of how satisfied the Bodines are with our services. And our good treatment of the unpleasant creature in the cargo hold. Captain Oolo would be most appreciative. Are you reluctant? The Captain will feel badly about a reluctance to dine with him."

Yes. She was reluctant. What if questions were asked? What if she was revealed as a stowaway? Or spotted by the Skirni?

"I don't know... I'm not very good... with crowds." She stared hard at Jules. "You know, Jules, with lots of people. *Looking at me.*"

Finally, the dolphin caught on.

"Ah, yes, this is true," Jules said slowly, thinking. "But it's a costume party. You could hide your shyness. Behind a mask."

Yed said, "Yes, indeed. I can provide this. The ship has a wide selection of costumes for guests. We stock a wide variety of maskings and ornamentation."

Zenn racked her brain to formulate some other credible excuse, but nothing came.

Yed shuffled his feet, a pained look on his wide, rubbery face. "Our Captain Oolo will be most disappointed if you decline," he said. Taking a step closer to her, he lowered his voice to a conspiratorial whisper. "No one declines such an invitation. Please. It is not done."

Later that evening, Zenn stood before the archway leading into the ship's Grand Ballroom. Jules had stopped outside the hall to check his costume one last time. He surveyed Zenn's outfit. "You are most appropriately attired. Shall we proceed?"

"I look ridiculous," she said, staring down at herself. From inside the ballroom, music, voices and laughter spilled out into the corridor. It was too late to back out now. But why hadn't she spent more time selecting her disguise? She didn't even understand the origin of the obscure Earther legend about half-fish women who wore bikini tops made out of coconut shells. Now, on the verge of dining at the Captain's table in front of hundreds of people, Zenn felt silly, oddly vulnerable and decidedly chilly.

"But you are an excellent and convincing mermaid. This is both festive and exotic," Jules told her tactfully.

"I feel like a genetic experiment gone horribly wrong," she said, picking irritably at the bulky sequined-cloth tail that tapered down to her ankles and made walking almost impossible. The costume's long black wig concealed her hair effectively, though, and the sea-shell-encrusted mask covered most of her face.

Jules ignored her complaint and fussed with the belt holding the scabbard of his sword. His pirate costume included a long red velvet coat stained with gunpowder splotches over a peach satin shirt with clouds of frilly lace sprouting at neck and wrists. One mech-hand had been replaced with a large plastic hook, and his mech-legs sported thigh-high synth-leather boots. A plumed, tri-cornered hat perched jauntily just behind his blowhole. The only distracting element was the gray tail flukes extending out between his coattails.

Why couldn't *you* be the mermaid? she thought irritably. You're already halfway there…

"You are forlorn," Jules said. "Is it due to our conversation before? About us leaving your friend Liam Tucker in the unhappy situation of the steerage decks?"

"I should've found some way to contact him today. I told him I'd go back down to see him." On the other hand, keeping her mind on finding Warra had kept her mind off worrying about Liam.

"But we could not proceed to the steerage level undetected without the assistance of the steward Yed. And he was otherwise engaged in duties all the day long. It is not your fault."

"But he'll think I forgot."

"We will arrange to see Liam Tucker tomorrow. And you can explain your failure as a friend then." She gave him a "thanks a lot" look. "Come. We'll be the talk of the party."

"That's what I'm afraid of," she said. But there was nothing to do now but plunge in and make the best of it. The truth was, she still felt a little giddy from her discovery about the sickbay. And even if she had no immediate solution to her father's whereabouts, at least this new clue gave her something concrete to hold onto. She peered into the hall full of chattering partygoers and took a deep breath.

"Are my coconuts straight?"

"Entirely. Let us go in. This will be... fun." He offered her his arm. Smiling at the dolphin's oddly comforting mimicry of human customs, Zenn put her hand on his metalloy arm and they waded into the noise and motion of the ballroom.

The sight that greeted them inside the spacious hall made Zenn immediately forget about her costume. The Grand Ballroom was vast, with a tall ceiling capped by a faux stained-glass dome. The room held dozens of tables with ornate centerpieces and individual nametags for each place setting. At the far end of the hall a single long, linen-draped table sat on a raised platform. Swirling around the tables were scores of passengers in varying degrees of flamboyant disguise, all talking and laughing as they hunted for their nametags. Flower garlands and streamers hung from the ceiling. In one corner was a quartet of musicians – two human females with violins, a young Procyon male bowing a cello and a tall Sirenian coleopt, all four upper arms playing a double-necked bass viol.

They were playing old-fashioned waltz music, but it was barely audible amid the guests' talking and laughter. The sight of the coleopt brought to mind the hulking insectoid who'd confronted her down in steerage, and then made her miss Hamish and wonder how he was getting along without Liam to help out with the cloister's never-ending list of chores.

The boy, his dark hair worn long on one side in the Procyoni fashion, sparked memories of Fane Reth Fanneson, the Procyon youth who Zenn had first met several weeks ago at the cloister. Fane was an under-sacrist – a sort of chamber assistant to a starship's Indra Groom. He was on Mars to pick up the whalehound owned by the royal family of the Leukkan Kire and transport the huge beast to its new home in one of the Kire's planet-wide nature preserves. Zenn and Fane hadn't exactly gotten along. They'd argued about the Procyon's spiritual beliefs – or, as Zenn would have it, Procyon superstitions. She wondered if Fane might even be at the party but, after considering the possibility, decided it seemed unlikely. He wasn't exactly the costume ball type.

Here and there, Gliesian waiters and waitresses trotted among the partygoers, proffering trays of drinks and appetizers. Zenn took a glass of punch off one of the passing trays, and Jules helped himself to a tall mug of frothy ale.

"Ahoy and avast," he declared as he clinked his glass against Zenn's and downed his drink with a flourish.

"If you say so," she said doubtfully, taking a sip of punch and scanning the scene. Humans and Asents of all sizes and body shapes paraded past – a Reticulan, its great bulk draped in a fairy costume complete with little wings; a colonist woman dressed as what seemed to be a zombie ballerina; another human with the uniform, helmet and muon-pick of an asteroid miner. Some unidentifiable short being – a Skirni? – buried beneath the stuffed tentacles and multiple eye-pods of a Kiran millivipe almost ran into her, swerved at the last second and veered back into the mass of revelers.

A brilliant red dinosaur-like outfit teetering atop two pairs of double-jointed insectoid legs wobbled past, with two voices inside offering muffled apologies as they bumped into those in their path. Whatever they were meant to be, Zenn decided they were enjoying themselves.

"Look there," Jules said, excited, pointing to the far exit. "A Skirni. Is that the one you seek? Is that this Pokt person?"

Zenn's pulse rate raced at the thought. The squat little alien who entered the hall was dressed as an Earther circus clown, complete with baggy yellow pants, floppy shoes and a red, bulbous nose. The effect was vaguely sinister. But no. It wasn't Pokt.

"It's Thrott," Zenn said. "The one you were gambling with before. See behind him? His slave?"

"Yes. My mistake."

It appeared for a moment that Thrott had spotted Jules. Had he recognized Zenn in her costume? If so, he didn't acknowledge the fact. A moment later, both he and his slave vanished into the milling throng of guests.

At the nearest table, Zenn's attention was drawn to a pack of Alcyons. They were squabbling over who sat where. Their gangly lizard forms were all cloaked in identical rodentlike costumes, their pointed snouts and flicking tongues sticking out of fuzzy-eared hoods. Zenn wondered if they thought it humorous to dress as their own prey. It struck her as kind of creepy.

She was about to ask Jules his opinion about this when one of the Gliesian waiters turned around to offer them appetizers. It was Yed.

"There you are." He seemed relieved they had shown up. "The Captain is eager to meet you. And also, I can confirm that I relayed the communication to Mars which you gave to me. It was sent off by the ship's comm officer this same hour."

Now that the *Helen* had moved well beyond Mars orbit, Zenn had decided it was safe to let Otha know what she'd done. It would be too late now for her to be sent back.

"Thank you, Yed," she told the steward. "I appreciate your help."

"It is my honor. Please…" He gestured to a small circle of guests standing near the central raised platform. "This way."

In the circle's center stood a tall human male in a dazzling dress-white uniform. Broad-shouldered, his craggy, weathered face wore a close-cropped white beard that perfectly complemented his sparkling blue eyes. He was every inch the ideal ship's officer. In fact, he looked more like a cartoon of a Captain than the real thing. As she approached him through the crowd, Zenn saw that the man's entire body shimmered with the minute, telltale static of a personal holo-projector image.

"Guest Bodine, Guest Vancouver," Yed said eagerly, "may I present Captain Yoolis-En Oolo of the Lumiliner *Helen of Troy*."

"A pleasure. Glad to have you both aboard." The Captain spoke in a deep, husky Earther drawl as he extended a hand for Zenn to shake. Zenn was certain it wasn't his real voice. And the hand she shook clearly wasn't human. Beneath the holo-projected pixels, her hand was gripped by what felt like thin, bony digits with leathery skin and small, sharp tips – a bird's claw? "I can't tell you how much I appreciate what you did for my Cleevus. She's never sounded better! You'll hear for yourself later tonight. She's doing excerpts from Tlanpoh's 'Ecstasy of the Hatchling Pool'. Do you know it?"

"Um, no, sorry."

"An operetta. Gliesian, actually. Selected in honor of the *Helen's* indispensable stewards." The Captain rested a hand on Yed's shoulder. "Especially this one." Yed's smile threatened to overflow his cheeks. "It's thanks to you and Yed that my little mudlark is able to show off her talents tonight. You're obviously an exovet who knows her fungal-animoids. Where did you study, if you don't mind my asking?"

"The Ciscan cloister, near Arsia City," she told him. But before she could explain she wasn't a full-fledge exoveterinarian yet, they were interrupted by a high, piping sound like a tin whistle.

"The signal for dinner. We'd best head to the table," the Captain said. "You'll be on my left." He gestured, and Zenn realized the Captain's table was the one set up on the raised platform. She wished yet again she'd made a more understated costuming choice as she hiked up her awkward tailpiece and struggled up the steps to take her seat.

Glancing out at the room, her attention was drawn by something approaching through the milling crowd. It proceeded toward them with an unusual bobbing movement. It took Zenn a moment to realize it wasn't a costumed passenger she was seeing, but something much more interesting.

TEN

A glimpse of a translucent dome with aquamarine zebra striping was visible over the heads of the partygoers. Zenn saw then that the strange, undulating movement of the approaching creature was because it wasn't walking on legs but was instead hovering several feet off the floor.

The Cepheian's face reminded Zenn of a blowfish, with two pale eyes, no nose and a permanently pursed-lipped expression on the tiny mouthpart, all crowded into a small area beneath the bulging, dome-shaped mantle above it. The body resembled nothing so much as a huge jellyfish: a five-foot-wide half sphere of see-through tissue, with multiple pastel-colored organs and gas sacs visible within. Hanging down from the dome's circumference were dozens of delicate, string-like gripping appendages and, most extraordinary of all, four ovoid globes of transparent skin. Suspended in each sphere was a single, diminutive consort – the water-breathing males of the species.

A chorus of high-pitched Transvox voices emanated from the males.

"Excuse us." "Coming through." "Tight squeeze." "Make room here, feh?"

Floating in their individual compartments of nutrient-rich fluid, the males looked like foot-long brine shrimp, each one waving four spindly arms tipped with feathery filaments that were once hands but had long since lost that function. Their blood-red eyes blinked as the males pressed up against the membranes of their spheres, straining to make out the surroundings beyond.

As Zenn had only recently learned in Otha's comparative physiology class, this kind of bizarre female/male symbiosis was a rare, but not unheard-of, survival technique. It was a kind of sexual dimorphism where the larger female animal carried her male counterparts along with her. It had been documented in a number of deep-sea fish on Earth as well as several marine creatures in the under-ice oceans of Jupiter's moon Europa. The Cepheian's gas giant homeworld of Eta Cephei, with its vast, sparsely populated cloud realms, was in some ways similar to the barren underwater deserts of the Earth and Europa. In these environments, locating a mate in all that empty water or air could be a life-or-death proposition. Still, it was an amazing thing to consider – solving the problem of how find a breeding partner by having your would-be husbands literally attached at the hip.

"Do you know what that is?" Jules whispered in Zenn's ear as the Cepheian wafted its way toward their table. "I'll wager you do not."

"Jules," Zenn whispered back. "It's a Cepheian drifter. And I'm not sure they'd appreciate us betting on what they are."

"Sorry. You're right," Jules said. "And I see now I would have lost my wager. Thank you for your frankness."

It was, however, the first drifter Zenn had ever seen outside of a v-film, and she had to admit it was a most remarkable sight.

"Ambassador Noom," the Captain addressed the hovering creature when it reached the front of the platform, "you'll be here on my right."

The Cepheian's self-generated mix of methane, hydrogen sulfide and other lighter-than-air gases filled its large balloon-like mantle and acted as both a lifting agent and propellant. The mechanism was much like the gas bladders that lined the undersides of the wings that bore giant Kiran sunkillers aloft. Zenn's nose crinkled at the rotten-egg aroma that descended over the table as the drifter drew closer.

The Cepheian rose up over the platform and settled lightly on the back of the chair next to the Captain. Zenn saw then it wasn't a chair but a specially constructed perch like a tall, sculpted "T" rising from a weighted base. Several of the Cepheian's gripping tendrils wrapped themselves around the upper crossbar, anchoring the body in place like a large, tethered balloon.

"Grab there." "No, there." "Too close." "Squashed here, feh."

The agitated males all spoke more or less at once, making it difficult to understand them. It occurred to Zenn that carrying your multiple mates around with you all the time was clearly a mixed biological blessing. Apparently the female was of a like mind. She reached a tendril up to the Transvox unit attached to her side and dialed down the volume on the translator. The consorts continued to complain and mutter, but at a much lower level.

"This is Ambassador Noom Surishta Voikunoybo," the Captain said to Zenn and Jules. "She and her staff are en route back to Eta Cephei. The ambassador has just come from a rather historic visit to Earth." The Captain sat, then addressed the Cepheian. "I understand congratulations are in order, Ambassador. I believe you've achieved a breakthrough of sorts."

"Of sorts, yes, Captain," the ambassador replied, her pleasing, velvety voice at odds with her – their? – exotic appearance. Unlike her consorts, she didn't use a Transvox, and Zenn was impressed at her lack of accent. If you couldn't see who was speaking, you might well mistake her for a native Earther. "This was only an initial contact, of course," she went on. "But I can honestly describe our talks as both wide-ranging and constructive."

"Can we now hope starships of the Accord will once again be welcomed in Earth orbit?"

"Time will tell, Captain. If future meetings are as productive, it's certainly a possibility."

"Providing," the Captain said, "the Ghost Shepherds leave us one or two ships to get around in."

"Captain Oolo–" Noom's tone was reprimanding "–as you well know, the Indra problem is of unknown origin. Suggesting otherwise only leads to wild speculation. Ghost Shepherds! Seriously, what next? Tales of Indra ships whisked away by goblins?"

"Ghost Shepherds," Jules said. "I have heard this name. They are thought to be spirit-beings of some form, yes?"

The ambassador swiveled to face Jules. "It is a religious belief among the Procyoni who attend the Indra. The Indra starship grooms and their sacrists believe the Shepherds are an ancient supernatural race who first harnessed the power of the Indra. Ghost Shepherds are alleged to keep their stonehorses stabled in a distant, uncharted star system so remote no other sentient being has ever set eyes upon it. This fact, these Procyoni say, explains why no one has ever actually seen a Ghost Shepherd. Very convenient, wouldn't you agree?"

"But, it is true that the appearance of the first Indra ship remains a peculiar and unresolved mystery, is it not?" Jules said. "That first vast ship was discovered simply floating about at the very boundary of mapped space all those years ago. And it was found empty of all life except for its great Indra, so it could not be said who built it. Or who left it for the Procyoni to find. Perhaps it was left by these haunting Shepherds."

"Yes," Noom said. "The Procyoni stumbling upon that first ship so close to their homeworld was a nice bit of fortune, I will admit."

That's an understatement, Zenn thought. Finding the first, derelict Indra ship within sublight distance of Procyon was the only reason interstellar flight existed at all. Up until that moment, no science known to human or Asent had been able to unlock the riddle of how to travel between the stars. The distances were simply too vast, the power requirements too huge, the technological obstacles too baffling. But after the Procyoni discovered the astounding ability of that single Indra, they were then able to take their first tentative steps into space beyond their star. The following discovery of the Indra herd feeding off the dark matter whirlpools circling a nearby globular cluster meant more Indra ships could be built, and they soon were. But it was that first colossal stroke of fate, that first abandoned Indra vessel, that led to the Procyoni making First Contact with Earth. That single ship became the seed of the fleet that now knitted together the planets and civilizations of the Local Systems Accord. It was almost enough to make one believe in ghostly aliens and supernatural doings… if one were inclined in that direction.

"And there are more suitably mystical facts," Noom went on, clearly enjoying herself. "According to the sacred books of the Procyoni, every now and then the Shepherds return to round up their far-flung Indra herds and drive them home again. This is in order to bring their stonehorses back to their hidden breeding grounds, to produce more Indra. And if the Shepherds should not perform this epic task, so the texts tell us, the Indra will be offended and refuse to grant the Procyoni or other Asents the power of star travel. A pretty fairytale. But only that." The Cepheian paused, then looked from Jules and Zenn to the Captain.

"Oh, forgive me, Ambassador," the Captain said, gesturing at his guests. "This is Jules Vancouver, of Earth."

"Pleased to meet you, Ambassador Noom… voykin…" Jules stammered to a halt.

"Omma Tsantis Iph Sharor Tus Florim Shardahla Noom Surishta Voiykenoiboh Noomdrass-Liquissi," the Cepheian said. "But please, you must call us Noom."

"We're Noom Noomdrass." "All Noomdrass." "Liquissi as well." "Liquissi family of Noomdrass, feh?" the male consorts babbled softly.

"And this is Miss Zora Bodine," the Captain said. "A Ciscan exovet, recently come aboard from Mars."

"*Novice* exovet, actually," Zenn said. "I'm still in training."

"A novice exoveterinarian?" Noom rose a few inches into the air to make eye contact with Zenn. "A Ciscan." "Creature physician." "From Mars." "The famous cloister, feh?"

"A Ciscan cloister novice," Noom said. "That would be the Arsia Valley Chapter, correct?"

"Yes, the Arsia Ciscans," Zenn admitted. She was surprised the Cepheian's knowledge extended to a tiny, almost defunct exovet training facility on a backwater planet in a marginal star system. "You've heard of our cloister, then?"

"Oh yes, we're well aware of the Arsia Ciscans and their… good works." Noom regarded Zenn with an odd expression. Was the Cepheian trying to imagine the face beneath the mermaid mask? Or was it, Zenn thought, just her own anxiety making it seem that way? "And what," Noom said then, "do your Martian compatriots make of Earth's new openness to contact with the rest of the Local Systems Accord?"

Zenn certainly had her own opinions about the Rift between Earth and Mars – and the Earther push to resume contact with their former colony on the Red Planet. But to debate the point here, on a raised dais at the center of several hundred people, dressed as a mermaid? Her face grew warm with color.

"I think most Martians are ready for contact again with Earth," she said. "But I also think the Earther Authority needs to understand how we do things," she added quickly. "You know, not impose their ways on Mars just because we do things differently or because we have alien patients at the cloister."

"Frankly, Ambassador," the Captain said, shaking out his napkin and placing it in his lap, "that's what puzzles me about your mission. The Temp Exec Authority has no love for Cepheians or any other Alien Sentients in the Accord. Why would Earth push for resumed contact with Mars and the Asent planets now?"

"It's the members of the Temp Exec Authority who wish to reopen trade with the other planets of the Accord. The extremists of the New Law faction are the only ones who wish to maintain the Rift and keep Earth cut off from outside contact," the ambassador said.

The Captain pressed his point. "I think what worries some within the Accord is the motive of the Cepheians in these negotiations. It's no secret that Eta Cephei wants to expand its trade networks. It needs more ships to do that. A deal between your species and the Earther Authority would make some in the LSA… deeply unhappy."

"I assume you refer to Procyon," the ambassador said, her voice gaining a slight flinty edge. "The Procyoni grooms have long held what can only be described as an inappropriate monopoly of Indra-drive ships and the profits that entails. But it seems self-evident that the open market is where issues of interstellar transport should be negotiated. All these rumors about Indra routes and secret dealings and such, this is simply the Procyoni stirring the pot, don't you agree?"

"Even so..." The Captain refused to be put off. "The fact is, the Authority seems to have reached out specifically, quietly, to Eta Cephei, Ambassador. Not to the Accord as a whole. This is bound to raise questions, wouldn't *you* agree?"

Any answer from the ambassador was prevented by the sight of a figure emerging from the crowd and approaching their table. It was one of the few passengers Zenn actually knew.

"Lieutenant, glad you could join us," the Captain said, rising from his chair. "Everyone, this is Lieutenant Stav Travosk, official envoy of the Temp Exec Authority."

The new arrival was the young soldier who'd been playing cards with Jules. Apparently, he'd decided his red-coated uniform was costume enough for the party. He ascended the stairs and stood behind the seat next to the ambassador.

"Hello again," the soldier said, acknowledging Jules.

"You two have met, I take it," the Captain said.

"Yes. Earlier. And the little mermaid?"

"Miss Zora Bodine," the Captain said. "From Mars."

"I believe we met earlier as well. You were the one looking for Jules in the card room?"

"Yes. That's right," Zenn said. The soldier gave her a nod and brief smile.

"The lieutenant accompanied the ambassador on the shuttle from Earth," the Captain said.

"Yes," Noom said. "The Authority was most generous in sparing Lieutenant Travosk. He is a highly skilled science officer and someone who understands the value of Earth resuming contact with the worlds of the Local Systems Accord. He is, as well, a man determined to help end the Indra problem afflicting us all. One could describe it as a driving obsession with him. And well it should be."

"Guilty as charged," the soldier said. "But it's not like I'm alone in wanting to see the disappearances solved. It simply can't continue. And there are many on Earth like me, working day and night on the solution. We will put a stop to it." The soldier's eyes grew, if possible, even steelier as he spoke. "You have my word."

"I can believe it, coming from you," the ambassador said. "In any case, the Lieutenant has been an invaluable asset to us, both a formidable mind and faithful bodyguard during our visit."

"A bodyguard?" Jules said, leaning forward to see the soldier better.

"On Earth?" the Captain said. "Was this necessary?"

"Simply a precaution," Noom said. "You know, the New Law and others with... strong opinions about any treaties the Earth might attempt to enter into. An overabundance of concern, I'm sure."

"But this is bold and thrilling," Jules said. "I should like to be a bodyguard." He turned to Zenn. "I can act as Miss Bodine's body-shielder. Like a horse-riding man covered in metal skin – a knight of olden days. So you will have no worries." He put one mech-hand softly on her shoulder. "I will go wherever you go, at the ready. To guard your body."

"Jules, I'm not important enough to need guarding," Zenn said quietly, not wanting to attract any more attention than she already had.

"You underestimate yourself, Novice," the Captain said.

"Novice?" The soldier turned his silver eyes back to her.

"Yes," Noom said. "We have a novice exovet to grace our company, Lieutenant. From the local Ciscan cloister, no less."

"The cloister on Mars? Still in operation? I didn't realize." The soldier's striking eyes rested on her in a way that made it difficult for her to look away. "But I'm glad to hear it's still functioning."

"Yes, Novice Bodine helped to revive my ailing Cleevus, didn't you?" The Captain beamed at her.

Zenn blushed beneath her mask, wishing again that everyone would just ignore her.

"In that case," the soldier said, raising his glass to her, "we must thank the fates that Miss Bodine came aboard when she did." Another smile for her, beneath the ice-gray glance. "So, where are you headed, Novice?"

Zenn's mind momentarily blanked.

"Oh… to… Sigmund's Parch," she said. "I'm traveling with my father, to return his sandhog boar to the seller."

"So, the animal became ill?" the soldier asked. "And required your attention on the journey?"

Zenn tried to think…

"Yes. A parasitic infection," she said, grasping for a reason she'd need to accompany the hog. "Affected his behavior and made him difficult to handle… He was aggressive, kept burrowing out of his pen, that sort of thing."

"Well, your father's a lucky man to have an exovet in the family," he said. He turned then to address the table: "Now, if you'll all excuse me for a moment, I'd better check in with my adjutant before we eat. He's handling all the paperwork for our excursion from Earth, and it makes him cranky if I don't update him on a regular basis."

The soldier stepped down from the dais and spoke into his sleeve screen as he walked a short distance into the crowd.

ELEVEN

An hour or so later, they'd all finished their main courses. The ship's stewards were weaving among the guest tables offering trays arrayed with assorted dessert dishes.

"...and in your exciting role as bodyguard," Jules was saying to Stav Travosk, "are you often called upon to heroically defend Ambassador Noom by shooting down nefarious assailants, blazing at them with your pistol?"

Zenn noticed then the soldier did in fact wear a holster on one hip, whatever weapon it held hidden discreetly beneath a wide flap.

"The ambassador exaggerates my position. I'm just here to represent the Authority and provide a courtesy escort. Nothing more heroic than that."

"And what's your take on the ambassador's negotiations, Lieutenant?" the Captain asked.

"Only time will tell," Stav said. "But Eta Cephei makes a compelling case. I think she may have persuaded a lot of people back on Earth, people who have a long history of not being persuadable."

"Yes, so I hear," the Captain said. "But I wonder. Is their case compelling enough to offer them exclusive control of the starship routes to Earth?"

"Captain Oolo," Noom interjected, rising a foot or so into the air. "You will embarrass the lieutenant."

Stav shook his head dismissively. "There are always rumors kicked up in this sort of negotiation: that the Cepheians are trying to control all Sol space routes, that the Authority is planning an end run around LSA trade law, that sort of thing. All I can say is that the Authority is the one who's reaching out. We have nothing to hide."

Noom then rose further into the air to address the table. "Precisely. And I think we can all agree that Accord politics are too spicy an addition to civilized dinner conversation." She gave Captain Oolo a significant look. He seemed on the verge of contesting her point when she went on, "Now, Captain, what about this mudlark of yours I've heard so much about? It will be performing tonight, will it not? I'm sure we're all anxious to hear this rare exhibition." Her attempt at changing the subject was successful, and the Captain happily launched into a discussion of Cleevus's lengthy pedigree.

After the dessert course, a Gliesian waiter came through the crowd wheeling a small trolley. On it was a portable aquarium, complete with a tiny purple velvet curtain.

The Captain descended from the raised dais and went to introduce his pet to the audience. Standing next to the trolley, Zenn saw him touch one hand to his belt. His holographic human-ship's-captain costume deactivated, revealing his true physique. Zenn had guessed right. The Captain was a bird of sorts – he was an Ornithope; six feet tall, his long neck topped by a smallish, round head with a massive hooked beak and hooded hawk's eyes. His leather-booted legs held a body covered mostly with brown and white feathers. Where a bird would have wings, Ornithopes had evolved feathered, claw-tipped arms. His white, vest-like captain's uniform was cut away at the chest, allowing him to show off the characteristic rainbow-hued breast feathers Ornithopes used for displays of various emotions. The chest feathers were now rippling with pride as he drew the curtain back to present Cleevus standing alertly within her small glass enclosure.

"Honored guests, allow me to introduce my fungal-animoid, Cleevus." The Captain's speech was now no longer the deep, bass drawl that had been manufactured by his holo-costume. Instead, he spoke in his natural voice: a bubbling Ornithope warble. Much like an Earther parrot or mynah bird, his heavy, black beak moved only slightly as he spoke, the sound produced by the complex, flexible membranes within his avian syrinx – the equivalent of a human's voice box – located deep in his chest.

"Tonight," the Captain continued, "Cleevus will be performing a program of symphonic, popular and operatic works by composers from across the Local Systems Accord. For her first selection, a concerto for Alcyon harp and orchestra, by Ghilic Sha."

By the time Cleevus had completed her final number, a soothing choral rendition of a Procyoni folk lullaby, Zenn was fighting to keep her eyes open. She leaned over toward Jules.

"I'm ready to call it a night," she said. "And I'm definitely ready to get rid of this tail. No offense."

"None taken. You do look on the verge of sleep. I should accompany you, should I not, if I am to serve as your body-guardian?" But as Jules said this, Zenn saw he was gazing at something across the room. Through a gap in the crowd, she could see he was watching a corner table with several costumed guests sitting around it. They were playing cards.

"Would you rather stay?" Zenn said, grinning at his obviously conflicted state.

"Would I be derelict if I did so? In my guarding duties?"

"Of course not. Go play cards. But Jules…" She waited till he turned to face her. "Do not gamble your walksuit away. Promise?"

"My walksuit? That would be folly."

"Yes. It would."

"So, if you are certain, then," he said, standing up from where he'd crouched at the table. "Sleep comfortably. I will see you in the morning." He then raised his voice so the others could hear. "I will bid you all good evening. Zora Bodine, when you return to your cabin, please wish your father good evening as well for me."

"Yes," Zenn said, thinking this was overplaying the part just a bit. "I'll do that."

He leaned in to whisper to her, "A subterfuge. I am deceiving those present by leading them to believe you now go to your own cabin."

"I get it, Jules," she whispered back. He engaged his legs and strode off toward the card game.

She rose from her seat, thanked the Captain and said goodnight to him and the others. Noom also excused herself, saying her consorts were growing weary and she needed to retire.

The soldier took his cue from the ambassador and said he was leaving as well. He rose and approached Zenn.

"A pleasure to meet you, Novice Bodine," he said, politely taking her hand in both of his and giving her a smile, locking his gray eyes on hers. "Travel safely," he said, held her hand a moment longer, then released her.

"I will, thank you," she said. She watched him go, momentarily flustered by their exchange. There was, she decided, something intriguing about this Earther soldier. Leaving the dais, she made her way through the partygoers toward the corridor. She was about to step into the passageway when the crowd parted and she saw the Captain's mudlark, surrounded by the pack of Alcyons. They were demanding an encore.

"Sing," one of the rodent-clad reptiles hissed, leaning in close to the aquarium.

"Yes. The Alcyon anthem. Sing that. Do it now," another lizard said, poking at the mudlark with one claw-tipped finger. The mudlark shrank into itself, its color blanching pale.

"The Alcyon anthem." The mudlark repeated the reptile's words back to him, perfectly mimicking the reptilian tones and timbre. "Sing that. Do it now," it said, again a perfect match.

Zenn looked to see if the Captain had noticed, but he was conversing with one of the waiters.

The mudlark was clearly terrified, Zenn thought, and its mimicry was just a fearful attempt to ward off the hostile group encircling it. When that didn't work, the mudlark seemed to panic, picking up any sound it could hear, replicating more and more voices from the partygoers in the room. Within seconds, the creature was emitting a babble of dozens of voices all at once. This only seemed to annoy the Alcyons, who drew in even closer around it as they continued to hector their victim.

Zenn was trying to work up the courage to intervene when it hit her, the feeling immersing her, sapping her strength to the point she had to lean against the nearby wall for support. The lights in the room grew faint, and all at once she was in total darkness. A wave of overwhelming fear hit her, a dreadful sense of being exposed to danger but unable to flee.

She had linked with the mudlark again, or it with her, as it was tormented by the Alcyons. But there was more. A roaring in her ears, a growing onslaught of incoherent sounds. Squeals. Clicks. Gurgles. Garbled words. Tones, rising, falling in the darkness that engulfed her… She was hearing… voices, human and Asent, distorted, impossible to sort out, ten, twenty, dozens of voices, all speaking at once, in a babble of different languages. She was hearing the conversations of everyone in the room, hearing through the exquisitely sensitive audio receptors of the frightened mudlark.

In the cacophony and darkness, she struggled to keep her balance, forced herself to remain still. Then, through the din of alien tongues and snatches of sentences, came words she recognized.

"...no, it is her. I'm certain... she's on board." The voice was faint, indistinct, and Zenn couldn't even tell if it was male or female, human or not. It faded in and out in the cascade of sound ebbing and flowing through the room.

"But how...?" This new voice was guttural, rasping, but clearer, easier to hear. "When last I saw her, we were at the launch port on Mars." Zenn knew then. It was voice of her Skirni abductor – and he was talking about her.

"...doesn't matter how," the other, unidentifiable voice said. Then it submerged, only to re-emerge. "...back on schedule, no thanks to you. Now, we can proceed as originally – we will take the ind– You will release the... into the chamber... you gain access?"

The Skirni again: "Do not concern yourself; Pokt knows... around a starship... will achieve access... deliver the nexus... And all Skirni... have their reward... justice..."

Then she lost all traces of the conversation as it blended into the churning sea of chattering voices. She fought to find it again, made herself reach out through the confusion and noise, searching, straining. But it was no use.

"...mistress?" A new voice. Closer. Clearer. "Can you hear me ?" Unusual accent. Female.

Abruptly, the strange sensations drained away from Zenn, the hundred voices went silent, vision returned – she was leaning against the wall of the hall, near the exit. She must have been "gone" for just a second or two.

"Are you unwell?" It was a Fomalhaut; yes, the Skirni's slave, concern lining her face, one hand on Zenn's shoulder.

"I'm OK," Zenn said, pushing away from the wall, trying to clear her head. "It was just… a dizzy spell. I'm fine now."

"I am pleased to hear it. For I come to you in my master's name," the slave said, her crescent eyes looking off into the corridor. "I am called Carm Sivit. And I bear a message to you."

"Yes?" Zenn said, her thoughts still clouded, unable to imagine what Thrott's slave could possibly want.

"I am to say: forgive me, mistress, for disturbing you," the Fomalhaut said, eyes now cast down. She raised her head, gave Zenn a quick look of pained misery, looked away again, and began speaking very rapidly, hardly stopping for breath. "Master Thrott's Encharan slug – the one you saw – it has been injured, *grievously* injured in a fight. My master beseeches you humbly to come at once and attend to its wounds which consist of deep slashes to vital organs. It will surely die if you do not come. My master states he will pay extravagantly for your services. Please do not allow this innocent animal to perish by refusing to come. My master thanks you."

In her shaken state, Zenn had to concentrate to comprehend the Fomalhaut's words.

"The slug… it's hurt? How long ago?"

The slave started in again on her memorized speech. "Master Thrott's Encharan slug – the one you saw–"

"If it's wounded… I'll have to come." Inside the room, she saw that the Alcyons had given up harassing Cleevus and had gone off into the crowd. "But I'll need to go get my field kit."

"Yes. Thank you. Quickly, please, mistress."

At Jules's cabin, Zenn changed out of her costume, checked on Katie – sound asleep on her bunk – and then hurried back into the corridor, where Carm Sivit waited.

On their way to Thrott's cabin, Zenn tried to organize her scattered thinking enough to extract further details about the slug's condition. But between the aftereffects of her link with the mudlark and the slave's near-panic, she could learn nothing new. The distressed Fomalhaut would only repeat her earlier words about deep wounds to vital organs. Zenn realized Thrott must have seen Jules at the party and deduced that it was her with him. Maybe he'd been at the dinner in order to arrange a fight with another animal owner. That would explain the slug being wounded. Apparently, he was willing to forgive her earlier behavior, at least when his prize slug was at risk. She would make sure he promised no more fights as a condition for her services.

They stopped in front of a cabin door.

"The animal... is inside," the Fomalhaut said, motioning for Zenn to enter.

Zenn had just stepped into the room when the slave's voice stopped her.

"My master Thrott," Carm Sivit said, eyes down, in a voice so low Zenn had to strain to make out her words. "He... holds my family in bondage. I must do all that he says or they perish. I wish you to understand this."

"But, that's terrible, can't you go to the authorities and–"

"No. I am sorry. I am so sorry," Carm said, her voice a pained cry. Then she toggled the outer door switch, and it hissed shut.

The interior was so dim Zenn couldn't make out any details. Moving further inside, she told the lights to turn themselves up, but nothing happened. She turned and told the door to open. No response. She went to the wall, flicked the manual override, still no lights. And the door also refused to respond.

"Master Thrott?" she said, setting her pack down on a chair. "Your servant said the slug was injured. Hello?"

A faint sound came from a dark corner of the room: a liquid, rasping intake of breath. Zenn squinted into the shadows.

"Thrott? Are you there?"

There was movement at the back of the room and a soft sputtering sound. A shape lifted itself up beyond a table, emerging into the scant light. The Encharan slug. It was... out of its cage! The creature's broad muzzle swung slowly to and fro. Had it picked up her scent? She kept still and held her breath.

Keeping her eyes fixed on the slug, she then risked a step backward and felt behind her, hands searching for the manual door switch. She found it, toggled it frantically. Again, nothing happened. The slug's eyestalks extended, raising the weak eyes upward, where they slowly panned across the room. Panic flooding through her, Zenn gauged the distance to the cabin's nearest high point – a shelf running along one wall. If she could reach it in time, it might let her get out of the slug's striking distance.

She eased her foot back until it contacted the door behind her, braced herself to make a run for it. The eyestalks swiveled, catching the motion. With an ear-splitting, high-pitched squeal, the slug reared and fell forward, toxic slime splattering off its body as it humped toward her.

Zenn sprang for the shelf, reached it, hands scrabbling to gain a grip on the smooth metal. Would it hold her weight? She hurled herself up, rolled her body onto it, knocking books to the floor, felt the impact of the slug hitting the wall beneath her. She forced herself into the small space, barely able to hold herself in place.

Below, the slug raised itself, its boneless form narrowing, extending, reaching up towards her. It was just inches away. Now, the barbed ribbon of the slug's radula-tongue shot out from the oral opening, scraping on the shelving beneath her, leaving deep gouges in the metal where it struck. The radula slid out again, hit the shelf – and stuck, embedded in the surface. The slug pulled its radula back into its mouth. It was hoisting itself up, its entire weight coming off the floor. It was climbing up to get at her.

Zenn realized she couldn't stay where she was. There was nothing else to be done: she pushed away from the wall, threw herself off the shelf and into the air. Passing just over the suspended slug, she landed hard and came up against the front of a table. She dove through the opening between its legs and turned to see the slug release its grip on the shelf and drop to the floor. It hit with a fleshy splat opposite her, re-oriented itself, eyestalks fully extended, the head waving back and forth.

The head stopped waving – it had spotted her. It heaved itself into motion, snorting and gurgling, wet body slapping hard on the floor as it came.

Zenn looked around frantically. No. There was no other place to hide. She was trapped. She turned again toward the door where she'd entered. Even if she could reach it, it was jammed. Then, she saw – the door… was open! Yes, she could see into the corridor beyond.

With no time even to stand, she scrambled madly backwards on all fours, crab-style. The slug slid around the corner of the table, zeroed in on her and pursued, squealing, the spiked radula sawing in and out. But the door was too far. She'd never make it.

"Get down." A man's voice, booming behind her. "Down, now!" She obeyed, dropped to the floor, drew her body into a ball, covered her exposed face with her arms and waited for the feel of slashing spikes and burning acid.

The sound of the onrushing slug filled her ears. It would be on top of her in another second. Then a shocking blaze of blue-white light filled the room, a sensation of searing, concentrated heat rippled through the air inches above her and a short, sharp animal shriek was followed by the sound of a something big and wet hitting the floor next to her.

Zenn lifted her head. The front of the slug's body lay six inches away. The creature was dead, a steaming, oozing stump of flesh where its head had been. Turning, she saw a figure silhouetted in the doorway. It wore a red soldier's jacket and held a flux-pistol in one hand. A wisp of smoke curled into the air from the gun's faintly glowing tip.

Later – Zenn wasn't sure how much later – she was out in the corridor, sitting on a bench set into the bulkhead. Someone had draped a blanket around her shoulders.

Jules had arrived and had located a cup of hot tea for her. He stood over her now, fidgeting nervously, and, for once, apparently speechless.

A short distance away, Stav Travosk spoke in low tones to Captain Oolo. "I overheard two of the stewards talking. Something about a disturbance on this deck. I… thought I'd investigate."

"Well, a lucky thing you came along, Lieutenant," the Captain said. "Wouldn't you agree, Novice Bodine? Lucky the lieutenant came along?"

"Yes. Lucky," Zenn said, forcing a smile, her emotions jumbled. The young lieutenant had dropped the slug in mid-lunge. Obviously, the man had just saved her life. But the animal hadn't attacked her out of malice; it did what came naturally to a creature bred to fight, trained to attack. Instead of feeling glad to be alive, she felt sick to her stomach.

"Sure you're not hurt?" Stav asked her, his piercing look now edged with concern.

"No, I'm OK," she said, her voice still wavering. She added, almost inaudibly, "I just wish… you didn't have to kill it."

"Not much of a choice," Stav said. "It was almost on top of you. You could have been badly hurt. Worse." He regarded her for a few seconds. "You really do have a… special feeling for creatures like this, don't you? For creatures in general. I suppose it goes with the territory. Being an exovet."

She nodded, let her eyes stray to the slug's smoking carcass, then looked quickly away.

"I don't see how it could have gotten loose." The Captain craned his long neck to peer into the cabin. "Guest Thrott would have been apprised of ship's regulations regarding the transport of dangerous animals." The Captain shook his head, turned to Stav. "Thank the gods you came along when you did. If the creature had escaped into the passageways, there's no calculating the damage it could have caused."

"Just lucky, like you said," Stav replied.

"Guest Bodine, I apologize again for this entirely unacceptable event," the Captain chittered, his warble rising half an octave as his he turned his hooded eyes to her. "If there's any way I can make it up to you, anything at all, you must not hesitate to let me know."

"It wasn't your fault, Captain."

"No, no. The *Helen* is my ship. All that happens aboard her is my responsibility." He smoothed his chest feathers with one claw. "Please, you must allow me to make it up to you."

"No, really," she said, not wanting any special attention, not wanting any attention at all. The only thing she wanted was to be away from everyone, back in Jules's cabin, safe, unnoticed.

"Actually," Stav said, addressing the Captain, "I have a suggestion. The Novice is clearly someone who appreciates… exotic life-forms. I understand that under certain circumstances, a guest might be invited to visit a starliner's Indra chamber, to have an up-close encounter with a stonehorse. I understand you'll be conducting pre-tunnel preparations tomorrow morning? What do you think, Captain?"

The Ornithope's head bobbed in agreement.

"Outstanding idea, Lieutenant," he said. "That would be the perfect opportunity. Novice?"

"The Indra chamber?" Zenn's unsettled state cleared considerably at the words.

"But only if you feel up to it," the Captain said.

"No, I mean, yes, I'd love to. Thank you."

"Guest Vancouver as well. And your father, naturally."

"Oh..." she stammered, "...Dad's not feeling so great just now. All the excitement of traveling. The strange food, you know, his stomach."

"I'm sorry to hear it. But it does affect some passengers that way," the Captain said.

A pair of stewards had arrived and were now gingerly covering the slug's body in what appeared to be a sort of plastic body bag.

"I can only repeat, I'm mystified how this could have come about," the Captain said.

"Perhaps Thrott's servant can shed some light on it all?" Stav Travosk said. "You did say it was his slave who brought you here?"

Zenn nodded.

"Yes. Perhaps," the Captain said. "When we locate her."

"You can't find her?" Zenn asked.

"No... " the Captain said, eyes squinting as he scratched his lower bill with one taloned finger. "I suspect this tragic affair has to do with her master's illicit animal fighting. Guest Thrott has a fondness for gambling, I'm told, legal or otherwise. He too seems to have gone missing. There will be hard questions for him when he is located."

"Well, if you don't need me any longer," Stav said to the Captain, "I'll turn in for the night." His silver gaze turned to Zenn. "Novice, you'll be a bit more careful wandering about the ship? Please?"

"Yes. I'll try," was all she could manage. She focused on sipping her tea, but her thoughts were a fractured mosaic of conflicting images: the slug's ferocious form bearing down on her, the heat of the soldier's weapon scorching the air above her – and now, the giddy prospect of again being in the presence of a *Lithohippus indrae*. The combination created in her the uncomfortable sensation of no longer being anchored in her own body but standing somewhere outside it, looking back at a trembling, red-headed girl sitting on a bench, covered in a blanket.

TWELVE

"The mudlark," Zenn said to Jules as they finished their breakfast in his cabin the next morning. "It was afraid, and it was picking up all the voices at the party. That's when I heard the Skirni's voice. Pokt. He was there, in the hall, or nearby. They recognized me somehow."

"They?" Jules said, going to the sideboard in his cabin for another helping of oysters. "You heard more than one?"

"Yes. I couldn't identify the other one. Too many voices, too much interference."

"And you say these two spoke of being on a schedule, to deliver a nexus to someone, or someplace? Do you know what they mean by this?"

"Jules, I have no idea. All I know is that they seem to think I have this nexus. But I don't even know what it is."

"A nexus, I believe, has the definition as being a point of intersection," he said. "Like a central thing that connects one thing, or many things, to some another things. Is that of any assistance to your understanding?"

"No," she said. "Whenever a link happens, I can't even think straight, after. Makes me tired and foggy. It's hard to even remember exactly what happened. And then the slug, in Thrott's cabin. I'm having a little trouble… organizing."

"That is why I go to the pool on this ship. It helps my thinking to become more ordered."

"So," Zenn said, "did you enjoy your swim?"

"Swim? No, no, I was not engaged in swimming this morning." He gave a mournful chirruping sound. "I was feeling remorseful. About not escorting you from the party gathering last night. It was my duty to bodyguard you and I went to gamble. This was selfish behavior and thus you were nearly slain by the poison-slug."

"Jules, I told you," she said, shaking her head at him, "that was not your fault. And besides, I'm OK now. So, if you weren't swimming, why go to the pool?"

"I went to stand at the edge and observe," he said. "There are often lizard children at play in the pool at this early hour. It is entertaining to see their antics. And I find the water has a calming effect, as I said, on my thinking. I thought of my failure at bodyguarding and how I might improve my future behavior. Have you had any news during my absence? Of Master Thrott or his servant's whereabouts?"

"No, nothing," she said. "I told the Captain about the animal fight, about stopping it, what Thrott said. The Captain thought if Thrott was really behind the attack, he'd probably go into hiding down in steerage. Apparently, a person can disappear for weeks down there."

"Yes, your Liam Tucker is fortunate in that regard, at least."

The door to the corridor chimed, then, and it announced a visitor. It was Yed.

"Good morning to you, Guest Vancouver," the steward said. Then, seeing Zenn, he added, "Ah, Guest Bodine! I come with news for you." The steward stood grinning and rocking back and forth on his wide flipper feet. "Captain Oolo requests that you both join him for your visit to the Indra chambers."

"Oh," Zenn said. "Right now?"

"Yes, if that suits you," Yed said. "I can take you to the Captain as soon as you are prepared."

Retreating to her bedroom, Zenn wrapped her scarf around her face. Now that the Skirni Pokt knew she was aboard, she would have to be more careful than ever to avoid being identified. But a trip to the Indra chamber? It was simply too enticing to resist. Besides, she rationalized, her refusal now could also raise suspicions.

They were about to leave the cabin when Katie confronted her, plopping herself down in front of the door.

"Friend-Zenn goes now?" she signed, sitting up on her hindquarters.

"Yes. But only for a little. Coming right back."

"Katie go with?"

"No. Sorry! Not this time."

Katie's ringed tail whipped in agitation. "How soon coming back?"

"Very soon," Zenn spoke the words to her, to see if she recognized them, which she apparently did.

"Friend-Zenn! Friend-Zenn!"

"Yes, Katie?"

"Katie have breakfasty food? Food now?"

Zenn sighed.

"Friend-Zenn brings Katie treats when she comes back," Zenn told her.

"Big promise?"

"Big, big promise," Zenn spoke and signed just to be sure she understood.

This seemed to satisfy the rikkaset – barely. She jumped into one of the chairs and curled up, watching as Zenn and the others left the room.

The steward led Zenn and Jules on a circuitous route going down through the ship and back toward the stern. At every corner they rounded, Zenn half expected to run into the Skirni Pokt, but it was early enough that they met only a few passengers. When they'd gone almost as far as they could go in the passenger section, they found the Captain standing in the corridor, speaking into his sleeve screen. He looked up when he saw them approaching.

"Novice Bodine, Guest Vancouver, I'm pleased you could join me." He preened his chest feathers as he spoke, smoothing the multicolored feathers until they lay flat. "Are you quite recovered from last night? Feeling ready to be up and about?"

"We wouldn't miss it for the world, Captain," Zenn said. "Would we, Jules?"

"No, it is not an experience to be passed by, I am told," Jules said.

"It's very kind of you, Captain," Zenn said. "I know this must be a busy time, with the tunneling coming up."

"It is the least I could do. The very least. After last night. And what you did for my Cleevus as well." He turned to the waiting steward. "Thank you for guiding our guests down, Yed."

"Of course, Captain," he said, snapping off a brisk salute before turning to Zenn and Jules. " I trust you will enjoy your visit to the chambers." He stood smiling up at them. And stood. And smiled. At last, Jules realized what was called for. He held up his relay, and Yed held up his, accepting the tip.

"Thank you, Guest Vancouver," he said, and trotted back the way he'd come.

"So, Novice Bodine," the Captain said, gesturing for them to proceed down the corridor, "is this your first time aboard an Indra vessel?"

"No, actually." She had, of course, been aboard an Indra ship before. But the frightful details of that encounter weren't something she chose to revisit, at least voluntarily. "It was a long time ago," she told him, and left it at that.

"And you?" the captain asked Jules.

"It is my first journey on such a craft," Jules said. "I too am most grateful for your allowing us to see your wondrous Indra."

"Don't mention it," the Captain said. "Although I'm afraid I haven't had a chance to speak with Groom Treth about your visit to her chambers. But I'm sure she'll overlook the usual preconditions."

"Preconditions?" Zenn said.

"Groom Treth is strict. About who is allowed into her chamber. And when. But Treth, like you, Novice, has a special interest in non-human creatures. Well, it goes with the territory, wouldn't you say? I suspect you'll be welcomed as a kindred soul."

A minute later, they rounded a corner in the passageway and nearly collided with someone coming in the opposite direction. It was the young lieutenant, Stav Travosk.

"Captain," he said. "Glad I ran into you."

"Lieutenant, good morning," the Captain said. "We're just going aft to the chamber. You're welcome to join us."

"Thank you," Stav said. "But I'm afraid I'll have to decline. We just received new marching orders, I'm afraid."

"Oh?" the Captain said.

"Ambassador Noom informed me at breakfast. It seems we won't be heading back to Eta Cephei just yet."

"Really?" the Captain said. "I hope there's not a problem."

"No, no. Just diplomatic hair-splitting as far as I know. Loose ends in need of tying up. In any case, she tells me we've been recalled to Earth. We'll be going back on the last shuttle."

"The shuttle to Earth?" The Captain eyed his sleeve-screen. "It should be ready to cast off any minute. I'm sorry I won't be able to see you and the Ambassador off personally. Please, convey my wishes for a safe journey."

"I will, Captain." Stav offered them all a quick smile. "Now the Ambassador will be waiting for me at the docking bay, so I'll say goodbye. Thank you for everything." He shook hands with the Captain, then turned to Zenn, again taking her hand. "Miss Bodine, until we meet again." Zenn found this a quaint sort of thing to say. But, curiously, the way he said it made Zenn feel that they might very well meet once more. She also found that the prospect didn't displease her. Then he strode off down the passageway.

"I hope their return to Earth implies nothing too serious," the Captain said as they came to a lev-car door with a sign reading "No Admittance – Crew Only". This, Zenn knew, concealed the special car that would transport them astern to the distant Indra chambers. The Captain identified himself to the door, which opened to admit them.

Zenn wondered briefly about the ambassador being recalled to Earth. It would be a long sub-light flight for them. It seemed to Zenn that there must be more involved than "a little diplomatic hair-splitting" to demand such a trip, but, as the car gently accelerated, her full attention turned to what lay ahead, and the prospect of entering the sanctum sanctorum where the sleeping stonehorse waited.

The entrance to the Indra chamber was guarded by a ponderous slab of gleaming metalloy bristling with locking bolts and conveying all the solid heft of a bank vault door. The Captain leaned his head into the recess containing the door's bio-key. A bright white line of light played over his features as the door scanned his head and eyes and, with a brief sound of sucking air, took a sample of the minute molecules of aerosolized saliva in his breath. An instant later, the bio-key's analysis of the DNA in the saliva was complete, and a small red diode on the door blinked from red to green. The bio-key's voice reported the Captain was who he claimed, and the door's huge locking bolts clanged and squealed as they were pulled aside. With a misty exhalation, the door swung open. They stepped into a small airlock. The door banged shut behind them, and before them, another, smaller door swung open.

As with Zenn's first visit to a starliner pilot room, the air inside was bitter cold, the interior illuminated only by the weak light of the read-out panels and glowing monitor screens lining the walls. In the oversized pilot chair in the center of the room sat a shape with its back to them. The shape was encased in a helmet and bulky full-body interface suit made of some glossy dark green plastisyn material. Zenn let the ends of the scarf drop away from her face but kept it covering her head for the scant warmth it offered.

A sweet, smoky scent filled the room. As her eyes adjusted to the low light, she could just make out the source of the odor: a small altar made of reddish stone slabs, set up within a shallow alcove in the wall. The blackened remains of smoldering branches lay on top of the stone platform, prompting Zenn to wonder where the Groom's sacrist was and to consider that the most complex spacefaring machines ever constructed could be piloted by a cult of pagan nature-worshippers. This never ceased to amaze Zenn. But the fact was, it worked, and she had to give them credit for that extraordinary feat. A lot of credit.

Zenn went to the viewing window of foot-thick ballistiplast that overlooked the vast, hangar-like Indra chamber. It was empty, but she could see, almost hidden in shadow, the huge black oval that marked the entrance to the warren – the contorted artificial labyrinth of metal and dynacarbon that concealed the Indra deep within.

Turning toward the Groom, Zenn thought the Indra pilot didn't so much sit in the chair as grow out of it. A tangled assortment of wires, tubes and strands of a translucent spiderweb-like material connected the Groom's interface-suit to the chair's numerous ports and inputs. It was here the pilot participated in the almost mystical phenomenon of Indra-powered interstellar flight. Through the complex ritual of the threshold procedure, the Groom would convey the coordinates of the desired destination through the suit to the Indra. Through a process that was still only partially understood, the Indra would "read" this data and move up out of her warren – "hers" because all drive-Indra were female, as were all pilots. She would then occupy the main chamber and commence the improbable mystery of interdimensional tunneling.

"Groom Treth," the Captain addressed the unmoving figure in the chair, the tone of his voice assuming a slight but noticeable formality, "I have taken the liberty of bringing two of our guests into the chamber rooms. Novice Bodine here, you will be interested to learn, is an exo–"

With a single, sudden movement, the Groom came up out of the chair. Sparks burst into the darkened room like miniature fireworks as wires and tubing popped out of the sockets sprouting from the suit's torso and helmet. The wires whipped briefly in the air like angry serpents, then retracted into the chair with a series of metallic slithering sounds and sharp yelps of electronic alarms.

"Captain Oolo, this is not acceptable," the Groom snapped, pulling the helmet off and releasing an obscuring cloud of heated air that billowed out from inside the suit.

When the fog cleared, Zenn saw the pilot's striking face bore the intricate living tattoos and multiple piercings of the Procyoni. The woman was almost as tall as Jules on his mech-legs. She had brown, almond-shaped eyes, sculpted cheekbones and a waist-length rope of black hair that now uncoiled to fall down her back. Brushing past Zenn and Jules as if they didn't exist, she leaned into the Captain's face. The scattering of metal studs, rings and tiny chains ornamenting her face and ears glinted against her mocha-tinted skin. The Captain blinked at her, brilliant chest feathers fluffing out defensively.

"Union regulations are clear – for those who can read them." The Groom's voice was low but tense, and she bit her words off sharply, her clipped Procyoni dialect making her sound even more severe. "Advance permissions are required to enter the chamber."

"My apologies, of course, Groom Treth," the Captain said, his eyes going quite round. "But, as I was about to explain, Novice Bodine is an exovet, Ciscan-trained. I thought you would appreciate meeting her."

After a dismissive glance at Zenn, the Groom turned back to the Captain.

"No. It is not the point. I am in pre-tunnel. My sacrist and I should be engaged in preparatory meditation. Our minds should be stilled to feel the Indra and her state. Instead, I am unsettled and my sacrist absent. Where is he? He is with the meddling Skirni you sent to me, escorting him back to the passenger decks where he belongs."

"The Skirni I sent you?" the Captain said, head bobbing up and down once in surprise.

"Yes. That Skirni. And now there are more interruptions with these two... guests! It is not to be endured."

"What Skirni do you mean?"

"Pokt Mahg-something," Treth said. Zenn looked at Jules, who returned her glance but said nothing. "He was here. Just now. He came with only your note for admission to my chamber. Not advance permission as required." The Groom snatched up a small v-film lying on top of a monitor console and thrust it toward the Captain. He took it, and his eyes widened even further as he read it.

"This is most unusual – most unusual," the Captain said, blinking at the film. "I never received a request from this Guest Pokt to visit your chamber."

"Then why is the permission signed by you?" The Groom tapped the film with one gloved finger, then crossed her arms and stood steaming before them.

"I did not sign this," the Captain told her, chest feathers rising and falling in time with his words. "There must be some misunderstanding. Did he... give any reason for his visit?"

"All he wanted was to see the chamber and waste my time with questions that any child could answer. I told him to leave."

The Captain turned to Zenn and Jules. "You must forgive us. There has obviously been some sort of miscommunication here." The Captain lifted his sleeve screen and punched up the comm function. "I'll get this sorted out." There was a brief pause as he waited for the person on the other end to answer.

"Yes," he said into his sleeve. "This is the Captain. Put the Officer of the Deck on." There was the faint, unintelligible chattering of a voice coming softly from the earbud on the side of the Captain's head. "Flynn? Oolo here," the Captain continued. "I have a situation in the chamber. What? No. What do you mean?" The Captain swiveled his neck around in Zenn's direction. "She is here with me now, in the chamber." A jolt of apprehension ran through her. There was another pause as the Captain listened to the far-off voice. "Are you certain? I see. No. I'll take care of it. But there's something else. Hold on."

The Captain lowered his head to Zenn's level. "We've just had a message from Mars. From the Ciscan cloister. Someone claiming to be your uncle." He waited a moment, watching for Zenn's reaction. "It seems you've deceived me, Novice Bodine… or should I say, Novice Scarlett?"

THIRTEEN

No!

Zenn's heart thumped in her chest. She'd contacted Otha too soon.

"Captain, I can explain," she said, her head feeling light, her mind helplessly casting about for what to say next. Then the sound of the pilot room's inner airlock door swinging open drew everyone's attention. She turned in time to see the back of the person who'd just entered as they turned to shut the door. It was a male with dark hair. The hair had beads and feathers in it and fell down across the shoulder on one side. It was cut short on the other side, in the Procyoni style. He wore a yellow-gold tunic with knee-length leather boots – the uniform of a groom's sacrist. The boy toggled the door switch and faced them. It was Fane Reth Fanesson!

"The Skirni is returned to the passenger decks," Fane said to the Groom. "He is a most disagreeable creature. And he smelled worse than a–" He stopped when he recognized Zenn. A faint smile crept across his face. "...worse than a yote."

Zenn was certain she had gone quite red. But still, inexplicably, she was pleased to see the boy, despite his reference to that first meeting at the cloister, when a full-grown yote had covered her in a spectacular shower of well-seasoned vomit.

"So, Novice Scarlett," the Captain snapped at her. "We will deal with your situation in time." His big eyes glared at her, then turned to the Groom. "But first I will speak to the Skirni who entered your chambers and clear up–"

"Quiet, all of you," Treth said, raising one hand to silence them. "Listen."

They all held still, but Zenn heard nothing beyond the usual sounds of the ship.

"Treth?" the Captain asked, bobbing his head at her. "What is it?"

"Look, there," Treth said, pointing at the floor beneath the viewing window. Almost invisible in a shadowed corner, a fist-sized hole could be seen in the heavy metal sheeting of the wall that separated the pilot room from the Indra chamber. A line of dark, viscous fluid flowed from the hole, and its circumference was blackened and distorted, as if melted. The opening hissed with the faint sound of air being pulled into a vacuum.

"By the sainted Shepherds," Treth swore as she knelt on one knee and peered into the opening. "It goes through... into the chamber! Fane..."

But the boy was already in motion. He went to a compartment on the bulkhead and withdrew what looked like the old-fashioned fire extinguishers they used at the cloister. Returning to the hole in the wall, he pointed the device's nozzle at it and squeezed the release handle. The mist of particles that sprayed from it flowed into the hole, where it quickly thickened and expanded to plug it.

"Treth, what could have caused that?" The Captain's warbling voice had lifted to a high chirp.

"Oh!" Jules exclaimed. He was at the viewing window, pointing into the chamber. "There's something in there. Is it the Indra?"

Zenn looked into the chamber but saw nothing. "No, it can't be the Indra," she told Jules. "The Indra is huge. And it wouldn't come into the chamber yet." Then she saw what Jules had seen. A scurrying movement, something darting out of the shadows. "Jules is right. There's something there."

"That is not possible," the Groom said, pushing past Zenn to look.

The thing was two or three feet long and moving at high speed, scuttling across thc chamber floor on multiple legs toward the opening that led into the Indra's warren. It had a segmented body like a centipede, but with a large, spherical head section. It moved so quickly it was hard to make out any further detail. The others had scarcely caught sight of it when it disappeared into the opening of the warren.

"Captain, this breach," Treth said, pointing at the hole in the wall, "it is the Skirni's doing. It must be. He must have loosed that thing into my Indra's chamber."

"I'll get an engineering team down here. We'll get this contained, and quickly," the Captain said. He turned to Zenn and Jules. "I'm sorry, but I'm sure you'll understand that we'll need to cut your visit short. I'll escort you back to the passenger decks."

He told the inner door leading back to the lev-car to open, but its only response was a short, sharp buzzing noise. He quickly punched in a manual code at the wall panel. The door still remained shut.

"This is... unprecedented," he muttered, again entering the manual code. "It cannot be possible."

"The thing that entered the chamber," Treth said. "It may have compromised the circuitry."

"I'll alert the bridge."

He was about to activate his wrist screen again when Zenn let out an involuntary gasp, as if she'd been punched hard in the stomach.

"What is it?" Jules said, striding over to her. "Are you unhealthy?"

"I'm... not sure. It feels like..."

The familiar surge of dizziness and warmth now swept over her, coming on faster and stronger than ever before. She put one hand against the bulkhead to steady herself. In the past, she'd always been close to a creature when the feeling struck. Now, even though it wasn't in sight, she knew instantly she was "linking" to an animal she couldn't see – the Indra. But the stonehorse was too far off, she told herself as her vision began to shimmer and spark. She then had the unearthly sensation that she was rising up out of herself. Yes, even though the animal was hundreds of feet away, deep in its metal burrow, there was no mistaking what she felt.

At once, her field of view ignited into a shattering of light, then a shifting aura spangled with dancing, geometric shapes. The light scintillated with a ghostly display of multicolored arcing flashes that expanded and contracted. Then came a rush of unnamable emotion, not her own, but also clearly recognized by Zenn as an "otherness" she'd sensed once before, in exactly the same way, long ago, when she was nine – on the day her mother perished.

Yes. She'd felt it even then, though she'd not known it – the mind of an Indra. But Zenn had no time to dwell on this thought – the Indra's sense of urgency was too powerful to ignore, too filled with fear and uncertainty to allow any of Zenn's own thinking to intrude. Then, this river of emotion was overwhelmed by an even more insistent sensation: a ferocious, needle-sharp burning that seemed to radiate from the center of her brain. No, not hers: from the Indra's brain. The pain intensified, almost too much to bear – and then the sensation ebbed and vanished, and she was alone again inside her own head, realized she was again seeing the control room and those in it, breathing the chilly air, weaving on her feet.

"Novice? Novice Scarlett?" The Captain was speaking to her, a bony claw holding her by one arm.

"It's… I'm OK." But the aftermath of the feeling still constricted her stomach, made her vision blur in and out of focus. "I think it was the Indra," she told them, not sure she believed her own words, but unable to deny what had just happened to her.

The Groom strode over to her, speaking sharply. "My Indra? What do you mean?"

"The Indra. I think… it's awake, coming this way."

The Captain bobbed his head apologetically at the Groom.

"The girl means you no disrespect, Groom Treth. I'm sure she must be under some sort of strain. Or illness, perhaps." The Captain dipped his head down to Zenn's level. "The Indra won't awaken until Groom Treth makes interface contact. There are many call-and-response interactions to perform before that happens. It all proceeds by a routine that cannot be altered or–"

The Captain was cut off by a sudden, strange vibration in the air. With two quick steps, the Groom was at the bank of read-out screens on the wall.

"Something's wrong," she said, scanning the displays.

"Treth?" the Captain said.

"She *is* moving! This is not right." She went to her command chair, lay back in it and instructed it to reattach to the interface suit. The wires and tubing extended from their receptacles like a nest of striking vipers, plugging themselves into the suit. "The thing we saw, moving in the chamber. It has attached itself to my Indra. It is... interfering with her."

"Zenn Scarlett," Jules bent close to look into Zenn's eyes. "Are you healthy and in the pink again?"

Before she could answer, a booming, sub-bass note rose from the floor plates beneath their feet, from the walls surrounding them. As it grew in volume, it added higher notes, a chorus of unearthly keening, not coming from the air around them but seeming to vibrate from within them. Zenn covered her ears, but Jules seemed simply awestruck, swaying on his legs, transfixed by the rising sound.

"She's moving into the chamber," Fane called out, standing at the viewing window. Through the window,

Zenn saw something stirring in the chamber, and she moved to get a better view. Several long, filamentous strands emerged from the cave-like opening at the far end. The strands elongated, changed shape, vanished from sight, reappeared and stretched out again, as if feeling their way across the surfaces of the chamber. Zenn knew these fleshy appendages were the Indra's primary sensing barbels. Able to perceive its environment in the full electromagnetic spectrum, the Indra used its facial appendages to sense the universe on multiple levels. And the barbels didn't just test the physical objects around the Indra, but slipped in and out of existence, vanishing in a mesmerizing, prismatic display of light as they penetrated the skin of this universe to touch the other nine unseen, tightly curled alternate dimensions of quantum space.

More of the Indra's body now began to emerge from the metal warren. Zenn's pulse quickened as she watched the creature rise from the darkness. The gargantuan scaled head emerged, almost fifty feet long, shimmering with the surreal electric light-show of extradimensional energy that streamed around and through it.

The Indra's seahorse-like face was now fully visible. Instead of eyes, its long, narrow skull bore three matching sets of slits – its energy detectors. Along the plated muzzle and all down the tapering jaw, dozens of sensor barbels waved like a kelp forest in a rushing tide. Now, slowly, the rest of the lithe, seven hundred-foot body flowed into the immense chamber, coiling and uncoiling, its beaded coat of vermillion and bronze-colored scales glinting like burnished armor in the room's widely spaced spotlights. It was the body of a fantastical, muscular snake, but thicker and flattened, tapering to a mace-like tip spiked with the flexible, thirty-foot spines it used to anchor itself in its warren.

Once the Indra had coiled its entire body into the chamber, the facial barbels all began to throb with a single, purposeful rhythm, vanishing, reappearing, vanishing again in unison. The heavy, almost hypnotic cadence of low-frequency sound that filled the control room was matched by the ripples of flashing light that skipped across the Indra's head and body – the same rainbow lightshow Zenn had seen when the Indra first reached out to touch her mind.

"She is starting to pulse," the Groom shouted, waving her hands at a newly risen row of translucent virt-screens that wheeled up into the air around her head.

"How can that be?" the Captain yelled back, stepping to the thick window. "You haven't visualized the coordinates. Or initialized the antineutrino stream. She'll be tunneling blind."

The room vibrated more strongly, shaking until they could all barely remain standing. A few seconds more, and Zenn and Jules both had to lean against the wall to keep their feet, while the Captain and Fane gripped the railing in front of the viewing window. In her chair, Treth pulled a swingaway control panel in around her. From it, another flock of Virt-screens materialized in the air. Her hands shot back and forth between the screens.

"Can you stop her?" the Captain shouted.

"I cannot. She is being… directed somehow."

The Groom summoned another screen, ran her hands over the control surface that appeared, then looked up at the ceiling. She poked at the screen once more, and again watched the ceiling expectantly. Nothing happened.

"The blast shield is not responding."

"We've got to leave. Now," the Captain yelled at Zenn and Jules, herding them toward the door.

"No," Treth called to them. "She is about to tunnel. I cannot be sure of the damping field. You'll never reach the passenger levels in time. Fane. Safe room."

The Groom's free hand stabbed at another screen and a circular panel on the far wall irised open like an oversized camera shutter.

"In there. Move, now," Fane yelled, pointing.

Zenn staggered to the opening and went through. It was a space the size of a small closet with padded benches and harnesses.

"Emergency safe-room," Fane said as they ducked in. "Shielded. We will be protected here. Strap yourselves in."

The room was equipped for four human-size occupants, so it was only just large enough to contain Zenn, the Captain, Fane and a walksuited dolphin. Treth made no move to join them. "The threshold…" Treth shouted from the control room. "It's opening!"

The door to the safe room began to iris shut, and Zenn had one final glimpse of Treth as the Groom activated her suit's body-scrim. The scrim unit emitted a flash of bright blue light that instantaneously spread out from the suit's belt until it covered the Groom in what looked like a shape-hugging second skin of gleaming, translucent light. The scrim was all that stood between Treth and the colossal shockwave of radiation and electromagnetic forces generated by an Indra in full dimension-splitting mode.

"She is beginning to tunnel," Treth shouted. "Hold on!"

FOURTEEN

Treth's words were the last thing Zenn heard before the fast-rising sound and vibration merged into an avalanche of invisible force hammering at her body, pressing her backward against the seat as if she'd been hit by a wall of some heavy fluid. Then the unmistakable sensations surged over her once more – the warmth, the tingling pinpricks on her skin, the feeling of being out of synch with her own body and mind. It was happening again…

The next moment she was touching, being touched, by the otherness she'd felt before: it could only be the mind of the Indra. Yes. Now, there was cold on her skin-not-her-skin, the sting of frozen, airless space on armored scales. Visions rose before her-eyes-its-eyes, flashes of a huge, vaulted space – the Indra chamber, seen in gray, photonegative hues – ultraviolet vision? And now something else. Pain, fear, something burning, attacking, but not from outside, from inside its head. The pain flared in her-own-not-her-own head, blazed between her temples. It was tiny but fierce, this attacker. And it wanted more than to attack and harm. It wanted… control.

Then, with a single electric spasm, it was over. The vision before Zenn, the sensations engulfing her, drowning her, were gone. Also gone out like a guttering spark was the consciousness that had shared her own thoughts. This sudden absence was a physical pain to her, a void that she inexplicably found terrible to be without, unforgivable to part with. Nothing had ever been so close to her. Nothing could be. Now Zenn was alone, more alone than she had ever been, as if ejected into the lightless, mindless emptiness of space beyond the reach of any living being. A sound intruded into the frightful death-black silence that surrounded her. It was faint but familiar, the sound of the distant place from which she'd been swept.

"Zenn Scarlett, can you hear me speaking?" It was Jules's voice. She was coming back, falling down, or rising up, from wherever she had gone, returning to herself to land with a shudder in her own body. How small it now seemed, this body of moist, heated flesh and brittle bone; what a tiny, fragile thing to carry one through the merciless universe and all its worlds.

She opened her eyes. Jules's face was close to hers, and there was a smell that at first she couldn't place. Then it came to her, and she smiled weakly. Tuna fish breath.

The safe room was quiet now, the sudden stillness broken only by the muffled sound of alarm tones bleating in the distance. The Captain was already out in the pilot room, speaking to the Groom.

"Novice? Are you well?" It was Fane. He was in front of her, bending over, his hands on his knees as he looked into her eyes.

"Are you? Well? You are healthy and in the pink?" Jules asked.

She nodded yes.

"You are sure? You did not seem so just then," Fane said, frowning.

"Yes, I'm fine now. It's just... something that happens to me sometimes. Like a fainting spell." She didn't want to talk about it. Didn't want him to think... what? That she was sick? Crazy? "Really. It's nothing." She attempted a smile.

Satisfied, Fane went to join Treth and the Captain.

"We tunneled unexpectedly. Just like that," Jules said. "The Captain states it should not have taken place as it did. He was unhappy with it. But I found it exciting – thrilling to be exact. Were you not thrilled?"

"Jules... it's getting worse," she said, keeping her voice low, her words slurring as she fought to regain herself. "Whatever's happening to me."

"Oh. Your linking. Of course, just now. It was with the Indra?" The dolphin looked down. "I am sorry. I have been self-centered and insensitive to your problem. Worse, you say. How is it worse?"

"Stronger, scarier, every time it happens," Zenn said. Her brain was unwilling to think properly, and she fumbled unsuccessfully with the buckle on her safety harness. Jules reached over and pushed the release button, freeing her. "Every time now, it's getting harder and harder to come back. It's almost more than I can manage. And there was something else this time."

"What was it?"

"The first time this ever happened, the first time I linked with an animal–" Zenn struggled to remember, fought to make herself relive that terrible day "–I thought it was at the cloister, when Katie fell into the well pit and I got her out. It wasn't then. I know now the first time was on the starship, the one where my mother… where she went into the Indra." She looked up at the dolphin. "I know now that it was the Indra I felt, for just a second. That's when this all started. But why then? Why me?"

Jules sat quietly for a moment. "I am sorry for your distress," he said finally. "But I have no ready solution. Perhaps you will understand. With time."

"Yeah," she sniffed, telling herself to get a grip; this was no time to act like a little girl. "Maybe."

She rose unsteadily to her feet and stepped out into the pilot room.

"…So, you're telling me we just survived an uninitialized tunnel event?" the Captain was saying to the Groom. "Treth, what is going on?"

"She is gone," the Groom said flatly, staring through the thick glass of the chamber viewing window.

"The Indra? She went back into the warren?" The Captain raised and tilted his head, trying to see into the chamber's shadows.

"No," the Groom said. "She is not in the warren. My stonehorse is not aboard this ship. The thing that burned its way into the chamber; it forced her to tunnel, made her push the *Helen* here – and then it took her."

"Took her? Took her where?" The Captain's voice rose to a squeaking high note. His head now began bobbing rapidly in sync with the voice, and his chest feathers fluffed out, then lay flat and then fluffed again. "Where would she..." Head up. "...go? Indras don't..." Head down. "...abandon their chambers." Head up again. "She'd be exposed. She couldn't survive without... There must be an instrument malfunction."

Ignoring this suggestion, the Groom now whirled to face Zenn.

"How did you know?" The Procyoni's voice was harsh. "You knew she was awake, moving. How? Speak, girl."

"I don't know how." The Groom's ferocious anger drilled into her, hunting an answer she didn't have. "I get this feeling from animals sometimes. They connect with me."

"How? Some sorcery?" The Groom stepped over to her. "Are you a thought-caster?"

"No. It's not that. I don't even believe in... I'm *not* reading their minds. It's something else." Once again, Zenn was exasperated, unable to explain what was happening to her. "I don't know what it is. I just knew the Indra was awake."

"And what do you feel now?" the Groom said, so close Zenn could feel the heated air flowing up out of the open neckhole of the interface suit.

"I feel... normal. But that's just how it happens. One moment it's like I'm in touch with the animal, and then it's gone. I don't have any control over when this happens to me – whatever it is. It just happens."

"Treth..." The Captain had been punching at his sleeve-screen, but with no result. Now he went to the intercom on the wall. It produced only crackling static. "Intraship coms are all down. I have to get up to the bridge."

He went to the door control panel once more. This time, it responded.

"Treth, I'll let you know the system's status as soon as I can access the day logs. I'll need your report on… what happened here. Soon as you can manage."

Treth didn't speak but leaned her forehead against the glass of the observation window, eyes on the empty chamber.

"Novice Scarlett, Guest Vancouver, if you'll come with me, we'll get you back to your cabins." The Captain spoke as he manually keyed in the codes to the outer door leading to the lev-car beyond. Zenn looked back to see that Fane had moved to stand beside Treth. The Sacrist raised one hand as if to comfort the Groom. But he stopped in mid-reach and dropped his hand to his side.

A minute later, Zenn, Jules and the Captain stepped from the lev-car into the *Helen's* passenger area. The Captain tried the nearest wall-comm. There was only more static. The corridor was empty, and the low illumination of the emergency lighting made it look ominous. The next intercom was also useless. But by the time they had made three more stops at decks 3, and 6 – all equally deserted – it dawned on Zenn that the intercoms were the least of their problems.

"Where is everybody?" she asked. "Where are the passengers and crew?"

"I don't know yet," the Captain said. "We'll find out more when I can access the logs on the bridge. Until then, you both stay with me."

They moved on through the silent ship, down echoing passageways, past vast, empty halls and activity areas.

Occasionally, they would find a piece of clothing or a single abandoned shoe lying in the corridor. There were uneaten meals on the tables of the dining rooms. They met no one.

At last, rising through the ship past deck after vacant deck, they reached the bridge. The door opened and they entered a multi-level room filled with rows of control panels, numerous empty chairs and dozens of wall-mounted view screens, all seething with ghostly static.

"Can you say what has happened to us and this ship?" Jules asked the Captain.

"I am about to try and find out." The Captain went to a console and called up a series of virt-screens. After a few seconds, the Virt-screens flickered to life and began to display various graphs, meters and views of the interior and exterior of the ship.

Jules walked across the room to examine one of the wall monitors, and Zenn joined him. Any other time, the view it displayed would have struck her as beautiful, with the entire sweep of the starship's bow visible. Beyond the ship, arcing gracefully up across the view at some distance, a giant translucent nebula threw up huge columns of dust, gas and plasma, lit in delicate hues of blue and red from unseen stars within. Zenn attempted to orient herself, but the constellations she was seeing looked like none she'd ever witnessed in the Martian sky.

Then Zenn saw what had attracted Jules's attention.

Floating above the *Helen of Troy,* something vast and dark blotted out part of the view. Illuminated by the weak ochre light of a nearby red dwarf that was definitely not the sun, the structure above them was impossibly huge.

It consisted of a jumble of immense, indistinct forms that jutted out at odd angles. One shape seemed to merge into the next; the entire convoluted mass curving away for what looked like miles. The very scale of the thing made it difficult to judge its size.

"Jules? What is that?"

"I am looking at it. I have no words..." They both went to stand next to the Captain.

"Captain, do you know where we are?" Zenn asked.

"If these readings are correct... we're somewhere in the galaxy's Scutum Arm." He waited for a moment, as if trying to comprehend the meaning of what he'd just said.

"The Scutum Arm," Jules said, leaning in closer to the Captain and his screens. "That place is many thousands of light years beyond our home place, is it not?"

"Yes, it is. The instruments are behaving strangely," the Captain said, fine-tuning one of the screens. "But it looks like we actually tunneled past the Carina-Sagittarius Arm and re-emerged in the Scutum. Phenomenal."

"Captain," Zenn pointed to the view port, "What is that out there?"

He glanced up at the object she and Jules had seen, then looked down again. "I'm still collecting data," he said, then made an abrupt gesture to call up a new screen. Zenn sensed that whatever the huge object outside was, the Captain was in no mood to discuss it.

"What about the passengers?" Zenn asked.

"The Indra's violent tunneling action. Could it have vaporized them?" asked Jules.

"Jules," Zenn scolded. "What a thing to say. Of course it didn't." But Jules's words were alarming enough to bring a terrible realization to her.

"Katie." She'd forgotten all about her. "Captain," she said, starting for the door. "I have to get back to my cabin… Jules's cabin. I left Katie there, my rikkaset. She'll be terrified."

"Novice, stay here," the Captain said sternly, not looking away from his screens.

"I have to go," she pleaded. "She's deaf. She's all alone. I told her… I told her she couldn't come with me and that I'd be right back. She won't know what's happening."

"Novice Scarlett," the Captain said. "Ship sensors show the only life forms from upper decks to steerage are right here on the bridge."

"Steerage," she cried out. "Liam." She'd forgotten about him as well. "I know someone, he was down in steerage."

"Novice, even if your friend, or your pet, was still aboard, I would still insist we all remain here, in one place. Until I ascertain our situation, no one goes anywhere."

She did understand. It didn't make her feel any less frantic.

"But, Captain Oolo," Jules asked, "what about that Indra's radiation that it sprays about? Could it have harmed the passengers?"

"I can't be sure, but it appears Treth got the damping field up. Almost seventy-five percent. That should have screened most of the passenger decks when we reached threshold. But that only tells us what didn't happen. Not what did." The Captain waved up a new screen. "The lifeboats are still in their bays. No one got off the ship that way. But the ship's internal status devices went offline as we dropped out of tunnel. They were shorted out by… Wait. Wait wait wait! What's this…?" He enlarged one of the screens and made it float up closer to his face. He moved his head in a small circular motion, blinking at the screen, reading the data as it scrolled by at a rapid-fire rate.

"We need to find Groom Treth. And her sacrist," he said abruptly. But the next moment, the door at the far end of the bridge slid open.

Treth entered the room, followed by Fane. The Groom no longer wore the cumbersome interface suit but was clad in a close-fitting body sheath of black metal thread material. Her solidly muscled arms were bare from the shoulder down, displaying her intricately interwoven anitats. The animated tattoos swirled sinuously up and down her arms, the abstract flamelike designs brightening and fading, contracting and expanding. Fane seemed to be cradling his midsection with one hand, his body bent forward slightly. Zenn thought at first he might be hurt, but other than his posture, he seemed fine.

"It is certain," the Groom said then, struggling to keep her voice level. "She was taken. My stonehorse was ripped from the chamber. I will find who did this. They will pay."

"Treth, there's something else going on here." The Captain took one last look at the virt-screens, then waved them away. "We need to get off this ship. Now."

FIFTEEN

“We are to abandon ship?” Jules said, looking from the Captain to Zenn. “But this is thrilling and exciting.”

“Captain,” Zenn said, “do we have to?” Frightful images swam in her head. Katie, alone, lost. And Liam… “What if somebody’s still aboard, and we leave them behind?”

“I’m sorry. No time for discussion,” the Captain said, waving the virt-screens away. “I’ll explain as we go. Wait one second.”

The Captain trotted to a small room just off the bridge. He went to a safe in the corner, identified himself and told the safe to open. From within, he swept a small pile of mem-crystal shards into his palm and stuffed them into one of his vest pockets. Then, to Zenn’s surprise, he reached into the back of the safe and withdrew a small particle-beam pistol. He slapped it against his side, and it adhered to his uniform vest. He then hurried them all out into the corridor.

“But, Captain Oolo,” Jules said, “where are we to go?”

“Lifeboats,” he said. “This way.”

The next minutes were a chaotic blur of hurrying down passageways and crowding into lev-tubes. They were halfway to the lifeboat deck when Zenn spoke up.

"Captain," she said. "Jules's cabin. It's on the next deck down." This would be her last chance. Maybe Katie's last chance.

"As I already said. Your pet is not there."

"No. My vet field kit," she lied. "It will only take a second to stop and get it."

"Really," he told her. "We don't have time."

"It would contain medical supplies, would it not?" These were the first words Fane had spoken since they left the bridge. "These could be of use." She suppressed an impulse to kiss him.

The Captain considered for a few seconds. "Very well. Make it quick."

When they stopped, Zenn exited, with Jules behind her. They rushed to his cabin.

"Katie," she called when they'd entered. Katie couldn't have heard her, of course, even if she'd been there. But that didn't matter.

They searched, but the rooms offered few hiding places. There was no rikkaset.

"Zenn Scarlett, your Katie is not here."

"We can't give up."

"We must go. I am sorry. They await our return."

Zenn looked at him, then looked around the room one last time, willing Katie to appear. Finally, she grabbed up her kit backpack and went to the door.

"Katie…" she said softly into the empty room. Numb, she followed Jules out into the passage.

As the lev-car started up again, Zenn held the battered backpack close to her. It smelled of worn leather, and animals, and Mars. That's where she should have left Katie. Back on Mars. She shouldn't have let her come. Tears threatened. This was all her fault. The thought made her too angry and ashamed to cry.

They continued their hectic progress downward through lev-tubes and empty corridors, and as they went the Captain detailed what little he had been able to glean from the ship's log. As soon as the *Helen* exited the quantum tunnel, the ship had been scanned – he didn't know by who or what. All of the passengers, crew and any biologically viable organisms had been identified and, it appeared, rapidly removed from the ship. Again, he had no idea who or what was responsible. More urgently, the Captain's last read of the sensors showed a fleet of small craft approaching from the direction of the huge structure Zenn and Jules had seen nearby.

"Could these ships be coming to rescue us?" Jules asked, quite sensibly, Zenn thought.

"Those aren't rescue ships," the Captain said. "They appear to be unmanned salvage drones. I assume they mean to strip the ship."

"What of our stonehorse?" Fane said. "Where is she?"

"I can't say," the Captain said. "I couldn't risk a long-range probe of… whatever that structure is out there. They might be watching for signals from the *Helen*."

They'd just left the lev-car and entered another corridor when they heard something in the semi-darkness ahead. It was faint at first, but quickly grew louder – a sound of banging, and ripping metal. Then, a stark white spot of light flashed onto the wall of the intersecting passage ahead. The circle of light vanished, then reappeared, brighter, the clanging noise louder.

"Treth, what is that?" the Captain said, keeping his voice low. The Groom sprinted ahead, looked around the corner, quickly jerked her body back.

"Drone! In the passage, coming this way."

"We can't let it see us," the Captain said. "This way." And he started back in the direction they'd just come, stopping a short distance down the passage and craning his neck at the ceiling.

"Can you reach that panel, Treth?"

The ceiling wasn't high there, and the Groom easily reached the small lever on the panel and popped the access door open.

"Everyone in." He raised his head up on his long neck to look back down the passage. The approaching light spilled across the far wall, the banging noises growing ever louder. The drone was almost to the corner.

Treth jumped up, grabbed the edge of the opening and hoisted herself through the hole. Then she leaned back down and helped pull Zenn up, followed by Jules, who had some trouble but with Zenn's help managed to squeeze his walksuit through the opening. They were inside a low service tunnel filled with tubes and piping, with not quite enough room to stand.

The Captain pulled himself up next. Zenn was about to move away from the opening when she looked back down to see Fane trying, and failing, to jump up and grab onto the edge of the hole. He still held his stomach with one hand and so had only one hand free to try and grab with. But he looked weighed down somehow and unable to overcome whatever it was that held him back.

"Novice, I cannot."

Zenn could see the spotlight of the drone playing on the wall just behind him.

"Fane... hurry."

"Here," Fane said, and he reached under his tunic and brought out a small pile of odd-shaped articles. "Catch," he said, throwing something up into the open hatch. She bobbled the thing but caught it. It was a piece of stone. He held several more in his hands.

"There's no time," she called down at him.

"Get back," he said, and she ducked back a step. With a great effort, he heaved the rest of the stones up all at once to land clattering inside the lip of the opening. Then, a moment later, he was up and through the hatch. He pulled it shut behind him and they both held very still as the clanging sound of the drone approached, blundered by beneath them and receded down the passage.

Fane gathered the stones off the floor and took the one Zenn had caught.

"Thank you for your assistance," he said. Then he gestured at her to go ahead of him, and she jogged on, crouched over, to catch up with the others.

They continued to move ahead, and as they rounded a corner, Zenn realized Fane was no longer behind her. She stopped, but after a short pause, he appeared again.

"What were you doing back there?" She was starting to feel that she had to keep looking over her shoulder to make sure he was keeping up.

"Nothing to concern you. Go on, I'm coming."

After making their way through the tunnel for several minutes, they reached a metal ladder and descended one level. The Captain located another access panel, and they exited out into the corridor. As they hurried along, Zenn found herself trotting next to the boy.

"You know those rocks almost got us caught back there."

"Rocks? These are the Shuryn Dohlm," he said, giving her an incredulous look. "I could not leave the altar in the pilot room. It could have been found. And defiled."

Zenn resisted pointing out that maybe losing a few stones was preferable to being taken prisoner by whatever had been banging its way down the corridor.

"So, I guess you got your promotion," she said instead. "To sacrist."

"Yes. I wear the gold now." He indicated the rough cloth of his tunic. "That is the mark of a full sacrist."

"Well, congratulations."

"It was never in doubt. I fulfilled all the requirements." After a brief pause, he added, "Thank you."

They stopped, and up ahead Zenn saw Treth open another access panel. After they'd all clambered into the passageway, they went on to a narrow stairwell and started down.

"You said a sacrist gets his choice of starships," Zenn said as they descended. "So you picked the *Helen*?"

"Yes. She is one of the longest-serving stonehorse craft. And Groom Treth is famed among pilots. It was a natural choice to remain on board as full sacrist." They left the stairwell and took the corridor to the right. They could still hear the salvage drone, but it sounded far away now.

"And what of you?" Fane asked her. "I will confess my surprise at seeing you in the chambers. How did that come about?"

"I... stowed away," she said, not sure what he would think of that. "But I had to. My father's in trouble. I'm trying to find him."

"You stowed away. On a starship? You?" His tone implied this was even more shocking than seeing her in the Indra chambers.

"Yes. Me," she said.

"I simply mean that is no simple task, stealing passage," he said. "How did you do it?"

"I hid in the cage-crate of a sandhog, back at the launch port in Pavonis," she said. She looked back to see him raise an eyebrow at this. "No one checked. And it got loaded aboard. It wasn't that hard, really."

"Oh? Not that hard?" he said. "Heh..." But his laughter wasn't mocking as it was when the yote had unloaded its stomach's contents on her during his visit to the cloister. She saw him smiling broadly at her with his crooked grin. She smiled back.

"Yeah, heh," she laughed, mimicking him, and then they both laughed together.

"Why would you think to do such a thing – to stow away? And your father – he is missing?"

"It's a long story," Zenn said, starting to have some difficulty talking and keeping up with the others at the same time.

"I look forward to its telling," the boy said, adding, "A sandhog crate. Well."

The Captain called back at them to keep up, and they hurried on, not talking.

A few minutes later, they arrived, breathless, at the lifeboat bay, a broad, low-ceilinged room with a double row of dozens of small, oblong-shaped, bright orange craft lined up facing the bulkheads on either side. Stepping up to one of the lifeboats resting on its ejection-tracks, the Captain commanded the vessel to open its hatch and prepare for emergency launch.

"Captain Oolo, are you sure?" Zenn had to try one last time. "Sure no one else is on board? I mean, why were we the only ones left behind?"

"I have wondered something similar," Jules said. "Why is it we weren't scanned as you said and taken with the others?"

"I assume it was the safe-room shielding. And yes, I'm sure no one else is aboard," the Captain said. He motioned to Zenn to go ahead. Resigned, she climbed in through the side hatch as the lifeboat's lighting and support systems blinked and clicked to life.

"The safe room's radiation shielding would have blocked any probing field," Treth said as she and Fane followed Zenn into the lifeboat. "And my scrim field would have shielded me."

"Whoever took the *Helen* will certainly notice the ship's captain and groom are missing. They'll come looking for us. We need to get off the ship and find out what happened to the passengers and my crew. Until we learn more, we simply can't afford to assume the circumstances are benign." The Captain flipped switches and spoke to the lifeboat's computer. Zenn could hear the hatch closing behind them. Then there was a slight bump as the craft moved onto the rail that would guide it out of the ship.

"Secure for launch. Hold on, everyone. In three, two…" The deployment mechanism seized the lifeboat and, with a single massive lurch, propelled it ahead at bone-rattling speed. Then the acceleration dropped, and Zenn drifted up, weightless against the restraining belts as the lifeboat exited the *Helen*. The craft now began to tumble slowly, rolling end over end as it moved away from the starliner. Her stomach didn't approve.

She leaned out into the aisle to see around Jules. Too large for the seats, he had secured himself to the craft's bulkhead by holding onto a length of cargo netting attached to one wall. She was just able to glimpse the small view screen at the forward end of the cabin. It showed the colossal, shadowy structure directly ahead of them. The huge form filled more and more of the screen as they approached. Smaller details on the hulking shape began to emerge as the lifeboat coasted ahead. She could also make out other shapes floating in space around them – other lifeboats. They were tumbling as well. Finally, it was Jules who spoke up.

"We seem to be rolling about in an uncontrolled manner, Captain Oolo. Is there no steering engine aboard this craft?"

"Engaging thrusters would attract attention," the Captain said. "I had all the other lifeboats launched automatically when we left the *Helen*. With luck, it will look like a malfunction and we'll just be one boat among dozens."

Whatever the thing was that they were approaching, Zenn thought, it was bigger than anything ever built by humans – or by any Asent species humans had so far encountered. As they drew nearer the looming shape, she saw something on the outer surface nearest them, something that simply didn't belong.

It can't be. I'm not seeing this.

There was no mistake. Zenn could see script on the hull of the thing they were approaching. It read: *LSAS Nova Procyon*. Zenn remembered the name from news reports. It was a Procyoni military ship of some sort. About a year ago it had vanished in the Outer Reaches without a trace.

"Captain," Zenn said. "Is that... one of the Indra ships?"

"Yes. The *Nova*," Treth said. "She disappeared on a recon mission fifteen months ago. At the edge of the Enchara void. Her groom and I trained together."

"A ship from the Accord? Can it be?" Jules said, detaching himself from the wall and moving up to get a better look at the view screen. "But this is a very large spaceship, is it not? It goes on and on."

"What you're seeing isn't just the *Nova Procyon*," the Captain told him. "The *Nova* appears to be part of an assortment."

"An assortment..." Zenn said. "Of what?"

"Starships," Treth said. She had lowered her face onto the eyerest of a small binocular-like device protruding from the bulkhead at one side of the control console. "I have counted thirty so far. There are many more. Most are too far to see their markings, but many are LSA designs. In addition to the *Nova* I have identified the *Symmetry*

Dancer, the *Delphic Queen*, the *Mizar Five* and the *Antara*. They have all been connected one to the other."

"Are these all... the Indra ships that disappeared?" Zenn asked, finding the question almost too incredible to ask.

"It seems probable," Treth said. "There are also non-Accord craft I do not recognize."

"Can you detect damage, Treth?" the Captain asked.

"It is difficult to say. But I do see evidence of scavenging."

"And the ships' stonehorses? Our stonehorse?" Fane asked, going to stand by Treth. "Is there any sign?"

"I cannot tell."

"So it is true. These are the lost Indra vessels," Jules said. "Do you see waterships among them?"

"Not possible to say," Treth answered. Jules seemed to deflate. "We cannot view all the ships from this angle."

"Are there life signs?" Zenn asked.

"Too soon to say," the Captain said. "Using a full-strength probe would light us up like a beacon. Right now, we need to stow ourselves out of sight."

The lifeboat's slow-motion trajectory brought them up close to the side of the *Nova Procyon*. A torn piece of hull plating yawned like a black wound in the ship's side. The gap was filled with a jumble of large, round tanks and connecting hoses.

"This will have to do for now," the Captain said, bringing up a virt-screen from the control panel. "Treth, we can nudge ourselves in using air bursts from our atmospheric venting system. We shouldn't be detected."

He and Treth worked at the controls and soon the lifeboat was nestled into the cavity in the *Nova Procyon's* hull.

"Captain," Treth said once they'd stopped, "there is an access hatch in the hull, there." She pointed to the view screen.

"Let's not be hasty," the Captain said. "We may be able to modify the probe field." He called up another screen. "If we can dial the power down low enough, we could send a signal through the hull without alerting anyone. It might be enough to tell us what we're dealing with."

The Captain then pulled out one of the mem-crystals he'd taken from the *Helen's* bridge and slipped it into the reader on the control panel. A screen popped up, and a schematic of the lifeboat's circuitry appeared on it. "If we adjust the probe gain here... and here... we should be able to do a minimal scan of the *Procyon's* near-field decks."

The Groom leaned in to view the display. "Yes. But such a low-power probe will take time to resolve any meaningful image."

"How long?" the Captain asked.

"Ten minutes. Maybe more."

"Let's get started."

After several more minutes, the Captain declared the probe was functioning. Now, he said, they must simply wait for it to accumulate data about what lay beyond the other ship's hull.

"This would be a good time to check inventories," the Captain said, addressing them all. "Treth, if you'll monitor the probe, I'll see what we have in the supply locker. Sacrist, check the toolbox on the starboard side for anything that might be useful."

Zenn followed the Captain to the rear of the cabin, where he began sorting through the contents of a small locker.

"Captain Oolo, I wanted to apologize. For lying to you." The Captain said nothing but dipped his head at her, bringing his beaked face near hers. "I'm sorry I sneaked onto the *Helen*. But I had to." His eyes grew larger.

"You *had* to stow away on my ship?" the Captain said, chest feathers fluffing out. "And why was that?" he said, then returned to pulling things out of the cabinet, placing some of them into various pockets in his vest.

Zenn took a deep breath – and explained. She told her story as quickly and coherently as she could.

"This is… quite a tale," the Captain said several minutes later, running a claw through his feathers. She noticed Treth and Fane had come up close behind her.

"You are the daughter of the healer Mai Scarlett?" The Groom said. "There are few exovets who deal in the mindways of the stonehorse. Your mother's work is… was well known among the groom's union. The loss of her and her aide Travosk was noted and mourned by my union sisters."

"Travosk?" Zenn said. "No, mom's lab-tech was Vremya."

"Yes," Treth said. "Vremya Travosk. I recall from the inquest reports."

"That's the soldier's last name, the one who sat with us at the party," Zenn said.

"Yes, Lieutenant Stav Travosk," the Captain said. "The Authority's liaison with the Cepheians."

"Were these two related, do you think?" Jules asked.

"I have no idea," the Captain said. "I suppose it's possible. Though it would be quite a coincidence."

"Well, it would explain his feelings about figuring out what was happening to the Indra ships," Zenn said.

"He spoke of this?" Treth asked.

"Yes. At the dinner, the costume party on the *Helen*. He said he was committed to solving the Indra problem. He sounded... determined." The memory made her wonder where the Lieutenant was now. In transit? Already back on Earth? If so, he'd surely know the *Helen* had been taken. Could he do anything about it? It seemed unlikely, but she allowed herself a flicker of hope.

"Your own mother healed stonehorses?" Fane gave her an approving look. "You never said."

The computer's voice sounded from the front of the ship. "Data collection complete."

A minute later, they all stood waiting expectantly around the pilot's console as the Captain peered at the readout.

"There are life signs. Fifty or sixty, at a rough guess." The Captain pointed to the diagram on the hovering Virt-screen. "Most of them are here, amidships, in the main saloon."

"Saloon?" Jules said. "They are drinking?"

"No. It's what you call a large room on a passenger ship like the *Helen*," the Captain told him. "Treth, what's the standard crew complement on a Nova-class ship?"

"Two hundred fifty, including civilian contractors," the Groom said, scowling at the diagram. "But the number shown here is barely sufficient to man the ship's systems."

"Where are all the others, do you think?" Jules asked.

Neither the Captain nor Treth had an answer.

An ominous *crack* from the right side of the craft was followed instantly by a keening alarm and a bland but urgent digitized voice: "Interior atmospheric breach. Catastrophic pressure loss from the starboard hatchway. Estimated time to fatal depressurization: forty-five seconds."

"The seal on the access hatch is bad," the Captain said. He bobbed his head anxiously at one of the Virt-screens. "Take whatever you can and move to the airlock. Quickly."

As Zenn grabbed her vet pack and threw it onto her back, small pieces of paper and debris began to leap into the air, fly past her and land near the hatchway, plastering themselves to its edges.

Gathering together as tightly as possible, they all crowded into the lifeboat's small airlock, where the Captain quickly keyed in a code on the wall panel to close the door behind them. It began to swing shut, but slowly. The soft whooshing sound from the leaking seal grew louder.

"Pressure dropping fast," Treth said. "When the inner door opens, we must move."

With a loud *snik* the small access hatch of the *Nova Procyon* cracked open, sending a cloud of dust into the lifeboat's airlock.

The hatch ahead was so small they had to pass through one by one. And with every second, the sound of air being sucked out of the lock grew louder. Finally, after Jules had squeezed through, Zenn followed him, and then Fane stepped through. Treth slammed the hatch shut behind him.

"The mem-crystals," the Captain muttered, eyeing the hatch. "I left them. They could have been useful."

"You cannot retrieve them?" Jules asked.

"The airlock is impassable now," Treth said. "It seems we are left with but one path."

They all stared at the dim, narrow passage stretching away before them. The Captain activated the lightpatch he'd found in the lifeboat's supply locker and pressed it onto the front of his vest. In the pool of light it produced, they started down the corridor, the Captain leading the way, followed by Treth, with Zenn, Jules and Fane going next.

As they made their way deeper in to the ship, Zenn saw that the *Nova Procyon* was a very different craft from the *Helen*. The impression was one of Spartan military economy – the metal-walled corridor was crowded with tubing and bundled wires, the ceiling so low they had to crouch at times in order to proceed. Broken furniture, empty supply containers and other trash lay scattered here and there. The still air was stagnant, and cold enough that Zenn could see her breath.

The first cabins they peered into along the corridor had all been stripped of anything not fastened down. There was no sound except their own whispered exchanges and echoing footfalls as they picked their way down the litter-strewn passageway.

With the lev-tubes inactive, it took them almost half an hour of climbing over obstructions, navigating garbage-clogged stairwells and forcing several stubborn doors before they approached their goal. The deck's main saloon was now just ahead, and, as they edged closer, they heard the murmur of voices. The air became a bit warmer here and, strangely enough, carried the scent of smoke. The Captain put up an arm to bring them to a halt.

"We'll wait here. No talking," he whispered. "Treth, take a look. Be careful." The Groom nodded and crept silently ahead. The sight reminded Zenn of the stories she'd heard about the upbringing of the young Procyoni girls recruited to join the groom's union, the military training they underwent as part of their education, the harsh living conditions and strict codes of discipline. It made her glad the Groom was with them.

At the door to the saloon, Treth crouched, listening intently. Then she placed one finger to her lips to indicate silence and beckoned them.

Zenn estimated there were several dozen people crowded at the far end of the room, their faces faintly lit by small fires burning in metal barrels scattered around the room. The people in the room clustered in small groups around the barrels, warming their hands. The smoke from the fires rose to the ceiling and hung there. At the center of the room, a smallish figure stood on top of a barrel. Even without seeing his face, she was quite sure who it was.

"...and also," the Skirni Pokt rasped, "I have assurances. From the Khurspex. You will be treated with more... concern. There will be greater rations." The murmuring of the crowd grew louder at this, forcing Pokt to raise his voice.

"This you should know..." He waved his short arms in the air for calm, and the noise simmered down to a restless grumble. "Our delegation is at work. It forcefully seeks your release. And your return to LSA space. Until then, remain calm. Comply with the requests of the Khurspex."

"Requests? You mean orders." A hoarse male voice sounded from the crowd. The voice's owner moved into a pool of firelight. He was tall, slender, and wore the tattered remnants of a Procyoni officer's uniform. "They removed most of my crew. Tell us what is happening here." The angry buzz had begun to grow again, rising up and filling the room.

Many of those in the room wore ragged blankets around their shoulders, and were dressed in clothes that had been reduced to shreds, their faces unwashed, bodies undernourished and gaunt. It was only then, as her eyes adjusted to the fitful illumination, that Zenn saw there were also familiar faces mixed in among the crowd of strangers, passengers she'd seen on the *Helen*. Warming his clawed hands at one of the fire barrels was the Alcyon alpha who'd been playing cards with Jules. Among those standing around another barrel was Thrott's Fomalhaut slave, though the Skirni himself was nowhere to be seen.

"What about the others?" a woman's voice called out. "What have they done with my husband?"

Pokt again waved for quiet. "Your fellow travelers are quite safe. We are told they were relocated. To maintain other ships in this structure. That is all we know."

Another voice sounded from the darkness. "What about the rumors? That the Spex took them for slaves?"

A Reticulan female wearing a ragged evening gown and oversized winter coat clambered up on a table near the back of the room and yelled, shaking her horned head in agitation, "How do we know our companions are even alive?"

"As I said..." Pokt shouted down the rising commotion. "Spreading rumors serves no one. The Khurspex are not a murderous race. That is not their way. If they were killers, you wouldn't be here now." A grudging silence fell on the room, and Pokt lowered his voice again. "They are not killers but scavengers."

"They're pirates," someone shouted.

"Yes," Pokt agreed. "They have been taking ships. The LSA protests that. But they are not killers! Have they not kept you all alive?"

"Yes, barely," the Procyoni who spoke before called out. "And why? What is this thing they're building? Why do they hold us here at all?"

Another angry voice called out, "We've been captive here for months! Some of these ships been here for years! Why didn't the LSA send rescue sooner?"

"I repeat, your questions will be answered in time. Remain calm. Everything that can be done is being done."

Treth pulled back from the door, hissed through clenched teeth, "It is the Skirni who violated my chamber."

"The one who took our stonehorse?" Fane said.

"Then he is lying to those people," the Captain whispered, motioning all of them to move a safe distance back down the corridor. "If he took the *Helen's* Indra, he may well be involved in the other disappearances. Skirni – hijacking starships. It is beyond belief. There must be more to this. Maybe we should hear him out."

"And maybe he should die like the blood-sucking skeenflea he is," Fane muttered.

"Quiet," Treth said, nodding toward the saloon. "He speaks of us."

"...and we are concerned for their safety. There are five unaccounted for. They were not identified as being on board the *Helen of Troy* after it arrived in Khurspex space."

"You mean they weren't rounded up like the rest of us," a female voice yelled.

Pokt ignored this. "The missing ones include the Captain, who is an Ornithope. There are also a Procyoni groom and her sacrist. As well an Earther dolphin in a mobile-suit. We are most interested in the... safety of the young human female with them. She is seventeen Earther years. She stands of medium height, slender, with red hair. She and the others may have been disoriented in the confusion. I urge you to contact me if you see any of them. And your help will be rewarded. With additional food rations. I can be reached through your Khurspex hosts."

This was too much for the crowd.

"Hosts! Hosts he calls them." The commotion that rose was beyond Pokt's control. Ten or twelve of the survivors surged forward and encircled the Skirni.

"They are jailors! We are prisoners forced to do their labor."

"Where's the rest of the LSA delegation?"

"Why don't you get us out of here?"

As the angry group pressed in on Pokt, two previously unseen forms now stepped out from the shadows at the side of the saloon. Twice as tall as a human, moving on four legs, the creatures positioned themselves between the Skirni and the angry crowd, which now drew back like a wave receding from the shore.

"Tell the Spex we need more food," one of the throng yelled out, shaking his fist at the aliens.

"Tell them we have no fuel. We're freezing in here," another shouted.

The crowd's anger at the Skirni now turned to jeers at both Pokt and the aliens that Zenn assumed were the ones they called the Khurspex.

The two beings were tall enough that their heads brushed the twelve-foot ceiling of the saloon. They appeared to have both insectoid and mammalian traits, with an outer layer of leathery, ivory-colored exoskeleton over a dull white dermal layer. Their coloring was pale; so pale Zenn was reminded of permanent cave dwellers, their skin gone white in the absence of sunlight.

Fane now stepped by her. She saw his eyes were very wide, his mouth open as if in shock as he stared at the aliens.

When he spoke, it was in a reverent whisper, "Ghost Shepherds."

SIXTEEN

"The Shepherds," Treth whispered. "Could it be?"

Fane reached out and gripped the Groom by the arm, both of them staring awestruck at the looming Khurspex.

The aliens held themselves on four stout back legs, with two small, arm-like tendrils waving before their erect upper bodies, giving them the appearance of distorted centaurs. The two tendrils extending from the torso ended in four flexible appendages at their tips, something like an elephant's trunk.

Even in the present situation, Zenn found herself straining for a better look at these beings – it wasn't every day one encountered an entirely new species, let alone an intelligent, technologically advanced species.

As the creatures moved further into the light, she realized each Khurspex was not merely a single animal, but a symbiont – a cooperative unit made up of multiple individual creatures.

The "back end" appeared to be some kind of quadruped, its four triple-jointed legs holding up a separate, barrel-shaped creature that was topped by the large, projecting head. The central "torso" creature appeared to have a short, muscular tail that fit snugly into the length of a groove that furrowed the back of the leg section, holding the two animals tightly together. The head was a third, separate creature, slightly darker in color and almost all braincase and facial area, with a pair of tentacle-like arms gripping the central chest section below it. The face, long and flat beneath the globular skull, tapered to a narrow-tipped snout. There were two eyes: visible, bright pink, sunk in narrow slits. Within the lipless mouth, a small, shiny black beak opened and closed, as if tasting the air. Most remarkably, the smooth, rounded forehead flickered with a display of soft, multihued light that shimmered and flowed just beneath the surface.

Zenn could also see that the Khurspex's epidermal layer of skin appeared to be peeling off in ragged sheets and dangling strings, as if the animal was molting its outer layer. Occasionally, one or the other of the two would shudder slightly, then recover.

Zenn knew there were other instances of multi-animal colonies of organisms living as a single being, like the Portuguese man-of-war in the oceans of Earth and a few symbiont tree-dwelling crustaceans from the Sirenian rainforests. But these were lower-order examples, uncomplicated, and only functioning at the simplest level. And Cepheians like Ambassador Noom, of course, were symbiotic but consisted of the same species. The Khurspex, however, looked to Zenn like an example of complex multispecies integration that was undreamt of in Accord science.

As the creatures moved up next to Pokt, the crowd pulled back further. The jostling pushed one group of passengers away from the fire light surrounding their barrel, closer to the doorway where Zenn and the others crouched. In the shadows of the saloon, one of those in this group stopped, looked in their direction, and stared. Had he seen them? It was too dark to see the person's face or to know if they'd been discovered.

"Back. Go back," the Captain whispered, harshly. They returned down the corridor till they came to an open cabin. The Captain pointed and they crowded in.

"Captain Oolo," Jules said. "What are those creatures? Are they the Ghostly Shepherds as this sacrist says?"

"The Shepherds? No, I cannot imagine such a... We need more information." He preened nervously at his ruffled chest feathers. "Treth, what do you think? Treth?"

But the pilot stood as if she could no longer hear, her face an unreadable mask. Fane too seemed deeply affected and stood shaking his head slowly. Then, the Sacrist looked up at Treth, confusion and wonder in his eyes.

"Groom Treth, can this be?" Fane said quietly. "Have they truly come, as foretold?"

Treth frowned. "We know this much: somehow, the stonehorses are being taken. And these entities are somehow involved."

"Gathered," Fane said. "The herds are gathered. By the Shepherds. As the prophecy tells us, as it is written."

"It is... possible," Treth said.

"Treth," The Captain went to bob his head in front of her. "What are you saying?"

"I am saying..." She clasped her hands in front of her, her knuckles white. "The Foretelling in the Book of Staffs. It tells us the Ghost Shepherds will return one day from their distant realm. That they will come to reclaim their stonehorse herds and take them home again."

"I'm sorry, and I don't mean any disrespect, but... that's just a myth," Zenn said, unable to keep silent. "These creatures aren't gods. That's just not... They're a new alien race. And they–"

"They are doing as the Shepherds are prophesied to do," Fane said, a strange light in his eyes. "It is written that they will come without warning. That their aspect will be as flawless as the dawn, as pale as the light of moons. That they and they alone will call the stonehorse herds homeward."

"Yes, it's written, but who wrote it?" Zenn implored. "A Procyoni. A person like any other person, a person like you or Treth."

"She was no simple person that wrote these words," Fane objected. "She was the Prophetess Ry Reth Trassin of Sinnuron. She saw what no others could see. She had direct communing with the Shepherds."

"Please," the Captain said. He stepped between them and raised his talons as if separating two boxers. "We don't have time for this. Treth, we need to backtrack. Get away from the Skirni and those... creatures... until we know what we're up against. And how to fight it."

"If it is true, if they are the Shepherds," Treth said firmly, "we cannot fight them."

"What?" The Captain's chest feathers rose in agitation.

"It would be sacrilege," she said simply.

"Plainly," Fane agreed.

"But..." the Captain sputtered. "What will you do then? Give up? What about the *Helen's* passengers and crew? And your Indra? They took your Indra. Maybe they took all the Indra."

"And it was so written that they would," Fane said.

"If it is the Shepherds' will, it cannot be undone by us. Or anyone," Treth said solemnly.

"So, what are you suggesting?" The Captain was almost chirping with frustration. "That we just... wait?"

"The Shepherds are gods. Immortal. Unknowable. Our actions will not alter their plans, whatever they may be. If they are not the Spectral Anointed, it will be revealed to us. If they are, they will give us a sign."

The Captain clasped his talons together.

"Are they invincible, truly?" Jules said. "In that case, fighting them would be of no use. There are such beings in the old Earth paper-novel-books. Super beings. Several can shoot fire from their eyes. And have capes."

Zenn stared at Fane and Treth. They were just going to do nothing until... what? A magical sign? Until they were captured? If that happened, she would never find her father. Or Katie. Or Liam. She searched for an argument. There must something.

"Treth," she said abruptly, the idea coming to her like a gift. Treth and Fane both peered impassively at her. "The Shepherds take care of their flock, right? They look after their stonehorses?"

"Of course," Treth said.

"And the Khurspex, who you think are the Shepherds, they've been helping the Skirni steal starships, hijack them."

"Because the stonehorses are bonded to the Shepherds, from time long forgotten," Treth said. "So it is right and just that they gather them back. And so also must the ships be taken. The stonehorses would perish otherwise."

"But, when the Indra on the *Helen* was attacked by that bio-mech, the one released by the Skirni in your chamber, that Indra was hurt. Couldn't you tell your stonehorse was in pain when the bio-mech attached itself to her?"

"So it would seem," Treth reluctantly agreed. "But one cannot say with certainty."

"Tell me this," Zenn went on, "Do the writings say what the Shepherds will look like? Do they say they're... ten-foot-tall tri-symbionts with... with light pigmentation?"

"The Writings are vague as to how the Shepherds will appear once they assume corporeal form."

"Then maybe, just maybe these aren't your Shepherds. Maybe they're just aliens who happen to be... ghostly-looking. Maybe their coloration is due to being cave dwellers. Or their home star has a particular light spectrum. And maybe these aliens are hijacking Indra ships for reasons we just don't know yet."

"This is merely your conjecture," Treth said.

Zenn got the feeling she wasn't exactly getting through.

"Either way, we need more data," the Captain insisted. He stepped closer to Treth. "All I ask is that we retreat, regroup and take the time to learn more."

Treth looked at Fane, then back to the Captain.

"Very well," she said, "but only until we learn the true

will of the Shepherds. No longer." They all moved quietly to the doorway and filed out into the corridor. But they had gone no more than five feet when a shout sounded some distance behind them.

"Guest Zora Bodine!"

Zenn whirled around. There, froggish face creased with a huge, black, needle grin, hands on his hips, stood Yed the One Who Consumes Fat Meal-Larva With Lip-Noises of Pleasure.

"It *is* you. You are safe," he called out, grinning even wider. Panic flowed through her. She gestured at him frantically with both hands, willing him to be quiet. Then he hooked a webbed thumb over his shoulder, pointing back at the Skirni. "Guest Pokt is concerned for your well-being. He is seeking you. And Yed has found–"

From behind him, a hand shot out and planted itself over his wide mouth. A face appeared. Liam. He was alive. He was safe.

"Shut up," Liam growled at the steward, who struggled to pull away, his eyes swiveling wildly to see who was clutching him. Liam looked over his shoulder into the saloon, then back to Zenn and the others.

"He's coming," he yelled at them. "Run!"

The squat figure of Pokt appeared in the doorway next to Liam and Yed. The Skirni squinted in their direction. He hadn't seen them yet. Then, a narrow beam of light leapt from the Skirni's left eye – an implanted scanner? It swept quickly across the passageway until it came to rest on Zenn's face, a tiny blue-green dot dancing on her cheek. She crouched and pressed herself against the wall.

She knew this was the same pinpoint of light she'd seen before – in her bedroom at the cloister, just before he'd kidnapped her, ten thousand light years away, and what seemed like a million years ago.

"You," Pokt rasped. He raised his hand. It clutched a plasma stick, which he pointed at them, threatening. Zenn pushed herself to her feet.

"No," Liam yelled. She saw him grab at Pokt, trying to pull the weapon from his grip.

Pokt snarled at Liam and, with a powerful twist, tore the plasma stick out of the boy's hands.

"Stop! All of you," he shouted at Zenn and the others. "You will come with–"

A mass of white-hot sparks blossomed from the bulkhead next to the Skirni, forcing him, Liam and Yed to all duck back into the saloon. The Captain, standing his ground further down the passage, held his beam-pistol before him in one claw.

"Go," the Captain shouted, waving them on. He stepped behind two large supply crates stacked in the corridor and prepared to get off another shot.

But before he could fire, Pokt scurried nimbly out into the saloon doorway, brought up the plasma weapon and loosed a charge. The jagged white lightning bolt of energy arced down the corridor to strike the floor at the Captain's feet, kicking up a spray of molten fragments.

"Everyone, down," Treth yelled. She grabbed Zenn by the arm and dragged her to join the Captain behind the crates. Jules and Fane hurried back into the cabin they'd just left. Behind Pokt, the two Khurspex peered out into the passage cautiously. When they turned toward each other, Zenn saw their forehead areas light up with flickering lightshows of rapidly shifting colors.

The Captain leaned out, fired three times in rapid succession and dropped back. The shots missed but made Pokt and the creatures pull away out of sight.

"Captain," Fane yelled. "Do not anger the Shepherds." The Sacrist stuck his head out of the cabin door. "Sainted Ones," he called to the aliens. "Forgive us. We do not mean to give offense."

The Skirni poked his head out and fired a bolt into the wall above the crates. Melted debris sizzled in the air around Zenn and Treth.

"A warning shot only," Pokt yelled. "I do not wish to kill. Only to stop you. Cease your resisting. You will be… treated fairly."

"Like you treated my father?" Zenn shouted, furious. And terrified. They mustn't be captured. She had to convince the Groom she was wrong.

"Treth," Zenn said. "Would your Shepherds do this? Help someone like him?"

"The Shepherds' ways are… veiled from us," Treth said. But Zenn could tell she was less sure now than moments before.

"You have to believe me." Zenn turned so the Groom could see her eyes, see that what she said was true. "Your Indra was hurting when she was attacked. I swear I could feel her pain and fear. I felt it. You can't let them take us."

Another strike from Pokt's plasma stick hit the wall beside them, making them crouch lower behind the crates.

"Enough. Throw down your weapon," the Skirni rasped.

"You did feel it," Treth said, nodding, then looking hard at Zenn. "I could tell, even then. But I could not believe it was so. Perhaps I wished not to believe. She was my Indra, after all."

Zenn thought she saw a change in the Groom. The sign was small, fleeting. But it was real.

"Sacrist," the Groom yelled at the unseen Fane. "The Novice speaks truly. The Shepherds would never harm a stonehorse. Or ally themselves with one who would do this. It cannot be the Foretelling."

"Book of the Rope of Light, chapter nine, verse twelve," Fane shouted back. "'For the Shepherds' return will rise as a storm-bull raging. It will fall as a jewel-rain blessing. Many will doubt the Sainted Ones' coming. Few will see the Ninth Gate opening. But the faith-keepers will know. The truth-seekers will see!'"

He's quoting scripture now! Zenn thought, incredulous. *This can't be happening!*

Treth shook her head.

"Sacrist Fanesson," she shouted at him. "Book of Dohlms, chapter eighteen, verse nine-twenty-six: 'Keep keen thy wit against false claimants to the Shepherds' cloak. Turn from these deceivers, who come as dreadwolves to the herd'."

"But Groom Treth," Fane yelled back. "What of the words in the Book of–"

"Shut up this talk," Pokt screamed shrilly. "Cease this nonsense talk, I say." And he loosed another bolt of plasma over their heads. "Come out now and be done."

"I need a better angle," the Captain said quietly to Treth. "When I move, you take the others back down the corridor."

"No, Captain. You are not trained in arms. Let me–" But the Captain was already in motion, firing as he ran for the opposite wall. Pokt didn't hesitate. He stepped into the doorway, raised his stick and fired. It caught the Captain square in the chest, the super-heated bolt hurling him out of Zenn's sight, leaving behind a small blizzard of colorful feathers that drifted and swirled where a second ago he had stood.

"Captain!" Treth cried.

Pokt now strode into the corridor. Behind him, the two Khurspex loomed into view. In the saloon beyond them, Liam appeared, looking shaken, his face drained.

"You see the product of your foolishness?" Pokt said, shaking the plasma stick at the Captain's limp body. "Take them to the bridge and hold them there," he instructed the two creatures, pointing to Zenn and the others. "And take care the Martian girl is undamaged."

"No!" Treth threw herself out from behind the crates, diving to where the Captain had fallen. A second later, she crouched with his pistol in her hand.

She fired. The energy beam burrowed into the hind leg of the leading Khurspex, scorching the limb and toppling the creature to the floor. Then, the Khurspex… broke in two. The front half, supporting itself on its long tendril-arms, withdrew its thick tail section from a cavity in the back half and heaved itself clumsily to the floor. The wounded back portion of the creature then stumbled away from the forward section, trying to raise itself on its three good legs.

Before Zenn could quite process this bizarre sight, Fane was walking past her, exposing himself in the corridor, deliberately placing himself between Treth and the aliens.

"This is sacrilege, blasphemy. It cannot be allowed." He held his arms outstretched to either side, moving ahead as if in a trance, calling to the creatures. "Shepherds forgive us."

"Fane, don't," Treth hissed.

Pokt gestured to the other Khurspex next to him. The creature raised its arm-tendril. Attached near its waving tip was something like a shell. It gripped the Khurspex's "wrist" with an array of thread-like filaments. The shell split open. From inside, a long, thin rope of living tissue like a chameleon's tongue whipped out toward Fane. It tapped him lightly on the side of his neck, then recoiled, the shell snapping shut around it.

Instantly, the Sacrist collapsed, dropped by the touch of the thing.

Anger twisting her features, Treth looked up from Fane's fallen body, raised the pistol. But Pokt had already taken aim. He fired, the stream of lightning licking across Treth's forearm. The pistol spun from her grasp. Clutching her arm, she staggered back against the wall.

"You see?" Pokt hooted. "It is useless." They all stopped where they stood as he approached. Stepping over Fane, he nudged his body with one boot. "This one will recover. The whip-whelk poison does not last long. It is the favored weapon of the Spex. Activated by the merest thought. So simple, so effective."

He leered at Zenn.

"You have been long sought, human. And much trouble. But now we have you. And what you carry."

Zenn saw motion behind Pokt. It was Liam, in the corridor, running at them, fast. The boy tackled Pokt from behind, squeezing a loud grunt of pain from the Skirni and sending them both sprawling onto the floor.

"Go!" Liam yelled as he scrambled to his feet, scooping up Pokt's weapon as he stumbled toward them. He turned, fumbled with the plasma stick, tried to aim it at the Khurspex coming down the corridor. "How does this… Where's the damn trigger?"

Grimacing in pain, Treth pushed away from the wall, snatched the weapon away from Liam. She twisted the handle to maximum force and fired – not at the approaching creature, but at the ceiling of the passage. A massive, forking lightning pulse erupted from the weapon, atomizing the ceiling panels in a cascade of fire, fragments and acrid, black smoke. Nothing of Fane, Pokt or the Khurspex was visible through the choking cloud.

"Dolphin, Novice! This way," Treth yelled. Jules strode out into the passage. Liam ran to where Zenn crouched, helped her to stand.

"Fane," Zenn cried. "What about Fane?"

"We cannot help him," the Groom shouted, shoving Zenn and Liam down the corridor ahead of her. "Run!"

Zenn didn't argue. She ran.

SEVENTEEN

They plunged on through the frigid air of the unlit corridors for what felt like hours. Down deserted passageways, up through stairwells, along yet more endless tunnels of corridor, not speaking, breathing hard, footfalls echoing. At last, Zenn had to rest and said so. Reluctantly, Treth whispered, "Five minutes. No longer."

The Groom squatted down on her haunches. Zenn and Liam both dropped to sit on the floor. Jules parked himself nearby and busied himself redirecting the mist-jets on his walksuit.

"Captain Oolo… I can't believe that he's…" Zenn's voice broke, the words refusing to come. Her shock quickly turned to anger. "Why? Why would they do that? What do they want?"

Treth raised her gaze to look at Zenn, the Groom's eyes hunting something.

"They want you, Novice. The Skirni said as much."

"But why?" Even as she spoke, Zenn felt a surge of guilt, then fear. She suspected she might know why. Should she tell the others? No. She could be wrong. It was crazy. Yes, she was probably mistaken.

"Treth, your arm," she said instead, standing up. "Here, let me see."

"It is nothing," the Groom said, but she allowed Zenn to examine her. The Skirni's weapon had cut a thin line of charred flesh across her upper arm. Zenn slipped off the straps of her field kit, dug in it and located what she needed. After cleaning the wound, she applied a coat of antiseptic and sprayed on a dermal bandage.

"That should protect it until the skin grows back."

Treth flexed her arm, nodded in approval.

"Thank you, Novice," she said, then turned and walked off to scout the route ahead.

"Scarlett," Liam said from where he sat against the bulkhead. "Sorry. About your friends."

"The Captain was just... trying to protect us," Zenn said, sitting down again beside him. Her throat tightened.

"And the Procyon kid," he said. "Do you think he's..."

"He'll be fine," Zenn said. "I think he's just paralyzed, like Pokt said." Her hand rose to her neck. She was certain the shell-like thing the Khurspex used on Fane was the same thing Pokt had used to paralyze her that night in her cloister dorm room. "The neurotoxin will wear off in an hour or so. He'll just be a little sore."

"Well, that's good to know. And I've got something here that might cheer–"

Zenn felt something brush her cheek, and she pulled back reflexively from Liam. Then she felt pressure on her arm, but saw nothing. Something was on her, poking at her... something alive!

A purple-and-cream blur distorted the air, and then a

rikkaset materialized into view, her snout poking out of Liam's shirt, gold-green eyes blinking at her, small black hands reaching out to her.

"Katie," Zenn cried, her eyes filling with tears. Katie sprang into her arms, and Zenn held her tight, smelled her wonderful rikkaset smell. "Katie, Katie, Katie," The rikkaset licked her nose and signed up at her.

"Friend-Zenn – Katie alone, alone. No friend-Zenn came back right away. Not so nice. Not nice!"

"Katie, I'm so sorry." Unwilling to release her grasp on the animal for even a second, she forced herself to speak slowly so Katie could read her lips. "I… I couldn't come back. I tried to find Katie but… but you're here now." She pressed her face into Katie's warm, silk-soft fur, then looked up at Liam. "Where did you find her?"

"I was about to tell you – she found me," he said. "After they took us all off the *Helen*, everyone was herded into a big cargo bay. Next thing I knew, she was rubbing against my leg and begging for food! And then–"

"Silence," Treth whispered urgently, coming back down the passage toward them. "I heard something! Just ahead." The Groom knelt against one wall, the plasma stick raised. Zenn opened the top of her jumpsuit and pushed Katie down inside.

"Is it those Ghost-Spex?" Jules asked.

"Quiet," Treth snapped at him. They all pressed themselves into the shadows and strained to see up the black tunnel that stretched before them.

The sound that came from the darkened corridor made Zenn jump, adrenaline pouring into her system.

Then she realized it was the sound was of someone, something, laughing.

"Hoo-haha..." The voice was thick, gravelly, with an odd, lilting accent. "Spex? You think I'm Khurspex? I think not, thanky very much."

"Come out," Treth ordered, weapon at the ready. "Show yourself."

"Show myself?" the voice said. "Show me that burn-rod pointing elsewhere! Then maybe."

Treth considered for a moment, then lowered the weapon.

"See?" she said. "Now come out."

A figure shuffled into view, stopping just beyond the shadows, appearing ready to bolt at the first sign of trouble. The creature was a little taller than Zenn, two short legs, two long arms. Its apelike face was masked with grime, and its outlandishly long cheek whiskers and eyebrows drooped forlornly, the once-white muttonchop sideburns tinted a grimy brown-gray. It was a Loepith.

He – Zenn guessed it was a male although it was hard to tell – wore several headlamps and a magnifying glass attached to a band around its head, and a tiny signal dish protruded from one ear. Strapped to its body – or hanging from multiple crisscrossing web-belts – was an assemblage of mashed-up electronic gear, miscellaneous hand tools and a variety of pots, a tin cup and what looked like wineskins. Net bags bulging with food and other odds and ends hung from shoulder straps. The overstuffed pack on his back had a rolled-up blanket tied to it. His ragged clothes had numerous pockets, but the outfit was so shredded and dirty, Zenn couldn't even guess the original color.

"Who are you?" Treth said. "What are you doing down here? Away from the others?"

"Who am I?" the Loepith snorted. "And who is she to ask us questions?" He glared at Treth. "Eh? Who are you to ask, rude and groomish?"

Zenn saw Treth's jaw tighten.

"Her name is Treth. And yes, she's a groom," Zenn said quickly, standing and moving closer so the Loepith could see her. "We mean you no harm. We're just trying to get away. From the Khurspex. We're from the *Helen of Troy*."

The Loepith pulled the head-mounted magnifying glass down over one eye, making the eye suddenly appear huge as he examined her.

"That was the *Helen* just got snagged?" the monkey-like anthropoid said. He seemed to relax a little, pushed the glass away from his eye. "The *Helen* and all its many-many. Bad luck, but there it is."

No, not monkey, more like a mix of human and orangutan, Zenn thought, considering his lanky frame and powerful, overlong arms that reached well below his knees.

The Loepith's big brown eyes glistened from deep sockets, his gaze darting about the corridor as he spoke.

"So, then – sampled some Spex hospitality, have ya? Hospitality, heh heh." The Loepith laughed a cackling laugh and displayed a smile packed with large, tea-brown teeth the size of dominoes. Zenn guessed he was middle-aged for a Loepith, mid-eighties or so. He spoke with what she thought might be a Lunar Settlements accent.

Treth slowly approached the Loepith.

"You're an engineer?" she said, leaning down to examine the creature more closely. The Groom was looking at something on his shoulder – a patch sewn onto his shirt, barely visible through the grime. "From the Zeta Reticuli Lunar setts?"

"Yes. The Moonish one, me." He pointed to the patch, tapping it, his gaze restless, as if reluctant to make eye contact with any of them. During the past century, Loepiths had migrated to the Zeta system's lunar mining settlements in large numbers, from their Ophiuchi homeworld. Their legendary reputations as nimble, ingenious mechanics made them welcome throughout the LSA. If a "Loeper" couldn't fix it, the saying went, you might as well scrap it.

"How long have you been here?" Treth asked.

"Long enough for this." He picked at his shredded shirtsleeve. "And this." He pulled out a matted strand of cheek whiskers and let it drop. "Years on top of years." His voice dropped. "What does it matter now? Not much, eh? Hardly."

"What was your ship?" Treth squatted down next to him.

"Oh? And who are you to know about me?" Suddenly suspicious, the Loepith stared at the Groom, eyes no longer darting about but keenly focused. "And what's my ship to you, groomish?"

"Please," Zenn said. "We're just trying to figure out what's going on here. My name is Zenn. She's Treth. This is Jules. And he's Liam. Can we know your name?"

The Loepith regarded her solemnly for a moment.

"Charlie, I would be," he said. "Charlie Iph, as called by some. But not lately. No one calls, you see?"

"Yes. We see. Charlie," Treth said, making an effort to speak more softly, "are you all alone here? Are there others like you?"

"Alone? Us? Yes. Alone entire, actually."

"And you live here?" Treth asked. "On the *Nova Procyon*?"

"Oh, on the *Nova*. On some others. I go here. Go here and there."

"To other ships?" Treth said sharply. "You've been on other ships in this… structure?

"Some other ships. Here and there."

"Charlie," Zenn stepped in closer to the Loepith. "Have you seen a man on any of the ships, a human from Enchara? A man named Warra Scarlett? He has red hair like mine. And a red beard."

Katie poked her head out of Zenn's jumpsuit. She stretched out toward the Loepith, crinkled her nose and pulled back.

"Needs a bath!" she signed up at Zenn.

"Katie, shush."

"One man? With a name?" Charlie stared at Katie, extended a long, inquisitive finger at her. Katie sniffed once, sneezed and burrowed back down out of sight. Charlie shrugged his shoulders at Zenn. "Many, many men. On all the ships! Men and not-men. Who can say what names men have?"

"He would have come recently," she told him. "Maybe from the *Helen*."

"No way to know, is there? None. We only know what we know, eh?"

Her heart sank. She consoled herself with the fact that the structure was vast, and this Loepith might not be the most reliable witness to the comings and goings on it.

"What was your ship, Charlie?" Treth asked again, then added, "If you wish to say."

The Loepith squinted at her, then seemed to decide it was safe to answer.

"She was the *Belle Savage*. A good old ship, her. Not so good now. Stripped down. All the good taken off her."

"The *Belle*?" Treth said. "That ship vanished fifteen years ago."

"Fifteen, is it? So it was. Fifteen years and one month extra."

"Can you tell us," Treth said, "what the Khurspex are doing this for? Why are they taking the stonehorses, building this structure?"

"The Spex? Those crab-heads? They wanna go home," Charlie said matter-of-factly. "They take the Indra boats to sail em home again."

"Home? They're taking all these ships to get back to their native planet?"

"Have to, don't they?" Charlie said. "It's a long sail. Other side of the g'laxy. They need every horse they can get, don't they?"

"The other side of the galaxy? Truly?" Jules said, coming up behind Zenn.

"How soon?" Treth asked. "Do you know how soon they're going to… go home?"

"Oh, soon soon. From what I see, *Helen's* Indra is the last one, the last stonepony they need. Then they'll hook all those ponies into that giant trip-ship in the middle and make that long g'laxy tunnel."

Treth put her hands on the Loepith's shoulders and lowered her face in front of his. "Charlie," she said, speaking very slowly, "how soon is soon? When will they go?"

"Days, I'd say. Could be less."

"How do you know?"

"Food's run out, hasn't it? Spex food. Charlie's food. Indra's food. That darkly matter, most all gone. And when those crab-heads are gone on that center ship, then the rest of us are gonna have to stay. Stay right here. Forever, mostly."

"Maybe not, Charlie," Treth said. "Maybe we can help each other. If you would help us, maybe we can find a way for you and the all the rest to go home. How's that sound?"

"Help us all get back homeward?" The Loepith grinned at this. "You could do that, groomish?"

A loud bang echoed from the passageway behind them. They all froze, listening. Zenn strained to see into the darkness.

"Spex," Charlie whispered, and when Zenn turned back to him, he wasn't there.

EIGHTEEN

"With me," Treth said. "Move." She started off down the passage. Then another bang, metal on metal – a door thrown open? But this sound came from in front of them. They were boxed in.

"We cannot go in either way," Jules said, weaving about uncertainly on his mech-legs. "Those Ghost-Spex will find us here. What will they do? Will they be mean and unpleasant?"

Zenn wanted to tell him it would be OK. But she didn't really believe that. She saw Treth checking the remaining charge in Pokt's plasma stick.

A husky voice called to them from the dark.

"This way, groomish."

Charlie was gesturing from a gap in the bulkhead a dozen feet behind them. Zenn was surprised they hadn't seen this passageway when they passed it. Then, once they'd all squeezed through the opening, Charlie slid a metal panel into place, sealing off the gap behind them.

"A secret and hidden passage," Jules said to Zenn. "This

is an element of paper-novel mysteries! Although generally there is a moving bookcase activated by a handle on the fireplace. It is very clever thinking, Mister Charlie."

"Gotta be sharp, don't we?" Charlie said. "Gotta keep the crab-heads guessing! And I know how. Oh yes, I go here and there."

With Charlie leading them at a brisk trot, they continued down the narrow service passage, their path illuminated by one of the lights that Charlie wore.

"Charlie," Treth said after they'd put some distance between them and their pursuers. "How have you avoided them, the Khurspex, all these years?"

"Hid, didn't I? Down deep in the deeps. Down in the *Belle's* nether-hold at first. Down in the hard, cold places. Not even the crab-heads could catch me there."

"And you were by yourself, all that time?" Zenn asked.

"Years, by myself. No talking, no one listening, you see?" Zenn could tell the Loepith had paid a price for those solitary years of running and hiding. As they went, Charlie explained that the ship they were on, the *Nova Procyon*, was attached on one side to the *Prodigious*, a Vhulk starship taken some eight years ago. The *Prodigious* was a "crusher ship", designed for inhabitants of planets with high atmospheric pressures and temperatures. Accordingly, surface pressures inside it were staggering, with interior temperatures kept at a searing level, just short of the boiling point of water.

Charlie didn't seem to know much about the ship on the other side of the *Nova*. All he'd been able to learn was that it was an alien craft filled with a toxic cocktail of unbreathable gases.

Beyond the *Prodigious* and its hellish environment was another Earther-class ship, the *Symmetry Dancer*, which was in turn attached to the *Benthic Tson*, built for sea dwellers and filled stem to stern with vast reservoirs of fresh and salt water. Next in line after the *Tson* was the *Delphic Queen*. Beyond that, the *Ghestan Star* and then Charlie's original ship, the *Belle Savage*. That was as far as the Loepith's knowledge extended.

"But what about internal scans of the ships, and patrols?" Treth asked. "How did you escape detection?"

"I keep all my eyes on em. Keep outta their way," Charlie said. Then he pulled open one side of the dirty vest he wore and glanced down at something that lit his face with a faint glow. Before Zenn could see what he was looking at, he closed the vest again. "Besides, Spex don't use scans so much, don't hardly need em. All the many-many are stuck in their own ships. Can't move around. So the Spex don't care about scans. Why should they?"

Like the *Nova Procyon*, Charlie said, each ship was connected on either side to ships with incompatible environments. As a result, no passengers from one ship could survive the conditions of the ships attached to it. This apparently negated the need for the Khurspex to keep close tabs on their prisoners.

"You talked of the *Benthic Tson*," Jules said, quickening his pace to come up alongside Charlie. "Are there living ones aboard it?"

"There are. Some in the water still," the Loepith told him. "Can't say how many."

"But why?" Zenn asked. "Why keep everyone here at all?"

"Need em, don't they? Spex gotta keep every ship's systems up and ready, and they need crews for that. That's their plan. Keep the big chambers going, keep those stoneponies comfy. But not so comfy now, are we? Spex are getting sick. Can't keep systems up with their skin coming off, with stumbling around half blind."

They came to a steep set of stairs and Charlie led the way down.

"But this is like the Ghostly Shepherd story," Jules said. "Maybe these ones *are* those Shepherds in the writings."

"No. I think not," the Groom said. "I clearly wounded one. The true Shepherds are immortal. Their flesh incorruptible. They cannot be harmed by such weapons as mortals possess."

"And did you see their heads?" Jules said. "They had colorful lights moving inside them."

"It's how they talk, those crab-heads. Use skin colors."

"Talking with colors," Jules said. "Can this be true?"

"Well, yes, I suppose so," Zenn said. "There are cephalopods on Earth, like cuttlefish, that use color to communicate. They have microscopic chromatophores under their skin – tiny sacs of pigment. They expand or contract the sacs to create patterns. The Khurspex could be doing something like that, only more complex."

"Thank you, Doctor Knows-Way-Too-Much," Liam said.

"But the Khurspex are getting sick?" Zenn said.

"Oh yes. Skin comes off. Thinking goes bad to worse. They gotta leave soon or they all go offline. Dead, that would be."

Had the Khurspex evolved a reproductive behavior like Earther salmon, Zenn wondered, crossing vast ocean distances to return to their home stream to spawn… and die?

"But the other side of the galaxy – that must be at least a hundred thousand light years away," Liam said. "Indra ships can't tunnel near that far, can they?"

"No," Treth said. "At least, not in our experience. The Indra in all our ships have proved unwilling to travel beyond the Outer Reaches of the Local Systems Accord. We assumed they were simply incapable of venturing farther. It is clear now that our understanding of stonehorse abilities is… incomplete."

"And all those other Indra, they are still held within their ships, correct?" Jules asked. Charlie nodded. "So, where is the *Helen of Troy's* Indra?"

"They put her in the big trip-ship. In the middle. All the other ships in a big ring around it."

"So the ships surrounding the one in the center, those are all the disappeared Indra-drive starships, right?" Liam said. "But how did they all get here?"

"Wormy bio-mech," Charlie said, undulating his hands in a wavy motion. "Part alive, part machine. They put em into the ponies' heads. It makes em jump over here, then they hook em all together."

"Bio-mech controllers, I would say," Treth said. "The device that burned its way into my chamber and attacked my stonehorse. They must force the Indra to tunnel."

"Bio-mech," Liam said. "I didn't think Skirni had that kind of tech."

"They do not," Treth said. "They must be in league with others, those with access to advanced capabilities. Or the funding to purchase it."

"But who would team up with Skirni?" Liam asked.

"Is it not evident?" Treth said. "Those with a motive to take stonehorse ships. Those with a reason to stand against the Procyoni and the groom's union."

"You mean... the Cepheians?" Zenn said, resisting the idea, but unable to ignore the evidence: Ambassador Noom's species had the motivation and the money to buy whatever tech they needed.

"The Drifters have made clear their intention to secure more Indra ships by any means." Treth said.

"But would the Cepheians do that?" Zenn asked. "Make a deal with the Skirni to hijack Indra ships? Just to get control of the space lanes?"

"The trade routes are worth trillions. And why else would they be so secretive about their dealings with Earth? They obviously have something they wish to keep to themselves. The so-called negotiations with the Earth Authority could be a distraction to mislead us," Treth said, dark eyes flashing, her anitats throbbing violently up and down her arms.

"It seems an incredible thing," Jules said. "The Cepheians scheming with Skirni-types to steal Indra craft. This would be wild and reckless behavior. I am having difficulty believing it."

"Oh? Are you? There is one thing more," Treth said. "Just before the *Helen* was taken, the Drifter claimed she was recalled to Earth, correct?"

"Yes. Stav said Ambassador Noom told him she had new orders, at breakfast that morning," Zenn said.

"This is an unlikely coincidence. To be summoned away just before the *Helen* and all aboard her were taken. The scheming Drifter merely employed this ruse as a convenient way off the ship. The timing cannot be happenstance."

Zenn hadn't really put the pieces together before. But she had to admit that, at this point, it seemed to fit. Noom herself said the Cepheians wanted to break the Procyon monopoly on Indra ship routes. Equally suspicious: at the costume party the ambassador seemed very interested in Zenn's identity, that she was an exovet novice. And Noom appeared to know all about the Ciscan cloister on Mars. Of course, there could be other reasons she would know this. But when added to the other facts, it seemed to fill out the disturbing picture Treth was painting. Could Noom actually be working with Pokt? If so, Noom's was the unidentified voice she'd heard at the party when she linked with the mudlark.

The implications seemed logical. The Authority on Earth was sincere about wanting to rejoin the planetary community of the Accord. It was the Cepheians and Skirni using Khurspex tech to take the Indra ships, and being used in turn, as they all schemed to advance their own ambitions.

NINETEEN

"...but I am wondering about all these Indra, all these ships, no matter who is doing the taking," Jules said as they hustled down yet another dark stairwell. "Why take so many?"

"Spex have a tricky way," Charlie said. "A trick to make one pony rope up all the space-jumping of the other ponies. Then – whoosh! – the big jump."

"I don't see how that'd work," Liam said.

"Stonehorses are able to communicate over interstellar distances," Treth said from the front of the group. "In theory, they could link all of their brains in some way. Combine their abilities and increase their range. But it would require some kind of... coordination. A connecting interface. A source-point to funnel the power into a single massive tunneling event."

Treth's words provoked a twinge of anxiety in Zenn.

"Something like a..." She actually had difficulty saying the word out loud. "...nexus?"

"Yes. Nexus would be accurate," Treth said, giving her a brief look. "But there is no such nexus, not known to our science. Nothing could withstand the resulting forces."

"Our science? No, not ours," Charlie said. "Spex science."

"If they had such a focusing device," Treth said, "it's possible they could concentrate the energy needed for a cross-galactic tunnel. But we don't know what this race is capable of. We are blind here."

"Blind? No, no." Charlie said. "Not a bit blind, actually."

"What do you mean?" Treth said, stopping at the foot of the stairs.

"Not blind. That's the meaning." Charlie pulled open his vest again and held one side open. Fixed to the inside was a glowing, flexible view screen of some sort. He peeled it away from the vest, held it up and pulled at its corners. It was made of a substance that allowed him to stretch it like a thin sheet of taffy until it was two feet square. Then he pushed the entire thing against the bulkhead, where it adhered, and ran one finger along its edge. It instantly lit up with an oddly distorted camera view of a corridor. The image was grainy, black-and-white and difficult to read, but it was sufficient to make out three Khurspex, walking away into the shadows.

"That's the corridor we just came from," Liam said, pointing at the screen. "How'd you rig that up so fast?"

Charlie dug into one of the bags hanging from his various belts and withdrew a transparent, cylindrical jar with a spigot-like mechanism sticking out from it. Floating inside the jar were what looked to Zenn like a clutch of tiny, pea-sized frog eggs. Charlie turned the spigot and one of the "eggs" dropped into his open palm.

"Spex tech," he said, grinning his wide, brown-tooth grin. "For watching."

Then, he looked up and threw the small, round thing against the ceiling, where it stuck with a wet splat. He ran his finger along the view screen again and suddenly they were all looking at a grainy, distorted image of themselves as seen from the ceiling above.

"They're… little cameras?" Liam said.

"Bug eyes, I call em," Charlie said, picking the object off the ceiling and dropping it into Liam's hand.

Liam's face filled the view screen attached to the wall as he brought his hand close to his face.

"Hey. He's not kidding. It looks like a little eye! I mean, an actual, little eyeball."

Zenn peered into Liam's hand. He was right. It was a small, living, self-contained eye. Its narrow slit of a pupil hinted at a reptilian origin. Probably cloned. It had several very thin hairs rising from it. Transmitting antennae? A tiny, spiral-shaped growth like a nautilus shell sprouted from one side of it, looking very much like the semicircular canal inside an ear. So, it could hear as well as see? The little eye blinked at her, and she pulled away, startled.

"This is quite the invention," Jules said, admiring the eyeball. "How is it achieved?"

"Who knows? Not me," Charlie said, putting the jar of "eyes" back in his pocket. "I snagged em from a Spex supply room. Now I use em all over. Bug eyes to keep watch on crab-heads."

"Have you placed other… bug eyes? In this ship?" Treth asked.

"Sure, sure. Lotsa places. Here and there."

"Before, the Skirni said he wanted us taken to the *Nova's* bridge," Treth went on. "Do you have one placed there?"

Charlie smiled at her, danced his fingers on the view screen in a complicated pattern. The screen flickered, went dark, then faded up on a distorted image of a cramped starship bridge, as seen from high in one corner. The room was crowded with control consoles, readout panels and screens. There was only one crew person in the room, a Skirni, seated at a console, his back to them as he peered into a view screen.

"Bug eye up in the vent shaft, in the bridge room," Charlie said proudly. "Spex never knew we were there, did they?"

"We need to know what they're planning," Treth said. "Charlie, do you save a record of your... bug eye pictures?"

Charlie patted his sleeve screen. "Right here. Memory shards getting full, I can tell you."

"Can you search back? To the last time there was a meeting on the bridge?"

"I can," he said. He poked a long black finger at his sleeve, and the screen blurred into a fast-motion montage of images.

"Look," Jules said, pointing at the screen. "A Skirni coming in."

"Yes," Treth said. "Slow it down, Charlie."

There was no mistaking the little alien's identity.

"It's Pokt," Zenn said.

The Skirni crossed the cabin, shuffling to where a squat figure leaned over a holo-table. Another Skirni. Above the table hovered a ghostly green 3D image of the giant Spex ring of ships.

"Can you magnify the image?" Treth said.

Charlie swiped a finger across the flexible screen, and the view zoomed in on the pair.

"Master Felik," Pokt said. "You summoned me?" The audio quality was terrible but just barely clear enough to make out words.

The Skirni at the table spoke without turning to face him. "I am told you let the human girl escape. Again."

"They resisted," Pokt protested. "They had weapons."

The one called Felik turned to glare at Pokt. "They had *your* weapon. Is this not true?" The Skirni named Felik was missing his right ear, and the wound from its loss ran in a dull, gray scar down his neck. Over the customary Skirni robes he wore a wide bandolier, loaded with what looked like long, slender cartridges. At his waist hung a T-shaped sort of pistol Zenn had never seen before.

"That's twice you allowed a child to outwit you."

"I could not have anticipated such behavior," Pokt whined. "It is not Pokt's fault."

"And what of Thrott and his slime creature? The thing could have injured her severely, killed her. All would have been lost."

"The fighting slug? You put this also on Pokt's head? No. How was I to know–"

Felik grabbed Pokt's robes in both hands, drew him close.

"You brought the human aboard the *Helen of Troy*. You wanted the glory of her capture, but you then failed to safeguard the thing once it was aboard ship." He pushed Pokt away from him, smoothed his own robes. "Now, our allies begin to wonder if the Skirni are competent in this affair. I too begin to have doubts where you are concerned." He leaned forward into Pokt's face. "Are you, Pokt-son-of-Mahg? To be doubted?"

"I have said what occurred." Pokt stepped back. "The human's fleeing could not be prevented. The girl and the others cannot leave the *Nova* and hope to survive. The search parties will find them."

Charlie snorted at this. "They have not found me yet, skirnish."

On the screen, Felik ran his bejeweled fingers over his face.

"Search parties?" He almost spat the words at Pokt. "That will not do. *You* must find them, if you hope to redeem Skirni honor in this affair." He jabbed one hand at the holo projection. "Very soon the Spex expect to tunnel to their homeworld. They expect the delivery of the girl to make that possible."

"Yes, and she shall be delivered. But I fail to understand one thing, Master Felik." Pokt's tone said he hoped to divert the conversation from his own shortcomings. "At first, the human girl's parent was to be the nexus, was she not? And this plan failed. Catastrophically."

Zenn's heart rate accelerated at the mention of her mother.

"I am told the parent was a weak vessel," Felik said, turning back to the holo image, speaking more to himself than to Pokt. "An accident was engineered in the animal healer's lab on Mars. This much was successful. The stonehorse brain cells took root in her brain and grew."

"Then why was she not brought to the Spex at once? Why did the human woman not become their nexus?"

"A test run was performed, in the *Retic Crown* orbiting Mars. The healer's in-soma pod was altered. It was taking her into the Indra's brain. But the insertion was... premature. The implanted tissue was imperfect. The Indra detected the pod. The creature's response was unexpected. It was a setback. Our allies admit as much."

"Still," Pokt went on, "this failure... Our almighty allies too have their complications."

Felik held up two fingers to Pokt.

"Letting the girl escape? Twice? Then the encounter with the slime creature? These are more than complications, Pokt."

"I have said the escaping could not be foreseen. And we have the female's father, in the sickbay on the *Queen*." Zenn's breath caught in her throat. "Why do we not use him?" Pokt went on. "As bait? She would come to him, would she not?"

"No, Pokt. I told you. This has been settled."

"But why not?"

"The use of the human male is not your concern," Felik waved away Pokt's protest. "Listen and heed: we and our allies have bargained with the Spex. We assist in taking the Indra ships, the Spex return home, the Indra fleet remains behind."

"The fleet. Yes. Our valued allies, they still do not suspect?"

"No. They preen and prattle and issue orders as always. They continue to believe we are cowed and gullible, that we believe their lies. But we must be vigilant and bide our time. And you, Pokt, must remember, the girl is the key. She is the only one who can pilot the in-soma pod into the primary Indra."

"So you say. But you have never said why this must be. Do not these devices operate with automatic steering? Place her in the pod and let it take the nexus into the beast! Do this and be done."

"Pokt, you know all you need to know. And your duty now is clear. Are you too simple to fulfill it?"

Pokt huffed, slapped his arms against his sides, seemed on the verge of arguing.

"Pokt is no simpleton…" he muttered, the words squeezed out through his clenched teeth. "The human girl will be captured and delivered."

"Yes," Felik said, turning again to the holo image. "She had better be."

Pokt's fists clenched at his sides.

Felik said quietly, "Tick, tick, tick, Pokt-son-of-Mahg."

Pokt grimaced at Felik's back, swiveled on his short legs and stalked out of the bug eye screen's picture, his tail lashing angrily behind him. Charlie paused the screen's image.

Treth turned to Zenn, eyes narrowing. "What *are* you?"

The Groom's cold stare made Zenn flinch.

"She is Novice Zenn Scarlett and my good friend," Jules said, coming to Zenn and resting one mech-hand on her shoulder. "And we must now stand with her and be faithful, as friends do."

"The dolphin's right," Liam said. He pointed to the view screen. "We've gotta keep them from getting their hands on her. I mean, who knows what they'll do?"

"Yes. Of course," Treth agreed. "But we need to know what we are dealing with. Novice?"

"I… I'm not sure what they mean by nexus," Zenn said, not being entirely truthful; she was beginning to have a strong suspicion. "But Treth, he said they have my father. On the *Delphic Queen*."

"That is possible," the Groom said. "The *Queen* is among the taken ships. Just beyond the *Benthic Tson*."

"And does the sickbay there look like the one on the *Helen of Troy*?" Zenn said, hope rising.

"Yes, the *Helen* and the *Queen* are sister ships. The sickbays are identical. I have seen no facilities like them on other ships." But then Treth held up a hand to silence Zenn. "First, we must determine what they want with you."

Zenn wanted to argue, wanted to scream that they had to go and find her father. But she knew the Groom was right. She made herself stop, took a breath. "They… talked about Mom's accident in her lab," she said, struggling to keep her voice calm, to keep her thoughts from racing out of control. "She was working with Indra neural tissue. There was an accident, what we thought then was an accident… Some of the cells were aerosolized, became airborne. After that happened, they ran tests, to make sure she wasn't contaminated by Indra brain tissue. But it sounds like she was."

"But how could that affect you?" Treth asked.

"When the lab accident happened, my mother was pregnant. With me. It sounds like they engineered the Indra tissue or forced a mutation. She could have passed the mutation on to me."

"Your thought-sharing," Jules said. "Could these Indra brain-bits from your mother also explain how you link with the minds of others?"

"Maybe. Probably." It seemed obvious now. She was surprised and angry with herself for not seeing the truth. "If it is, that's why it's been getting stronger every time it happens. It's the Indra neurons. Growing. Forming new synapses. Making new connections."

It's me. It's inside me. It's all my fault…

Treth's stare grew even more intense.

"Charlie," Zenn said then, turning to the Loepith. "Do you have any of your bug eyes on the *Delphic Queen*? In the sickbay?"

"Could be. Not sure," he said. He touched the view screen. The images rapidly cut from shot to shot – a large cargo hold of some kind, an empty dining saloon, a small storage closet, a rusting airlock. And then a sickbay. And on a gurney in the dark at the far corner of the room, a figure. It was human, male, lying on his back. He was motionless. Charlie zoomed in on the figure. It was immobile. Held in a force field? It was impossible to tell. But there was just enough light to see the man's face, his beard…

"It's him…" Zenn breathed the words softly, almost unable to speak.

"Are you certain?" Jules said, coming closer.

"Yes, I'm sure." Tears came, then. She didn't try to stop them.

The screen suddenly flickered, went black, then displayed a cryptic symbol Zenn didn't recognize, accompanied by a low buzzing sound.

"What happened? Bring it back!"

"Nope, better not," Charlie said as he called up another image. "Alarm code. Got a problem." The new view was the shot of the corridor they'd just left. Two Khurspex could be seen. They were examining the part of the passage where Charlie had erected his false wall. Their glowing foreheads glimmered and flashed in agitation.

"Uh-oh." Charlie pointed to something coiled at the bottom of the frame. The Khurspex had another creature with them, restrained on a short, thick leash attached to a harness. The thing was long, the size of a large python but with hundreds of tiny legs along its belly, like a fringe. Its muscular body was covered with smooth, glossy yellow skin covered in brown diamond patterns. The triangular head was pock-marked with half a dozen tiny eyes, the mouth full of chisel-like teeth. Sprouting from the head were three fleshy stalks; they terminated in flared growths of some sort, like tropical orchids, but made of thin, flexible skin. The creature swept these "flowers" back and forth across the floor.

"What is that, Charlie?" Zenn said, trying to get a better look at the thing.

"Sniffer snake," Charlie said. He ripped the view screen off the wall, compressed it back down to a handkerchief-sized square and thrust it back into this vest. "We gotta go! Go right now."

"I thought you said the Spex couldn't find you," Liam said as they set off at a quick trot.

"Spex? No! Sniffers… maybe."

They came to the stairway's exit, rushed out into a short corridor, then into yet another stairwell, which they descended rapidly. Finally, they entered a wide passage that led to a dead end. Charlie slid aside another hidden panel, and they stepped out into a long, low-ceilinged room, its floor littered with great piles of garbage and discarded packing crates.

"Where are we?" Liam asked, peering into the darkness beyond the pools of light from Jules's walksuit headlights.

"Must be the lower deck," Treth said. "Lifeboat bay. Charlie, any lifeboats still functioning?"

"Lifeboats," Zenn said. "We could take one to the *Queen*, couldn't we? We could get to my father."

"Not likely," Charlie scoffed. "No boats left. No docking ports to use, anyway. They sealed most of em. And you only get to the trip-ship on shuttles. Only take a shuttle from the docking ports. All those dock ports guarded."

"The functioning shuttle ports," Treth said. "Where's the closest?"

"Down at the *Ghestan Star*. She's the one. But why even try? Every other ship is bad deadly. Breathe in one, can't breathe in the next, too hot, then too heavy, then too wet."

"But *you* did it," Treth said. "You made it through the other ships. How?" She reached out to take him by one shoulder. "Charlie, is there a way to reach the *Star*?"

"Could be, could be," he said, ducking out of her grasp. "But not for this many. Not the way I came. This many-many would have to go some bad, hard places to get that far."

Treth turned to the others. "We have no choice. We must reach the shuttle bay of the *Ghestan Star*. From there, we can access the central ship."

"But why?" Liam protested. "If Scarlett here is the damn nexus thing, the key to their whole plan, can't we just... hide her, keep her away from them?"

"We cannot remain concealed in this ship forever," Treth said. Zenn knew she was right. They had to leave or be captured.

"But didn't you say Indras can't tunnel all the way back to the Accord?" Liam protested.

"They cannot. Not with the tech we possess. We must find a way through these ships. After we are aboard the central ship, the Khurspex technology that brought us here will allow us to tunnel home."

"If we do this," Jules said, "if we indeed reach this central tripping-ship, do you know how to use the Khurspex science? To cross this large and horrible distance?"

Treth gave him a somber look. "One step at a time, dolphin."

"My father. We have to try and get to him. We have to!"

Treth leveled her eyes at Zenn. "Everyone, on all the ships, is depending on us, Novice. We cannot risk their lives for the sake of any one person. You understand what I am saying?" Zenn nodded yes. But she wasn't going to give up. Not yet. There had to be a way.

"Charlie." She turned to the Loepith. "What ships are between us and the *Ghestan Star*?"

"That would be the *Prodigious*, then the *Dancer* and the *Tson*, next the *Queen*, and, after her, the *Star*."

"So, the *Delphic Queen* is on the way to the shuttle ports on the *Star*," Zenn said.

"I know this, Novice," Treth said.

"I have an idea," Zenn said. She slipped off her backpack, set it down and began digging through the contents.

"But this crusher ship," Jules said. "It is a foul and broiling place, I believe."

"Foul enough," Charlie said. "Hotter than five suns, I'd say."

"Something in your bag of tricks, Scarlett?" Liam said.

"Acadarine; yes, here it is," she said, holding up a large tube. "It's a nano-augmented antipyretic administered to megafauna during some surgeries."

"Yeah, uh… in terms a towner school drop-out can understand, please?" Liam said.

"It's a drug we give to really big animals to bring down their body temperature when we operate. As the body cools, vessels constrict, slows blood loss."

"Big animals? What, like whalehounds the size of a house and stuff? Is it safe for us?"

"I don't actually know. I'm not a human-Asent doctor, Liam. I'm not even qualified to treat animals. Technically. But I think… if I cut the dose way down and mix it with a blood conditioner, it could help protect our brains and internal organs. Not sure if it'll do anything for the epidermis…"

"Scarlett?" Liam shook his head at her.

"We might get a nasty sunburn."

"Will the effect last long enough to traverse the *Prodigious*?" Treth asked.

"I'm not positive. This hasn't been tried before."

"So, that's our choice?" Liam said. "Captured by the Spook Shepherds, or roasted like a Solstice goose."

"Zenn Scarlett will not allow our roasting," Jules said. "She is a well-versed novice. Her methods will shield us from the oppressive heat." He bent to whisper to her: "Won't they?"

"Shielded from the burning of a crusher?" Charlie hooted. "Not likely in that ship."

"Shielding..." Treth said, but to no one in particular. She stared for a moment into the air before her, thinking, then she spoke fast, looking back the way they'd just come, "You will proceed to the airlock leading to the *Prodigious*. I will join you there."

"Join us?" Zenn was baffled and not a little alarmed. "Where are you going?"

"This ship's Indra chamber," the Groom said. Zenn wanted to protest, wanted to grab the woman and tell her she couldn't leave them, but she knew it would do no good – Treth was already squeezing past Jules and moving off.

"But why?" Zenn's mind raced as she tried to imagine what she could say to Treth to keep her there with them.

"The Loepith knows the way; go quickly," Treth said. "Wait for me there. I won't be long."

TWENTY

Charlie led them rapidly up several decks. At every blind corner, they paused to check the way ahead before setting off again.

"Zenn Scarlett," Jules said, "this all seems to me a risk-filled plan. I feel we may be gambling with unlucky cards in our hands."

"It's our best chance right now, Jules," Zenn told him, trying to sound confident. "We'll find my father. And we'll get to the center ship. And then… we'll all go home."

She hoped it sounded more plausible to him than to her.

"Scarlett," Liam said as Jules moved ahead to walk next to Charlie. "I didn't have a chance to say before. But it was good to set eyes on you again. I mean, really good."

"I was glad to see you, too, Liam," she said.

"So, it sounded like to make this nexus thing work, the Skirnis wanted you to go into the Indra's head?"

"Yes, apparently," she said, still reluctant to deal with the full implications of what they intended for her. "An in-soma insertion."

"Yeah, the thing you used to go into the body of the swamp sloo back at the cloister. But inside an Indra – kinda dangerous, right?"

"There's a lot of radiation in an Indra's skull," she told him. "But from what they said, they think I'd be protected. Because of the Indra tissue in… in my brain. When the in-soma pod enters the skull, the Indra will see me as part of itself. Won't spike an immune response. Seems to be the theory, anyway."

"Is it a good one? This theory? Will you be OK?"

"I don't know, Liam. It didn't do my mom any good."

They went on in silence for a while.

"Um… does it make you feel weird, what's going on inside you?" He gave her an anxious look. "Can you, like, tell what people are thinking?"

"No," she said, smiling at his sudden concern. "It's not like that. You don't have to worry. I'm not reading your mind or anything."

"That's a relief," he said, then added with his usual smirk, "Not that I'm thinking anything, you know, that I wouldn't want you to know."

"Oh. Really?"

"Look, Scarlett," he said, lowering his voice. "I need to say something to make sure you understand. I'm sorry for what happened back at the cloister. What I did to the animals, letting them loose, making you all look bad. I was stupid for not figuring the whole thing out sooner, for not figuring out a way to stop Vic trying to take your land. Maybe I was… Maybe Graad tried to scare me and it worked. But I wasn't scared for me. I was scared cause he said he'd hurt you if I told. I was more scared than I'd ever been… because if anything had happened to you, I'd never… Well, I just want you know that."

She knew how Liam felt. Of course she knew. The memory of his arms around her, his kiss, his scent, his body's warmth against hers in the cool night air outside the cage of the thirty-foot insectoid predator that had nearly escaped its enclosure, an escape that surely would have left them, and possibly everyone in the cloister, dead. No, it all remained as unforgettable and as deeply, profoundly unsettling to Zenn as the night it happened.

"Liam." She took a long breath and cast about, searching for words. "You may not have noticed, but I'm not like the girls you know. The girls in Arsia, the other girls on Mars."

His expression told her that these weren't the words he was expecting. But he soon recovered.

"Uh-huh. Most of the girls I know don't climb into a pod-capsule thing and let a swamp sloo swallow them. On purpose. They don't risk their life to keep a centipede long as a bus from getting out of its cage and slaughtering everyone in sight. Yeah, you're special. That's for sure."

"No. I mean, I didn't exactly grow up in a normal family. You know, doing the normal things. Playing with other kids, going to parties, worrying about what dress to wear to the dance… talking to boys."

"Oh. I get it. You're the snow princess. Living in her cloud castle. In Nevermore Land. Above the rest of us."

"I think you're mixing up your fairy tales. But no. I never once felt like I was above anybody. I felt like I was just too different for anyone to want to get to know. Like a permanent outsider."

"What? Outside looking in? You wanted to be a towner?"

"I didn't want that, either. No offense, but a lot of towners are narrow-minded and... well, let's just say they're people like Vic LeClerc. They'd just as soon she'd shut down the cloister and run us off our land. But..." She raised a hand to keep him from interrupting. "What I'm saying is that what happened that night – you can't just do that, just up and kiss me and expect me to have anything like a normal Arsia-girl response. I don't even know the range of responses an Arsia girl would select from."

"The range of..." Liam sputtered. "You make it sound like some kind of... science project."

"Yes," Zenn said, "That's exactly what I'm saying. Me having the totally wrong response. Liam, I grew up surrounded by scientists or animals. Then Mom died. Dad freaked out and left. And I was on my own. That's my childhood. Now, half the time I don't know what I'm supposed to feel around people. Make that ninety percent of the time. I'm not sure I'm even able to feel what I'm supposed to be able to feel about another person who... a person who's..."

"A person like me? A towner kid?" Liam did a good imitation of being insulted.

"Like a boy. A boy my own age with... hormones and all. I do know how sexual attraction works, you know. I've read the books."

"Nine Hells, Scarlett, why don't you just stick me under a damn microscope or something?"

Zenn shook her head, mad at herself and getting madder.

She wasn't explaining this right at all. She didn't know how to tell him what was going on inside her. She just didn't have the vocabulary.

"Faster moving," Charlie called back to them as he broke into a trot. "Groomish said to reach the *Prodigious* fast. Faster is better."

"Great," Liam fumed. "Now monkey-boy is giving us orders."

"His name's Charlie."

"Yeah. Sure. Sorry." He was quiet for a moment as they hurried to keep up with the Loepith and Jules. "So, let's just get your microscope off of me and my hormones for the time being, OK?"

"Good idea."

"About this crusher ship. Hot enough inside to make my head, like, burst into flames?"

"No. Not quite." She repressed a grin.

"They say there are places on Earth now that get almost that hot, you know, with the weather going totally crazy. Humans can't even live in the big desert zones anymore."

"Right," she said. "Along the equator, it's gotten pretty bad."

"Still, it'd be something to see. Earth, I mean. You ever want to go?"

"Well, sure. But there are other planets I'd probably rather visit first."

"Not me," he said. "I'd go there. See the places where forests just go on for miles. And oceans. Nine hells, can you imagine? So much water you can't even see across? That'd be something."

"So," he said after a few moments of silence, "inside the crusher is way hotter than a desert. But we wouldn't, like, burn up?"

"No, Liam, it's not that hot. It takes temperatures over five hundred degrees Fahrenheit to ignite flesh. Depending on fat and moisture content, of course."

"Right, of course. Well, how hot is hot?"

"Crusher ships are designed for thermal extremophiles. But even they can't survive anything above two hundred twenty degrees. So, flesh-igniting heat inside the ship? No. Hot enough to destroy the membranes lining your lungs? Likely."

"And this acadama-stuff," he said. "The medicine you have. It'll protect us from that?"

"It's never been tested for something like this," she admitted. "But it might just work."

"Scarlett," he said as the passage narrowed and he dropped back to trot along behind her. "You are such a comfort."

Fifteen minutes later, Charlie brought them to a halt in front of the airlock leading to the *Prodigious*. Too exhausted to seek out the nearest cabins with bunks, they found comfort wherever they could and settled in to wait for Treth. Zenn took off her backpack and stretched out on a length of dirty carpeting. Emerging from her pack, Katie inquired about when they were going to eat, and was told "later" yet again. After a frustrated snort, she nestled down to sleep next to Zenn. Charlie curled up in the darkest corner he could find, while Jules just locked down his walksuit where he stood and, one eye closed, was soon snoring softly. Liam said one of them should stand watch. Then he slid down against the bulkhead opposite Zenn and immediately fell asleep.

Zenn closed her eyes but was somehow too exhausted to doze off. Disconnected images tumbled through her mind like haphazard scenes from a blink-nov. There was also the distant clang and whisper of the ship – all sounding to her distracted mind like a squad of Khurspex guards coming down the passageway.

When at last she did fall into a fitful sleep, it was only to be startled awake by a hand on her shoulder. It was Treth. She held a wide, black mesh belt. Attached to it was an oblong metal device like an oversized buckle.

"So, that's gonna protect us from being broiled alive," Liam said through an expansive yawn. "What is it? Jar of sunscreen?"

"It is a scrim-shield," Treth said. "It shelters the body of a groom during Indra tunneling. I knew I would find a spare unit in the pilot's room."

Then she dropped into a squat and began tinkering with the shield, depressing invisible pressure plates that caused the device to open with a loud click, exposing its tangle of clockwork innards.

"I can expand its radius of protection for a short period. It should cover an area large enough to contain us all. In tandem with the Novice's medicine, we should have time enough to transit the *Prodigious* and reach the ship beyond. With luck."

"Luck?" Liam said, standing up. "Right…"

While Treth tinkered with the scrim, Zenn took the tube of Acadarine paste from her pack and attempted to quickly work out the lowered dosages required to avoid poisoning them all. After mixing it with a measure of powdered blood conditioner, she parceled out the individual doses for each of them.

"Put out your hand, Liam," she said. He obeyed and, using the tip of a scalpel, she placed a tiny amount of the mixture in his palm. "Now lick it off."

He raised his eyebrows at her.

"OK, but if I croak, I'm suing for malpractice."

He licked his palm.

"Gaaah!" His face contorted as if he'd bitten into a lemon. "Damn. You coulda warned me."

"No, I couldn't. I've never tasted it," she told him.

"Great. Tucker the lab rat, at your service."

"Somebody had to go first," she said, then she went around to measure out the drug to each of the others in turn.

Minutes later, Zenn could feel the effect of the antipyretic taking hold, as first her finger tips, then her arms, then her entire body beginning to feel chilled. Shivering slightly, she watched as Charlie twisted together a final pair of wires inside an open wall panel next to the airlock.

"Those Spex, they're in a bad way now," he said, examining his handiwork. "But they could still be looking at ship's systems. When they do, what'll they see? No open airlock here! Just a little data misfire."

"And if they don't see it that way?" Liam wondered.

"It doesn't matter," Treth said. "We cannot go back."

"How long will this groom-scrim protect us? From all

that heat?" Jules asked, his mech-legs fidgeting beneath him.

"The power cell should have sufficient charge for ten to twelve minutes," Treth said, buckling the belt around her waist and stepping over to the airlock. Jules bobbed his head in agitation, prompting Treth to add, "Ample time, dolphin."

"But all that heat! Zenn Scarlett, are you certain I will be capable?"

Zenn wasn't sure. But she couldn't say that.

"You're starting to feel the cold, right?" He nodded. "That's a good sign. You can do this, Jules."

"You are most positive? I am not."

"I'll bet you," she said. "Five units says you can."

"Oh?" His voiced quivered. "Five units?" Then, his voice a little stronger, "Let us say ten units. As between friends."

"Yes. Let's say ten." She threw her arms across his body to hug him, then stood back, giving him the most encouraging smile she could manage.

"So, Jules, you're a betting man, huh?" Liam said.

"A betting cetacean," Jules corrected him. "But this is the one wager I am hoping to lose. One must appreciate the ironic humor. Betting against one's own self."

"Well, I bet you'll do fine," Liam said. He patted Jules's flank.

Zenn tried to give Katie her small dose, but the rikkaset took one sniff of the mixture and refused to eat it. Zenn wiped the paste on her paw; Katie licked and spat.

"Bad, bad," she signed at Zenn, blinking her eyes. "Not good to eat."

"Sorry," Zenn told her. "But Katie needs it." Then she took a length of bandaging from her pack and started to wrap it around the rikkaset.

"Katie must stay in this cloth until I say to come out. Understand?" she signed and spoke the words.

"Katie understand," the little creature signed back. "Big trip? Katie going big trip?"

"No, little trip. Done soon. Katie stay." Then Zenn pulled the bandaging over the animal's head and tucked the balled-up cloth down securely into the pack before refastening the flap and slipping her arms into the straps.

At the bulkhead, Charlie pushed a key on the control panel and, with the groan of long-dormant gears, the huge airlock door slowly withdrew into the ceiling. They all looked at Treth.

"Gather around me," she told them. "The scrim's effective area will cover a space approximately ten feet by five. Do not step beyond that boundary."

"How do we know where the boundary is?" Liam asked as they all crowded into the airlock and huddled around the Groom.

"You'll know," Treth said, and she activated the scrim. A veil of faint blue-violet light shimmered to life, hugging the Groom's body. She dialed a small control wheel on the belt, and the light detached itself from her, lifting into the air and expanding until it formed a translucent dome just large enough for all of them to crouch beneath.

"When I open the second door, we will move as one. The exit airlock is directly opposite on this same deck."

They looked on intently as Charlie activated the lock control. The door behind them closed again, and the second door in front cracked open and slid up; a line of dull orange light appeared and spilled into the lock. The line of light grew wider and brighter as the door groaned upward; wisps of smoggy mist drifted in to swirl around the edge of the scrim's protective field. A sharp scent like scorched metal and burning oil rose up to fill Zenn's nostrils.

TWENTY-ONE

The ruddy light pouring in through the rising airlock door crept above Zenn's knees, and the heat climbed with it, hot, then hotter. By the time, the door was up high enough for them to move into the *Prodigious*, the temperature had soared. Zenn's shivering quickly ceased. Even with the scrim's protection, the air burned Zenn's cheeks and forehead, making her feel as if her skin was cooking. The scrim's shape was visibly deformed as they entered the heavy atmosphere of the ship, and they had to duck even lower to remain beneath the top of the shimmering bubble.

"Like I said," Charlie said, scurrying along behind Treth, "five-suns hot."

"Stay together. Jules, keep up," Treth called out as they moved ahead. Jules made a high-pitched squeaking noise and tried to move faster. But he was forced to stoop over awkwardly to remain below the scrim, and he bumped into Zenn, almost pushing her out of the scrim's field.

"Sorry. Most sorry," he squawked. "I'm so clumsy…"

"Jules, don't worry. I'll lean over so you can see where

you're going." The act of speaking drew a draught of searing air into Zenn's throat. Breathing through her nose helped, but only a little. Sweat ran down her forehead in rivulets, stinging her eyes. Then she realized the scrim bubble was slowly filling with steam – it was the water from the misters on Jules's walksuit, vaporizing into a hot, wet fog.

As they settled into an erratic, fast-walking rhythm, Zenn squinted to see ahead in the orange-brown gloom. The deck they were on had a high, curved ceiling of heavy, red-bronze-colored plating, giving her the feeling of moving through a gigantic artery. Huge pipelines and runs of tubing twisted along the walls before disappearing into irregularly spaced holes. A low-frequency pulsating sound pounded at them from somewhere, like a distant heartbeat at first, but growing steadily louder as they went deeper into the ship.

They rounded a corner, and something moved in the heat-shimmered murk ahead of them. The shape dodged into a dark recess behind a small forest of piping. The thing was flat, glossy black, eight or ten feet long. Zenn thought she'd glimpsed pincers.

"Did you see that?" Liam said, moving close behind Zenn. "What was it?"

"Fire-mite," Charlie said.

"Dangerous?" Liam asked.

"They hunt… in packs," Charlie said, spacing out his words to keep from burning his throat. "If this one… is alone… won't… bother us."

"What do they… hunt?" Liam wondered, wiping his sweat-soaked hair from his face. Zenn knew but didn't want to inhale the hot air it would take to tell him: native predators of the Vhulk homeworld of Dante Nine, fire-mites ate only live or recently killed prey. Zenn also wanted to say there shouldn't be fire-mites running loose in a passenger ship.

"We must not… waste breath," Treth barked. She had to raise her voice to be heard over the thunderous din coming at them in ever-stronger waves. "We will pass through… an engineering bay ahead. Then bear to the right."

The cavernous room they entered next was at least five hundred feet long. No ceiling was visible in the burning smog above them. Through the swirling haze, Zenn could now see the outlines of three large, squat forms in the distance, laboring before a bank of huge structures that took up the entire center of the space. As they hurried to cross the vast room, more details emerged. The three forms gradually resolved into identifiable creatures: Dantean Vhulks, their heavily muscled, silica-plated bodies well equipped to survive the heat and pressure of their nightless triple-star home planet.

Looking something like giant, prehistoric ground sloths, the Vhulks squatted before four plasma-fusion furnaces big as buildings, their huge, armored arms working at massive lever-type controls mounted in front of them. One of the furnaces was unattended; it bore the marks of an explosion, its metal walls ripped outward, leaving a ragged, still-smoldering hole.

In unison, the three Vhulks swiveled their heads, gazing at Zenn and the others with baleful, slightly bioluminescent eyespots set deep into their blunt-nosed faces.

"Are they… friendly?" Liam asked.

"Their concern… is the plasma boilers that heat the ship," Treth said over the noise from the blazing furnaces. "They should have… no quarrel with us." As they drew closer, the Vhulks lumbered away from their stations, and went as a group to stand looking at something hidden behind the damaged furnace. One of the creatures motioned at them to approach.

Zenn saw then that the three Vhulks had gathered around another of their kind. It lay on the floor, its upper body leaning against a bulkhead wall, eyespots dimmed, body still, except for labored breathing. The Vhulk's massive right arm was badly mangled and burned, the thick armor-like epidermal layer of skin charred black. A viscous gray fluid oozed freely from the wound's carbonized surface.

Zenn put a hand on Treth's shoulder. "It's hurt," she shouted, trying to ignore the pain from the scalding air. "The arm is burned… it looks bad."

The largest of the three Vhulks reached down to gently lift the arm of his wounded comrade, as if to display its injury.

"It's asking… for our help," Zenn said. "It will die… unless we do something."

"Five-suns hot," Charlie croaked. "No time."

"Treth, it will only… take a minute. Long enough… to seal the wound."

"Zenn Scarlett," Jules said, his overheated Transvox circuitry hissing with static. "It is too hot in temperature. Can you truly succeed in this?"

She didn't know. But she had to try. "Treth," she pleaded. "Please."

One of the other Vhulks raised its arms up towards them, in what to Zenn was an obvious gesture of desperation. This was too much even for Treth. The Groom held up her hand and brought them to a halt.

"Quickly, then. This way. Stay together."

Treth maneuvered them next to the fallen Vhulk until the creature's upper torso and damaged arm were brought within the edge of the scrim field. Its body radiated heat into their protective bubble, raising more steam, making it even harder to breathe. Zenn slipped off her backpack. Katie poked her nose out of her cloth wrapping, then withdrew again with a short, sharp squeak.

Sweat now pouring from her face, Zenn wiped at her eyes and bent over the appendage of the unconscious Vhulk. A foot-long section of skin had third-degree burns oozing fluid. This was worse than she'd thought. Maybe Jules was right. Maybe this was beyond her abilities. Panic wrapped around her thoughts like a constricting serpent, pulling tight, tighter. No! She pushed back against the fear.

It's not about me! Not about my fear! She silently repeated the mantra Otha had drilled into her during classes. It's about this patient! It's about what I can do for this patient, here, now!

It worked. The words and the memory of Otha, the image of him standing over her, guiding her, stilled her tumbling thoughts.

Yes. She did know what to do! She'd trained for similar wounds. Not exactly the same, but close enough. She conjured up the details of Otha's lecture on extremophile skin structure. A small oasis of calm bloomed and spread within her. She could do it. She would help this patient. She could only hope the artificial gelled skin she had would set up quickly enough to resist the heat and pressure outside the scrim.

Working as fast as she dared, she cut along the bleeding edge of the wound with the caut-shears, sealing the wound as she went, removing a large swath of dead skin and muscle, which she dropped onto the floor.

"That it?" Liam gasped. "You saved it. Good work. Can we... go now?"

"No. Just a little... longer."

The raw slash of subdermal tissue she'd exposed quickly filled with gray-green blood. Using dissolvable hema-clips, she pinched off the few bleeding vessels she'd missed with the caut-shears, blotted up the excess blood with several absorbent pads and took up the canister of dermoplast. Making certain the artificial skin was adhering to the edges of the wound, she sprayed the substance back and forth until the entire damaged area was covered.

Jules wavered on his mech-legs.

"Not breathing... well..." he said. "Breathing... badly."

"Almost... finished," She grabbed the largest gage pneuma-ject in her kit, shoved a vial of broad-spectrum anti-viral and stimulant into its barrel and injected the solution into the intact portion of the Vhulk's arm.

"We must go. Now," Treth said.

"Done." Zenn stood back from the Vhulk, slipped her pack on.

As they started to move, Zenn tapped the dermoplast patch with her knuckle. The patch felt hard and firm. It might just hold.

After they'd gone a short distance, she looked back to see one of the creatures helping the wounded one to sit up. It was coming to, the stimulant taking effect. The Vhulk lifted its arm to its face, examined it, turning it this way and that. The arm flexed normally, the seal unbroken. The plast seemed to be holding. Then all was lost in the thick haze as they hurried on.

Before they had traveled a hundred feet, Treth called out, pointing ahead. "There. Our way out."

Zenn could see nothing but superheated smog. But as the hallway leading to the airlock appeared in the wall ahead, she heard a bubbling, gasping sound from behind her.

"I'm sorry… but my… breathing," Jules wheezed. He was slowing down, having trouble walking. She could hear Liam also breathing hard and glanced back to see that he was supporting Jules under one of his mech-arms. Treth noticed too and had no choice but to slow down. Underneath the static of the Transvox, Jules's already high-pitched dolphinese now rose into an even higher register. "My breath… not… adequate." Zenn was startled to see a thin film of mucus bubbling up at the blowhole on top of his head. His tail flukes seemed to be spasming in short, jerky muscular contractions.

"It's the heat," Zenn said, "…his bronchial linings… going edemic." If the air burned her own lungs as she spoke, Zenn could only imagine what it was doing to the dolphin's delicate membranes.

"What is it… that ails him?" Treth said.

"His airways… swelling shut… excess fluid."

"He must… keep going," Treth said.

"It isn't much farther... Jules, you have to–" Zenn stopped speaking. In front, Treth had raised her arm to stop them again. Out of the seething mist, blocking the way forward, Zenn saw a low black shape scuttling from shadow to shadow. A piercing, inhuman scream knifed through the air. It was answered by another scream somewhere in the smoking mists.

Another shape appeared – but made no move to hide. Then there were three, then six of them. Flattened ten-foot bodies slung low to the ground, serrated pincers held at the ready, the fire-mites raised and lowered themselves on a tangle of slithering legs, their six spider-like predator's eyes following every move of the prey before them.

"Are they...?" Liam sputtered.

"A hunting pack," Charlie cried. "Mites hunt in packs."

TWENTY-TWO

"Everyone... stay still," Treth said as she drew Pokt's plasma weapon from her belt. She brought it to bear on the nearest mite. "After I fire... we will run... for the airlock."

The Groom squeezed the stick, and the lightning stream arced through the haze. It caught the fire-mite squarely in its central thorax – and glanced harmlessly off the creature's thick chitin armor. The mite shook itself and, unfazed, began to creep toward them.

"Fire again," Charlie screeched. "Fire, fire!"

Treth aimed and squeezed off another shot, striking the creature on one of its large claws but still with no visible effect. Zenn could've told Treth why: fire-mites were extremophiles, and their armor had evolved to withstand precisely the sort of super-heated energy the plasma weapon produced.

"We must find... another way. Go back." As Treth spoke, four more mites crept up behind them, cutting off retreat.

A rasping intake of air sounded behind Zenn and Jules lost his balance, teetered momentarily and tipped forward, falling into Zenn and Treth. Liam grunted with the effort of trying to keep Jules from knocking them all out of the scrim's protective dome. Huddling up closer to her, Charlie whimpered pitifully.

The circling pack drew in from all sides. The closest mite was almost inside the scrim. Zenn could hear the sound of its claws, the serrated pincers clacking inches from her face. Then Liam was pressing up next to her; he was trying to put himself between her and the approaching creature.

Then the snapping claws, and the mite they were attached to, were gone. Zenn shifted just enough to see around Jules and Liam. A few feet away, one of the Vhulk stokers held the attacking fire-mite in one massive paw. Lifting the struggling predator as if it were weightless, the Vhulk hurled it into the murky air and out of sight. It landed somewhere with a crunch of cracking chitin and a loud screech. Zenn saw that two more Vhulks had also waded into the pack and were flinging away any creature that hadn't already retreated into the shadows.

When there were no more mites to be seen, the three Vhulks stood waiting until Zenn and the others reached the corridor leading to the airlock. Then the Vhulks lumbered off into the hellish miasma and were gone.

"Stay with me," Treth shouted, moving close enough to the bulkhead to allow the scrim's outer boundary to make contact with it. "Charlie..." The Loepith popped the cover off the control panel and began rewiring the circuits inside.

"Treth," Zenn shouted, pointing to the scrim above their heads. "Look." The thin, purple-green bubble that surrounded them had begun to show tiny gaps on its surface, as if the delicate web were being broken apart in a dozen places.

"The scrim. It's tearing," Liam said.

"Get closer," Treth said. "Move in... closer to me."

Through the holes appearing in the scrim, the shocking heat stabbed like scalpel tips penetrating Zenn's face, the back of her neck, her hands. She felt as if the hair on her head was about to combust. Charlie frantically spliced together one last pair of wires, then punched at the airlock keypad.

"Simple as that," he said.

Nothing happened.

"Bad luck. All bad," Charlie muttered. He twisted another pair of wires, punched at the pad again.

Zenn's next breath seethed like molten metal poured down her throat. She didn't dare inhale again. Her consciousness began to stutter and fade. She was passing out.

Seconds later, she was lying on her side in the dark, gulping air into her lungs – stinging draughts of wondrous, delicious, ice-cold air. They'd made it! They were in the *Symmetry Dancer*. But after the *Prodigious*, it felt as if she was tasting air from the subfreezing Martian icecaps. It was glorious beyond words.

She rolled to a sitting position and saw Jules tipped against the nearest wall, his flanks heaving as he greedily sucked in the cooling air and expelled it rapidly through his blowhole. Liam sat next to him, head hanging down between his knees, chest pumping. Charlie lay flat on his back, also savoring the *Dancer*'s air. Beyond him in the corridor stood Treth, leaning with one arm on the bulkhead. Zenn no longer felt the chilling effect of the antipyretic; the intense heat must have forced their bodies to dissipate it quickly, but it had apparently lasted long enough to be of some help.

Zenn felt Katie squirming in the backpack. She reached behind her to undo the flap, and the rikkaset hopped to the floor.

"Friend-Zenn," she signed irritably. "Too hot for Katie. No fun. Stinky."

"Sorry," Zenn signed, and stroked Katie's tufted ears.

"Are you better now?" she asked Jules. "Getting enough air?"

"Enough, yes. Much better now," he replied, walking over to where she sat. "I must report I am very happy to be out of that place. I thought for a moment you would need to leave me behind. That was a frightful moment."

Zenn stood. She pulled the dolphin's smooth, velvety head down toward her with both hands and rested her forehead against his chin.

"You know I would never leave you," she told him quietly. "You know that, right?"

"You can never tell what another will do," he told her, not moving from her grasp. She held his beak in her hands and looked into his eyes.

"Well, unless they're your friend. And I'm telling you that I wouldn't have left you. I couldn't leave you. Do you know why?"

"Why then?"

She gave his smiling beak a gentle shake. "Because I won. And you owe me ten units."

TWENTY-THREE

One of the most technically advanced and luxurious private starships ever commissioned, the *Symmetry Dancer* had belonged to a succession of wealthy humans and Asents: a trillionaire Alcyon syn-gen inventor, several mega-star entertainers, one best-selling blink-nov writer and an Oortish mine-owner-turned-politician – who was currently learning about life in the penal colony on Titan after some rather serious computational errors in his tax returns. Just before the starship vanished a year and a half ago, the *Dancer* was purchased by the royal family of the Leukkan Kire. The Kiran ambassador to the Accord was aboard when it was taken, and the Kire's king and queen had offered a small planetoid as reward for his safe return. The reward was never claimed.

After allowing a few minutes for them all to rest and recover, Treth came back from her short recon trip to give them the bad news: the door leading into the interior of the *Dancer* was code-locked.

"Locked, yes," Charlie said, brandishing his twine at the Groom as he shuffled up to the door. "Knew it would be."

“You knew?” Treth said as the Loepith pulled an access panel off the wall and peered into the hole.

“Been here before, haven’t I?” He poked at his sleeve screen, then brought it up close to face, squinting at it.

“Charlie,” Treth said, “we need to get inside. Quickly.”

“Need to find the numbers, don’t I?” Charlie told her, not looking up. “Need the code. For the door. Not all here, though, is it?” He frowned at the sleeve screen read out. “Only a part left. The heat in that ship. Did some damage.”

He went to the door and typed with one finger at the keypad.

“Might remember the missing bits, though. Maybe.” He had barely spoken the words when a bell-like tone rang out, followed by a soft, lilting voice that seemed to come out of the air around them.

“Charlieee…” the voice said. It sounded happy.

“Oh no…” Charlie’s eyes went wide. “Lost data, lost too much. Didn’t mean to do that.”

“What just happened?” Treth asked.

“Made a mistake, didn’t I?” Charlie moaned, and covered his face with his hands, rocking back and forth. On the floor next to Zenn, Katie looked around apprehensively.

“What did you do?” Liam said. “Was it bad?”

“Charlieee.” The voice spoke again, sultry, female, emanating from nowhere. Then Zenn saw it, saw her, standing in the center of the room – which a second ago had been empty. “You’ve come back,” the voice said. “I’m so pleased to see you.”

The owner of the voice was a beautiful… no, a ravishing human female with intricately styled auburn hair and a slinky, very expensive-looking optiweave evening gown.

Seeing the apparition suddenly appear, Katie puffed up her tail fur and blended out of sight.

"I knew you'd come back," the beautiful woman said, then bent to take Charlie's whiskered chin into her hand.

"Awww, no, no..." he muttered miserably. Then, as Zenn and the others watched, the beautiful woman seemed to melt, turning transparent with a short burst of static. When she came back into focus, she was no longer a human woman. She had become a Loepith; a female Loepith, Zenn thought, by the body build and lack of facial whiskers. She wore a uniform similar to Charlie's but new and spotless.

"Did you think I'd forget?" The shape had altered, but the newly appeared Loepith continued to speak to Charlie with the husky tones of the human seductress she had been moments before. It made for a strange combination.

"Did you see this event?" Jules said. "She changed entire."

"It's a holo-projection, Jules," Zenn said, moving in to get a closer look. Katie reappeared next to Zenn, apparently reassured it was safe. She sniffed at the apparition but, smelling nothing, became suspicious again, her fur rising.

"Not a holo. Worse," Charlie said. "A simstriss. The *Dancer's* simstriss."

"They're an advanced AI construct," Treth said. "Used onboard the higher-grade ships. Charlie, she seems to know you. How is this?"

"From before," Charlie whined as he sat down despondently on the floor. "Been through it all before, haven't I? Now I'm back in it. Bad luck, bad and worse." As he spoke, the simulated Loepith sat down next to him and nuzzled into his shoulder.

"Charlieee..." The sim-Loepith purred, looking at him with what could only be described as adoration. "I was so hoping you'd return. I've been quite bored without you. The *Dancer* is so very lonely without my usual quota of guests to attend to. And, I must remind you, you promised to stay. When you left me, I was so bored and lonely with not a soul to take care of. But it doesn't matter. You're back now." She hugged him to her. He squinted his eyes shut.

"These simstriss types," Jules said, "do they always change in this way? As you look at them? It is disconcerting."

"They read the bio-signature of the species they interact with," Treth said, "then assume the most suitable appearance."

"Truly?" Jules asked. "Hello," he said, leaning down toward Charlie and the sim-Loepith at his side. "My name is Jules V Vancouver. What is your name? Testing. Testing."

The simstriss tilted her face up toward Jules and, after a brief fadeout, resolved herself into a dolphin that lifted into the air. The walksuit that materialized around the sim-dolphin was like Jules's rig, only sleeker and newer.

"My name is Lu, Guest Services Agent and Hospitality Specialist Zero-slash-delta-delta," the sim-dolphin said, the voice still unchanged. "Welcome aboard the *Symmetry Dancer*, Guest Vancouver. I do hope you and your companions will be with us for our entire voyage. However, I must admit I have not been informed of our destination. I'm sure this information will be forthcoming soon. In the meantime, if there is anything I can do to make your time on board more enjoyable, please do not hesitate to ask."

"Yes, Lu, there is one thing," Treth said, stepping between Jules and the sim. "We would like to exit this holding area and enter the ship. Can you assist us with that?"

"For your safety, this holding area has been locked," Lu said pleasantly. As she spoke, she transformed into a Procyoni groom, complete with intricate anitats and face piercings like Treth's but with a cascade of dark brown hair falling across her shoulders.

"Can you unlock it? Please."

"I regret to inform the guest that this holding area must remain secured until authorized ship's officers arrive," the sim-groom said. "May I offer you refreshments while we wait? Tea? Coffee? Kipfruit gelato?"

Zenn's mouth watered at the mention of iced kipfruit. Treth ignored the offer.

"Ship's officers? Do you mean the Khurspex?"

"Yes, the Khurspex code-admins. They are en route now. Estimated shuttle arrival time is fifteen minutes. I'm sure they will be able to answer all your questions."

"We should leave this place," Jules said. "Those Khurspex will come. They will not treat us nicely."

"Can we go back into the crusher?" Liam said.

"No," Treth said flatly, unbuckling the scrim-field generator and dropping it to the deck. "The power cells are depleted."

"Charlieee," the simstriss looked at Charlie and was once more a Loepith. "You must not leave again. Being here without you, it's simply not to be endured. You will stay this time? I so hope you will stay."

Charlie looked up pitifully at Zenn and the others, then lowered his face into his hands again.

"Lu," Treth said. "I am Treth Loreth Shansdaughter, Stonehorse Groom, LSA starliner *Helen of Troy*. I order you to open the code-locked door."

"I am so sorry to remind the guest that this holding area must remain secured until authorized ship's officers arrive," the simstriss repeated, smiling. "May I offer you–"

"This construct is obviously malfunctioning," Treth said, "to ignore the direct command of a union groom."

"Been tampered with," Charlie said miserably. "Had to make adjustments the last time, didn't I? To get through."

"What kind of adjustments?" Treth asked.

"Minor, so I thought. Spex had the *Dancer* all sewn up tight so no one could pass. Fiddled the simstriss config-sys to breach the lockdown protocol. And so, the sim, it... Well, then, as you see, it... attached itself."

"What?" Liam said, peering at the simstriss. "You saying this thing fell in love with you?"

"Love? With me? Well, then... How could it be..." Charlie's voice trailed off into a mutter.

"Our Charlie's a lady's man," Liam laughed, catching Zenn's eye. She laughed too and realized this was something she hadn't done in quite some time.

"You altered it once, Charlie," Treth said. "Can you do so again?"

"Not so easy," Charlie said "Lost my data. Wrong code changes could crash it all down. Crash ship's systems. Life support, too. Bad luck for all of us in here."

Treth was silent for a moment, then went to stand over Charlie and the simstriss. "Lu, I know this is a hard thing for you, but... Charlie wants to leave."

"This would be unfortunate. I am afraid it simply cannot be allowed." The simstriss hugged him closer. "You do not wish to leave me, do you, Charlie?"

"Uhh..." Charlie looked at Treth, who nodded at him. "Yes? Yes. I'm afraid I might."

"But I don't want you to leave, Charlie. The boredom. No one to care for. Please, you simply mustn't." She looked up at Treth. "We regret to inform you it cannot be allowed."

"We understand your situation, Lu," Treth said, speaking quickly. "And I have a proposition. Would you be willing to let the rest of us proceed into the *Dancer*... if Charlie promised to stay?"

"Treth," Zenn couldn't believe what she was hearing.

"Lu?" Treth ignored Zenn's protest.

"You would promise to stay with me?" Lu asked, the expression on her Loepith face hopeful and wide-eyed. "You would stay forever? To be my one and only guest? I would see to your every requirement."

Charlie looked from Treth to Zenn and back, his eyes almost rolling in his head.

"I... would promise," he said, his entire body seeming to shrink into itself at the prospect.

Loepith-Lu smiled a wide, brown-toothed grin. "Yes! He promises." Standing up to address Treth, Lu was once again the brown-haired Procyoni groom. "Central hatchway deck 3 is now unlocked for guest boarding. Welcome, and have a pleasant journey aboard the *Symmetry Dancer*. Please watch your step."

"Treth, no." Zenn was gripped by helpless rage. They couldn't leave him. Not after all he'd done to help them.

The Groom took Zenn by the shoulders and propelled her toward the doorway that now stood open.

"No arguments, Novice. We must go." Treth fixed her eyes on Zenn. "We must, if we are to have any hope of helping all the others."

Jules looked at Charlie uncertainly, then went to the doorway. Zenn knew Treth was right; this was their only choice, to get away, to help the others, to somehow make it to the *Delphic Queen* and find her father.

"Treth," she said, desperate.

"You must trust me, Novice," Treth said quietly, guiding Zenn through the doorway.

Lu draped her lanky Loepith arms around Charlie. At the doorway, Treth turned.

"Charlie?" He looked up at her hopelessly. Then, in one swift motion, Treth plunged her hand into the guts of the open control panel next to the door and yanked out a tangled, sparking wad of wires. A starburst of light bathed the room and the body of Lu-Loepith went white with static and vanished. "Run!" Treth yelled at Charlie.

"No! Not good," he yelped, leaping to his feet, holding his head in both hands and doing a little jig of distress. "She'll be mad now. Memware's not stable. She'll be dangerous mad."

"Too bad," Treth covered the distance to Charlie in three strides, grabbed him by the rags of his uniform and propelled him ahead of her through the door. "Everybody move, into the ship! The sim will reconstitute. We don't want to be on board when she does."

TWENTY-FOUR

"How long before the sim comes back?" Liam asked anxiously, running alongside Treth as they all raced through the *Dancer's* tidy, well-lit corridors; apparently, the ship's auto-maintenance systems were all still fully functional.

"Uncertain," Treth said. "Ten minutes? Five?"

"Five?" Charlie squeaked. "Maybe less. And then a mad, mad Lu." Some of the cabin doors they passed stood open, and as they passed, Zenn looked longingly at their sumptuous furnishings, their large, inviting bunks, their soft mattresses, pristine white sheets. They dashed by a dining saloon, tables still draped with spotless linens; she imagined the wonderful food that must be stacked on the galley's shelves. Her stomach protested. How long was it since she'd eaten? She couldn't remember.

They were all gasping for breath by the time they reached the airlock leading to the *Benthic Tson*.

"Well, Groom," Liam said, bent over, sucking in air, hands on his knees. "Anything up your sleeve for getting through this ship? Got some spare gills on ya?"

Treth activated a monitor screen on the wall. "All waterships of this class are equipped with auxiliary service craft," she said. "Pressurized submersibles for maintenance and emergencies."

"There's a submarine?" Liam said.

Zenn noticed the look of concern on Treth's face as she frowned at the screen. "Treth? What is it?"

"There is a problem," Treth said, dialing up another image on the monitor.

They all moved in to see what the Groom was seeing on the screen. It was a murky underwater cam shot of a small, bulbous craft suspended in a circle of gloomy green illumination. The service sub sprouted numerous utility arms and sensors from its dull yellow hull, and a thick cable could be seen running from the craft to the nearest bulkhead.

"The sub is moored near the opposite airlock. It is not responding to commands. Charlie?"

"You can repair it, perhaps?" Jules said, moving closer to look at the screen. "Maybe it is a fuse thing? Or it needs further computer input?"

Charlie poked tentatively at the screen's keypad. "Won't respond. Not from here."

"But what do we do, then?" Jules's voice had risen in pitch. "How do we get through the quantity of water inside the ship?"

"Charlie, is the service sub's interior still pressurized?"

Charlie punched up a schematic image. "Yes. But it will not detach from its mooring. Command link is dead."

"Won't be much help to us all the way over there, huh?" Liam said.

"Charlie, can you go around the direct command system, bounce a signal to the sub off the *Tson's* exterior com dish?" Treth asked.

"I suppose I can." He brought up a virtual keyboard that floated in the air before him and began typing, using his two index fingers. "But it will need two bounces, won't it? The signal, that is, bouncing it off the secondary com dish. Spex might notice that bounce."

"We've got to risk it," Treth told him.

Charlie typed in the commands. They all waited, watching the screen expectantly. Then an alarm tone sounded abruptly from the panel, and Charlie pulled his hands away as if he'd been shocked.

"Bad luck, bad luck."

"Nine Hells!" Treth pulled the engineer away from the screen so she could see it more clearly.

"What?" Liam said.

"Trip wire," Treth said, typing furiously at the keyboard. "They set a trip wire code on the com dish. They were expecting someone to try this. We need to go. Everyone, back into the *Dancer*. Maybe we can–"

A strangled, angry burst of garbled sounds behind her made Zenn turn to the door leading into the *Dancer*. There, blocking their way, was Lu. At least Zenn assumed it was Lu. The simstriss was indeed angry. Unable to maintain a single form, she rapidly changed her appearance, uncontrollably shifting through one organism's shape after another.

"Charcharch-harlie." The Lu that said this was a tall male Alcyon, lizard tongue flicking in and out. This form faded and resolved again into a Loepith, then a Reticulan, the alien's bovine face contorted.

"Software's gone unstable," Treth said. "Everyone stay away from her."

"Naught-naughty Charlieeeee." Another shift and Lu was momentarily a shrieking human child, then a Cepheian Drifter, then a massive, tri-horned Gargani, which lumbered into the airlock chamber on two thick, furry legs. "No more tricks from you," the sim-Gargani bellowed, then she grasped the rags of the cowering Charlie in a huge, clawed hand and lifted the Loepith off the floor.

"Charlie, no," Zenn screamed. As Lu made for the doorway, the simstriss blurred once more but was unable to fully re-form again, becoming a disjointed, unfocused composite creature, part Loepith, part writhing Cepheian tendrils, part Gargani legs and torso, part beaked-and-feathered Ornithope. Zenn watched in horror as the departing sim-monster bore Charlie back into the *Dancer*, holding the weakly struggling Loepith aloft in a claw, a tendril, a paw, until the sight was hidden by the closing door.

"Charlie..." Zenn said, her voice breaking.

The sound of an incoming message drew their attention back to the wall monitor. They all gathered around it in time to see an image take shape on the screen. Pokt's jowly face filled the screen.

"You are all in attendance? Good. Oh, all but the ape. Before the sim-slave malfunctioned, it expressed a desire for the Loepith. I obliged it. Now you will want to sit for your safety. The airlock will fill with a sleeping gas. You will rest until the Spex and I arrive. We come on a shuttle. Then I am afraid there will be consequences. Of a harsh nature." The Skirni's image vanished. The sound of inrushing air came from above them. Zenn looked up to see threads of mist descending in lazy spirals from vents in the ceiling.

"There – gas." Liam pointed.

"Novice Scarlett," Treth said, "the intruder-defense gas on this craft will be morphazine; do you have an antidote?"

Zenn tried to remember, her thoughts a sudden jumble, the ghastly image of Charlie held aloft by the sim still vivid.

"Novice Scarlett," Treth shook her by the shoulders. "An antidote?"

"I think… I might, yes." Zenn unslung her kit, scooted Katie to one side and dug frantically, searching for the vial. "Naloxin. Here it is."

Zenn pushed the vial onto a facemask nebulizer – and then she too was going down, her knees suddenly too weak to hold her.

"Scarlett." It was Liam, close by, strong arms lifting her, propping her to sit with her back up against the wall. Then his legs went limp and he crumpled to the floor next to her.

Zenn could now no longer lift her arm. Treth's hand was on hers. She took the facemask. But the Groom succumbed next, stumbling backwards away from Zenn to sit down hard before slumping over.

Like a swimmer slipping beneath the water's surface, Zenn watched the room go indistinct, watched it recede into the distance and, finally, watched it go black.

When Zenn opened her eyes again, something was pressing down on her nose and mouth – the nebulizer mask. The mask pulled away, and a fishy smell filled her nostrils. Khurspex! Her body jolted upright. The blurry object bobbing in front of her face came into focus. No, not Khurspex – dolphin breath, Jules.

"Alert? Yes, I did the correct thing." He pulled the mask away from her face. "Quick, wake up completely, please."

Zenn stood, endured a brief rush of vertigo and shook her head to clear it.

"Jules… how…?"

"Better to wake up these two and quickly. Those Khurspex will be coming."

Zenn revived Treth first, then Liam. The both got shakily to their feet. Opening her pack, she was about to give Katie the antidote, but the rikkaset had apparently been buried deeply enough to avoid the sedative's affects. Jules tried to help Zenn put the pack back on, but he moved strangely, one mech-arm hanging at his side, one mech-leg dragging behind him.

"Jules, what's wrong?"

"My half-brain. The drug-fog put half my thinking to sleep."

Of course! The dolphin's sleep defense mechanism. Only half his brain had been affected by the gas; the other half stayed awake. Zenn reached up and held the mask over Jules's blowhole and told him to breathe slowly. Treth was already at the airlock panel.

"The way back to the *Dancer* is locked," the Groom said. "But I still have control over the airlock into the *Tson*. They saw no need to close it off. We might have time before the Skirni arrives."

"What about Charlie?" Zenn said.

"As I said. That way is secured. We cannot reach him," Treth said. "If he is lucky, the simstriss' ethics memware will prevent any serious harm."

"But her memware is corrupted," Zenn said. "We don't know what it will do."

"We must concentrate on what is possible," Treth said, typing furiously at the virtual keypad. Without looking up, she said, "Dolphin, how far can you swim underwater?"

"Swim?" Jules reared back on his mech-legs, as if the Groom had taken a swing at him.

"Underwater?" He looked from Treth to Zenn. "How far can I go underwater? This is what she wants to know?"

"The sub is roughly four hundred feet distant," Treth said, her eyes on the screen. "Can you reach it and return?"

"Reach it?" The dolphin shifted nervously from mech-foot to mech-foot.

"What about the pressure in there?" Liam interjected. "Won't it crush him?" Jules gave Liam a wild-eyed stare.

"It is the equivalent of two hundred feet in depth," Treth said. "Cannot dolphins swim at that level?" Jules didn't answer but waved his head back and forth in agitation.

"Yes," Zenn said, a little reluctant to join the discussion with Jules so obviously upset by it. "They can go as deep as twelve hundred feet. As long as the pressure on them rises gradually."

"The lock is equipped with an equalization chamber." Treth pointed to a thick observation porthole that looked into the chamber. "Water is pumped in until the pressures are the same on either side, then the exit door into the *Tson* will open." The Groom stepped over to Jules. "You are the only one among us who can reach the sub and release the mooring cable. But you must go now." Jules shrank back from her again, emitting a twittering squeak that his Transvox didn't even attempt to interpret.

"Jules." Zenn went to him and pulled his head down to her level. She could feel his body trembling with fear. "What is it?"

"Zenn Scarlett, do not stand apart from me now!" There was stark panic in his voice.

"Jules, what's the matter?"

The dolphin's black eyes stared into hers. The Transvox was barely audible.

"Zenn Scarlett... I do not know how to swim."

TWENTY-FIVE

"Seriously?" Liam said, unable to control his disbelief. "A dolphin who can't swim?"

"It's not his fault." Zenn was in full protective mode now, standing next to the quivering dolphin with her hands on his heaving flank, hoping her touch would calm him. "He just told you. He was taken from his family right after birth. He's spent his entire life in walksuits."

"The institute thought it would be counterproductive. To the walksuit program. If my body got used to swimming. They wanted me to learn walking. I learned very well, you have certainly seen. Walking I can do."

"There is no time for this, dolphin." Treth waited until Jules met her gaze. "We have only one escape path." Jules stared, imploring, at Zenn, then looked back at Treth again, and his trembling seemed to diminish. Zenn could sense him struggling with his fear.

"If you can't do it," she told him, "we won't think badly of you."

"No, of course we won't," Liam said, but his nervous laugh betrayed what he was really thinking. "But, um, you *are* a dolphin, aren't you? I bet you've got the lungs for it. What if… What if I bet you? How's this – five units says you can do it."

"Liam," she scolded.

"Hey, it worked before."

"Jules," Treth said. "We understand. It is no easy task we set before you. We will not think badly of you. But it is the only way out for us."

"I have practiced at holding my breath," Jules said, as if admitting a secret. "Simply to see how long I could do it." Treth cocked her head at him, waiting for him to come to his own decision. "Swimming would be like that, yes? Holding my breath, I mean, and… moving… through the water." He gave his tail fluke an experimental twitch, glancing back at it uncertainly.

"Yes, something like that," Treth told him. Zenn gave the Groom a look, and Treth added, "It could be more involved than just holding one's breath."

Jules looked at the pressure chamber as if it was the mouth of a large, hungry animal.

"Will it be a complicated journey – getting through the water to the sub?"

"No. It is a straight route to the other side," Treth said.

"Jules." A thought had occurred to Zenn. "Do you know how to echolocate?"

"Yes, I have done that." Some of Jules's former enthusiastic tone returned. "I often put just my head below the surface of the pool at the institute. I could sound-see many yards into the water and learned to recognize many things."

"Sound-seeing is good, Jules," she told him. "That will help you navigate inside the ship. It will be dark."

"Oh? Very dark?"

"Yes," Treth said. "At least until you reach the sub. It is illuminated. Swim to that light." Treth opened the hatch leading into the pressure chamber and told Jules the manual key code he would need to detach the mini-sub's umbilical from its outer hull. The keypad was designed with large pressure pads, and she thought he would be able to manipulate them with his beak. She made him repeat the code to her. Then, she said, he must turn around and come back quickly before his breath ran out.

The equalization chamber was dank and smelled of mold and seawater. Jules hesitated a few seconds, then crossed the threshold and turned to look back at them.

"When the water is halfway up the wall, release your walksuit and let yourself float up as the level rises," Treth told him. "Just before the water reaches the ceiling, take your last breath, a big breath, and prepare to swim out of the exit hatch when we open it. Ready?"

He gave the hatch leading into the *Tson* one last, apprehensive look.

"I am ready."

"Jules," Zenn said. "I know you can do this." He bobbed his head at her in reply, then the hatch swung shut, and Zenn could hear the sound of a rushing torrent as the chamber filled.

Treth brought up an image on the monitor, and they all watched as the foaming water quickly mounted up along Jules's mech-legs, then up over his body, until with a twist, he pulled himself free of the walksuit. As if reluctant to get his face wet, he held himself in a rigid vertical position, keeping his head well out of the rising flood. But when the water was almost to the ceiling, he had no choice. He took his last breath, and his smooth form ducked beneath the surface. Treth touched the panel, and the chamber cam showed the hatch opening into the *Tson*. It yawned wide, an oblong hole of perfect blackness.

After a glance back at the camera, Jules flicked his tail, tentatively at first, and then, with a single powerful thrust, he arced gracefully down toward the open hatch – and slammed into the wall a foot from the opening. Floating stunned and motionless for a second, he gathered himself, rotated in the water and tried again, this time moving carefully through the hatch until his tail flukes vanished into the lightless interior of the watership.

Treth punched up the cam shot of the distant sub again.

"He is a brave one, your dolphin," she said to Zenn.

A sudden tide of emotion made it impossible for Zenn to reply, and she stood with the others, silently watching the image on the monitor, waiting for Jules to swim into sight. Zenn realized she was holding her own breath and forced herself to relax. After what seemed like much too long, a shadow flicked past the camera.

"Look," Zenn said, pointing.

Then, there was another movement on the monitor. A long, slender object, undulating across the camera's field of view.

"That him?" Liam said, squinting at the screen.

"No. Loose wiring. Or debris..." Treth didn't sound convinced.

"That's not debris," Zenn said. Then a huge, flattened, saucer-shaped body glided past. There was no mistaking the tapered wing tips and leopard-spot markings. "Lurker!"

"A what?" Liam asked.

"A black-smoke lurker. Hydrothermal vent predator. Big, really big, like a giant manta ray, with feeding tentacles. Smart. And mean." Zenn felt numb, her mind spinning back to the lurker they had treated at the clinic. It was an immature female, small for its age, just a bit over fifteen feet in diameter. But the memory of its vicious nature and lethally effective feeding tubes had made an impression even on Otha. The creature was almost impossible to approach, let alone work on. And it was a small specimen. An adult lurker could stretch fifty feet from wingtip to wingtip, with feeding siphons that extended twice its body length.

"Will it interfere with him?" Treth asked. "Will it prevent the dolphin from accessing the sub?"

"It could kill him," Zenn snapped, unable to disguise her anger and fear.

"Then why do they let that thing swim around in there?" Liam asked. "The *Tson's* a passenger ship, isn't it?"

"Guard dog, I would assume," Treth said. "Let loose by the Khurspex to prevent ship-to-ship crossings. As they did with the fire-mites in the *Prodigious*."

The lurker, in fact, was the perfect choice for protector of the *Tson's* pitch-black depths. Zenn could imagine it on patrol, its immense, lidless eyes sifting the darkness for any stray photon, for the faintest trace of prey. And Jules, with no idea what awaited him, was swimming straight toward it.

Abruptly, a familiar torpedo shape glided in and out of frame. Then Jules's smiling face filled the camera shot. He bobbed his head up and down excitedly and, Zenn thought, proudly. Her heart was pounding and she wanted to shout at him to swim away, to hide.

They watched Jules go to the docking control panel next to the sub. He poked the buttons with his snout but got the sequence wrong, or pushed too many keys at once, because the umbilical remained firmly attached.

Hurry, Jules! she thought.

He paused, then started again. This time, he got it right. With a flurry of bubbles, the umbilical popped off and the sub was floating free.

"Yes," Liam shouted, pumping a fist into the air. "He did it."

Come back – get out of there, Zenn thought, imagining the lurker gliding toward her friend, silent, hungry.

Treth keyed in a sequence at the control panel, and the sub's lights blinked to life. Its props spun into motion and it propelled itself out of the cam's range. Jules flashed his smile to the cam again.

"Jules," Zenn shouted at the screen. "Watch out!"

The feeding tube was rising up from the darkness below the dolphin. Moving with the speed and agility of a snake, it circled his body, drew itself tight, then jerked him down and out of sight, leaving only a swirling vortex of dirty green water.

"No," Zenn gasped. "He'll be killed…"

This time, the storm of warmth and dizziness enveloped her more quickly than ever before. Her vision telescoped to a vanishing point, then went black. All sound ceased, her body's warmth replaced by a wet, freezing cold, a cold that penetrated like needles all over her. Then the silence was invaded by a curious, rapid-fire clicking and a more distant cacophony of other indistinct, water-borne sounds.

Zenn knew instantly this was unlike the earlier linkings with other animals. Something even more powerful and disconcerting was happening to her. Consciousness began to slip away, lifting like a paper-thin tissue of thought that threatened to be carried off on a cresting current. She fought to stay in control, to keep her thoughts her own and, for a moment, it seemed she could do this. But it was too difficult; it took more strength than she had. A confusion of unnamable emotions broke through, flooded her mind, and the blackness around her began to shimmer and vibrate with shapeless images that almost came into focus before receding back into shadow.

A painful tightness gripped her lungs, a force that grew more unbearable with every second, increasing its hold, compressing the very bones of her ribcage. Another pressure was also building, inside her head, growing slowly, then expanding faster, rippling outward, now feeling like a flower opening in her brain, now exploding like fireworks in a starless sky. Then the energy pulsing out of her mind cut itself loose from her, grew beyond her. She felt it push out of her head somehow, felt it advance like a widening, laser-hot circle of light moving through the skin of her face, or what should have been her face but wasn't. It expanded across her strange-feeling skin, along the projecting beak where her cheeks and jaw should be, down along the extremity where her legs should be but weren't. It then leapt away from her, leaving her-body-not-her-body and continuing to expand into the water beyond her, a cast-off skin of pure light. She now knew the energy wasn't expanding out of her own mind and physical self but out of a different body – Jules's body! She was inside of Jules's mind, looking out through the dolphin's eyes.

She saw the expanding circle around her as a fiery globe of energy now, rippling out to surround her body, Jules's body, which hung in the center of it, like a sculpture on display, an ornament in a glass bubble, all bathed in the hazy dream-light of the green-black water.

She understood then – the pressure on her chest, on Jules's chest, was one of the lurker's feeding tubes, constricting in a muscular loop. She watched in growing terror as another slender appendage tipped with rasp-like teeth undulated toward her, toward Jules, searching, scenting molecular clues as it wove its way through the water. The feeding siphon.

The grip of the lurker was unbreakable, and Zenn could feel the life being squeezed from the lungs of the body she inhabited. A darkness blacker than the watery gloom began to creep in around the edge of her vision. Jules was losing consciousness. Zenn knew with a chilling clarity that when that spark was gone, it would not return. Her paralyzing sense of helplessness spiraled up into impotent fury.

And then another consciousness was there, pushing into her mind, joining with her in the searing cold and suffocating dark. Like a doorway spilling out warmth and light, the other mind opened up into her own mind, shining its uncanny consciousness into hers. She knew immediately what it was. It was the Indra, the same stonehorse whose thoughts she had shared aboard the *Helen of Troy*. Now Zenn was suspended between Jules and the Indra, her own mind becoming a doorway too, a connecting thread, a conduit for the Indra's unfathomable intentions. And she knew… no, didn't know… she felt that if she tried hard enough, if she gathered all the will she could find within her, she could help Jules. Or be the instrument, the channel, of the action that could help him. Yes, just a little more… more intention, more willing that it happen, even if it hurt her, even if this action cut the tenuous bond tethering her to her own body and her world, even if she never found her way back from the place she floated now, just a little more… With a sharp spasm, she was pierced by a lance of burning pain and brilliant, arcing light. And it was over.

TWENTY-SIX

When her vision returned, Zenn hadn't moved from where she'd been before. She was crouched stiffly in place in the *Dancer's* lock, just outside the equalization chamber leading into the *Tson*. Her body was shaking, and pain hammered between her temples. Liam held her close against his chest. Treth's face was next to hers.

The Groom was saying something, but Zenn couldn't make it out; there was a ringing, hissing sound in her ears, as if she'd been deafened by a loud explosion. On the floor of the chamber, something lay in a pool of water. A dolphin! Jules was arching his back in small movements, trying to orient himself so that he faced her. There was something coiled around his torso – the lurker's feeding tube, or what was left of it. Still and lifeless, it ended in a stump that appeared to be cleanly cut, the raw edge sealed shut as if cauterized by intense heat.

Treth's voice came to her faintly, as if from far away. "… feeling? Are you injured?"

"I'm good. Jules… is Jules…"

"The dolphin is unharmed. Mostly."

Zenn worked to focus on him and could see raw red patches where the lurker's grip had abraded the skin.

"But he was caught." Her words were coming more easily now, though her head continued to throb. "How did he... get back here?"

"You experienced some sort of... seizure," Treth said. "There was an atmospheric disturbance. It enveloped you. When it subsided, the dolphin was here."

I did it! I helped him I thought it, and it happened.

"It was the Indra," Zenn said, trying to comprehend what has just occurred. "The *Helen's* Indra. She did it. Through me."

The idea was almost enough to make her forget the excruciating pressure in her head.

Treth tapped Liam on the shoulder, gestured at the equalization chamber. "Assist me," she said.

"You OK?" he asked. "Can you stand?"

"Yes. Go help Jules," Zenn replied.

He left her side and went to help Treth drag the walksuit to where the dolphin waited on the floor.

"On the *Helen*, you said you sensed the Indra," Treth said, as she and Liam helped Jules into the contraption. "You knew she was about to tunnel. This thing that just happened – was it the same?"

"I think so, sort of," Zenn said, but already the event was receding, dreamlike. "I'm sure it was her. I was in Jules's mind, then the Indra was in my mind. It... wanted to help. No, it knew that I wanted to help and–"

"Scarlett," Liam said as he cinched up the body harness

on the walksuit, "you saying an Indra read your mind and... zapped Jules back here?" He seemed unable to suppress his disbelief. "That's some pretty hefty magic."

"But I believe this is so," Jules said, adjusting his Transvox connections. "I felt Zenn Scarlett's thoughts. I felt her thinking – planted inside my head. It must be the Indra brain-cell material inside of *her* head. That is what saved me from that hungry swimming thing."

"Indra link with each other," Treth said. "There is no mystery to that. Impulses are sent by sub-quantum carrier wave. The science is known. But this event..." She looked at Jules, then at Zenn. "Matter transphase executed through another life form? Is this possible?"

"Yeah, well, I guess anything's *possible,*" Liam said. "I'm just pretty damn impressed. Whatever it was." He patted Jules's side.

An insistent beeping came from the control panel on the wall.

"The sub," Treth said. A few more keystrokes from her and the circular hatch in the floor leading down to the submersible irised open with a gust of pressurized air.

"The dolphin will be a tight fit," Treth said, going to the open hatch. "We will need to assist him."

"Right," Liam said. "You first, Scarlett. Guide his legs down the ladder."

"I think you'd better go first," she said, still shaken from what just happened to her. "You're stronger. Go ahead. I'll help from up here."

"Hey, you're the boss," he said as he vanished into the hatch. "I'll save you a window seat."

"Here," Treth said, following him down the ladder. "We will both take the weight of the dolphin from below."

"Zenn Scarlett," Jules said, approaching the hatch. "I tried to call out to my First Promised inside that water-ship. As I was swimming. I thought she might be there and hear me."

"Good idea," Zenn said, trying to keep his walksuit arms from getting hung up on the hatch as he descended into the sub. "Did you get an answer?"

"I am not certain. That hungry swimmer made a loud noise. It was violent and unpleasant."

Zenn was about to follow Jules into the sub when she heard a trilling sound behind her. Across the room, she saw Katie, sitting up, holding the severed length of lurker feeding tube in her two front paws, nibbling eagerly.

"Katie," Zenn said.

"Come on, Scarlett," Liam yelled up at her. "We're all set down here."

"Give me a second," she said into the open hatch, then ran over to scoop the rikkaset into her arms. "Bad girl..." Zenn whispered, hugging the animal to her. She'd just reached the hatch when something hit the sub hard from outside, the impact knocking Zenn off her feet. She scrambled up again just in time to see the hatchway to the sub begin to close.

"The hatch – it's sealing," Liam yelled from inside the craft.

"No! Wait," Zenn shouted. Holding Katie in one arm, she ran for the hatch, only to lose her footing on the water-slick floor. She scrabbled ahead on knees and one hand, but was too late. Liam was fighting his way back up into the hatchway, arms reaching out toward her, when the hatch irised shut above him.

Leaping up, she skidded over to the control panel. Katie jumped from her arms to sit on the console. What Zenn saw on the view screen made her faint with fear. The lurker had its tentacles wrapped securely around the sub, its feeding tubes scrabbling against the hull, trying to force a way in. A second later, the creature gave a powerful flap of its winglike fins. With a loud sound of rending metal, the craft was torn from the docking port. Another push from its wings and the lurker vanished down into the inky depths, pulling the sub behind it.

Zenn hunted for the comm button but couldn't find it. Wild with panic, she pounded at the panel with her fists.

"...taking on water – turn that valve." It was Treth's voice. "No, that one, dolphin. Move aside, let me – no, no, I can't..."

The voice was drowned out by the sound of rushing water, then a confusion of garbled voices shouting, static, and silence. She strained, waiting to hear a voice, waiting for a sound, a signal. There was nothing.

A loud scraping came from behind her. Zenn knew without looking what it was: the *Dancer's* airlock door being forced. Pokt and the Khurspex.

"Katie, in," she signed, and Katie burrowed into Zenn's backpack. With a grinding of metal on metal, the door swung open. Zenn turned to face them.

TWENTY-SEVEN

Numb, exhausted and heartsick, Zenn allowed herself to be herded back through the *Symmetry Dancer* by Pokt and the half-dozen Khurspex with him. There was no sign of Charlie or the simstriss. Time passed in a disconnected jumble – a shuttle ride, a docking port, a quick march to a smaller intership ferry, Pokt saying nothing, pushing her ahead of him, the Khurspex crowding into the ship, occasionally stumbling into one another in their deteriorating state, their dank sea smell now tinged with the scent of accelerating decay. The ferry eased into motion, and with no other place available, she slumped down to sit on the floor, unable to stop the horrifying images that refused to stop replaying in her mind: the sub in the grasp of the furious lurker, dragged out of sight to vanish into the black, hopeless depths of the *Tson*.

"Where are you taking me?" she asked finally.

"To the service ship," the Skirni said. "From there you will be placed into the stonehorse."

"Why? What will happen then?"

He bulged his eyes at her. "Pokt knows. Pokt knows much more than you. I have read your diaries. On the shards from your room. You did not suspect what was placed within you, even when it should have been clear. The joinings you shared? With the animals? Yes, I know what grows inside you. The time is ripe. You will enter the stonehorse. These hideous Spex will go homeward. And this business will be concluded."

Even in her dazed state, the thought of an in-soma run into the skull of a living Indra was enough to provoke a cold stab of fear. "What business?"

"That which ends the years of wandering." He shook his head at her. Suddenly animated, he hopped up out of his seat. "Years of the Skirni homeless among the worlds. Worlds that turned us away, made us scrape and grovel. And we, we who were denied a planet of our own, we will say who can have a world. We will possess the Indra ships. And we will say who can go from star to star. We will say who walks on green grasses and who lives their life in the cold arms of mother-void. The Skirni will say."

So that's what the Cepheians promised them.

Zenn almost pitied him. Almost.

"That's not true, you know." She tilted her head up at him.

"What is not?"

"Your allies won't let the Khurspex hand over the Indra fleet to you. Or to anyone else."

"You don't know what you say," he said, snorting.

"Why should they? Why would they give you the ships when they could keep them for themselves?"

“Lies. Pathetic lies.” But she could see her words struck a chord. “The friends of the Skirni know our value. The Skirni have long survived in the ships of the Accord. We are everywhere yet are so despised we are noticed nowhere. The scorn of others has become our hidden strength.”

“Yes. But what about when you’ve served your purpose? Why won’t these friends of yours just toss you away?”

“You know nothing,” he scoffed, but his mottled color darkened, his hands clenched and unclenched as she spoke. “You simply fear such power in the hands of the Skirni.”

“Oh? What if it is the Skirni who are fools? What if your friends deceived you? Then the Skirni get nothing.”

“No. That is not how it will go.” A wicked smile split his pug-face. “The Skirni have taken steps. To assure we get what is deserved. I am done listening here.” Then he waddled forward to stand next to the Khurspex operating the ferry, muttering to himself.

A short time later, the ferry docked. Pokt ordered Zenn through the side hatch. They entered a larger ship with an open deck area holding a scattering of supply containers. Along one side of the deck was a row of nine or ten compact surgical bays set into alcoves. In them, Zenn could see operating tables, banks of diagnostic scanners and other equipment. The ship was probably a mobile medical unit or rescue craft. Beyond the surgery bays, she could see all the way forward to the pilot’s console at the bow. The pilot’s chair had its back to them.

“The *Tson’s* mini-sub has gone offline.” The sound of the voice from the unseen person in the chair drew a gasp of shocked recognition from Zenn. Then, the chair rotated, revealing a human male. He wore a vermillion soldier's jacket. "Your friends should have surrendered," Stav Travosk said matter-of-factly, the silver-gray eyes showing no emotion.

"You? You're the ally?" Zenn said.

"Ally?"

"You and the Authority… the Skirni."

He gave Pokt a scornful glance. "Oh, the valiant Skirni network. Allies, yes. But the Authority? Hardly."

"I don't understand."

"Clearly." He smiled at her tortured look. "You're surprised? That the New Law refused to stand by and watch humanity be overwhelmed. The Authority is finished. Or they soon will be."

"You're a spy," she said, the terrible truth dawning. "For the New Law."

"I prefer 'patriot'. Someone who refuses to let my species succumb to a tidal wave of alien filth."

Behind her, Pokt emitted a snort. She turned to see him glaring at Stav, who appeared oblivious to either his insult or the Skirni's reaction.

"Now it's time." He stood and came toward her. "The Indra is ready for you." Her shock was overtaken now by stark fear closing around her chest like a deathly cold hand. "Pokt, your presence is no longer required. Go to the *Delphic Queen* and wait. I'll contact you when I want you to bring him."

Zenn's throat tightened.

Father!

Pokt regarded Stav, then went the hatch leading to the shuttle they'd just come from.

"I should enjoy seeing it," the Skirni said. "The placement of the nexus into the stonehorse. Why do I not wait?" His beady eyes flicked to Zenn, then away again. "I could wait until you have made the interface and the Indra ships are secured."

"No."

"Is there some reason I should not see it? It will be a shining moment. When the Indra fleet is taken and we divide our prize."

"I said no."

"Are we not allies, the New Law and the Skirni?"

"What? Of course we are. Pokt, we don't have time for this."

"But if we are? Equals? Why should Pokt not stay and witness the ending of our plan?"

Stav clamped his eyes shut, turned his head away, then swung back to the Skirni.

"I do not explain myself to you, Pokt." The Skirni didn't move. "I said go and wait on the *Queen*." There was brittle anger in his voice, silver eyes flashing.

Pokt met Stav's gaze and gave him a hostile smile in return. He glanced again at Zenn, back at Stav, and then he turned and went through the hatch.

Visible through the bow view screen behind Stav, the vast Khurspex structure was suspended in space, floating like an immense, ungainly wagon wheel. At its center was what had once been a starship, but was now a surreal composite vehicle of spires, connective struts, loops of massive ductwork and bizarre engineering permutations, a free-form construction with no visible bow, stern, up or down that Zenn could identify.

Stav saw her staring at it. "There, in the center." He pointed to the viewport. "The meta-ship. Built for the Asyph, what the Spex call the *Helen's* Indra. Built so the Asyph can take the Spex back to wherever they go to spawn more of their kind."

Now, in the shadow below the meta-ship, extending out into space, Zenn saw her, the *Helen's* Indra. The whole of the creature's mighty head was exposed, floating serenely in the open vacuum, looking strangely vulnerable despite its size. There were four small bronze-gold spheres moving in lazy orbits around the Indra's head – sedation satellites, keeping her calm and docile.

"Nearly in position," Stav said, leaning into the console to make a final adjustment for their approach.

"But you… the Encharan slug. You saved my life."

"Couldn't let you be damaged, could I?"

"How did you even know?"

He looked up at this.

"Microtransmitter. At the party. Once I knew it was you behind the mask, I needed to keep track of you. Your hand?"

Yes. She remembered now, the feeling that he'd held her hands in his a little too long. That's when he planted it. She examined one hand, then the other. In the center of her right palm, a tiny black speck, no bigger than a dust mote, just under the skin.

"And, of course, that's why I mentioned the visit to the Indra chamber to the Captain. It all fell nicely into place. The safe room there. Most protected site on the ship during a forced tunnel event."

"But if you had a tracker in me this whole time..."

"It went offline when the *Helen* tunneled," he said, his attention back on the console. "We'd anticipated this might happen. It shouldn't have mattered. But the Spex drones were late getting started. And the Captain was a bit too clever for us. And, as it turned out, too clever for himself. Enough chitchat."

He came and took Zenn roughly by the arm and led her aft. He gestured to a long, narrow object stowed in shadow near the far bulkhead. The sight of the thing made Zenn pull back against Stav's grasp. He only gripped her harder.

"You'll be familiar with the instrumentation on this."

The in-soma pod was a gleaming new Royce Insomic, smaller and sleeker than the aging Gupta-Merck unit in which she'd trained. Top-of-the-line equipment. Any other time, Zenn would have been thrilled to see what it could do.

"I'm not checked out on this model," she said flatly, searching for anything to say that would delay him, put off the inevitable. "It's newer... too complicated."

"Not a factor. The pod's autopilot is preprogrammed. Your only job is to facilitate system ops. That and compensate for any anomalies on the way to the hypertrophal lobe."

The HT lobe. The organ at the center of the Indra's brain, the living quantum field-generator that enabled the stonehorse to outrun the laws of physics – and carve a path through the very fabric of space and time.

"What do you expect me to do in there? If I survive?"

"Nothing. Nothing at all. The Indra will engage the nexus once you're in position. It's a homing reflex, hardwired into their behavior."

"I won't do it," she said, trying to hide the dread growing inside her. "You can't threaten me now."

Zenn thought of Jules and the others, water pouring into the sub, the lurker dragging them down into the icy black; limp, cold bodies floating somewhere entombed, deep, soundless... No, Stav couldn't use her friends as a weapon against her. Not now.

"I had a feeling it would come to this," he said. "And I've taken steps to help you overcome your reluctance. You will do your part. You'll become an agent of purification, in spite of the alien corruption growing inside you. In spite of your small, selfish desires."

He motioned at the console and a virt screen rose up into the air. An image came into focus – a human body lying on an operating gurney in a sickbay, the *Delphic Queen's* sickbay. The air around the body shimmered and heaved with the energy of a restraining field. The body immersed in it moved sluggishly, as if in fitful sleep. Her heart began to pound as she saw the long braid of hair suspended in the field – hair the same color as hers. The figure's eyes were closed. The facial muscles twitched ever so slightly.

"Father." She spoke the word in a half whisper. "What have you done to him?"

"He's restrained, that's all. To keep him manageable."

Zenn stared at the sleeping face, her mind a whirlwind of emotion.

Stav spoke to the screen, pronouncing his words with exaggerated clarity, making sure whoever was listening on the other end understood.

"The Skirni Pokt is on his way. I will contact him when I want the prisoner brought over. Then you can join the others on the Asyph's ship. Understand me?"

From off-screen, a Khurspex's pale, eyeless face leaned into the image. A noise from somewhere out of view attracted its attention and it turned away.

"No, wait..." Stav said. But the Khurspex had already pulled back out of camera range to investigate. "Tell Pokt to–" Then the screen abruptly went dark.

"These creatures..." He growled to himself, turned to the view screen at the bow. "It's almost time for the Asyph meta-ship to leave. Makes the Spex even more worthless and unpredictable than usual."

Zenn followed Stav's gaze to the screen at the front of the cabin. She now saw that several ferries and shuttlecraft had disembarked from the surrounding ring and were all making for the central ship, like moths to a flame.

"No one wants to be left behind," Stav said, eyeing the small armada. He smiled at her. Zenn looked away.

"I won't," she said, but this time, her voice wasn't as steady. "You can't do anything to make me."

"What I can do to *you* is only part of what can be done."

Stav pushed a pressure point on his sleeve screen, and a small opening in the ceiling of the nearest medical bay slid open. What descended from it was alive. Coiling down from the opening were half a dozen thick, knobby gray-green vines, each one terminating in a three-way assortment of talon-like hooks, scissoring claw blades and suction cups, all writhing in the air with a slow, precise menace.

"The Khurspex aren't killers. But this ship we're on, hijacked along with the others, must have belonged once to a race much less squeamish than the Spex. When properly stimulated, the bio-med devices aboard this craft produce effects on a living body that are nothing short of unbelievable." He regarded Zenn calmly as she watched the vicious-looking vines. "Your father will be here shortly. What becomes of him then – " he patted the surgical bay, "– is up to you."

TWENTY-EIGHT

She knew it had been futile. But she had had to try. Now he'd played the card she'd known all along he would play. After several minutes of silence, as Stav maneuvered the ship closer to the central ship and its Indra, Zenn admitted defeat.

"I'll do it," she said.

"You never had a choice. But it will be easier. This way." He walked to the in-soma pod and told it to begin pre-op checks. It split apart, the lid opening with a soft hiss. Zenn slipped off her backpack and set it carefully against the nearest bulkhead. She felt for Katie; the rikkaset twitched against her hand, a small, black nose appeared, two bright eyes blinked up at her. Preoccupied with the pod, Stav didn't notice.

"Stay, Katie," Zenn signed quickly, whispering the words to be sure Katie would obey, her voice breaking. "You stay. Friend-Zenn… will be right back."

She pulled the cover over Katie's face, then she took a deep breath and went to the pod.

A soft alarm tone pinged from somewhere, and a mild jolt rocked the ship.

"What now?" Stav looked up from his console in irritation.

A creaking rasp of machinery came from the other end of the craft, and the rear airlock hissed open.

"No. Not yet," Stav said, taking a step toward the hatch.

"I have brought the Earther." It was Pokt. He didn't enter but remained half visible in the hatchway.

"I told you to wait," Stav said, his voice even but seething.

"Yes. I thought it better I come now. To observe the process."

"*You* thought…?"

"To see that all goes as promised. With the stonehorse and the fleet."

"Pokt, I don't know what you're getting at…" he said, keeping his eyes on the Skirni as he edged away toward the front of the ship.

"Getting at? Yes, I will tell you what I am getting at, Lieutenant Travosk of the New Law. I had a thought just now. As to the nature of our alliance." He looked at Zenn, then away.

"You? Had a thought?" Stav gave Pokt a thin imitation of a smile.

"Yes. A thought. That the purpose of this alliance might not be what it seems. Not what you claimed it to be."

"Pokt, you're not making sense. And we're running out of time." Stav had reached the pilot's chair.

"Am I not? Making sense?"

"No, Pokt. You are not," Stav said, then he sat down in the pilot's chair and leaned back as if to make himself comfortable.

"My sense is this: perhaps you do not intend to keep your word," Pokt said, stepping into the cabin to keep Stav in sight, walking with his hands held behind him. "Perhaps you will not honor our bargain, and keep the stonehorse fleet for yourself. When it should clearly go to the Skirni."

"That's ridiculous, Pokt." Stav said calmly. "Why would I lie about this? You said yourself, the Skirni and the New Law are allies."

"Allies?" Pokt's voice now dropped to a low snarl. "We do not need allies such as you. You who treat Pokt as dirt. You will not deal honorably. We must take what is ours!"

Both Pokt's hands now jerked up into view. Clamped onto his wrist was a Khurspex whip-whelk, its dull brown shell just beginning to crack open, the fleshy appendage writhing out to test the air.

"The Skirni *will* have that fleet," Pokt screamed, raising the weapon to aim at Stav. "And you will pay for your contempt and lies."

Stav leaned over quickly in his chair. When he rose again, there was a flux-rifle gripped in one hand. Before Pokt could activate the whip-whelk, Stav fired. The razor-flat ribbon of purple, ionized gas scored the Skirni along the side of his head, pitching him backwards to hit the wall, where he slid down and lay still. The smell of burned flesh drifted in the cabin's air.

Stav rose from his chair and went to look down at the body.

"Poor little Pokt," he said, then came to stand next to Zenn. "Did he really think the Skirni were going to... what? Rule the universe? That we would allow that? It's almost tragic."

He grabbed her shoulder in one hand and pushed her toward the in-soma pod.

"His behavior proves the point, I suppose," he said. "Treachery. Betrayal. No surprise, is it? Humans could never ally with Asents. Not in any real sense. Get in." He gave her a shove. "We need to get started."

She did as ordered, stepping into the pod and lying down on her stomach on the lounge seat. She buckled the safety harness around her and rested her hands on the control surfaces hidden on either side. This new unit had the same general layout as the cloister's older pod, and she'd memorized the various controls' positions during her in-soma training. Stav likely knew the designs of both pods, but she could try to stall him.

"I'll need time to get familiar with these," she said, feeling dead inside as she put her hands on one control and then another. "It's different from the one we had."

"No, it's not. At least, not in any way that concerns us just now." Stav leaned close to her. He nodded at the open hatch Pokt had entered from. "He's right there, your father. Fail this, do anything foolish, and you'll live just long enough to watch me take out my disappointment on him. Do we understand each other?"

Zenn said nothing and toggled a switch. The pod door swung shut with a soft, breath-like sigh.

Inside the cramped pod, Zenn was alone; alone with her thoughts of her father and her stupid, girlish daydreams about saving him, her hopes twisted into the nightmarish bargain she had made in order to see him once more, alive and unharmed.

"We're there," came Stav's voice, then his image materialized on the small view screen just in front of her face. He was seated in the pilot's chair. "Prepare for insertion. And make sure you–"

The transmission was severed by a loud, high-pitched electronic screech. The screens flickered off and on again as the pod was seized by a shaking so violent Zenn nearly had the breath knocked out of her.

"What was that? What's happening?" she said into the mic mounted on the pod wall near her left cheek.

"It's the restraining satellites." She saw Stav wave his hands at a screen and the pod stopped shaking. "The Indra is resisting their control. I've boosted the levels."

"Resisting?" A terrifying thought swept everything else from Zenn's mind. "Is she spiking a fever? What's her internal D-rad level?"

"Yes, she's feverish. But the Dahlberg radiation is within limits. It's survivable."

"For how long?" Zenn said, not quite able to believe she was heading into a lethally stressed Indra.

"The sedation sats will hold until the nexus is needed. It's not your concern."

Before Zenn could protest that it was very much her concern, the in-soma pod lurched into motion, and the unit's bow-cam view screen showed the med ship's outer hull door sliding up. Barely fifty feet away, the armored mass of the Indra's head filled the opening, scales gleaming dully in the faint starlight, its colossal body out of sight, hidden within the huge bulk of the meta-ship that cocooned it.

The launch arm pushed the pod out into the void, and Zenn's body lifted up, weightless against the safety harness. With a slight lurch, the arm and the attached pod came to a stop. The tip of the pod was resting lightly against the Indra's skin.

The arm jerked into motion, extending again, and the pod was carried toward a dark spot just below the crease where the creature's giant skull met the first node of the spine. Hidden in a fold there, Zenn knew, was one of four cranio-mitral valves spaced around the base of the Indra's skull.

Made up of two muscular flaps that opened and closed to relieve pressure in the skull, the cranio-mitral valves kept the Indra's head from literally exploding during the awesome forces generated by quantum tunneling. The valves led directly into the foramen magnum – the hole that admitted the spinal cord into the skull. The foramen opening was the critical boundary. If the Indra perceived her and the pod as a foreign body at that point, it would be all over. That's where the immune response would trigger, the same response that lit up the Indra chamber when her mother, in her malfunctioning pod, had been lost doing what Zenn was about to do now. Unless the tissue inside her own brain deceived the creature, it would release a pulse of radiation no amount of shielding could withstand, a deadly particle-wave no living organism could survive. What had her mother felt when she saw the radiation gauge in her pod leaping into the red zone? Did she feel heat? Pain? Panic? Astonishment?

The nose of the pod had just penetrated the Indra's body when both view screens went black. Zenn's pulse rate galloped.

Claustrophobia enfolded her like a heavy, suffocating blanket. She gasped out loud at the sensation and fought to remain calm, made herself draw the air of the cabin deep into her lungs, then slowly exhale. The pod slid ahead. She was inside the Indra's body.

The pod's exterior headlights switched on, the beam playing across the space ahead, the bow-cam showing the smooth, dull pink membrane lining the spinal interstitial space.

"Cranial temp holding steady," she said softly to herself, as if hearing the words spoken aloud made the information somehow more reassuring. "Hull integrity nominal." Her jolting heartbeat slowed. "Internal stats nominal. Forward velocity two thirds." Her breathing slowed to a steady rhythm. She would do this and come back out and she would see her father again. That was as far as she could think.

The autopilot light blinked steadily on and off, and a low hum sounded as the pod's exterior coating of millions of tiny artificial polycilia fibers came to life, pushing it ahead, moving slowly, soundlessly forward.

The cranio-mitral valve came into view just in front of her. It was large enough for the pod to squeeze through, but not if its three valve flaps remained shut, closing off the opening. The musculature would be much too strong for the pod to penetrate without a relaxant.

A pinging sound above her signaled the pod's surgical computer had come online.

"Inject eight point zero cc's atropoda via intramuscular?" The computer's gender-neutral voice was maddeningly blasé and relaxed, but she was glad nonetheless that this newer pod model was equipped with the latest medical AI system. It made her feel less alone.

"Yes, inject eight point zero," Zenn said.

One of the pod's exterior surgical arms extended until it contacted the surface of the bulging valve muscle. A large pneuma-ject emerged from the tip of the arm, and with a visible effervescent puff of bubbles from its compressed air, a measured dose of atropoda venom was propelled into the valve wall. Harvested from a species of free-swimming seaweed found only amid the sentient reefs of Bensarus Oc, the atropoda produced a unique variety of highly potent, fast-acting muscle relaxant. Very similar, she noted grimly, to the paralyzing toxin of the whip-whelk used to paralyze her, Hamish and Fane. Fane... with his bright, off-kilter smile. Where was the Procyoni sacrist now? Was he safe? Injured? Was he still alive?

She was pulled back to the present when she saw the valve before her relax and yawn open. The polycilia microfibers coating the pod vibrated to life again, carrying her forward through the opening of the foramen magnum. This was it. The entry into the skull. No turning back now. She held her breath as she felt the pod sliding through the muscular valve.

A moment later, her entire body, every cell, every molecule, was bathed in a throbbing stream of energy – the Indra sensing her. But this was different from the other linking events. She wasn't overwhelmed. She didn't lose hold of her own mind; her thoughts remained her own, remained clear, maybe even sharper than usual. Now Zenn, in return, was able, was allowed, to sense the Indra's being. She felt the creature's ancient, unfathomable consciousness, its mind reacting in vague surprise at first, then questioning, a rapid, probing study of the strange presence within her. Would the Indra react? Would it reject her? Kill her? Kill them both?

Zenn held her breath, watching the D-rad gauge. The gauge ticked up, then back down, stayed down.

No fatal surge of radiation. No lethal immune response. The nexus tissue inside her had done its job. The Indra was aware of the invader in its body but accepted it.

Zenn breathed out at last, scanned the readout dials glowing in front of her, made herself focus on what would happen next. The autopilot reengaged, and the pod moved forward. Now it would enter the narrow open space that ran along the spinal cord. Unlike a mammal's brain, the Indra's cerebral material was arrayed like a tree's leafy branches sprouting from the central trunk of the cord. This open cavity would take her in turn to the brain's lateral ventricle, a fluid-filled area that, it had always seemed to Zenn, resembled the outline of a butterfly with wings outspread. It should be just twenty feet or so from there to her final destination: the hypertrophal lobe.

The pod slowed to a halt then, held tightly between the innermost part of the double-layered skull walls and the *dura mater*, the tough membrane that enveloped and protected the brain.

Zenn double-checked to make sure she hadn't misread the gauge. No, no mistake. The Indra's fever was generating

274 rads of Dahlberg radiation; 312 rads would disable all the instruments on the pod, and 330 rads would kill any life forms inside her.

"Execute maser-caut incision to *dura mater* with minimum-length for pod ingress?" the computer inquired.

Zenn told it to go ahead and another thin, metal arm reached out from the pod's hull. The maser-cauterizer built into its tip crackled to life, and it slit an opening in the tough, white *dura* tissue. Surface tension pulled the two sides of the incision apart as the maser made its incision, its heat sealing the edges of the wound as it cut, the fluid around it boiling and bubbling in response. A few seconds later, there was an opening large enough to allow the pod to squeeze through. As the pod moved beyond the *dura mater*, the enormous brain itself came into view, the mushroom gray and off-white of its convoluted surface billowing away into the dimness. She read the D-rad gauge: 292 rads. Still rising.

Freed suddenly from the grip of the *dura*, the pod escaped into the open space of the lateral fissure with an unexpected spurt. Before Zenn could react, the pod was knifing through the cerebrospinal fluid so fast, she had to slam her fist onto the emergency braking jet control to keep from ramming the brain tissue ahead of her. The pod slowed just short of impact and coasted to a halt with a slight bump against the soft, spongy mass. She tensed, staring at the monitor dials for any sign of response from the Indra. None came. She made herself relax.

The autopilot resumed control and reversed the pod's direction, pivoting and moving ahead, passing from the tunnel-like lateral fissure into the more expansive ventricle. The space was about the size of a small, narrow swimming pool and filled with straw-colored cerebrospinal fluid.

Moments later, the outline of the hypertrophal lobe emerged on the view screen. Protruding into the ventricle, the HT lobe was a dangling, six-foot-long sack of heavily veined tissue. Thin bluish threads of interdimensional energy rippled across its surface, appearing, vanishing, appearing again in a pulsing, hypnotic display. The autopilot slowed the pod, allowing it to drift momentarily forward, then stopped, the beating polycilia holding it in position a foot or so from the lobe.

She toggled a switch, and the view screen displayed the cabin of the med ship. Stav was working at one of the science station consoles off to the side of the pilot's chair.

"I'm at the lobe," she said into the mic. "What now?"

"Now?" Stav said, looking up from the console and giving her an unsettling grin. "Now you save the human race."

"How?" she said bitterly. "By giving you control of the Indra fleet? You think that will keep the Earth pure? You think the other planets of the Accord will let you do this? They'll find a way to take back the ships. You won't be able to stop them."

"You believe that's what we intend? To take the fleet?" He shook his head, as if he pitied her.

"I know you're not giving the ships to the Skirni. They're aliens. The New Law wouldn't do that."

"Of course we wouldn't. The Skirni's compliance was necessary. Over the years, they'd infested most of the Indra ships in the Accord. They had nowhere else to go. And that made them useful. Once. But you're wrong about the New Law. We don't want the fleet. We never did."

"You don't?" Zenn said, baffled.

"You really have no clue, do you? About what's inside of you. About what it can do. About the miracle you're about to perform."

"What miracle?" She didn't want to know. And she was desperate to know.

"The Indra mutation your mother passed along to you? It affects more than simple neural tissue. We equipped it with a little clock. Ingenious, really. And it's been ticking away ever since it took root in you."

Unnamable fear reared up in her, tightening her throat, making it hard to breathe, hard to speak. She forced the words out.

"A biological clock? What for?"

"For the moment when you would become the nexus. The nexus. What a marvel. That small bit of cultured tissue that lets a single mind connect the minds of all the Indra in the galaxy. The Spex, of course, think it will take them home. I'm afraid they're in for a little disappointment."

"They're not tunneling to their planet?" Zenn said, still not understanding. "Then where?"

"Nowhere. The clock inside you? It's about to turn the nexus into something unique, unprecedented. A knife, a scalpel. A tool to cut away the alien pollution that threatens the very essence of what it means to be human. What's about to happen is the end of humanity's longest war. A war fought for hundreds of years, undeclared, unseen, but war nonetheless. And you, Novice, are the Trojan horse that will win that war for us."

"But... how?" Zenn's voice stuttered.

"By destroying every Indra in the galaxy."

TWENTY-NINE

Stav's words sent fear like a drug coursing through her.

Destroy all the Indra? He can't. They wouldn't.

"When the nexus tissue links the mind of the Asyph with all the others of its kind, the little time bomb inside your head will activate. When that happens, you'll no longer be seen as 'friendly' by the Indra. You'll be detected as a foreign object, the enemy within. Her immune response will generate a massive Dahlberg radiation burst."

"Like my mother," Zenn whispered. But Stav heard.

"Yes. The loss that day was unforgiveable." She saw Stav's face darken. "She shouldn't have died." For a second, Zenn thought he was talking about Mai. Then he went on, his voice suddenly different, softer. "But she knew the risks. She knew what was at stake. She gave her life for all of us."

"Vremya."

Zenn saw his eyes close, his face contort. "Do *not* speak her name." After a few seconds, he turned back to the console, took a deep breath and waved up another Virt-screen, his voice steady again, his expression emotionless, businesslike. "This time will be different. Because of you. The radiation surge will be channeled by the nexus to every Indra within several hundred thousand light years. It will vaporize the HT lobes and most of the adjacent brain tissue of any Indra within that range. At least, that's our best distance estimate."

No!

Zenn's hand went to the autopilot control, toggled it frantically. She had to stop the pod or turn it around. She had to keep this from happening. The toggle clicked uselessly.

"I'm afraid that's inoperable," Stav told her. "I assumed you might have a change of heart once you were inside."

"You'd do that?" Zenn said. "Destroy the Indra? Cut off all the worlds, all the beings in the Accord? Imprison everyone on their home planets – forever?"

"It's the only way," Stav said, "to keep the alien corruption at bay. To keep human culture from being chipped away, bit by bit, until there's nothing recognizable left. Those who think like you have never understood: humans and aliens were not meant to mix. The behavior of the Spex for the past centuries proves that."

"What behavior? What do you mean?"

"I suppose you deserve to know," Stav said, as if about to grant her some precious gem of knowledge. "When the Spex first tunneled through to Accord space, eons ago, it was a freak accident. They discovered they were far beyond the distance their Indra could cover to get back home. Their engineers devised the nexus to cross that distance. And the most suitable host, the organism that best served their need, was a human being. Stunning, really, the odds. The one species in all the galaxy with a brain most hospitable to Indra tissue… was us. That alone tells you that humanity is unique. One doesn't allow something that extraordinary to be defiled."

"The Spex were taking humans?"

"It hasn't dawned on you? Earth's history of unexplained alien encounters? Unexplained abductions?"

"But there's never been any evidence! UFOs? People taken aboard spaceships? No one took any of that seriously."

"That's right," Stav said. "Who would believe some ranting backwoods rube saying he'd been probed by aliens? Or a farmer babbling about mutilated cattle? Why do you think the Spex chose those people, those places? There were times the truth almost came out. A Spex scout ship went down in what used to be called New Mexico. Another ship had an engine malfunction over Tunguska in Sino-Siberia. Knocked down an entire forest. But the Spex were smart. They covered their tracks, planted diversionary evidence."

Zenn had heard the stories. But she'd always considered them no more likely than other human fantasies – unicorns, sea monsters. But all that time, all those years, it was the Khurspex trying to get home.

"They finally made it back to their world," Stav said. "But it was a close call. They lost several ships on the way. One of them just beyond Procyoni space."

"That was the first ship," Zenn said.

"Yes. The abandoned Indra ship that brought star travel to all the races in this sector. The one that opened the floodgates of alien contamination. It was then that the

New Law had its beginnings. Of course, no one believed them about the threat. But it didn't matter. We watched. We waited. We knew the Spex would be back someday. And when they turned up, we made sure that it was us, and only us, they dealt with. Well, with the occasional Skirni, as I've said. We were only too happy to help them secure a fresh nexus." Stav shook his head. "And now, because of you, because of what we've made you, Earth will at last be safe. Separate and safe. Forever."

He's right. It's because of me. All the Indra will die because of me. This horrific thought extinguished all other thoughts.

"It won't be long now," Stav said, peering at a readout on the console. "Then it will all be over. In a flash, so to speak."

Zenn struggled to speak, panic and anger twisting like living things inside her.

"You... You'll die, too," was what came out of her mouth. "You'll be trapped here. With all the others. When the Indra are gone." She at least wanted that much. To see him admit that he would pay for what he was about to do.

"It would be a small price to pay, wouldn't it? My life spent to purchase the future of all the lives of my species?" Stav paused, considering the prospect. "But no. That's not how it will be. We've modified the nexus to ensure the Asyph herself will survive the extinction of the rest of her kind. She'll then transport me and my crew back to Sol space. Then she'll be sacrificed. And the last Indra ship will become an empty, drifting relic. A symbol of the priceless gift the New Law has bestowed on humanity: the gift of remaining human."

A sharp buzzing sound came from outside the pod. Static crackled through the cabin, and Zenn felt the hair lift from her scalp. Just the pod's D-rad repulsers, she told herself, activating in response to the rising radiation. Then a loud *zap* sounded above her, a shower of sparks hissed and ricocheted around the cabin, piercing heat stung her shoulder. She thrashed violently against the seat harness, trying to get away from the pain, then froze as the pod interior was plunged into total, heart-stopping darkness.

Zenn stared into the black silence, which became heavier and, somehow, blacker and more silent with every passing second. All the pod's systems were dead. What now? Maybe the pod was too damaged to proceed. Maybe she would be spared the task of wiping out the most complex and mysterious life form in all the galaxy. A second passed, two seconds. But then the lights in the tiny cabin blinked on, off, on again. With a low electric groan, the pod's systems came back on line, the repulsers whining into action.

"Still there?" Stav's voice, then his image displayed on the view screen. "Just some initial D-rad flux. She's building up to the threshold. The nexus will make its final synaptic link inside you any minute now. The radiation spike will follow just after." He looked up from the console. "I'm afraid that earlier, I lied. You won't survive. But don't despair. It's a great thing, a noble thing you're doing. Think of it as your contribution." A tone rang from the console, drawing his eyes back down. "Ah… here it comes."

The pod bucked as if hammered by giants, the impact throwing her painfully against the harness straps. Alarms hooted frantically in the cabin, the radiation gauge swung wildly into the red, then dropped down, then shot up again, and Zenn was certain she would die the very next second.

Instantly, without the usual warning rush of warmth and confusion, the interior of the pod vanished; her field of vision flared with a seething rainbow of convulsing, swirling colors, and her consciousness was plunged directly into a mind not her own. The colors dissolved, and there was blackness, stars and something else, huge, circular – the immense wheel of the interconnected starships of the Khurspex structure. But Zenn wasn't *seeing* it. She was sensing it in some other way, receiving images, but not transmitted by anything like her human eyes – not received and processed by mammalian rods and cones responding to photons from a puny, narrow spectrum of visible light. She was receiving information through other organs of perception, organs capable of conveying a reality no human mind ever imagined. She was sensing as a stonehorse sensed.

Flowing in fluid, dreamlike motion, the image before her now blew itself apart, the Khurspex structure spinning away, lost in dizzying, fast-receding distance, leaving only stars rushing at her. And not just the light of stars, but radiation-falls of blooming magnetic fields made visible, spreading like ripples; towering star-geysers, pushing cascades of boiling plasma up out of bottomless gravity wells; spiraling quark trails of throbbing, subatomic forces seething out in torrents from every iron-burning stellar forge, her-vision-not-her-vision gathering it all in, hurtling forward, propelled through a sea of a million million suns beating like as many cosmic hearts threaded through the never-ending dark.

Overlaying this bewildering impulse stream came the sensation of the mind behind the rushing sensory river – the Indra's consciousness, again reaching out to touch her mind, mingle its essence with hers, moving into her awareness with a feeling like a delicate, stinging-cold net thrown across the crown of her head and penetrating her skull, reaching down into the soft, delicate folds of her neo-cortex.

Just when it seemed too much to endure, too terrible, too ravishing for a single mind to contain it, the scene collapsed into another vista, endless pulsing ranges of nebulae lit by hidden, primordial nuclear fires, one plane of vision appearing and rushing past, only to be replaced instantly by another panorama of swirling energies, then more blackness, then more luminous shoals of stars, until she was unable to breathe, unable to keep from losing herself in all she was feeling, on the brink of finally disappearing once and for all into the nameless forces pouring into her.

And now the careening vision changed again, began to coalesce, to focus on a single bright red point glittering fitfully in the streaming void. The pace slowed as she saw three, four, five gas giants, all with attendant moons, all whirling past, all suspended in orbital ballet around their red Goliath of a central star. Closer to the star now, and she was surrounded by a seemingly endless vista of shattered fragments, rocky planetoids, jagged mountains of rocky, slow-tumbling debris – an asteroid belt? And now she saw them. Indra. Dozens of them. Hundreds. Long, graceful bodies extending out of fissures and caverns in the asteroids. No, thousands of Indra.

And Zenn knew then, at once, as the Indra knew, where this was. This was the unmistakable familiarity and perfect sweetness only one thing could evoke, one thing in all the frozen infinities and fierce glowing arms of the great, wheeling galaxies: this was home. And she was witness to it: the fabled breeding grounds of the *Lithohippus indrae*. No wonder the Khurspex were bound so closely to the stonehorses. The mind of the Indra, the Asyph, communicated this to her: they originated from the same planetary system. Both species felt the same irresistible pull to return, to renew, to regenerate, to live. Fane's words came back to her. He was right, in his way. The Khurspex were shepherds, come to reclaim their far-flung herd.

But now the Indra felt something else, and Zenn felt it, too. Something dark, painful, and it dawned on Zenn that this wasn't a homecoming. Not yet. The Indra, Zenn realized with a shock, hadn't physically moved at all. It dawned on her that everything she'd just experienced was only a prelude – the Asyph wasn't physically traversing the gulf of distance she had just witnessed; it was plotting its course, preparing to tunnel, mapping the way it would go. Using the facial barbels that flickered in and out of this place and time to appear in another, the Indra had penetrated the continuum to plot out the path that would, when the time came, bring it to the destination it ached to reach.

Then, at once, Zenn was back at the Khurspex meta-ship, seeing, as the Indra saw, the sprawling ring of ships, sensed now in a flowing spectrum of wavelengths that ebbed in and out of visible light, falling into infrared heat, rising to ultraviolet, shifting to high-energy microwaves and then cascading back and starting the sequence all over again.

And Zenn could feel it – the nexus inside her, almost ready, almost completed, but not quite online, not yet, almost, almost. And contained within it, hidden, the tiny molecular clock, the lethal trigger: Stav's time bomb, ticking down to the end. The end of this beautiful, uncanny Indra, the end of all Indra, the end of her own fragile, tiny body. Almost time. Only seconds now. Seconds.

Zenn's thoughts lurched, her mind flailing; she felt the Indra sensing her fear, her despair and then something worse, infinitely worse… she felt the Indra… recognize her, as the other, as an invader!

THIRTY

Zenn froze where she lay in the pod, exposed, helpless, as the Indra's mind burrowed into hers, pouring through her with all its merciless, relentless anger. She could feel the creature's unfathomable power focusing, gathering itself to annihilate the trespasser within its body. Stav's plan would work. The Indra would do as he'd said. And all would be lost. There was nothing she could do in the face of the Indra's unthinkable, irresistible onslaught against what it now saw as a mortal threat. There was nothing to do but die.

Then Zenn was seeing the face of her mother; but no, not her face. Rather, the sense of her, but clear, unmistakable, and so real, so beautiful, so filled with compassion and loving, and it was as if Mai was right beside her. Then, her father: the warmth, humor and strength of him filling her mind. She felt the strong hands that had once lifted her up, the affection that lifted her higher. And somehow… yes, she felt her father's mind, she was *in* his mind, she was with him on the ship where he was held fast, trapped. And she felt his love for her, felt his anguish, not for himself but for where she was that instant. And then other minds, opening to her, letting her in. Like cold, clear streams tumbling into a single river of sensation and thought. Fane, Jules, Liam, Treth. Still alive?

They must be. They must be… Please, let them be alive.

Her thoughts were now touching the thoughts of the passengers from the *Helen of Troy*, then all the beings on all the Indra ships, all their minds, welcoming, flooding into her, overwhelming her with their longings, their fears, their desperation. Even Stav, his single-minded obsession burning away all other concerns within him. The teeming Khurspex, frantic with their need to return home. All the mighty Indra in their ships. All connected. To each other. To Zenn. To the measureless webs of animated matter thrown out to every corner of the universe to conjure the mystery and the wonder that was life itself. All this life. All these beings who only wanted one thing. To live. To live and… to go home!

They must not die. This must not happen.

Then the time was almost up. Something like a shadow's edge rushed at her, speeding, coming fast, then faster, she felt it surge toward her like an irresistible avalanche of sheer intention. Her time was up. The ticking clock inside her ticked to zero, the nexus completed its circuit, time stopped. The universe held its breath.

She waited to be ripped apart. Waited for the killing tidal wave of energy to crash into and through her, to blast through the minds of every Indra in the galaxy, killing them all. But the thing that should have happened next… didn't.

Zenn knew at once why. It was the Asyph. The *Helen's* Indra. The Indra knew. Of course. Of course. And Zenn knew then with perfect clarity what the Indra knew: she, Zenn, was not the enemy. Not the invader. The Indra had seen into Zenn's very core, knew Zenn's mind, and more: knew her heart. And now the Indra was reaching deeper, searching, showing Zenn what was there all the time, hidden deep within her own tattered consciousness. Diamond-hard and true at the center of Zenn's being. It was simple. So simple. Unadorned. Uncomplicated. It was right there. It was what Zenn felt. For all those beings. For all those dreaming minds. For all those lives that only wanted to live, to go home again and live and regenerate and continue, all those lives that did not deserve anything less. The New Law was wrong. Alien and human were not enemies. They were *connected*. They were one. They were alive. They were life. So simple.

And now Zenn felt more, as if this new knowing brought with it new strength. And the possibility of control. She felt her will growing. And the Indra's will, too. Melding, intertwining, each reinforcing the other, growing strong, strong enough, together, to bend the course of events. And something else, just as strong but dreadful: the cost. The price for opening herself to the unthinkable forces pressing in on her, fighting to get out of her. Zenn knew deeply, unquestionably, that if she let this happen, if she united with the Indra this time, she might not come back, might never return to herself, might whirl away, dissolving into atoms, vanish utterly into... what? She couldn't guess. Didn't dare.

Still, the decision came without hesitation. The choice as simple as the knowing of it. She joined with the Indra. And it began.

In the instant of decision, the tangle of connection deep in Zenn's brain exchanged the last signal that was required, the final synapse bridged. Now, the fulcrum's balance was at last overweighted. The astonishing strangeness within her mind blossomed into the nexus. And then she was the one, the single living point through which the awesome quantum force of first one Indra, then two, then a dozen, then an entire species, flowed – colossal, unstoppable, unknowable, joyous!

The final focused stream of energy broke its final barrier, and the threshold was crossed. Like a universe-snake uncoiling for the strike, a dark energy chain reaction of immeasurable power slipped the bonds of physical law, the force exploded out, time doubled back on itself, swallowed its own tail, disappeared. Sound, sense, awareness all hurtled to an unbearable crescendo, roared, thundering headlong into the infinite abyss, soared up and out again. Certainly, no being made of flesh could survive this. No mind made of matter could experience such an inhuman journey, touch so many beings, look so deeply into the shocking mystery of existence and ever be whole again.

A single quick breath later, however, Zenn was whole again, somehow returned and held within the preposterously insignificant bounds of her own puny primate's body.

Alive... I'm alive!

She wanted to laugh, shout at being enfolded again in the warm, living world. And she wanted to sob, her heart breaking at the thought of the minds she had been torn away from, the bewildering number of beings, all the creatures whose innermost longings she had momentarily felt and lived as her own.

As reality seemed to congeal and take shape around her, she saw she was still lying in the in-soma pod. But the bow cam view screen showed something else. What? The interior of the med-ship. She was no longer in the Indra's brain. Stav stood at his console, not looking at it, but holding onto it with both hands as if to steady himself, weaving on his feet like he'd just been through something that had knocked him off-balance.

Zenn toggled the pod door to open. Cool, fresh air flowed into the musty interior. She unbuckled the safety harness, sat up, almost passed out from the effort, her head aching, her body weak, scarcely responsive. Stav turned to her, his eyes unfocused. He lifted his gaze to look beyond her, seeing a sight that, judging by his expression, made no sense.

Zenn realized with an odd detachment that something was different. There was a smell in the cabin that hadn't been there before: a heaviness in the air, rank, wet, a scent that instantly evoked a memory – the lock leading into the *Benthic Tson*. The smell of seawater. Zenn rose up in the pod to see what Stav was seeing behind her. There, impossibly, still rocking slightly to and fro at the far end of the cabin deck sat a large oblong object.

Water sheeted off its sides to run out and ripple across the floor. The object was yellow with a dull-green slime of algae coating. It had numerous mech-arms, and booms sprouting from its hull and several small portholes. It was the service sub from the *Benthic Tson*.

The hatch on top of the sub creaked open, and Treth rose into view. There was the sound of movement behind Zenn. She twisted to see Stav drop behind a cargo crate, the flux-rifle at his shoulder.

"Treth, look out!"

The rifle bolt tore into the plating near the sub's hatch, spraying hot fragments. But the Groom had already launched herself into midair. She hit the deck hard and rolled into the nearest medical bay. Zenn saw she carried Pokt's plasma stick.

Rising to her feet, Treth aimed and fired, and the lightning pulse snaked across the cabin to strike the bulkhead next to Stav's head, sending him to the floor. Zenn saw her chance. She pulled herself up out of the pod and scurried around to the other side of it, putting it between her and Stav.

"Novice Scarlett," the Groom yelled.

"Treth," she shouted back. "The sub. How did you…?"

"We did nothing. We were sinking, the hull imploding. Then we were here."

"And the others?"

A blond head poked above the sub's hatch.

"You OK, Scarlett?"

A bolt from Stav's rifle skimmed the side of the sub, and Liam disappeared back inside.

Another bolt split the air above the Groom, and a gush of molten metal sprouted from the wall. Stav, leaning around the pilot's console, was taking aim when Treth leaned out and fired first. She missed, but the impact forced Stav to retreat farther behind the console.

"This is pointless," Stav shouted. "You are outnumbered. Kill me, and my crew will kill you. You cannot prevent what is coming." Stav rose just long enough to let off another blinding volley, then ducked down again.

"It is already prevented," Treth yelled, firing, then pulling back out of sight. "You failed. The Khurspex ship tunneled. It is gone."

Stav gave a harsh laugh. "You're insane. There is no way that–"

"Look, Treth, there." Zenn pointed behind Stav. There was no mistaking the blood-red orb that filled the view screen. "It's Mars!"

Stav twisted to see.

"No," he murmured. The scream that followed as he turned back to them was less than human. "No!"

He crouched and, with the rifle gripped in one hand, loosed a series of wild shots at the alcove where Treth was concealed. A round from Treth's weapon made him drop back behind the console.

"Novice," Treth called to her. "How can this be?"

"It was the Indra," Zenn shouted. She knew what had happened. She'd felt it. She'd helped do it. "She understood! She knew. She sent us home."

"You," Stav shouted, turning his weapon toward Zenn. The shot jolted the in-soma pod off the floor. It landed inches from Zenn's face, smoking, flames rising from within it. He fired again, and the pod skidded into Zenn's side. She couldn't stay there.

"Novice," Treth yelled. "Run. Now!"

The Groom stepped out, exposing herself to unleash a firestorm of lightning at Stav. Zenn had just enough time to throw herself into the nearest surgical bay. She turned to see Stav's next shot rake Treth's side. The Groom collapsed out of sight.

Zenn's backpack lay just outside the bay. There was movement inside it.

Katie...

Zenn hooked the pack with one foot and pulled it to safety. Katie's nose emerged.

Stav was on his feet now, working his way toward Treth's position. Zenn saw Treth sit up, gripping her side but still managing to fire. Her shots went wide of the mark, and Stav returned fire from the hip. "It's over, Groom," he growled, his voice seething. "You will all pay for what you've done."

Treth got off another round, but her aim was getting worse. She must be badly wounded. Soon, Stav would be close enough to finish her. Zenn saw movement near the far bulkhead. Something small, brown. The Khurspex whip-whelk. It had detached itself from Pokt's dead arm and was trying to crawl away on its multiple spindly legs. Zenn made a tentative move toward it, but a round from Stav forced her back into the bay.

"Wait your turn, Novice." Stav spat the words at her, then returned his attention to Treth. The Groom was firing blindly now, but that was just enough to slow Stav's progress toward her.

At Zenn's feet, Katie struggled free of the backpack and looked up at her.

"Friend-Zenn, Katie hungry," she signed. "Have treat for Katie?"

No, she thought dully, no treats for Katie.

But a second later, another thought came.

"Katie. See the little oyster thing?" Zenn signed rapidly, then turned Katie's head to make her look directly at the creeping whip-whelk.

"Oyster-bug! Good for Katie eat?"

"No. Not oyster. Not good to eat," Zenn signed. "But Friend-Zenn needs. Katie brings it? Yes? Katie brings."

"Katie big hungry," the rikkaset signed. "Certain? Certain no good eat?"

"Big certain," Zenn signed back, growing frantic, starting to think this wouldn't work. "Please Katie. Bring it to Zenn. Don't eat, bring. Ready?"

Katie considered for a moment, huffed irritably and signed, "Katie ready."

"Good. Katie? Blend!"

A purple-cream blur, and the rikkaset vanished. Zenn signed at the animal's last position.

"Get the oyster. Bring it to Friend-Zenn."

Stav and Treth traded two more volleys. All Zenn could do was huddle in the bay. And wait. After a few seconds, Zenn realized something was wrong. It was quiet. No firing. She peered around the edge of the alcove. Stav was walking across the center of the room, moving toward

Treth. The Groom must be unconscious. Or dead.

Zenn saw the whip-whelk jerk once across the floor, then rise a few inches into the air and begin to float toward her.

By now, Stav was standing over Treth. He kicked at something. The plasma stick skidded across the floor, beyond the Groom's reach.

Then, the whip-whelk was close enough for Zenn to grab. As soon as it was in her hands, she pushed it onto her wrist. It responded instantly, the many spider-like arms wrapping her forearm in a surprisingly strong grip; she could also feel a faint prickling like an electrical current emanating from the creature into her skin. Subdermal neural connection?

Katie rematerialized. Zenn stroked her, then, with a twinge of conscience, gathered the rikkaset into her arms. Stav had seen Pokt with the whip-whelk and cut him down before he could activate the creature. She would have to use Katie to hide the weapon until she was ready.

She rose and stepped out into the cabin.

"You, Novice, are a great disappointment." Stav raised the rifle to his hip, swung its tip toward Zenn.

As he raised the gun to his shoulder, Zenn dropped Katie to the floor and thrust her arm out in front of her. She had time for only one thought:

Stop him!

That was enough. The whip-whelk's shell opened, the rope of flesh leapt through the air and brushed gently across the side of Stav's neck. A slight, astonished exhalation escaped his lips, his eyes rolled back in his head and he dropped senseless, falling on his side, the rifle clattering onto the floor. The whelk's appendage retracted back into its shell, and the two halves snapped shut with a soft *clack*.

THIRTY-ONE

The Khurspex had, in fact, gone home, just as Treth said. The meta-ship had vanished. The *Helen's* Indra had channeled the unified strength of all her kin through the nexus, inside Zenn, to bear herself and the Khurspex home. At the same instant, the Asyph had sent the *Helen* and all the other Indra ships home, too – actually, to Mars, which was home to Zenn, at least. Now all that remained where the meta-ship had drifted was empty space and fragments of debris. The dozens of hijacked interconnected ships still circled this emptiness at the center, in a high orbit above the Martian surface.

Within a day, crews on board the ships were already busy making repairs, the ships' Indra resting in their chambers after their contribution to the Khurspex's galaxy-spanning effort. The general consensus was that, tended by their grooms, the Indra would all be plying the spacelanes again in a matter of weeks.

For a day and a half after her final link with the Asyph, Zenn descended into a long, dreamless, blissful sleep. At last, she had come fully awake earlier that morning, sitting up in her own bed, in her own dorm room at the cloister. Through her open window, she could see the cloister grounds, the ruins of the chapel and, beyond it, the canyon walls of the pressurized valley that snaked its way into Arsia City. The air wafting through the window smelled of freshly mowed switchgrass and gensoy blossom.

Katie was curled up on the pillow next to her, dozing. When anyone entered the room, the rikkaset would wake, eye them up and down and, once satisfied they weren't a threat, plop down and resume her nap.

"...and you'd asked about Jules," her father was saying from where he sat at the foot of her bed. Her father. Sitting there, on her bed. Like this was a normal thing. In fact, Warra Scarlett had just returned from a meeting of the ships' captains and civilian leaders. He summoned up an image on the virt-screen hovering near her bed. "The captain of the *Benthic Tson* listed several cetaceans on her roster and I was able to track him down. Do you feel strong enough to say hello?"

"To Jules? Of course." Zenn turned eagerly to the screen as it floated over to her. It glowed to life with the image of a dolphin's smiling face. Jules was immersed in a large body of water, and she could see a Transvox unit attached by a strap just in front of his dorsal fin. There was a great expanse of water behind him, roofed over by an immense ceiling.

"Zenn Scarlett." She had never in her life been so happy to hear a Transvox voice. "You are healthy and in the pink?"

"Yes! Yes, Jules, I am. But where's your walksuit?"

"It's being repaired. For the moment, I am swimming – aboard this watership. I can now tell you: I like swimming. It's thrilling. And guess what else I am able to say? I will wager you cannot guess it."

"Please, Jules," Zenn said, laughing. "No more bets. Not right now."

"Very well, but I would have won this bet. What I have to tell is of my First Promised. She was in fact here on this ship. You will remember, I called out to her when I was doing my first swimming, to unhook the small submarine. She heard me within all that water. It was she who came to help us when the submarine was taken by the hungry swimmer-lurker-fish."

"But Jules…" Zenn's mind roamed back to the sight of the sub in the lurker's grasp, the sound of the failing hull. "I saw the lurker; it was huge. I saw it pull the sub down. Your First Promised – how could she help you?"

Another Transvox sounded from off-cam, a female voice with a lilting, unidentifiable accent.

"*Ja*, I hunted that lurker since first I was placed aboard the *Tson*," the voice said. "This jävla fiskar's attacking of the submarine made a quantity of noise. This was its grossa mistake." The cam shot zoomed out. Floating in the water next to Jules was a sleek, thirty-foot, black-and-white patterned body.

"Zenn Scarlett," Jules said, "I wish you to meet my First Promised. Inga Hammerfest, I introduce my very good friend Novice Zenn Scarlett."

Zenn understood now how Jules's First Promised had been able to help.

"An orca," Zenn said. "Your First Promised is a killer whale? That's... great."

"It is thoroughly great, is it not?" Jules beamed at the whale, and it nuzzled at his side with its broad, toothy face. "Inga killed that lurker thing as it held us. But the submarine ship still continued to sink in the water and she could not hold us up. We were being crushed severely by pressure. Water came in at all sides. But then there was a bright light, and a strange feeling, and the sub was all at once aboard the medical ship. Myself, and Treth and the boy Liam. Aboard and not crushed. And you were there, too. And we had all come back here to Sol space."

The mention of Liam made Zenn wonder again where he was. No one had heard from him since the Indra had transphased the ships home again. Where had he gotten to? Would he come back to Mars, face the charges against him for his unwilling part in sabotaging the cloister?

"And now," Jules said, "Inga and I will proceed onward to the ocean-world of Mu Arae, as was her plan in the start. Its seas are awash in wonders. The coral reefs of the Bensarus Oc archipelago are in fact intelligent, but I am told their language is inscrutable even to a Transvox unit. In any case, it will be a majestic environment to witness. We have a multitude of expectations. I will visit you before we go on this trip."

"You'd better," she said.

"I will come down as soon as my walksuit is repaired and functional. I will say farewell for now and wish that you continue to improve your health."

The screen flickered off, and a voice drew Zenn's attention to the doorway.

"Novice Scarlett, recovering well, I trust?" It was Ambassador Noom, peering in from the hallway. She fluttered in to hover at the side of Zenn's bed.

"Thank you, Ambassador. I am."

"We are all gratified to hear it."

"Gratified," one of her consorts chimed in from where he floated in his clear-skinned sphere. The others agreed: "Pleased." "Overjoyed." "And relieved, feh?"

Noom addressed Zenn's father. "I have just come down from the infirmary on the *Nova Procyon*. Lieutenant Travosk is being held there. Attended by a military guard. He seems to be suffering from some sort of post-traumatic shock."

"He's admitted his part in the plot to destroy the Indra fleet?" her father asked.

"Oh, he's proud of the fact," Noom replied. "Insists he'd do it all again. That he owes it to someone. Valia? Lena? I can't recall."

"Vremya," Zenn said.

"Vremya Travosk," her father said. "I looked into that. I just got the full story from the Authority on Earth."

"So, she must have been Stav's wife, or sister," Zenn said.

"Sister. Sort of," her father said. Zenn gave him a questioning look. "Turns out Vremya was Lieutenant Travosk's opposite-gender clone. Part of a secret breeding program of some kind. The details are still foggy. Illegal, of course. Just one more black mark for the New Law."

"She was an op-gen clone?" It was Treth's voice, followed by her walking into the room. The Groom winced as she smiled down at Zenn, favoring the side where Stav's shot had caught her. "It is said the bond between such beings can be unnaturally intense."

"That's what I've heard, too," Warra said. "I suppose the way she died would explain Stav's obsession with taking down the Indra fleet. And using Zenn to do it. Of course, it won't mitigate the charges against him. He'll be going away for a very long time."

"I should hope so," Noom interjected. "And of course I must say that I am utterly mortified by my own part in all of this, unaware of it as I was."

"But how could you have known?" Zenn said.

"I come from nine generations of Cepheian diplomats, Novice. My instincts should have alerted me. When he said I had been recalled to Earth, it was just a ruse to get himself off the *Helen* before it was hijacked. I was used. There is no excuse. I should have sensed his duplicity."

"So, what will happen to him?"

"The lieutenant will stand trial in the Accord Central court," Noom said, adding quickly, "I have already agreed to provide evidence against him. It is the least I can do. And when the Skirni leaders hear of their betrayal by the New Law faction, I feel certain they will testify against their former co-conspirators as well. To save their own flesh, if nothing else."

"What about the rest of the New Law, on Earth?" Zenn asked.

"Once the truth is known, it is certain the Authority will purge them," Noom said. "With the New Law xenophobes discredited, the Earth will certainly allow Indra ships back into Sol space. And I, of course, will have much explaining to do when I return home. My lack of awareness in this affair is unforgivable, a diplomat of my standing."

"Most unfortunate." "Decidedly awkward." "Hardly bearable." "Feeling regretful, feh?"

"It is a difficulty of your own making, Drifter," Treth said. "And in any case, our attention should be on the Novice. You are experiencing no ill effects?" Treth tapped the side of Zenn's head.

"From the Indra tissue?" Zenn's hand went to her temple. "No. It's just sitting in there. Taking up a little space."

"Otha ran a full brain and body diagnostic," her father said. "There's no sign of damage, or any residual effect from the Indra neurons. The working theory is that the tissue became inert after the Indra tunneled."

"I am curious," Treth said. "The communion you had with the Indra, and with the other creatures. Will you miss it?"

"Yes… and no," Zenn said. She'd been thinking hard about it, but couldn't decide if the sensation was one she'd ever want to experience again. "I think maybe I'm glad to just have myself to myself again."

"You're no longer sharing brain-power with the Indra?" Noom said. "That is probably for the best, lest you transphase additional submarines hither and yon."

"Submarines." "Transported." "Perilous." "Extremely dangerous, feh?"

"I couldn't agree more," Zenn said.

"And what of the Indra themselves?" Noom rotated to face Treth. "Are they all viable? Able to tunnel?"

"Several are in need of attention, but nothing life-threatening," the Groom answered. "Generally, they are all in good health. We can at least thank the Khurspex for their vigilance in that regard."

"Excellent," Noom said, drifting toward the door. "Then I will be able to say that Indra-ship traffic will soon be back to acceptable levels. A favorable report on this matter will go some way to helping my case on Eta Cephei."

"Normal traffic." "Healthy Indras." "Best outcome." "All's well, feh?"

Noom's consorts continued to chatter as she propelled herself out of the room.

"Now, then, Novice Scarlett." The Groom crossed her arms, her anitats putting on an especially colorful display. "The Indra I mentioned. While none face imminent danger, several suffer from malnutrition and minor injuries. Once you are strong enough, my sister grooms and I could use the services of an experienced exovet like yourself."

Zenn grinned at the words.

An experienced exovet. I like the sound of that.

"Of course. I'd be happy to help." The mere prospect of being near an Indra again, of being useful again, was enough to make Zenn feel that she'd recuperated quite enough. "I could start now, today."

"Easy, kid," her father said, patting her shoulder with a soft laugh of the sort Zenn hadn't heard from him since... she couldn't remember when. "There's plenty of time for you to get stronger first. The ships have to be separated again; lots of work to do before they'll be going anywhere."

"And speaking of this work," Treth said. "I am needed elsewhere just now. Rest and be well, Novice."

"You'll let me know how I can help?"

"Yes. But there is ample time. Our Indra will survive until you are up and about."

Zenn settled back into her pillows. Her thoughts returned to Liam, but she consoled herself that he was one towner boy who could probably take care of himself. She just wished he'd let her know he was OK. She had to admit that, at last, all things considered, it was permissible to luxuriate a bit in her surroundings – familiar faces, familiar food, the clean, soft, pleasantly scented sheets. Yes, there was ample time, now. Time to heal, time to attend to the Indra, to get reacquainted with the animals in the cloister clinic and, best of all, time to get to know the father she'd nearly lost.

THIRTY-TWO

Later that night, Zenn was reviewing a V-film status report on the cloister's patients when there was a soft tapping at the room's open window. Startled for a second, she then saw a blond sheaf of hair. Liam! She went to the window.

"Scarlett. Thought I'd drop by." She could only stand, staring. "Mind if I come in?"

She stepped back from him, shaking her head in wonder. He pulled himself through the window, crossed to her and brought her body to his, giving her a brief, tight hug. He released her, and they stood close but not touching, grinning at each other, then laughing out loud.

"Liam, what are you doing here? How'd you get onto Mars?"

"Oh, nice to see you, too. I'm fine, thanks."

"I can see that," she said. Same old Liam. "I mean, you just disappeared. No one knew what had happened to you."

"Remember that Fomalhaut with the waspworm?"

"Yes, the one down in steerage."

"He actually turned out to be a pretty good guy. Except for the animal fighting thing. He had business here on Mars. He'd won a couple of berths on a private ferry drop. Don't ask how, OK? Anyway, I came down with him. Nobody else knows I'm here."

"That would explain the window," Zenn said.

Katie had jumped off the bed and came to sniff at the boy's foot.

"Hey there," he said, bending to pet her. "How's my rikkaset?"

"Oh, so she's *your* rikkaset now? She's fine. And I'm doing fine, too," she said. "Thank you for asking."

"You? I never doubted it. It'd take more than a New Law plot to destroy civilization to keep you down."

Katie was up on her hind legs, sniffing Liam's back pocket. He pulled out a small paper bag.

"Dried grasshopper," he said.

"Crunchies!" Katie signed. "Crunchies for Katie?"

"I happen to know they're her favorite," he said.

Trilling loudly, Katie snatched the bag from him, hopped up on the bed with it and began feasting intently.

"You know they're looking for you, right? Will you stay on Mars?" She realized she wasn't prepared for him to say no.

"Turn myself in, you mean?" He made a sour face.

"Liam," Zenn said,"Vic and Graad forced you to help them sabotage the cloister. And you exposed what they were doing. And then you helped us escape, helped stop Travosk and all. You're a hero. There's no way they'd do anything to you. They'd never put you in prison with Graad."

"Yeah. Maybe. Maybe not. Fact is, guys like Graad always know other guys like Graad. Guys who aren't in prison."

"But what would you do? Where would you go?"

"That's kinda why I'm here," he said. Zenn gave him a puzzled look. "Liph Kenis, the Fomalhaut I came down with. He's got this idea. Now that the Rift is going to be over, he wants to go to Earth and start a business. He's asked me to help."

"You? What sort of business?"

"Waspworms. He says Earthers will be ready to buy off-world pets again. And his worm is apparently some kinda champion bloodline, you know, a purebred, with papers and all."

"Liam, what makes this Kenis person think you know anything about business or breeding insectoids?"

"Well, I told him about my work here at the cloister clinic, you know, with the animals."

"Mucking out stalls and hauling feed?"

"I might've tweaked the details of my resume a little. The main thing is, I've got an escape plan. And this might be my one shot, you know, to see Earth."

"But what if you talked to Ren? He's a constable, Liam; he must have ways of protecting people like you. People who did the right thing and deserve–"

"Ren Jackson? He can't hardly patrol the territory he's got now. And Graad Dokes has a reputation for getting even with people he doesn't like. I'm at the top of that list. No. No choice, here. I've got to get off Mars. And, Scarlett..." He took her hand in one of his. "You should go with me."

"Me?" She let go of his hand and stepped back. "Go to Earth?"

"Hear me out. Just hear me out," he said, pacing in front of her excitedly as he spoke. "I told Liph all about you, about what you did aboard the Spex ships, the Indra in-soma thing. And all your training here at the school. He said an exovet like you would be really valuable to his operation at the waspworm farm or whatever you call it."

"I'm still just a novice. You know that. It'll be years before I can legally practice medicine."

"Hey, Liph isn't the kind to worry about that kinda thing, trust me."

"Liam, listen to me... you know I like you."

"Yeah, well, I was kinda hoping we'd gotten that far."

"No. I really do. Like you. Everything you've done for me, for all of us. But there's something I've been trying to explain, about me–"

"Oh, no." His face darkened. "This isn't the 'it's not you, it's me' talk is it? Tell me it's not that, Scarlett."

"What? No. I mean, sort of. But not like you're thinking."

His expression shaded from disappointment to utter confusion.

"Nine Hells, Scarlett, what is it, then?"

"I'm sorry, that's what it is, Liam. That I can't go with you. That I can't be what you want me to be. I don't know how."

He turned , faced the wall, then spun around and leveled his gaze at her.

"You don't know how, or you don't *want* to know how?"

"I just can't, Liam. I just don't know what to do, how to act." She went to sit on the bed next to Katie, who was still focused on her treats. "I know it's supposed to come naturally, that it's built-in, instinctual. We're mammals..." She picked up the rikkaset and set her on her lap, stroked her fur. Katie kept eating. "I should know how to behave like one. But right now, I feel like I'm just learning how to be around you, in... that way. But I'm a slow learner."

"You?" Liam said, "Zenn Scarlett, who devours books like candy? Who has more medical stuff crammed into her head than an entire school library? You. Learn things slow. Give me a break."

"Liam, this isn't something you find in a book. This is me, growing up like I did, with the experiences I had. More to the point, experiences I *never* had. In a place with not all that much chance for me to learn the finer points of... the romantical element."

Liam came to sit beside her.

"Fine. So you're slow. I can wait. I'm a patient guy. Sorta. But if we had time and a whole new life on Earth–"

"Liam. I can't just drop everything." She put Katie back onto the bed between them. "I'm going to be an exovet. I'm going to finish school, do my internship, get my license and be a full-fledged exoveterinarian. It's all I've ever wanted. I've worked really hard just to get this far. And I owe it to myself to see this through. I owe it... I owe it to my mom, Liam."

"Your mom?"

"She devoted her life to the animals that needed her. She died doing that. She didn't get to have the time she should've had, to live the life she wanted. I can do that for her, Liam. I can help all those she wasn't able to help."

"Nine Hells, Scarlett." He stood up again. "OK. I get it. About your mom and all, but... I just thought we could make a fresh start. I never thought about... I'm such an idiot." He shook his head. "I never thought about you, about what school means, why you're so damn intense about it all."

"Yeah, I guess I am. Intense."

"No kidding." He went to the window, leaned against the sill, looked back at her. "But, Scarlett, I've gotta go. I can't stay here. I may never get this chance again."

She went to stand behind him, put her arms around him and leaned into his back, felt his warmth, realized that even after all his time off-world, he still carried the faint scent of fresh-cut hay. She thought again of her mother's words, that sometimes, making the right choice was the most frightening thing you could do. Her mother hadn't mentioned it could also break your heart.

"You'll send word of how you're doing?" she said, still pressed in close, not looking up, afraid of what would happen if she did. "I want to know all about what Earth is like. And how your wasp-farm turns out." Her voice was breaking now. She took a long, deep breath to steady herself before she pulled away. He didn't face her but continued staring out into the night.

"Damn, Scarlett, you're really killing my ego here, you know that you don't you?"

"What?" she said, smiling to keep the tears back. "Your girls in Arsia didn't act like this?"

"No. They did not." He turned to her. "But, hey, you warned me before. You're not like the other girls in Arsia."

"So, when do you–"

"The ferry back up to orbit leaves at dawn."

"I'm serious, Liam," she said. "You send me shards on a regular basis or I'll..."

"You'll what?"

"I'll send my attack rikkaset to hunt you down and..." She'd tried not to; she told herself she wasn't going to. But it was no use – she started to cry, shoulders heaving, vision blurring. He was next to her a second later, arms tight around her.

"I'm sorry," she told him. "I wasn't going to get all... I didn't want you to see me cry."

"Scarlett." He leaned back so he could see her face, ran one big hand under her eye, wiping at her tears. "You've never looked better."

He lowered his face to hers, kissed her lightly on the forehead and let her go. Going to the window, he hefted his body up and out onto the ledge. He stopped there, swiped the hair out of his eyes and said, "When I'm a wealthy waspworm farmer, I'll send my private ship for you, OK?"

"You'd better," was all Zenn could manage to say without breaking down again.

"Be careful around your animals. Especially the big ones. And keep an eye on Katie for me."

"I will."

"OK, then, well... bye, Scarlett."

She ran to the window, leaned out to hug him hard,

once, and then he dropped out of sight. She listened to his footsteps on the gravel path until they faded away.

Suddenly, she was alone with Katie, the sound of grasshoppers being crunched and the scent of blooming gensoy sweet in the night air.

THIRTY-THREE

At the evening meal three days later, the cloister's great refectory hall was filled to overflowing with humans and Asents at every long table. This, of course, was a sight Zenn had heard about from Otha but never witnessed. Sister Hild had explained that tonight was a special event, to acknowledge all that had happened, to bring everyone together and celebrate with what she described as a victory dinner. It was so strange, Zenn thought, looking out over the crowd; it was like it must have been in the old days, before the Rift with Earth, when the cloister school teemed with students and every night saw the hall packed to the rafters with eager diners.

As the first dishes were brought out, Zenn recognized some of the servers as towner kids. She was surprised, and gratified, to see that Otha's community outreach program seemed to be working. If the locals were letting their children wait tables at a Ciscan cloister dinner, they must have started to reconsider their suspicions about the alien "monsters" housed in the cloister's pens and pools.

Zenn and her father were seated with Otha, Hild and Hamish at the room's head table. Before all the dishes had been brought out, they were joined by Ambassador Noom and a newly ambulatory Jules. Liam's absence was painfully apparent to Zenn, but she tried to tell herself he was a big boy, he knew what he wanted, he'd done what he felt he must. Still, it was hard to see all of them together again without seeing him in among the familiar faces. Fane was missing from the assembly, too, but she'd had word that he was in good health and once again working alongside Treth aboard the *Helen of Troy*.

"Inga, my mate-to-be, is regretful she could not be here," Jules said as he parked himself near the table. "Her walksuit was damaged beyond repair during the ordeal. But I am paying to have a new unit constructed for her. I do not mind the paying, as she is my First Promised. This goes without saying. Despite its impressive expense. And look..." He spread his mech-arms wide. "My own suit is now fully refurbished and with a special coat of polishing wax. It shines."

"Very impressive," Zenn said, smiling at her friend. "And please tell Inga 'hello' when you see her."

"So, Novice Scarlett," Noom said, wrapping several tendrils around the large chair that Otha had adapted into a perch for her. "I'm told your thwarting of the conspiracy of the New Law and the Skirni is the talk of all Mars, of the entire Accord."

"Heroic actions." "Bold exploits." "Great deeds." "Worthy of blink-novs, feh?"

Zenn felt color rising to her cheeks.

"It wasn't just me, you know," she told Noom and the others. "I had lots of help."

Otha heard and slapped his hand onto the table. "Yes! But how you rose to the occasion." Her uncle had trimmed his beard for the evening's festivities and wore a brand new linen shirt woven for him by Sister Hild, with a sleeve-screen made from spare parts she'd scavenged from one of the clinic's old diagnostic computers. "One could say you were born to do what you did. Literally born to it." Her uncle had already downed several glasses of Hamish's latest batch of home-brewed ale, and he was feeling gregarious. "Here's to our own heroine, blood of my blood." He raised his mug into the air. Hamish sat next to him, and the big insectoid now lifted the foaming mugs he held in three of his four upper arms to clink against Otha's glass.

"Excellently done, Novice Zenn." Hamish's Transvox translated his Coleopt whirrings. "And welcome home to your cloister. May you remain here with us for an extended period."

"My sentiments exactly," Sister Hild said, reaching over to squeeze Zenn's shoulder. "You've been missed, child. By all of us, including your animals."

"Dad," Zenn said quietly, turning to her father, "Charlie? Any news?"

"Oh, I didn't have a chance to tell you. I heard just before dinner. Your Loepith was still aboard the *Dancer* when they checked him off the list of the missing. He was already helping out with refitting the ship's Indra chambers and getting systems back on line. He did have an odd request, though."

"I'm so glad he's OK," she said. "What did he want?"

"A lawyer. One skilled in interstellar divorce law," her father said. "Something to do with the marriage rights of AI entities. You know what that's all about?"

"Actually," she said, smiling to herself, "I do."

When the last of the dishes were just being cleared away, the murmuring of the crowd increased to a low buzz as a group of very tall women and one boy entered the room from the large double doors at the front of the hall.

"What's this?" Zenn asked.

"Just a little surprise," her father said, a glint in his eyes.

Everyone turned to watch as the new arrivals approached the table where Zenn and the others sat. Treth walked at the front of the group of eight other women, all Indra grooms. They all wore their formal dress uniforms of iridescent blue-black synthweave bodysuits topped with vermillion cloaks, the cloaks draped over their left shoulders, their right shoulders bared to the arm to show off their anitats. As they drew closer, Zenn realized with a surge of emotion that the boy who walked with them... was Fane. The young sacrist wore one arm in a sling and walked with a slight limp. When he saw Zenn, the crooked smile he gave her almost made her burst into tears of relief. Fane, lopsided smile, feather-beaded-hair and all. He wore a new gold sacrist's tunic. In his uninjured hand, he carried what looked like an oblong silver-bronze bowl. The group stopped behind Zenn's table, and Treth raised her hands to address the crowd.

"I would speak." The room grew quiet. "We are all still coming to terms with the momentous events of recent days. We faced a terrible challenge. The worlds of the Accord balanced on the knife-edge of apocalypse. But we triumphed over the forces arrayed against us. Forces of intolerance, greed and evil. I stand before you now to credit one among us who, more than any other, made our victory over these forces real."

Treth placed her hands on Zenn's shoulders.

"Novice Zenn Scarlett," she said. "In recognition of acts of valor and selfless daring, I am privileged this night to make this announcement before my Union Sisters and before all others assembled. I announce here your induction into the Sacred and Exalted Procyoni Union of Stonehorse Honorary Grooms. So saying, I welcome you as Honorary Starship Groom, Irullian Class."

A thunder of applause filled the room, the diners rising to their feet. Zenn turned to look up at Treth, her heart almost too full for her to speak. She managed to whisper, "Treth, thank you."

"Rise, Groom Scarlett." Zenn got to her feet, and the noise in the hall died away. "Extend your right arm." Zenn obeyed, giving her father and the others a quizzical look. Treth reached out to roll up the sleeve of Zenn's shirt until her forearm was exposed.

"Sacrist, the Irullian Indraydith-Tull," Treth said solemnly. Fane stepped forward. He gave Zenn another quick, furtive smile and handed what he carried to another groom. The surface of the metal bowl was engraved with runelike symbols.

"Groom Fareeth," Treth said to the woman who had taken the device. "I confirm this one worthy of the mark. Proceed."

The one named Fareeth placed the device against the skin of Zenn's arm, midway between her wrist and elbow.

"Attend me now as I give you the mark," Fareeth intoned, staring into Zenn's eyes. "By the Shepherds' grace, I give it. By the ancient ways, I make it. By your willing soul, you receive it. I make the mark of the stonehorse Groom. The mark is yours. The mark is ours. The mark will make you known." She pressed on the device and Zenn's arm prickled with a quick, fierce heat followed by icy cold.

Fareeth lifted the device away. The room again echoed with applause as her father moved to stand behind her. She held up her arm for him to see. The animated tattoo on her skin was small, just a few inches across. It was shaped like a tiny, intricately detailed Indra, curved into a ring, chasing its own tail. The anitat seethed with the gemlike color of living flame, shifting red, blue, yellow, then red again as the hues glowed and faded, rose and fell, the stonehorse circling around and around in endless, timeless flight.

ACKNOWLEDGMENTS

Thanks to: my agent Adam Schear at DeFiore & Co, my editor Amanda Rutter at Strange Chemistry, all the publishing support elves/warlocks/selkies at Strange Chemistry/Angry Robot Books, my extended family alive and passed, all my friends, all my teachers, all the readers of the first Zenn Scarlett book and all the cats, dogs, ferrets and many equines here at the Schoon Ranch and, as always, to my endlessly supportive wife, Kat.

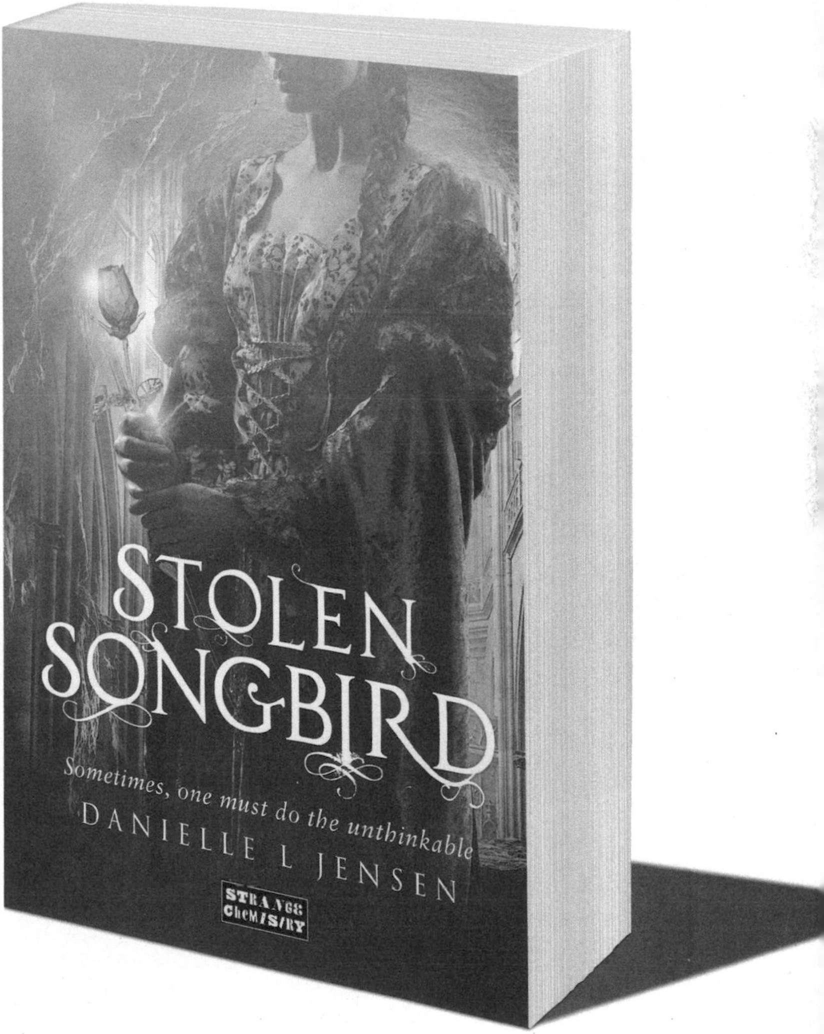
STOLEN SONGBIRD
Sometimes, one must do the unthinkable
DANIELLE L JENSEN
STRANGE ChEMISTRY

EXPERIMENTING WITH YOUR IMAGINATION

Fifty-six lifetimes to explore...

EXPERIMENTING WITH YOUR IMAGINATION

"For the first time in what feels like forever, I find myself wanting a YA paranormal series to never end."
Emily May, The Book Geek

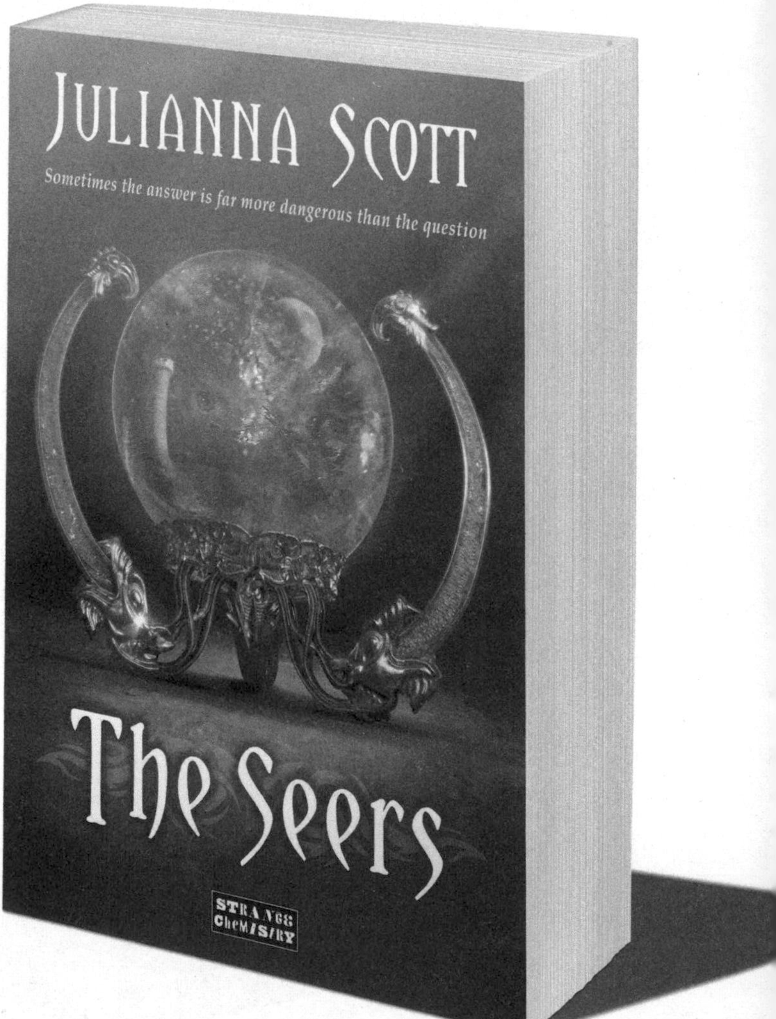

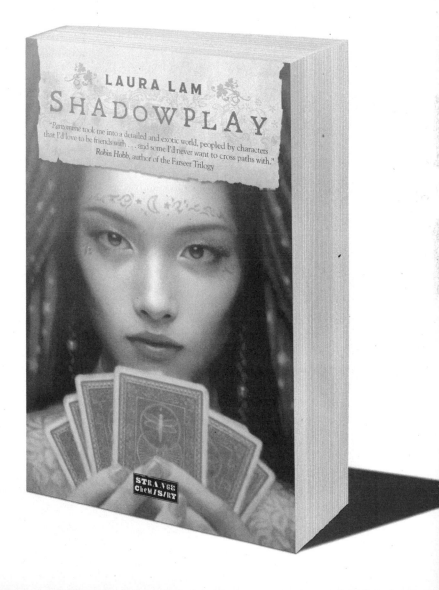

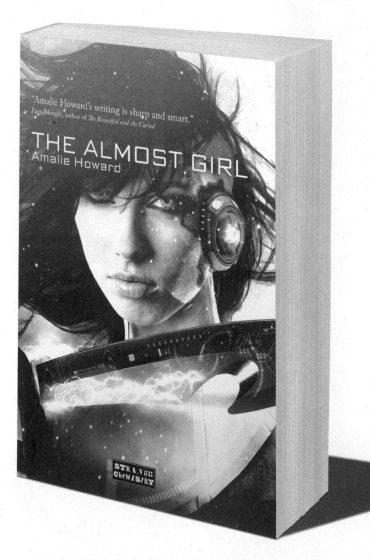

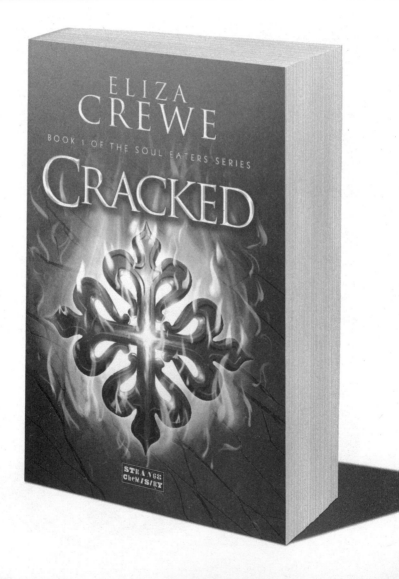